IN THE WORST WAY

Mercy Watts Mysteries Book Five

A.W. HARTOIN

CHAPTER ONE

Death changes you. It's changed me. I didn't think it would, but I killed a man and I'm different. At first, I thought I was fine. After all, People have tried to kill me before. I was sort of used to it or, at least, it didn't bother me much. But I'd never killed any of my previous attackers. The worst I'd done was kick them in the junk or pepper spray them. I'd say I handled the death well until I went on a diet. Diets happen and then unhappen for me, except this one didn't end. I couldn't go off my diet. I couldn't. I ate lettuce, lots of it. Then I ate tofu. I hate tofu. But I kept eating it. Death makes you eat tofu. Who knew?

"Doesn't that hurt?" asked a low voice in front of me.

I focused on Felix behind his vegetable stand under the slim red girders of Soulard Market. He held a bunch of radishes and had a bit of straw in his scraggly blond beard. "Huh?"

"Your dog is biting your leg," he said.

And he was. I had a big black fuzzy poodle gnawing on my calf. He chewed on my legs so often I didn't even feel it anymore.

"He's not my dog," I said. "He belongs to my...my... He's somebody else's dog."

"He's still gnawing on you."

"He's got separation anxiety."

Felix raised his unibrow. "You're right there."

"It's not me that he misses," I said.

Pickpocket tightened his grip while gazing up at me with shiny dark eyes. He belonged to my cousin by marriage, Chuck, who I'd kissed and then managed to alienate while working on a poisoning case in New Orleans. My father was a famous detective and sometimes I was called on to run down a suspect. In the case of New Orleans, I was paying back a favor for a friend. I solved the case but was nearly knifed. A hooded stranger with ties to the Costilla gang wanted information about Stevie Warnock, a guy who ate rocks for money and told everyone I was his best friend. As it happened, I didn't know where my best friend Stevie was, but the Costillas' emissary was willing to slice and dice me anyway so I shot him in the face. That was two months ago. Chuck had taken off on an undercover assignment and left me his dog, the slobbering Pick. It was a promise that he'd come back to me, but the promise had ruined three pairs of jeans, six pairs of tights, all my leggings, and my going-to-court pantyhose. I paid twenty-five bucks for that panty hose and he ruined them five minutes before I had to testify at a competency hearing for a serial killer. It was a bad day.

"You want these radishes or not?" asked Felix.

"I'll take two bunches," I said, trying to shake Pick off and failing yet again.

Felix bagged my radishes and I put them in my marketing cart, a gift from my godmothers, Myrtle and Millicent Bled. They supported my diet by buying me my cart and not saying a word about it, which is more than I can say for anyone else in my life.

My shiny new cart was an upright chrome affair that folded flat and could fit thirty pounds of vegetables. I tested it. So now I fit right in with the old ladies and mothers of five weaving their way through the vendors of the old outdoor market. Soulard was a comfort. It'd been the same for over eighty years, a produce paradise in the heart of St. Louis. Myrtle and Millicent had started bringing me when I was still in diapers. My mom never had the time and my godmothers had all the time in the world so I knew the vendors well even before the unfortunate events in New Orleans.

I paid Felix and attempted to walk down to my favorite lettuce vendor. That I had a favorite should've concerned me but it didn't. I was mostly worried that April wouldn't have enough to feed my habit. There was a mother with a passel of little ones eyeing the red leaf and arugula.

Back off, woman.

Pick dug in his heels and his warm slobber soaked through the leg of my only remaining pair of skinny jeans.

"Let go. What is your deal? We need lettuce," I said while trying to pry his jaws apart. No luck.

I pulled out my cell and texted Chuck. "Your dog is biting me again. Come home and do something about it."

My fingers stayed poised over my phone's keyboard. I'd sunk to a new level. Next I'd be claiming a deadly illness, the black plague or Lyme disease. Not that it would work. My phone remained depressingly silent. No vibration. No Train belting out "Drive By." Chuck didn't answer. He hadn't answered for two solid months, despite my daily texts. I kept expecting him to. Every single time I expected him to answer. I'm crazy that way.

Pick sat down while I texted Chuck, but he didn't let go of my leg. You'd think his mouth would get dry, but drool was always in good supply.

"He didn't answer," I said. "I know you're shocked. Try to contain the disappointment."

Pick shifted his jaw to get a better grip and I gave in. I always did. Pick expected it. He was smarter than me in many ways.

"I'll buy you donuts after the lettuce."

That nutty poodle let go and licked his chops.

"You're despicable and getting fat. What's Chuck going to say? You know how he loves fitness."

Pick yipped and began tugging on his leash. The mini donut shop sat at the end of a long row of healthy stuff and the smell of fresh frying donuts made both of us drool.

"Alright, alright." I let him pull me to April's ornate lettuce stand.

She liked to arrange her lettuce into pictures. Today it reminded me of the ocean, waves of green going on forever.

"Back so soon," said April. She acted like she was surprised. She wasn't.

"I ran out," I said.

She nodded and wisely said nothing. Going through twenty heads of lettuce in four days wasn't normal even if my apartment was infested with giant rabbits.

I picked out an assortment of normal stuff, reds, greens, arugula, and chicory. Then I got some frisée and mizuna to shake it up. Twenty-two bunches to be on the safe side. Running out was not fun.

April wrapped it all up and I filled my cart, placing the lettuce on top of my other staples, cucumbers, tomatoes, and whatnot. I paid April and calculated how many apples and turmeric I needed for juicing. Pick tugged harder, dragging me to the right.

"Hold on," I said, trying to picture how many wormy-looking turmeric roots I had left in the fridge.

Pick began prancing and making his I-see-someone-I-know whine. I looked up and spotted my dad standing at a stand with specialty greens like watercress and baby beet. He had his gun holster on and his hand poised like he was ready for something to happen at any second. Soulard market was pretty dangerous, all those vitamins and such. Dad was against vegetables as a general rule. He used to pay me to eat his when I was a kid so my mom would think he was eating them. A dollar per serving unless it was beets. I charged five bucks for beets. Dad called it extortion. I didn't know what that was but even at six I knew beets cost extra.

Dad saw me, but he didn't move. He scanned the area looking for something that he didn't find, then he gave me a little head cock to tell me to come over. Pick dragged me to him and wagged like he hadn't seen Dad in a month instead of a week.

"What are you doing here? Not buying veg, I assume."

"You assume right. Let's go," said Dad, not looking at me but still scanning.

"I'm not done," I said.

"You're done."

"No, I'm not."

Dad grabbed my arm and looked me in the eye for the first time. "Have you seen anyone following you? Anyone unusual?"

"All my stalkers are unusual." I smiled. Dad didn't.

"I'm not talking about the Marilyn Monroe fanatics. Anyone who doesn't want you to see them?" Dad was back to scanning.

"I had a couple of DBD fans yesterday. They just wanted an autograph." Through another series of unfortunate events I ended up being the band Double Black Diamond's new cover girl. Their fans outnumbered Marilyn Monroe's and were happily less odd.

Dad wheeled my cart around and began taking long strides toward the exit, dragging me along with him. I yanked my arm out of his grasp. "I told you I'm not done."

"We identified the guy," he said under his breath.

My heart seized up. "What guy?"

"Who do you think? The guy you shot."

"And?"

"It was Richard Costilla. The youngest of the brothers."

I felt like vomiting but I said, "So?"

"So you have to be locked down until I fix this."

"Define locked down."

"You're coming home with me. No going out." Dad glanced around. "Sure as hell no wide open spaces. The Costillas' want you dead."

"Are we sure about that?"

Dad yanked me close. I hadn't seen such fear in his eyes since I was little and ran off in Disney World. "We're sure. You need to come home."

"You mean your home," I said.

"My home is your home. It always will be. The Costillas don't play. You killed their baby brother. You think they're just going to forget that? The kid was seventeen."

"He was trying to kill me."

"They don't give a crap." Dad spun me to face him. "You're coming home right now if I have to wrestle you to the floor and hogtie you with zip ties."

"No, thanks."

"You're coming," he said between gritted teeth.

Richard Costilla's face flashed in my mind. I needed a salad so bad. "I get it."

The edge left Dad's eyes. "I'll buy you donuts."

"I don't want any donuts, but Pick wants some."

He touched the lacy greens of my carrots that draped over the edge of my cart. "I can see that, but do me a favor and tell your mother that I bought you donuts."

I shrugged. "Okay."

"And that you ate them."

"Obviously."

"Good." He took Pick's leash from me and we walked to the donut guy. The smell of sizzling dough filled the air as he dropped a fresh batch in the fryer.

Dad bought a bag and leaned over to me, his broad forehead wrinkled under his red hair. "Are you sure about the donuts?"

"I'm sure."

"How long are you going to punish yourself?"

"I'm not!" I gave my cart a hard shove and I dashed ahead of Dad and Pick. Pick yipped and his nails scraped the concrete floor of the market as he tried to follow me. My heart twisted a little. Somehow in the long weeks since Chuck left Pick with me, he'd become my dog and I hated to leave him behind but I couldn't talk and I couldn't think about talking. So the Costillas had marked me. I should've been frightened. Terrified would've been an appropriate response. Instead, I felt empty. I needed a salad. A salad and maybe some tofu.

CHAPTER TWO

I'd just opened my truck door and grabbed my carrots when Dad reached me.

"Leave the freaking veg and get in the truck," he said, huffing and puffing. Dad was rail thin but had the endurance of a guy with one lung.

"I paid for this stuff. I'm not leaving it." I hauled out the bags, careful not to damage my delicate greens.

Dad shoved me out of the way and tossed the bags in. They bounced off the dash and windshield. He had no respect for my frisée.

"Knock it off." I tried to worm my way back in but Dad took up a lot of space for someone so skinny.

He ignored me as usual, finished wrecking my dinner, and then tossed my cart in the bed of my truck without even folding it. I froze and stared at him. My truck was a 1958 cherry Chevy with original paint. He bought it for my sixteenth birthday, but it was really for himself. He thought a girl would never want to drive an old truck and he would end up with it, but I was on to his game and took the truck just to piss him off. He was always worrying about the maintenance and the paint since I refused to give it back and drove it every day. He obsessed like a fifteen-year-old girl with a crush on a lifeguard. "Is that a scratch, Mercy?" "Don't eat in the truck." "What kind of wax did you use?" He was crazy so when he threw that metal cart in the pristine bed of my truck, without a thought to the damage it would cause, I knew it was beyond serious.

"They'll kill you," he said. "And you won't even see it coming."

"Okay."

"Follow me home now."

"Okay."

He turned to his car parked beside mine and his phone went crazy. It was the red alert signal from the original Star Trek series and not like something Dad would put on his phone at all.

"What the hell?" He dug it out of his pocket and glanced skyward. "Freaking Morty. He screwed with my phone again."

I suppressed a laugh. Uncle Morty was my dad's best friend and a computer guru of supreme ability. He loved Star Trek and all things nerdy.

"Morty can put ringtones on your phone?" I asked.

"Yes. Get in the truck now." He looked down at the screen and paled. Now that's saying something. Dad had zero color to begin with.

"What is it?" I asked.

"Get in my car," he said.

"What about Pick?"

"Him, too."

"What about the leather? His nails—"

"Get in the car!" he yelled and everyone in the parking lot stared.

I locked my truck, put Pick in the backseat, and got in. Dad revved the engine and peeled out while simultaneously telling the car to dial Morty.

"Yeah," said Morty after picking up on the first ring.

"How come you got this before me?" asked Dad.

"Does it fucking matter?"

"No. How long ago?"

"Came in five seconds before I texted you. You think I'd sit on this?" asked Uncle Morty, managing to sound petulant.

"What's going on?" I asked.

Both Dad and Morty told me to shut up. Fine. Shutting up.

"Morty, I want all you got on this."

"I'm on it."

I could hear Uncle Morty heave himself out of his chair. It was quite an operation. Dad ended the call and glanced at me. "Do The Girls keep an inventory at the house?"

"Huh?" I stared at him. The Girls? What did my godmothers have to do with anything?

"Pay attention, Mercy. Is there an inventory of The Bled Collection at the house?"

"Um...I think so. I saw one in the library a couple of years ago. Why?"

"Someone broke into the mansion and cracked Lester on the head."

"Oh my god. Is he okay?"

"He's old as dirt. What do you think?"

"Shit. Were The Girls there? What about the rest of the staff?"

Dad stared at the road as he weaved through the traffic. "Lester was alone. EMTs are on their way."

I banged the dash with both hands. "Hurry up."

"There's nothing you can do."

"Wanna bet?"

Dad hit the accelerator and yanked the steering wheel to the right, taking us up onto the sidewalk. Somehow, we squeezed between a fire hydrant and the store fronts to bypass the traffic stopped at a red light. We lurched back onto the street as the light turned green and Pick slid across the backseat. I winced at the sound of nails on leather, but Dad didn't seem to notice. He yanked right again and Pick slid to the left, making a tiny yip when he bumped the door. We hit a curb and he flew into the air only to land on all fours and slide to the right. Pick was doing that smiling pant that dogs do when they're happy. Maybe he was used to it. I'd seen Chuck drive and he wasn't exactly slow or smooth.

I turned to face the front and screamed as Dad cut off a delivery truck while lowering his window and popping his old cherry on the top of the car, flashing like crazy.

"Didn't they take that away from you when you retired?" I asked while clutching the door handle for dear life.

Dad gave me his evil Grinch look. "They tried."

"They're the police. How could they fail?"

"Oh ye of little faith."

I screamed as we narrowly avoided a woman walking six dogs. "Hail, Mary, Mother of God, pray for us sinners."

Where's my rosary? I need my rosary.

"Now at the hour—"

"Stop that!" yelled Dad. "We're not dying today."

"You just clipped a light pole."

"It deserved it. You want to get there or not?"

"I want to arrive alive!" I yelled.

"I trained for this."

"Was there a test? Did you pass?"

"They said I was too aggressive," Dad said.

"No, shit!"

"Watch your language."

"Are you kidding me?" I hit my head on the window as Dad made a sharp left onto Lindell Boulevard. "I'm telling Mom you tried to kill us."

"She failed the test, too."

"What is wrong with you people?"

One minute and thirty long seconds later we drove onto Hawthorne Avenue. Lucky for us the street's big ornate gate was open for another car or Dad might've driven straight through it. We careened down the quiet street, passing the Lexus and its astonished driver. Hawthorne didn't get many out of control cars or police cruisers and it was a banner day for both.

Dad passed our house so fast it was a blur and then slammed on the brakes in front of the Bled Mansion. Pick flew between the seats and landed on the console with his paws on the dash.

"You almost killed the dog!" I yelled.

"He's a police dog. He's fine."

"He's a poodle."

"Close enough." Dad jumped out. "I'm pumped. Let's kick some ass."

I got out much more slowly, acutely aware of our audience, five uniformed cops and two detectives. Pick jumped out behind me, spun in a circle, and barfed in the gutter. Dad stepped over the heaving Pick and yelled, "What have we got, fellas?"

The cops stared at Dad, even the ones that knew him well. I guess nobody gets used to my dad. I certainly didn't. The detectives, Sidney Wick and Nazir, recovered the fastest. They walked down the long brick walk and Nazir flicked his hand at me.

Oh, right. The light.

I slipped around the car, popped the light off the roof, and tossed it into the backseat none too gently. If it broke that was just a darn shame. When I came back around, Dad was through the gate and talking to Nazir and Wick with big expansive hand gestures. I snagged Pick's leash, gave him a soothing pat, and trotted past them.

"Hold on, Miss Watts," said Wick. "Where do you think you're going?"

"Are the EMTs here?" I asked.

"Arrived about forty-five seconds before you did."

"Good." I dashed toward the front door with Wick yelling, "Wait!"

I wasn't waiting. It was Lester. I'd known him my whole life. He'd handed out the cigars when I'd been born upstairs. Waiting wasn't happening.

The door was locked, but the alarm wasn't activated. I unlocked the door with my key and, in an instant, saw that the alarm hadn't been tripped. It simply wasn't on. Weird. Dad programed his specially-designed system to be armed at all times since a guy named Jens Waldemar Hoff started sniffing around. He was the agent of a non-profit, The Klinefeld Group, who were suing the Bleds to get control of their extensive art collection. The Klinefeld Group looked like a solid organization if you didn't look too closely. They were willing to say or do anything to get their hands on the multi-million dollar collection. Lately, they put out attack ads, slandering my dad and his police record and accusing the Bleds of stealing from the Jews before the Nazis arrested them during WWII. The lawsuit was all over the news and it was getting dirtier by the day because it didn't look like the lawsuit would get anywhere. My adventure in New Orleans had come at just the right time. All the arrests stemming from my investigation made us look like saints and The Klinefeld Group like scumbags, which they were.

I swung open the big heavy door. "Where is he?" I yelled to Nazir. "Kitchen!"

Wick punched Nazir in the shoulder and began stomping up the walk after me. "Don't tell her that, you moron. She's corrupting our crime scene."

Dad waved for me to go in and I winked at him. I wouldn't corrupt anything. I wasn't some nitwit, despite what The Klinefeld Group said about me.

I tightened up on Pick's leash and we headed into the cool interior of my first home, my birthplace. Pick's nails clicked on the gleaming hardwood and he sniffed the Egyptian dog's head that made up the armrest of the bench next to a display of family pictures on a rosewood table. Stella and Nicky were safe in their gilded frame, smiling in front of a Venetian gondola in 1938. Stella was The Girls' cousin and she linked my family to the Bleds, but I still didn't know why or how. I'd discovered in New Orleans that she and Nicky had met with my ancestors, Amelie and Paul in Paris, a meeting that was concealed just like Stella's activities during the war.

We dashed into the receiving room first and I could see in a glance that all the art was intact. Myrtle and Millicent did rearrange the collection according to their mood and the current setup had been in place since I got back from New Orleans. My godmothers played everything close to the vest, but the minute I saw the Whistlers and Caillebottes come out of the attic, I knew they were angry. Gone were the warm Monets, Bazilles, and Gauguins. Cold paintings in grey scale and jagged cubist works were in their places. It was the only indication of their deep upset at being accused of crimes that they abhorred.

Pick tugged me through a series of rooms, all undisturbed, until we entered the kitchen. There was a cluster of EMTs and a couple uniforms standing by the wide marble pastry table.

One of the cops pointed at me, "Stop right there. Who—"

He realized who I was mid-sentence and began stammering.

"I'm the goddaughter of the owners, Mercy Watts." I tied Pick to a chair and walked over. "What's his condition?"

"Who?"

"Lester Hodges, your victim."

"You know him?" He was talking to my breasts and I wanted to give him a swift kick in the shin.

"Naturally. He's the chauffeur." I pushed past him and my breath caught in my chest. Lester was lying in a pool of blood while the EMTs tried to resuscitate him. The only blip on the monitor was manual, done by the EMT doing compressions on Lester's narrow chest.

Why? He's so old.

Another EMT readied the paddles and yelled, "Clear!"

Lester's body spasmed.

"I've got a rhythm!" The EMT shouted stats into his radio and they brought the gurney in. They lifted Lester onto it without much effort. He weighed about a hundred pounds in the heavy chauffeur uniform he insisted on wearing. My last glimpse was of his thin face, slack jawed and unresponsive. An arm came around me and pulled me back. I breathed deep Dad's cologne and said, "They got him back."

"Details?"

"Blow to the back of the head. They brought the weapon with them," I said staring at the blood.

"How do you know?"

"I know this kitchen. Nothing's missing." I pointed to the armchair beside the window. "He was sitting there. Probably asleep until they came in. He always snoozes here while The Girls bake. Do we know where they are?"

Nazir and Wick came in. Wick sighed and looked at the ceiling for a second. "Neighbor called it in. She saw the owners get in a car service about two hours ago. Maybe you can tell us where they are."

I got out my phone and checked the calendar. "The cathedral fête starts this weekend. They're probably working on it."

"Doing what?"

"Organizing. Lester doesn't drive them much anymore. He can't see over the wheel very well. They just call a service. Which neighbor?" I asked.

"Excuse me," called out a refined voice.

Mrs. Haase waved at me through the window. She had gardening shears in her hand and wore her usual floppy hat. She wasn't as interesting as the broken window I was looking through. I walked around the pastry table and waved to her. The hole was the size of a mug and, sure enough, there was a heavy mug lying in the rose bed at Mrs. Haase's feet.

Wick came to my elbow. "We think Mr. Hodges threw the cup when they hit him. She heard the breaking glass."

I called to Mrs. Haase, "I'm coming out."

The cops, including Dad, stayed in the kitchen discussing the point of entry. I untied Pick and went out into the garden. Mrs. Haase shocked me with a hug and allowed Pick to sniff her hand. "How are you, dear?"

"Okay. So you heard the breaking glass."

"I did and I came right over. There were two men in suits going out the back gate."

Suits?

"Did you see their faces?" I asked.

"Sadly, no. But there wasn't a car. They just went out through the stables to the alley."

"Did they use a code to get in the stables?"

"No. The door was open." Mrs. Haase took off her hat and a lock of thick grey hair fell in her face. She tucked it behind her ear and leaned in. "The stable is always locked and alarmed. The cars are worth quite a bit."

"I know. Were they carrying anything?"

"Like what?" she asked.

"A weapon. Maybe a hammer. Something like that," I said.

"Now that you mention it, there was something in the larger man's hand, but I couldn't see what it was."

"Did he have it in the alley?"

"I didn't pay attention. I heard Lester moan and I called 911. The poor man. He wouldn't have threatened them. He could barely see. What do you think? Will he survive?" she asked.

"I couldn't say."

"You must have some idea. You are a nurse."

"It doesn't look good."

She hugged me again. "I'd like some tea. Can I have Bethany make you some?"

"Bethany?"

"Our new cook."

"No, thanks. I'm fine."

Mrs. Haase headed for her own Tudor-style mansion and I went for the stables. The door was unlocked and the alarm was in sleep mode. The lights were on. Whoever they were, they weren't nervous or particularly sneaky.

I checked the door to the alley and it was wide open, the entry point to the grounds of the estate. The lock wasn't jimmied. How did they get in? I made a circuit of the entire stables. First the cars. They were all there and undisturbed. The keys were in the house. They wouldn't be hard to find. Maybe they planned on driving off in the 1921 Maybach or Millicent's Borgwald Isabella and the broken window ruined the plan.

Since the cars were all there, I checked the stalls. The building had originally been a stable and The Girls kept the stalls their ponies used filled with fresh hay for sentimental reasons. I used to do my home-work out there, lying in the fragrant heaps. The smell was soothing when I was struggling with statistics.

Pick tugged on his leash and barked, dragging me past the stalls. They were all normal. Their brass plaques engraved with horses' names were shiny and untouched. No. Not quite. The stall at the end, my Statistics study stall, wasn't quite closed. Pick went wild as we got closer and found the bolt thrown open. I used my sweater sleeve to open the door. The hay was heaped evenly, except for one spot in the corner under the empty trough. Pick sniffed and began baying like a bloodhound. Maybe the poodle was a police dog. I tied Pick to the black bars of the stall, got down on my hands and knees, and slid my hand under the straw until I felt something hard.

"Find something?"

I glanced back at my dad. He was smiling.

"Maybe. The straw was disturbed."

"Don't touch it." He called Nazir and he came in, gloved up, and felt around until he came up with a small metal pry bar with blood on it. "Huh?"

"What?" I asked.

Dad crossed his arms and tapped his foot, staring at the bar in Nazir's hand. "It's too small for almost everything. You can't pry a door open with that."

"Or a window," said Nazir.

"They weren't worried about getting in."

I frowned. "They had a key? How?"

Dad called Uncle Morty and told him the Bled Mansion had been hacked. The cursing that came out of Dad's phone was loud and colorful. Uncle Morty could probably hack the US Treasury if he cared to put the time into it, but there weren't many guys like him. Whoever hacked the Bled Mansion was very very good. Spidermonkey was my cyber snoop and he was just as good as Morty if not better, but he knew the Bleds personally. So he wouldn't do it and there was still the matter of the key.

Uncle Morty bellowed about the system until Dad hung up on him. "He's pissed."

"No kidding," said Nazir. "But what's it got to do with him?"

"It was his firewall they breached. He thought it was impenetrable."

"Nothing's impenetrable."

"Clearly."

"Hello." I waved my key ring at them. "What about the key? The Girls have deadbolts on every exterior door. If they didn't break a window or pry open a door, how'd they get in?"

Dad blew out a deep breath in a whoosh. "There may have been a fault in the system."

"What kind of fault?" asked Nazir.

"When Morty originally designed the system he was worried about the deadbolts. The Girls are getting up in years. Their manual dexterity isn't what it used to be. Using a key to get out of the house in an emergency, like a fire, could be difficult."

"So?" I asked.

"So we had the locks wired into the system so I, your mother, and the security company could unlock them in an emergency so they could get out and the authorities could get in." Dad flushed to the roots of his red hair. He was almost purple like someone was strangling him but his voice remained calm.

"Are you crazy?" I yelled. I don't know what gave me the balls to yell at my father. Nobody yelled at Dad. It just wasn't done.

Dad stared at me, the blood draining out of his face.

"I'm glad you said that and not me." Nazir edged away. "Step away, Mercy."

"I don't care! He made it so some dude in Pakistan can open the damn door if he has the brains to figure out the system!"

Dad sucked in a breath and let out a string of curse words so fast I couldn't make out any individual one, finishing with, "We disconnected the system!"

"Apparently not! Did you physically cut the wires to the locks?" I asked, now strangely calm. I'm surprised my life didn't flash before my eyes. Dad was that mad.

"The security company was ordered to do it!" he yelled as Wick and two uniforms ran in.

"Did you follow up?"

"No!"

"That's insane."

"Son of a bitch!" Dad pointed a long finger at me. "You're right!"

Did my father just say I was right?

"Huh? What?"

Dad dropped his arm and his shoulders slumped. "You're right. This is my fault. Is Lester going to die?"

"Most likely," I said softly. "But it's not you who whacked him."

"I gave them access." He walked away toward the cars and we all watched him in silence.

"What'd I miss?" asked Wick.

Nazir gave him the rundown and they bagged the pry bar. I doubted if they'd be able to trace it or find any prints. Whoever the suits worked for wouldn't be stupid enough to leave evidence if it could be traced to them.

"So," said Wick, looking at the pry bar. "They wanted access to something, but the house wasn't it."

Dad's shoulders twitched at his words and I said, "Something small like a cabinet. They left great art on the walls. Small pieces. There's a Renoir in the back hall. It could fit into a pocket and they had to pass right by it when they went to the kitchen. They wanted something in particular. Something hidden."

"Like what?" asked Nazir. "Why not just take the easy stuff?"

"You can't sell it for one thing. Not easily anyway. There are some collectors who'd have no problem buying a Renoir known to be part of The Bled Collection, but it's not an easy sale. The point of having a Renoir is to tell people you have it. Stolen art must be hidden."

"What do they have that's worth more than a Renoir or whatever else they've got in there?" asked Wick.

I crossed my arms. "I don't know, but I know who wants it."

CHAPTER THREE

I stood in front of the desk and held the tiny gold key in my hand, but I didn't need it. The suits had used their pry bar and it hurt my heart to see the damage. It was devastating. The cops had missed it on their first pass through the house. Millicent's desk in the library had been wrenched open and the papers thoroughly gone through. It was a Biedermeier writing desk circa 1840 and they'd just ripped open the drawers like they were nothing instead of irreplaceable.

Wick leafed through the piles of paper. "They went through pretty much every cabinet, closet, and drawer in the house, big and small. These drawers won't fit anything but paper." He looked up at me, his round face sweaty. "What was in here? All I got is receipts and some charity stuff."

"The inventory," I said. "There was an inventory of the entire contents of The Bled Collection."

"Which would presumably have what they were looking for on it," he said.

"We'll have to call the rest of the family."

"What for?"

"There are pieces in other houses. They have to be warned," I said.

"And the list says which pieces are where?" asked Nazir.

"Of course. It doesn't change much. The family doesn't loan out pieces to museums as a general rule, but sometimes a family member wants a certain piece for an event. There is restoration work to be done from time to time, too."

Wick closed the drawer and ran his beefy finger over the splintered mahogany veneer. "And you really have no idea what this Klinefeld Group is after?"

I shook my head. "I don't and neither do Myrtle or Millicent. Aunt Miriam says they want a box or rather something that would be in a box."

"Maybe your aunt is wrong," said Nazir.

"Have you met Aunt Miriam?"

Nazir did an involuntary shudder and I laughed. Aunt Miriam wasn't wrong. A couple of months earlier she received a visit at her convent from a man calling himself Jens Waldemar Hoff. He wanted information about The Bled Collection and specifically about some box that The Girls hadn't opened. He threatened to out Stella Bled Lawrence as a Nazi collaborator unless the Bleds handed over all the pieces Stella smuggled out of Europe for Jewish families. The Bleds refused and The Klinefeld Group added their false accusations to the lawsuit. The Bled family was all over the news and not in a good way. Talking heads on CNN and Fox News were discussing what an evil traitor Stella might've been, but Millicent and Myrtle didn't waver. They didn't have to. The one thing The Klinefeld Group didn't know was that our government knew all about The Bled Collection and the pieces Stella smuggled out. They were all labeled by Stella herself and there was a thorough inventory at the end of the war. All information about Stella's activities as a spy for the US and Britain were still top secret and the courts weren't looking on the lawsuit with a kind eye.

"I don't know how we protect something if we don't know what it is," said Nazir.

"It's enough to know that they didn't get it," said Dad.

"Do we know that?" I asked.

"They took the inventory. If they had it, they wouldn't need the inventory." He took the little key from my hand and placed it on the desk. "We have to call The Girls."

"By *we* you mean me, don't you?" I asked.

"I can do it, but..."

"But I'm their girl. I'll do it. How much should I say?"

"Everything. This is their house and their collection. Tell them everything."

I didn't call my godmothers. That's not the kind of news that should be delivered over the phone. I delayed by eating half a bar of Amedei Prendime dark chocolate. Millicent kept a stash for emergencies and this was definitely an emergency. Then I tried to call a cab to take me down to the cathedral. Dad caught me in the act and put me in a squad car. A uniform drove me down with strict orders not to let me out of his sight.

I'd planned on giving Officer Samson the slip, but when I caught sight of the cathedral all the wiliness drained out of me. Something about those solid grey walls, gothic arches, and green tiled roof made me want to be good. Maybe I expected Aunt Miriam to come charging out in full habit to catch me, but, for whatever reason, I just got out of the car and let Samson follow me.

The fête was in the school adjacent to the cathedral. It was a dull modern building compared to the cathedral it served, and I never liked it. Millicent and Myrtle were in the musty, cold gym discussing how much a primitive painting of an orchard would bring in. Not much in my opinion. The painting was atrocious.

I got their attention and told them what happened. At first, they didn't react. They were like statues wearing prim Chanel suits and little hats with netting pinned to their elegantly done silver hair.

Finally, Myrtle said, "Are you alright, dear?"

"Me? I'm fine. How are you?" I asked.

"I believe we're ready to go," said Millicent.

"Where are we going?"

"To the hospital, naturally."

"Oh well. I called on the way over and they were taking Lester into surgery. There's nothing for you to do," I said.

"You're quite wrong. The Hodges will be there and we must express our sympathy. You know that. We taught you what to do in times of crisis."

I suppose they did, but I only listened with half an ear most of the time. I was a Watts and proper behavior didn't come easily. I gathered their coats and put them in the squad car for the trip to the hospital. They talked Samson into using the siren and we made it in record time.

The Hodges family was there in full force. Millicent and Myrtle expressed their regrets and sympathy while I got the scoop from the attending. I'd worked with Dr. Gagnon several times. Since I was a PRN nurse I got around and knew everybody. Being a temp had plenty of advantages. Getting the real story from the source that day wasn't one of them. Gagnon was upbeat with the family but painfully honest with me. If Lester made it out of surgery, he had a chance, not a good chance, just a chance. The crack on the head had caused a significant bleed in the brain. They were going in to repair it, but the position made the surgery difficult and Lester's age was a huge factor.

I left the hospital with a terrible weight on me. The Girls didn't realize how bad it was and I didn't enlighten them. I let them think it could all be fine. They didn't need to know about the possibilities. I wished I didn't.

Samson drove us back to the Bled Mansion and I introduced them to Wick and Nazir. Millicent produced another inventory from a hatbox in her closet and I was tasked with going through the house and verifying the location of every piece. It took me six hours. All the pieces were there, but The Girls had moved them around so they could be anywhere in the mansion, including bathrooms and the attic.

When I was done, I gave Dad the list and went upstairs to my room. The doors on the wardrobe were open and my clothes had been rifled through, but nothing had been taken or ruined. I laid down on the floor and scooted under the bed. The names were still there, printed in Stella's handwriting on a yellowing label and pasted to the side rail. The Wahle family. It was their furniture that I lived with and slept on. I didn't know what had happened to them after Stella took possession of their things in 1939 and I didn't want to know. They hadn't come to claim what belonged to them and that was more information than I wanted. Was it something that belonged to the Wahle family that The Klinefeld Group wanted?

I touched the label and knew that I was going to find out and it would bring no peace. Chuck wasn't there to help. It was just me. What if this had to do with my parents? My godmothers had given them our house and it was an extraordinary gift. Something had happened to make them do it and I'd been searching for the reason ever since I found out. Dad had flown to Paris with Josiah Bled, The Girls' uncle, the year before I was born and the old man had never been seen again. While Dad was gone The Girls' signed over our house's deed to my mom, a woman they'd never met.

The weight of those names, the break-in, the possibilities of what my parents had done to earn our house settled on my chest, pressing me into the thick Turkish carpet. I was about to wallow and there was only one thing to do when wallowing came to call; I had to make a salad or tofu or a salad with tofu, the ultimate cure.

I wiped a tear from the corner of my eye and heard my door creak open wide. Pick's fluffy feet scampered in and he followed my trail to the bed, got down, and belly crawled to me. His red tongue flicked out and touched my cheek.

"It doesn't help but thank you," I said, scratching him under his chin.

Beyond his panting head, a pair of pearl grey Prada pumps walked in, circled the bed, and then found a place at the Wahles' rocker next to the full-length mirror.

"Don't let them haunt you, dear," said Myrtle. "They will if you allow it."

I bit my lip and then said, "Who?"

"The Wahles. You shouldn't be under there. They'll take you to places you shouldn't go."

Pick sniffed the label and I pushed his snout down in case he smeared the old ink. "And where would that be?"

"Darkness."

"You know that?"

She sighed, a sad and lonely sound. "I spent my life with these names surrounding me, weighing on me. My parents searched for the Wahles and when they died it fell to Millicent and myself."

"But you never found any trace," I said.

"Oh, no. We picked up the trail in 1986."

I jumped and bumped my head on the slats. "So they're dead."

"I said I found the trail, not the end of it. Millicent and I found many clues over the years, but none led us to their fate."

"What clues?"

"We found a man, who was eleven in 1939. He remembered the SS coming for the Wahles in the middle of the night in Hallstatt. He was reluctant to speak of it. His shame was deep."

"He was a child."

"His parents weren't. They watched their friends being dragged out of their house and thrown in the back of a truck and didn't lift a finger. He never saw the Wahles again. It was our first clue. It took six years to find another."

My heart was pounding. They found a clue about the Wahles the year before I was born, the year Dad and Josiah Bled flew to Paris and took the train to Hallstatt, the Wahles' hometown. "And what was that."

"No," she said, her voice sharper than I'd ever heard it.

"No?" I whispered.

"It's too hard."

"You've given up?"

"Never and, in the future, the same will be expected of you."

"Of me?"

"Naturally."

A pair of Italian loafers walked in and Dad said, "There you are."
Dammit, Dad. Go away.

He leaned over and peered at me in the gloom under the bed. "What're you doing under there?"

"What do you think?" I asked.

"I don't know. You were always a weird kid."
Gee, I wonder why.

"Lots of people think I'm normal."

He chuckled. "Name one."

"Um..."

"That's what I thought. Get out here. I've got a plan," said Dad.

Oh, no. Not a plan.

"A plan for someone other than me."

"Yeah, right. What did I say? Get out here."

Pick belly crawled backward and I rolled out, away from his slurping tongue. "What's your plan? Did the techs find fingerprints? Do I get to go kick somebody in the crotch?"

Dad crossed his arms and lowered his eyelids to half-mast. "Yes, that's exactly it."

"Really?"

"No. Think, Mercy. The Klinefeld Group aren't idiots. There won't be any fingerprints and we don't kick men in the crotch."

Speak for yourself.

"You punch sleaze bags in the ear," I said.

"That was different."

It always is when it's you.

"So what's the plan?"

"You're going away for a few days. It's all arranged," Dad said.

I jumped to my feet. "What? Why?"

"We were going to keep you with us for the duration but the situation has intensified." Dad glanced at Myrtle, who watched him intently. I could tell she didn't know about Richard Costilla yet, but it wouldn't take long for her to get it out of Dad and he knew it. He sighed and continued, "There have been multiple inquiries about you."

"What does that mean?" I asked.

"Men have shown up at your agency, Kronos, and three hospitals looking for you. Five hours ago, a man was observed waiting outside your apartment building."

"You don't know that was about me."

Dad looked at me like I was too stupid to breathe. "Of course it's about you, moron. You're out of here."

My phone started ringing. It was the theme from *The Godfather.* I really was a moron. "I can't. I have work and stuff. I have stuff." I fumbled for my phone.

Button. Button. Where's the damn off button?

"Whose ringtone is that?" asked Dad.

"Nobody."

Dad snagged the phone before I could press the button and he looked at the screen. "Who is Great Butt?"

Oh my god!

Myrtle's ring-laden hand fluttered over her chest and I wanted to crawl under the carpet. You didn't say butt in front of my godmothers. It was derrière at the very worst.

"Well?" asked Dad.

"Um...it's a guy," I said.

"I assumed that. Who is it?"

"He's Italian."

"Also a safe assumption. What's his name?"

"Er..."

Dad leaned over me with a brittle smile. "His name is Er?"

"No. It's...it's Felix."

Felix? What the hell, Mercy?

"You know an Italian guy named Felix?"

"Italian guys can be named Felix," I said.

"They can, but they're not."

My phone was still ringing in Dad's hand, having started up again after my voicemail picked up. Dad made a move to answer it and I snatched it out of his hand. "Hi, Felix. How are you?"

"Felix?" asked Oz Urbani, a man who couldn't have been farther from a Felix. Oz was the nephew of Calpurnia Fibonacci, the head of St. Louis's most notorious mafia family. Oz claimed he wasn't a part of the family business. I had my doubts on that. He did have a great butt though.

"Of course I remember you, Felix," I said.

"Oh. Your dad is there, isn't he?"

"Sure thing."

"Alright. I'll make this quick. My aunt just told me that the Costilla organization has a hit out on you."

Be calm. Look calm. It's only Felix. He wants to date you, not tell you about your impending death.

"Oh, yeah. That sounds great, but I don't like horror. How about *The Woman in Gold?*" I asked.

"That looks boring," he said.

Oh my god.

"I don't think it's bad," I said.

"It's bad."

The movie?

Dad moved in closer to try and listen in and I backed up nearly falling over Pick who yelped.

"The starting price on your golden locks is fifty thousand," said Oz.

Not the movie then.

"Good to know."

"So you killed Richie Costilla."

Damn. That was fast.

"Well, you never know until you see it."

"Huh? Oh, right. The movie. Look, Mercy, I just wanted you to know. Keep your head down."

"Thanks. See you later."

"Good luck," he said and hung up. Is there anything more ominous than ending a phone call with good luck? I don't think so.

I tucked my phone away. "So...you were saying, Dad."

"What did *Felix* want?"

"To go to the movies. We have different tastes. You said I'm going away."

He cocked an eyebrow at me. "Suddenly you don't seem to mind."

Hell, no, I don't. Fifty thousand isn't chump change.

I shrugged. "I can fight you, but I won't win."

He threw up his hands. "Finally, she admits it."

Myrtle smiled and I grimaced. I'd never live this down and Dad would expect to win forever. Not going to happen. This was a onetime thing.

I rolled my eyes. "Fine. Go ahead and rub it in. Where am I going? Prie Dieu? Grandma's house?"

"A girl trip. Your mother has arranged it all," he said with a diabolical grin.

"A girl trip? With who?"

"Your cousins."

I went cold. My toes were probably blue. "But...I only have three girl cousins."

"That's right. You, Mercy Watts, are the lucky winner of an all-expenses-paid trip with your only three female cousins."

"Weepy, Snot, and Spoiled Rotten? What did I ever do to you?"

"We don't have that much time," Dad said, the grin growing wider.

Myrtle handed me a thick packet of Amedei Prendime dark chocolate bars. "Good luck, dear."

"No way. I'm not doing it. I can go somewhere that they're not. How about federal prison?" I asked.

Myrtle stood up and hugged me. "May God give you the serenity to accept the things you cannot change."

Oh my god!

CHAPTER FOUR

Dad let me get my truck from Soulard Market's parking lot, but only because my veg would rot and ruin the upholstery. I was not allowed to go alone. Officer Samson accompanied me and stuck so close I felt like a toddler with a helicopter mom.

I pulled in the alley behind my parents' house after dark and closed the garage door on the trio of squad cars behind me. I retrieved my phone and checked for messages. There were plenty of messages. None were from Chuck and he was the only one I wanted to hear from.

"Dad's sending me off with the Troublesome Trio," I texted him.

I waited and nothing. Of course. Of course, there was nothing. I screamed and banged on the steering wheel. Samson whipped open the garage side door with his gun drawn.

I waved and got out. "Sorry. I just had a moment."

His eyes darted around the dim garage like he didn't believe me. "Yeah?"

"Yeah. It's been a bad day. Aren't you off shift?" I asked.

"We're doing Detective Watts a favor."

Dad was still Detective Watts. I guess he always would be. Samson helped me gather up my cloth bags and lug them down the long brick walk past Mom's lush gardens. The tulips were blooming, fat and heavy. The cold spring air accentuated the scent of the flowers. For a moment, I forgot the break-in and the rest of it and just breathed in the fruits of Mom's labor.

We tromped up the back stairs before I said goodbye to Samson and unlocked the door. I picked up my umpteen bags, walking sideways into the butler's pantry at the rear of my parents' house. It was ice cold as usual. Dad stood at the marble counter pouring himself a generous glug of whiskey and watching me out of the corner of his eye. Pick trotted in from the parlor and sat on Dad's foot. Dad looked down and frowned. "Why does he always sit on my feet?"

"It runs in the family," I said. "You want to help me with these bags?"

"Hell, no. I'm not taking the blame for that."

"I don't know what you're talking about."

"You will." He put the highball glass to my lips. "Drink. You'll need it."

I took the smallest of sips. It was nasty, but I smiled and choked back a cough for Dad's benefit. He swore that when I was a real adult, I'd appreciate whiskey. Not going to happen. Burning throat liquid wasn't for me.

"Tommy, is that you?" Mom's voice came right through the kitchen door along with the faint smell of her beloved ragu bolognese. It took four hours to make and contained, to my dismay, chicken livers.

Dad raised his glass to me and said, "No. It's a crazy sick maniac, drinking all your handsome husband's good whiskey."

"My husband is just okay. You can drink his whiskey."

"What?"

Mom laughed in the kitchen, but Dad couldn't stop frowning.

"Don't come in. My boyfriend's still here," she said.

Dad began some serious muttering.

I nudged Dad out of the way. "Hello. She's joking."

"It could happen," said Dad.

I rolled my eyes at him and turned the old brass doorknob. It couldn't happen. Not that Mom couldn't get a boyfriend. She could get twelve plus two. But she wouldn't. For some reason, she was devoted to my father, a six foot four redhead that wouldn't eat for days, if she didn't watch him. Seriously, my father had a feeding schedule. He was that skinny.

I opened the door and the bolognese smell rolled in like a thick fog and enveloped me so completely that I was light-headed for a blissful moment. It smelled like we were Italian, which we weren't.

Mom twirled around, holding a wide wooden spoon and wearing one of Dad's white dress shirts that came to her knees and a pair of black leggings. Even though she'd been cooking for hours, her hair was perfectly done and never looked more like Marilyn Monroe, cat eye makeup and all. My mother never looked bad. I, on the other hand, had no makeup, dog slobber on my jeans, and spider webs in my hair. Sometimes people confused me for Marilyn, but nobody ever mistook me for my mother.

I hauled my bags to the kitchen table and heaved them on. Vegetables were heavier than they looked. "Hi, Mom. Sauce smells great."

"What do you expect me to do with all that lettuce?" She jabbed the air with her spoon. "Don't even bring those in here."

"What am I supposed to do with them? Leave them on the porch to rot? This cost good money." There! I was using my mother's own words against her. Did she ever hate wasting good money.

"How many heads of lettuce did you buy?" she asked.

"A few."

"Define a few."

"I don't know," I said.

"You don't want to tell me," she said.

Correct.

"I'd tell you if I knew."

I did know. I had twenty-two heads of lettuce in my bags. In retrospect, it was a lot of lettuce. At the time, it seemed like a snack portion.

Mom stalked over and whacked my bags with her spoon in rhythm with her words. "This. Has. Gone. Too. Far."

"It's just lettuce, Mom," I said, trying to hide the radishes, cucumbers, kale, and carrots. "You love salads. You eat salads all the time."

"How much weight have you lost?" she asked.

I groaned. "Do we have to talk about this again?"

"How much?"

"A little."

"I'd say it's closer to twenty-five pounds," said Mom.

Holy crap! Right on the money.

"It's not that much."

"You're starving yourself."

"I am not. I eat."

"You eat nothing." Mom picked up a bag of arugula and threw it at Dad. "I told you to talk some sense into her."

Dad held the bag up like a shield. "We had a situation."

"We have a situation right here. Look at her. She looks like a scarecrow." Mom plucked at the waist of my jeans. It was bunched up under the belt.

"Thin is in, Mom. You don't know," I said.

"I know something's wrong and it ends here. You're eating my bolognese tonight."

"No, I'm not."

"Why not?" Mom asked with her face an inch from mine.

Because I have to eat a salad.

"Because...because I ate with Millicent and Myrtle."

"You ate at a crime scene where Lester may very well have been bludgeoned to death." Mom looked at Dad. He grimaced. For a man, who lied to suspects with an aplomb people wrote articles about, Dad sucked. Any fool could tell I didn't eat and Mom was no fool.

"I have talked and talked to you," she said.

Then you should be done.

"You can stop. I'm fine. I'm just eating healthy. Healthy is good," I said.

Mom's plump lower lip quivered and her big eyes filled.

Oh, no! Here comes the Mom guilt.

"I'm sorry. I'll do better," I said quickly.

Dad heaved a sigh and dared to come in the kitchen. "See,

Carolina. She'll eat and we're all happy again."

My cat, Skanky, chose that moment to enter the kitchen. Actually, it wasn't so much a walk as a terrified scamper. His rear end was completely bald, including his tail.

I scooped him up. "What the hell?"

"Watch your language," said Dad.

"I will not. What's he doing here?"

Mom crossed her arms and didn't look at me. "I picked him up for you since you have to go away. I was doing you a favor."

"Some favor. Look at him. What happened?" I asked.

"Nothing."

"Nothing?" I squeaked. "His butt looks like a plucked chicken."

Skanky hid his head in my armpit and Mom rolled her eyes. "That's what he looks like. You bought him from a homeless man for twenty bucks and a leftover latte."

"This isn't an issue of price tag," I said. "He was fine this morning."

"It's probably his breed, whatever that may be."

Dad stepped back into the butler's pantry and snagged the whiskey bottle.

"Just because my cat doesn't have a pedigree, it doesn't mean his fur just magically falls out," I said.

Mom shrugged. "It could."

"I know what happened and so do you."

"Nothing happened."

Mom's evil Siamese stalked into the kitchen, side-by-side with their skinny aristocratic tails stick straight and fully furred.

I pointed a finger at them. "Your Siamese did it."

"Don't you blame my babies," said Mom and Dad took a drink straight from the bottle.

"I'm your baby. Those are just cats."

Mom gasped. "Just cats? I'll have you know they are best in show winners."

"They licked my cat's fur off. Again!"

"Do not yell at me," said Mom, drawing up to her full five foot two.

"Dad!"

He shook his head. "Don't bring me into this."

"Tommy!" said Mom.

"Apologize to your mother," he said.

What a coward. He knew those cats were evil. Everyone knew it, except for Mom. The Siamese each stuck a hind leg in the air and began cleaning their rears just to show me what they thought of me. I already knew and had the scars to remind me in case I forgot.

"I'm not apologizing for her cats being evil," I said.

"Carolina Grace Watts!" roared Mom.

If I called Dad evil, it wouldn't have bothered her, but the Siamese were out of bounds.

"Using my real name won't change the fact that they are evil. I'm taking what's left of my cat and going home. And I'm going to eat lots of lettuce, too."

Dad blocked my path. "Okay. Okay. I don't understand what's happening here and I really don't care. I guess eating salads is bad, which is what I've been saying for the past twenty-five years, but whatever. Mercy, you're not leaving and you will eat the bolognese. Carolina," Mom glared at him and he swallowed "You will admit that your... cats aren't very nice to Skanky."

"Not very nice?" I stomped my foot and put Skanky's butt in Dad's face.

He cringed and took my cat. "I could've done without that. I'm taking Skanky to Mr. Cervantes. I'm sure he can take care of him for a few days and he will grow his fur back." Under his breath, he said, "He's had to do it before."

"What was that?" asked Mom.

"Nothing. I'll be right back. Try not to talk about religion, food, or politics while I'm gone."

I ran around him to the pantry. "I'm going, too. I have to pack."

Mom waved her spoon again. "I already packed for you."

"What?" I asked. "You went through my drawers? Ew."

"Why ew? I'm your mother."

"That's why it's ew," I said. "I'm an adult. I have a private life. I would like some privacy."

Mom narrowed her eyes. "How come? What are you trying to hide?"

"Nothing, but I could have stuff in my drawers."

"What kind of stuff?"

Letters to Chuck. Diaries. Mom's face on a dartboard.

"Just stuff. Private stuff."

Mom banged her spoon on the table. "Do you have drugs in your apartment? I knew it, Tommy. Look at her. I think her hair is falling out."

"It is not. And there are no drugs. Just leave me alone for once."

"I can't. I'm your mother," said Mom.

"I don't need your help."

"Clearly you do. Look at your cat."

I pointed at the evil Siamese. "It's their fault."

Dad grabbed me and marched me out of the kitchen and down the hall to the stairs. "Go upstairs and be quiet."

"She's driving me crazy," I said.

"It's mutual. You worry her sick. Now she's going to be crying all night."

"Yeah, right. Mom doesn't cry. It ruins her makeup."

Dad squeezed my arm until I yelped. "Listen to me. In the last two months, you killed a gang member, got a price on your head, broke up with your boyfriend, and stopped eating. You won't talk to us or to anyone. You work ninety hours a week and you started jogging. Don't tell me something's not wrong."

I teared up and bit my lip.

"Now we're going to work this out, whatever it is. You're going on this trip your mother arranged and you're going to like it. You're not going to try and escape. I'm going to take care of this Costilla thing."

"In four days?" I asked.

"Just between you and me, there's a sting operation going down. The Costillas are going to have bigger things to worry about than you. We just have to snap them up."

"You really think an arrest will fix it."

"No, but a war over who's in charge while the surviving Costilla brothers are in prison will."

"Just four days?" I asked.

"Yes, but first, you will apologize to your mother?"

"For what specifically?"

"For everything you've ever done wrong," he said with his best-dimpled grin.

"That could take a while."

"Tell me about it. You say whatever you have to say. I have to live with that woman. I can't listen to another lecture on the brain's need for fat and calories."

"Okay."

Dad gave me a nudge up the stairs and turned away.

"Wait," I said. "How did Mom get the cousins to go on this trip anyway? This is short notice."

He shrugged. "It's Snot's bridesmaid trip. They wanted to go."

"Huh?"

"Snot's getting married. You really do need some calories."

"No, no. I remember that, but it's weird that I'm going," I said.

"It'd be weird if you weren't there. You're the maid of honor."

"What? I am not. I'm not even in the wedding."

Dad laughed. "You are now. Congratulations."

I did apologize and I ate the bolognese. Well, I moved it around on the plate and Mom fell for it. She was distracted by all my apologizing. I covered it all, including peeing into her flower beds when I was five. Boys peed outside. I thought I'd give it try. If they could do it, so could I. It was the first of many notions that didn't work out for me. There are some things that one just has to have a penis for. Standing up and peeing is one of them. My socks and shoes didn't survive the attempt and neither did Mom's bluebells.

Dad watched us through the dinner, pushed back from the table with whiskey in hand, ready to make a break for it if another fight broke out. He hated it when we fought. When I was a teenager, he would be suddenly required to put in even more overtime than usual and when he did come home, he brought pastries from the Missouri Baking Company. Sometimes we pretended to fight just to get the gooey butter cake. Despite being a stellar detective, Dad never figured it out or maybe he just thought an influx of sugar helped keep things calm.

After dinner, he offered to wash the dishes, leaving Mom and I momentarily speechless. We quickly retired to The Oasis, Mom's bed. I would say it was my parents' bed, but The Oasis was all Mom. Dad just got to sleep there if he was good. My mom knew how to make a bed. She believed in the best linen, the comfiest mattress, and pillows imported from heaven.

We curled up and Mom turned on *Grantchester*. I wasn't much of a mystery fan, having enough real-life mysteries to contend with, but I said nothing and let Mom ogle Sidney Chambers. During a scene with a doctor, Mom put her arm around me and whispered in my ear, "I want you to see Dr. Witges." I nodded. Mom took that as an agreement. It wasn't. I was merely acknowledging that I heard her. We could fight about it later when she figured it out. Dr. Witges couldn't help me. Talking to her wouldn't change a thing. That kid would always have tried to kill me. I would always have killed him.

Dad brought us Ghirardelli hot chocolate and backed out of the room. I took one sip and immediately wanted to eat an entire cucumber in penance. Luckily, Mom was so entranced by Sidney that she didn't notice when I tipped my cup into the orchid on her bedside table. I thought that would kill it, but a couple of months later it sent up shoots and had crazy twisted blossoms. Mom thought she'd invented a new species.

I don't know what time I went to bed. Pick and I slept in my third-floor bedroom, smelling the paints wafting in from the studio across the hall. Aunt Tenne's boyfriend Bruno worked there, creating his masterpieces. That sounds snarky, but they really were masterpieces. Bruno was a genius and the art world was abuzz with his talent. He preferred to block it all out and closet himself in the attic while Aunt Tenne basked in the limelight. She was a natural at promotion and had taken over my so-called career, too. I was still Double Black Diamond's cover girl, although I was on hiatus since I lost so much weight. Aunt Tenne fielded Mickey Stix's calls and complaints, swearing that I'd get my Marilyn curviness back. I wasn't so sure. All I wanted to do was sleep, work, and eat lettuce. None of those things was going to bring back the body that Mickey and the DBD fans loved. I fell asleep with my nose buried in Pick's fluffy neck, thinking about pouring Ghirardelli into that orchid. Who was the girl that did that? I didn't know her, but I couldn't find my way back alone.

CHAPTER FIVE

"Mercy," said Dad, poking me in the ribs.

"Huh?" I inched away from his insistent voice in a pointless attempt to escape. I should've known better. There was no escaping my father.

"Get up now," he said.

"No."

"Yes. It's time to go."

"I'm going back to sleep," I said.

Another jab to the ribs.

"You can sleep in the car."

"Go away. It's midnight."

"It's four a.m."

I smacked his hand as it came in for another jab. "Oh my god. Are you crazy?"

"Everyone's waiting," said Dad. "Get the hell up."

"Everyone's waiting for what?"

"You, idiot." Dad hauled me upright and I slid onto the floor. "Get dressed and come downstairs. We'll go out the side door. Sandy's waiting."

That woke me up. "Sandy?"

"Yes. Get a move on."

"Where are we going?"

"The bridesmaid trip," said Dad with an exasperated sigh.

"Now? At four in the morning."

"I'm not going through this again. Get up. Your bags are down-stairs." Dad left and I looked at the clock. It really was four a.m. Why was this my life? I'd been mostly good when people weren't looking and yet here, I was getting dressed to go on a bridal party trip for a wedding I didn't know I was in until yesterday.

I slipped on a pair of flats and stomped down the stairs, trying to formulate a way to get out of it. After a little sleep, the Costilla threat seemed unreal. Would they really go to so much trouble to kill me? I mean, why bother? They had bigger fish to kill, federal witnesses, rival drug lords, innocent bystanders.

"Mercy!" Mom yelled up the stairs.

"I'm coming."

And I'm going. To jump out of the car at the first opportunity.

Mom and Dad were at the newel post. Dad had at his feet two full-size suitcases, a garment bag, a carry-on, and my purse.

"Wait a minute," I said. "You said four days."

"It is four days," said Mom and she was looking me in the eyes. Not lying or at least she was getting a whole lot better at it.

"What do I need all that stuff for?"

"For whatever you do."

"Which would be..."

"How should I know?" asked Mom. "It's your trip."

"It's not *my* trip. I don't even know where I'm going."

"Cairngorms Castle," said Dad.

I backtracked up three stairs. "That better not be in Scotland."

"It's not in Scotland," said Mom. "We wouldn't send you to Scot-land for four days."

I wrinkled my nose. "Oh really?"

"Well, we wouldn't this time. Cairngorms is on the edge of Johnson Shut-ins State Park. We took you there when you were thirteen. Don't you remember?"

I did remember after some effort. Cairngorms Castle was the

creation of a mining baron who decided it was a swell idea to build a Scottish-style castle in the middle of nowhere. The estate put him into bankruptcy and two years after it was finished, he threw himself off the parapet. It was said to be bad luck as well as haunted by a succession of ill-fated owners who never lived more than three years after purchase.

"I thought it was abandoned?" I asked.

"Not anymore," said Dad. "It's a world-class retreat."

"Wouldn't I be safer here with you than at a retreat? There'll be all kinds of people there."

"My friends own it now."

"Your friends own Cairngorms Castle?" I asked. "Don't all the owners die in hideous ways?"

Dad pulled me down the stairs. "Not all of them."

"Which one didn't die?"

"Julien Delancy. He sold the castle to John and Leslie," said Dad.

"Why'd he sell it?"

Mom pulled me past Dad. "Never mind that."

"No. No. I mind. What happened to Delancy?" I asked.

Dad shrugged. "It was just an accident."

"The kind of accident that only happens in Cairngorms Castle?"

"He was in the armory. He safetied a flintlock pepperbox revolver."

I crossed my arms. "And..."

"It wasn't loaded, but he heard a rattle so he was checking it out and shot off his ear," said Dad all nonchalant.

"Was his finger on the trigger?"

"No."

"Did it at least have powder in the pan?" I asked.

"Not so much," he said. "Let's go."

"People actually pay money to stay the death castle?"

"Yes and handsomely, too. John and Leslie will take good care of you," said Mom.

I glared at my parents. "What kind of friends are John and Leslie? Work friends?"

"You could say that," said Dad.

"*Would* I say that?"

"Yes, they're work friends."

"What work?" I asked. Dad had friends in every walk of life. If John and Leslie had been cops, he would've just said that. They were something else and that made me nervous.

"They're retired."

"From what?

"That's all you need to know," said Mom. "Pick up a bag and let's go."

I grabbed the garment bag. "Wait. Where's Pick?"

"He's fine. Come on," said Dad.

"Where is he?"

"You're not taking him."

I dropped the bag. "Pick! Pickpocket! Come here, fuzzball!"

"Mercy!" said Mom. "People are waiting."

"Well, they can keep waiting. Chuck left his dog with me, not you."

Mom and Dad followed me through the first floor, protesting that I needn't worry about Pickpocket. The more they protested, the more I worried. And I was right to worry. I finally found Pick in the butler's pantry, trembling in a corner, surrounded by the evil Siamese. Swish had a tuft of fuzzy fur in his chops and Swat had all his claws out.

I grabbed the broom and brandished it. "Not today, you freaks. One bald pet is enough."

"Mercy!" said Mom. "If you hit my babies, so help me, I will—"

"What Mom? What are you going to do? Those cats are evil and mean and evil."

She squinted at me. "You said that already."

"I'll smack them into next Tuesday!"

Dad wrestled the broom out of my hand. "No, you won't." Then he whispered in my ear. "Because I have to live here."

"Give me that broom," said Mom with a strange glint in her eye. She was going whack me with it. I could tell.

"No, I don't think I will," said Dad. "Mercy will take Pickpocket with her. Problem solved."

I took Pick's leash off its hook and Mom gathered up her babies and took them cooing into the parlor. They hissed at me over her shoulder, but, of course, she didn't notice.

"Your friends won't care about bringing Pick?" I asked.

"I'll explain it to them. Get a move on," said Dad.

We got my ridiculous number of bags and went out the old servant's entrance. It was a concealed door that you'd never know was there if someone didn't open it for you. Our house hadn't seen a servant since Josiah Bled had lived there. He moved out and disappeared, then my parents moved in. Josiah designed the house with secret doors and hidden staircases. As we stepped out into the cool morning air, it occurred to me for the first time that the secret of why Millicent and Myrtle had given the house to my parent's might be hidden in the house itself.

"Hey, Dad?"

"Yeah?"

"Do you think you've found all the hidden stuff in our house?" I asked.

"How would I know?" He laughed. "The building plans he filed with the city are practically blank."

"That's weird."

Dad shushed me. "Keep quiet. Why do you think we're getting you out at this hour?"

"You're crazy," I whispered.

"I'm hoping that if the Costillas have anyone watching the house, they'll be lax at this hour."

"Is that why we're going to Sandy's?"

Dad nodded and we went through Mom's side garden. There was lots of ivy, good for concealment. All the outdoor lights were off and Dad was very quiet about opening the gate to Sandy's house next door. Her house was built about the same time as ours but was a Tuscan-style villa. Every house in the Central West End was as unique as its owners.

We went through Sandy's sculpture garden and Dad knocked softly on her side door, which wasn't concealed at all.

The door cracked open, showing a young woman only five years my senior. Sandy was a celebrated young sculptor and heir to a small paper company fortune. "Hi," she whispered and waved us in.

Sandy brought us through the main floor of her house to the

garage, attached at the back through a long walkway. She gave Dad the keys to her Jag and said, "Good luck."

The garage door opened and we drove out into the alley. Dad was all concentration, but there wasn't anybody about. We left Hawthorne Avenue and were downtown at the Hyatt Regency in fifteen minutes. Dad pulled into the hotel's underground parking after getting the nod from the attendant, who didn't look like that was his real job.

As we drove down the ramp, I asked, "How well did you know Josiah?"

"What makes you think I knew him?"

"You have the building plans."

"I got them from the city."

"Oh. So you didn't know him?"

Dad glanced at me and I tried to keep my expression neutral. I'd never asked Dad directly about Josiah Bled before. Until a few months ago, I thought Dad hadn't known him at all. Myrtle and Millicent gave Mom the house, not Josiah, even though it was his house originally. Spidermonkey had discovered that Josiah signed over the house to The Girls the day he and Dad had taken off for Paris and The Girls in turn signed it over to Mom. No one would say why.

"We met," said Dad. "He was an unusual man."

"Did you like him?"

"Why all these questions about him of all people? We're trying to slip you out of town so you don't get murdered. Why aren't you worried about that?"

"I am."

Sort of.

"Doesn't seem that way."

"There's nothing I can do about it. You're handling it. So about Josiah?"

Dad grinned. "There they are. Perfect." He pointed to a long black limo parked in a corner of the garage. There was a uniformed driver standing beside it and four plainclothes cops positioned around the area.

"A limo? That's a little over the top," I said.

"Your mother and Aunt Christine cooked it up," said Dad.

"And they decided I'm Snot's maid of honor?"

"Bingo."

"Why me?" I asked. "She has two sisters."

"They were fighting over it." Dad pulled up beside the limo.

"She doesn't even like me."

Dad cocked his head at me. "Bridget likes you just fine."

"No, she doesn't. She and her sisters used to duct tape my legs together every Christmas and put me in a closet."

He laughed. "Oh, that. That was bonding."

"For them. What about me?"

"They were bonding with you."

"I was their victim."

"Potato potata."

"I don't think that works here."

The chauffeur opened my door and I had a moment of panic. Years of duct taping flashed before my eyes. "What about Myrtle and Millicent? What about Lester? He just barely made it out of surgery. I can't leave. I'm the nurse in the family."

"Mercy, my girl, I can say that trio would rather have you gone and safe than here and in danger."

"But—"

"Get out of the car," growled Dad.

I got out, but I made a fuss about it, lots of grumbling. Dad and the chauffeur removed my many bags from the trunk and stowed them in the limo's trunk next to the Troublesome Trio's flowered matching luggage. My luggage looked like it'd been thrown from a train and stomped on by a horse. I wasn't entirely sure it hadn't been. I inherited my luggage from Great Uncle Ned who was once a rodeo clown and thought train tickets were for those too slow to jump on.

Sadly, all the luggage fit and I was fast losing my chance to get away. Of course, I could just jump out at some point and make a run for it. I could hole up in some seedy motel for the four days and call it good. My eyes darted around the garage. It was just the limo. No other cars were there.

Dad laid a big hand on my shoulder. "What are you looking for?"

"The tail," I said in a moment of surprising honesty.

"No tail today."

"Yeah, right."

"I'm not bothering to tail you, Mercy," he said.

"Why not?"

"I know where you're going and I've taken steps."

Oh, no. Not steps. Steps is bad.

"What steps?" I asked.

"Don't worry about it. You're not to leave the estate for any reason for the next four days. The property is secure. John and Leslie will be watching."

"Swell," I said. "This'll be fun. So you're saying no bodyguards."

"Nope."

"What about Aaron? Isn't he going to be dogging my every step?" I asked. The good thing about Aaron was the food. Besides bothering me, he owned a restaurant, Kronos, and was the best cook ever. I'd been avoiding him since New Orleans in case he tried to feed me.

"Aaron's got other things to do. You want him watching you get a manicure?"

"I have to get a manicure? What about the Shut-ins? Am I allowed to go there?"

"Absolutely not." Dad squeezed my shoulder. "You don't need to go anywhere. You're going to be girly. They have a spa. Do that."

I rolled my eyes. "Four days?"

"Four days."

The chauffeur opened the limo's back door and I gave in to the inevitable. At least the inevitable until I managed to jump out. I sighed as Sorcha aka Weepy peeked out. Her long red hair brushed the floor and she tossed it back over her shoulder. "Mercy, what's taking so long? Let's go."

Dad gave me a thumbs up. Great. The last time he did that was at my eighth grade graduation a second after I got my diploma. He gave me the thumbs up and I proceeded to fall down the stage stairs, flashing everyone my polka-dotted panties and giving myself a fat lip. I won't even discuss the time before that. Dad's thumbs up were a harbinger of doom. My doom, specifically.

"Thanks, Dad," I said.

"No problem."

Not for you.

I got in the limo and doom was right. Sitting in the forward seat between my cousins, Bridget and Jilly, was Uncle Morty. No one in the history of the world has ever looked more out of place. I would say that he looked miserable, but he always looked like that. Think grumpy old toad. In comparison, my duct tape wielding cousins were lovely. They all had the Watts red hair and skinniness like my dad, except on them it was swan-like elegance.

I sat on the backseat with Sorcha. Pick jumped in behind me, spun around three times, and laid on the floor.

"Why on earth are you here?" I asked.

Uncle Morty snorted. "'Cause you're gonna try to jump out of this freaking limo."

Ah crap!

Bridget and Jilly stared at him with wrinkled noses, but he didn't smell any different than usual, pizza, cigars, and Irish Spring soap.

"I'm not going to jump out," I said with a good amount of astonishment.

"I know. 'Cause I'm here in this freaking ridiculous limo."

Jilly ran her fingers over the suede roof liner. "Our mom made sure to get a good one."

"A good what?" growled Uncle Morty.

"Limo, of course. There are different levels, you know."

He stared at her in a way that made me think that Jilly was going to show up in his next novel as a sniveling twit soon to be killed off.

"You wouldn't want to go in one of those limos they rent out for proms. They can't ever get the vomit smell out." Jilly shuddered. "We totally deserve a good limo."

Sorcha rolled her eyes. "You think you deserve a limo for a trip to Kroger."

Jilly tilted her head and showed off her two-carat diamond earrings. "But it would be hard to park."

"Un. Freaking. Believable," said Uncle Morty and he belched. It smelled like pickled eggs. We all leaned back and Pick put his snout under his paws.

Bridget smiled brightly. "Morty's just here for the ride. He's not going on our special weekend." She sounded sure, but her eyes were worried.

"Ya damn skippy," said Uncle Morty.

My cousins all smiled at me with a look I'd never seen them have before. Something like a cry for help.

"Why didn't Dad just come?" I asked and the Troublesome Trio perked up.

"He's got shit to do, saving your butt and what all. I sit all day anyway." He patted the laptop bag at his feet. "I'm gonna work and keep an eye on you. I ain't even getting out of this limo when we get there."

Bridget nodded, her bobbed hair swinging wildly. "It's a two-hour ride. We can get lots done. What've you been thinking?"

"Um...what?" I asked.

"For the wedding. I want to hear all your ideas."

A mischievous grin spread across Uncle Morty's face and he cracked his knuckles. "Let's have it, Mercy. What are your ideas?"

You and me, fat man. One of these days, I will—

"I brought these," said Sorcha as she dropped a pile of bride magazines in my lap. Then her voice hardened, "From when I was maid of honor."

Oh, lord. I am so going to get taped.

"Ow, um, thanks."

Uncle Morty got out his laptop. "I'm sure Mercy has been through all...seventeen of those freaking awesome magazines. Since she's not dating my wizard anymore, she has lots of time to focus on the wedding."

And there it is. I'm being punished.

Jilly lacquered her thin lips with a layer of gloss and eyed me over her mirror. "You were dating a wizard?"

"My wizard," said Uncle Morty.

"I thought you were dating a doctor," said Sorcha, wistfully.

"She was," said Bridget and then she lowered her voice like someone could overhear, "Then she kissed Chuck on that porny video. Don't worry, Mercy. I don't mind."

"Don't mind what?" I asked.

"Well, you're notorious. But my mom says you'll lend a kind of je ne sais quoi to the wedding and that's good."

"Er…"

"Je ne sais quoi translates to I don't know what," said Uncle Morty with his big hairy hands poised over his keyboard. "Come to think about it, that's pretty accurate."

"That's not what it means," I said.

"It does when they're talking about you. Who knows what you'll add to that freaking wedding."

I sneered. "Thanks."

"You're welcome for ruining my life."

"Right back at you."

I had not ruined Uncle Morty's life any more than he had ruined mine. I made a mistake. I kissed the hell out of Chuck. It was caught on video, which wasn't porny by the way, and my then boyfriend, Pete, saw it. He dumped me and his Dungeons and Dragons cronies a.k.a. Uncle Morty. Pete was their wizard and apparently irreplaceable.

Morty pressed the intercom. "What the hell's the holdup? I got four women back here and no booze."

The back door opened and Dad leaned in. "I got it." He handed me a pizza box from Louie's with a rank smell coming out of it. "Have a good time, girls."

Dad slammed the door, thumped the roof, and the limo started rolling.

Morty grabbed the pizza box, dropped it in Jilly's lap, she only squawked a little, and lifted the lid. Noxious fumes rolled out and Jilly recoiled. Sausage, anchovy, and onion. Extra onion by the look of it.

Uncle Morty rubbed his hands together and said to me, "And now we're even."

Gag.

CHAPTER SIX

Two hours in a limo sounds like cake, except we didn't have cake. We had an obese fantasy writer, a stinky pizza, the air-conditioning on high because said writer was hot, and the constant clatter of typing. The muttering and cursing didn't help either.

I didn't think this would ever happen, but, after an hour and a half, I turned to Sorcha and said, "I'm sorry."

"For what?" She glanced at Morty, who was muttering something about a freaking dwarf. "It's not your fault."

"It kinda is."

"It's okay. We're family." Then she grinned at me, popping out the famous Watts dimples. "Besides, we brought duct tape."

I winced.

"I'm kidding."

Jilly shook her head. "She's not."

Bridget plopped a magazine in my lap. "So we've agreed?"

I nodded when normally I would've said no way. The bridesmaid dresses that my cousins wanted was a short, busty girl's nightmare. Even after losing twenty-five pounds I could not pull off a satin column dress. The thing was backless. Backless! I'd be using Sorcha's duct tape to secure my breasts. Nightmare.

"I love love love it," said Jilly.

She would. Jilly and Sorcha were five foot ten, had no breasts to speak of, and zero body fat. They would look like Audrey Hepburn with their long swan-like necks and I'd look like a badly upholstered sofa.

But I owed them. They put up with Uncle Morty in the form of a smelly, loud troll for a long time with no complaints. These were not the cousins I remembered. They did not live up to their names of Weepy, Snot, and Spoiled Rotten and nobody had taped any part of me to any other part.

"It's the one," I said.

"Success," said Bridget and we toasted the decision with tiny Cokes out of the mini fridge.

"And the color matches the green of your eyes," said Sorcha, her own eyes red from tearing up over how beautiful Bridget's dress was. Sorcha wasn't dating anyone and had no prospects. Her career in law wasn't helping. She didn't want to date another lawyer and they weren't keen on her either. She'd probably make partner by the time she was thirty, but I had a feeling that wasn't the sort of partner she aspired to be. Sorcha was meant to be a wife and mother and she knew it. I wished I was as sure about anything as she was about that.

"Eyes. Yeah, that's important," muttered Uncle Morty without looking up.

"What?" asked Bridget.

"Nothing. He said nothing," I said.

Sorcha finished up the list of wedding decisions we'd made and tucked it in her laptop bag. "There. The first stage is done."

First stage? What can be left?

I decided it was better not to ask and pressed the intercom. "There's a gas station. I've got to go."

Everyone agreed to take a pit stop, even Uncle Morty after I kicked him in the shin. We pulled into a little one-pump gas station with a rusted awning and lots of beer signs. The chauffeur opened the door for us and Uncle Morty pointed at me. "Get me some beer and a pizza."

"I doubt they have pizza at six-thirty a.m." I looked at the Quik Mart. "Or ever."

"Tommy got it at four-thirty."

"That was Dad in St. Louis."

"I need a pizza and beer. I'm creating here."

Bridget and Jilly suppressed smiles and Sorcha rolled her brown eyes. I couldn't believe it. My cousins were the practical ones.

"You'll have a frozen burrito and you'll like it," I said, getting out.

"Listen here, you—"

Sorcha slammed the limo door and sucked in her lips like a bad little girl who just dumped dirt on her neighbor's head. Not that I would know anything about being a bad little girl with a bucket.

"Do you think he'll get out and yell at us?" asked Jilly.

"Are you kidding? He's so immobile he practically has bedsores." I waved to Terrance, our chauffeur, as he lit up a cigarette. "Be back in a minute."

He took a super long drag, burning down half the cigarette in one go and was on me in two steps. "Alright. Let's do it."

"Are you kidding me?" I asked.

"What do you think?"

"I can go to the bathroom by myself."

"Until you're on the estate, you're my responsibility," he said.

"You're not coming in the bathroom with me," I said.

"We'll see."

Fantastic.

I dashed for the door, but Terrance outpaced me, grabbing the rickety metal handle. "My responsibility."

"You're not really a chauffeur, are you?"

"How'd you guess?"

I sighed and he opened the door with a creak. An elderly man jolted awake behind the high laminate counter. "Good morning." He glanced outside and saw the limo, but it didn't faze him. With Cairngorms Castle so close it must not have been unusual.

"Can I use your bathroom?" I asked.

"With a purchase," the man said.

"Do you have any frozen burritos?"

His bushy grey eyebrows shot up. "*You* want a frozen burrito?"

"Yep."

"In the freezer at the back. Microwave's right there."

The cousins came in and I told them about the purchase for peeing thing. They wrinkled their brows but began looking through the racks of Corn Nuts and Pennzoil. I went for the bathroom with Terrance on my heels. I picked out a couple of questionable burritos and popped them in the microwave while Terrance looked in the bathroom. It was the size of a small closet and he declared it safe.

When I came out, I expected a line but the Troublesome Trio were talking to Terrance over by the counter. Sorcha was smiling and flipping her hair. Terrance was pretty handsome. I hadn't noticed before what with all the following me and sniffing around the bathroom.

I microwaved Uncle Morty's stank burritos. They were almost as bad as the pizza he'd slowly consumed over the space of an hour and a half just to let the stink last longer. While I was trying not to burn my fingers, a couple of voices came through the racks.

"Cherie, you need to listen to me now." The voice had the rasp of an older man.

"I'm doing this my way," said Cherie.

"You're not thinking straight. We can't afford this. You can get a refund."

"Anthony, please."

"Please what? We're going to be there in a half hour. We have to have a plan. We can get out of it. How did you pay for this?"

"I have a plan," she said. "You just take care of the boys."

"Taylor deserves this and God knows we need it, but we should go home. I've still got connections."

"I've decided what's going to happen. They think they'll take it just because they are who they are, but I know what I'm doing," said Cherie.

"I'll throat punch those dickheads," said Anthony.

"That'll help." Cherie heaved a sigh and came around a corner. I'd seen women with newborn triplets with more energy. Cherie's skin was loose and sallow as if she hadn't slept in days. Her boxy t-shirt and jeans were as limp as the rest of her. A bright orange headband held her auburn hair back from her face, exposing her grey roots. Her dark brown eyes landed on me for a second and then flicked away to the soda case where she picked up a six-pack of Mountain Dew. Something about Cherie didn't sit right and she made me nervous.

She left the soda case and went for the counter with an older man picking up her trail after the sunglasses rack. His arms were full of chips and he looked as tired as Cherie. His mostly bald head had a few strands of silver hair plastered to his scalp and his Wrangler jeans were so loose there were several inches of material gathered up under his embossed leather belt.

I watched them for a second. Their backs were tense and ramrod straight. What was it with those two? I had the strangest feeling something wasn't right. They paid for their purchases and I braved the burning hot burritos and dropped them in a bag. Morty wanted beer, but I just couldn't do it. Who buys beer at six a.m.? Drunks, that's who. Not gonna do it.

Terrance slid out of the knot of cousins and came over. "You ready?"

"I've got to pay first."

"What's wrong?" he asked.

"Nothing. Why?"

Terrance glanced around the store. "Did someone say something to you?"

"No. What is your deal?" I asked.

"You look worried."

I was worried, but it was probably the drive, the stress, the smell coming out of the bag I was holding. "I'm worried Morty will take another hour and a half to eat these burritos."

"We're only a half hour out. You know I could smell that pizza through the glass. I'm surprised you all weren't asphyxiated."

"I think that was what he was going for," I said. "I'll pay and be right out."

"I took care of it," said Terrance.

He led me out of the little store with eyes darting every which way and he needn't have bothered. The only vehicle in sight was a beat-up Dodge Caravan with Illinois plates at the lone gas pump. It was filled with kids and the back door was up. The trunk was stuffed with battered luggage that made Great Uncle Ned's look good. At least they got to travel. There were battered old stickers from England and France and a brand new one from Ecuador along with some airline tags that they hadn't bothered to take off. Cherie glanced at me and pumped the gas while Anthony stared into the thick forest across the road. His sweatshirt hung on him. It'd been washed from black to mottled grey and the emblem for Lion's Baseball was peeling off. His face, much older than Cherie's, wasn't just tired. Sorrow filled every line and crevasse. He wavered on his feet as if he could barely stand under the weight of it.

In contrast, a couple of cheerful teenaged boys were next the van. They were tall, well-muscled and in boxing stances, giving each other jabs to the chest and laughing when they connected. The side door of the van rattled open and a pretty girl about sixteen leaned out and said, "Knock it off. You're so stupid."

"What do you care, Laniac?" said the boy with dark hair and an easy smile.

"I care because you're an idiot and I've been stuck in this van with you for hours. I didn't even want to come on your stupid thing."

Anthony turned around and his face lit up when he looked at the kids. "Taylor, stop calling Lane that. You know she doesn't like it."

"You get it, right?" said Taylor. "Laniac. Maniac."

"Yes, I get it. Just get in and leave her alone. It's been a long drive."

Taylor punched the other boy again and jumped in, knocking into Lane and making her squeal in protest. The other boy, a blond with short spiky hair, saw me and watched as Terrance opened the back door of the limo. I got in with the cousins and then watched the boy get in the van and pop open a Mountain Dew. Yuck.

"Where's my beer?" bellowed Uncle Morty when I gave him the stinking burrito bag.

"In the store. You gonna do something about it?" I asked.

He grumbled and peeled open a hideous, greasy burrito and took a slow bite, but he didn't make a move to get out for beer. From the look of it, those burritos were going to last until Cairngorms Castle. A half hour was way too long to spend with them or him.

The Cairngorms Castle gates were grand to the extreme, twenty feet high and done in ornate ironwork. They were also electrified. There was a discreet sign warning of high voltage like they didn't really want you to know and they'd be very pleased if you fried yourself.

I got a good look at the gate and the concertina wire on the top of the high stone walls on either side because my head was out the window. Uncle Morty started gassing ten minutes after the first burrito. I really should've known better. Mom had banned him from ever eating Mexican food in her presence.

Terrance glanced back at me as he pushed the button on the little metal box next to the drive. "Get back inside."

Before I could answer, a tinny voice came out of the box, "State your name and business at Cairngorms Castle."

Terrance told the box who we were.

"Press your right thumb to the pad."

He did and there was a sharp beep before the voice said, "Welcome to Cairngorms Castle, Watts family. Proceed to the castle and prepare to be searched."

The gate made a clacking noise and I had a flashback to Hunt Hospital for the Criminally Insane. At least they had a reason for their gates. What was the castle keeping in or out? Maybe somebody was a little paranoid, but I got why Dad thought I'd be safe here.

Terrance yelled at me again and I sucked in a breath before going back inside. The stink had cleared somewhat with all the open windows, but the pizza/burrito combo had soaked into the seat leather. When I sat down, a poof of stench came up. The Troublesome Trio had tissues pressed to their noses and Uncle Morty wore an expression of malicious delight as he pounded away on his keyboard.

"Almost there," I said.

"Good," choked out Bridget.

"The grounds are beautiful." Sorcha wiped her eyes. She made it through almost the entire drive before her mascara ran. It was a record. Weepy cried at everything, including adorable kid's birthday cakes and sappy commercials. I don't know how she lasted over two hours with Uncle Morty and bride magazines.

I stuck my nose out the window like a cocker spaniel and agreed. The grounds were beautiful. Plenty of dense trees and rolling hills dotted with spring wildflowers. After ten minutes, the castle came into view, just as I remembered it, gothic and a bit cobbled together. Cairngorms Castle wasn't a traditional castle. The main part looked like a cathedral with a long peaked roof, a cross on top, and a rose window. Under the window was a pavilion with cutout crenellations on the top like a medieval tower. Inside the pavilion was the main entrance with enormous arched black walnut doors. The rest of the castle was a smaller cathedral-like section with two towers stuck together on the side, another cathedral, another tower and so on. Each tower was different and the castle gave the impression that a child had put smaller buildings together to make one big one, but somehow the whole thing flowed well.

Terrance stopped at the pavilion behind a white Toyota Sienna with two blue-uniformed guards standing beside it. We got out without waiting for him to open the door. If it meant thirty seconds longer in the Morty stink, we weren't waiting. Pick leapt out and began shaking, presumably to get the smell out of his hair. Uncle Morty had offered the poodle some burrito, but Pick had the sense to turn it down and snort in derision.

"What are they doing?" asked Sorcha.

One of the guards was holding a mirrored stick under the van while the other one loaded the luggage on a cart.

"Looking for explosives," I said.

"Seriously? How do you know?"

Hunt Hospital for the Criminally Insane.

"I saw it on TV."

Bridget hooked her arm through mine and craned her neck up to look at the high limestone walls of the castle. "Wow. Can you believe this place? Your mom said it was good, but I had no idea. It's bigger than your house."

"My house is an apartment," I said.

Her eyes roved over the multiple stained glass windows and little gargoyles. "No. I mean your parents' house."

"Your parents' house is bigger than my parents' house."

It was too true. Uncle George opened a medical supply company about the time my dad became a cop. He worked ninety hours a week while my cousins were growing up and he made the business a success through pure toil. Until Dad retired and went private there was no question about who was the more successful brother. George built a house out in Ladue that our house would fit into with room to spare. Jilly was six when they moved. She barely remembered the cracker-box-sized house they had in Dogtown when her dad was struggling to get a toehold in the business world, which was why she was known as Spoiled Rotten. Bridget and Sorcha remembered it very well.

"Not that house," said Bridget. "The Bled Mansion."

"That's not my house."

"It may as well be." She said it with the snotty tone I expected of her. She hated the birthday parties that Myrtle and Millicent threw for me, and I suspected they were the reason I got duct taped so much.

The guard with the mirror straightened up. "All clear." He closed the rear lift-gate. There were all kinds of bumper stickers on it. The most popular was Steel Vipers Baseball and Immaculate Heart Varsity Baseball. The back window only had one thing on it, a memorial sticker.

Rest in Peace
Beloved
Q
March 3, 1987

1987. That was a long time to mourn. To be fair, my high school boyfriend had disappeared nearly ten years ago and was presumed dead. Sometimes it felt like yesterday so who was I to judge. I once wanted to put a memorial sticker on my truck, but Dad threatened my life.

"Good morning, ladies," said the guard. "You're the Watts bridal party?"

We said we were, but he required two forms of ID before he ran a metal detector over us.

"You're clear to go in, ladies. Have a wonderful time at the castle," he said.

"What about our luggage?" asked Sorcha.

"We'll bring it to your rooms after we've x-rayed it."

"You're x-raying our luggage? Why? We're a bridal party," said Bridget.

He nodded and smiled pleasantly. "It's just a precaution. Security is our top concern here at the castle."

"And why is that?" I asked.

"As I said, it's just a precaution."

The security should've made me feel safe. Instead, I felt like a prisoner. The Girls and I had an easier time getting into Israel.

"Leslie is waiting for you," said the guard and he got out a piece of equipment made for sniffing bomb-making materials.

I stared at him until a warm voice said, "Ladies, may I introduce myself. I'm Leslie, one of the owners of the castle."

I turned to find a man around fifty standing under the pavilion. He had long silver hair feathered back from his face in a way that didn't seem outdated at all, wire-rimmed glasses, and an outfit that made me want to date him despite the fact that he was the same age as my father. The man could rock a vest. He wore a white crisp shirt under a tailored pin-striped vest. The fitted jeans didn't hurt either.

"Oh," chirped Jilly and a fierce blush crept up her neck. Sorcha tossed her hair and Bridget just stared. I stared too, but I recovered quicker.

Sorcha whispered to me, "He looks like he should be on the cover of *Forbes*."

"Or *Rolling Stone*," I said.

Leslie smiled, showing even white teeth so perfect they had to be caps. "Morty."

"Leslie."

There was a grunting behind me and I spun around. Uncle Morty heaved himself out of the limo. Crumbs rained down on the pristine pavement.

Bridget yanked on my arm. "Mercy, please."

"Um...right. Uncle Morty," I said in a wheedling tone that I wasn't going for but couldn't control. "What are you doing out of the limo? You said you were staying in there and not coming out."

"I changed my mind." He wasn't looking at us but at the facade. Oh no. The creative wheels were turning. It was nearly impossible to stop him once his brain latched on.

"But I bought you burritos," I said.

"They sucked."

"I'll buy you more burritos. Better burritos."

Uncle Morty scratched his belly, exposing the hairy expanse and I could feel the panic in Bridget. Uncle Morty and his...stuff was not good in an isolated castle for four days or ever, if I'm being honest. Morty was an acquired taste and my cousins had not acquired him yet.

I peeled Bridget's hand off my arm and threw my hands up. "Darn. It's too bad you didn't pack anything. You don't have any of your stuff. Your dragon models, your swords, your helmets. And clothes. You don't have clothes. Clothes are essential to the writing process."

"No, they ain't," he said. "I'll just wear this."

"For four days?" asked Jilly. Her mouth hung open wide enough for me to see her dental work.

"That ain't nothing. When I'm on a writing streak, I've been known to wear the same shit for two weeks."

"Oh my god," said Sorcha.

"Oh my god is right. My damn book ain't working and this place is already getting my juices flowing. I'm all juicy.

Ew.

"I'm sure the castle is booked. Way booked." I glanced back at Leslie, who gave me a slight shrug.

"Leslie can find room for me. Can't you, *Leslie*?" said Uncle Morty.

What's that about?

"How do you guys know each other?" I asked.

Morty got his laptop, tucked it under his arm, and belched. "We met in another life. One of many."

"What does that mean?"

"It means we're old friends," said Leslie.

Uncle Morty snorted.

"And we understand each other. We'd be honored to accommodate Mr. Van Der Hoof."

"Damn right." Uncle Morty stomped past us and whipped open the big arched door to take up residence.

"But..." said Bridget.

"Our weekend," said Sorcha.

"And the smell," said Jilly.

"I'm so sorry," I said. "I'll...I'll..."

Leslie touched Bridget's shoulder. "The bride-to-be, I presume."

She nodded like crazy.

"You need not worry. If I know Morty, he'll hole up in a tower and you won't see him at all. He'll be working. Isn't that right, Miss Watts?"

"Yes. He does hole up when he's on a streak," I said.

"Okay," said Bridget. "You don't think he'll want to go to the spa with us, do you?"

"Not on your life."

She blew out a breath. "It's going to be great. He can work and we'll do our activities."

Leslie took Bridget's hand and looked deep into her eyes. "It will be perfect."

People said my dad and Chuck were charming, but them combined couldn't hold a candle to Leslie. He morphed into exactly what Bridget needed and then he did it with Jilly and Sorcha. He said all the right things. No. Not the right things. Perfect things.

When he was done, they were smiling and going through the front door without a care in the world. Five Mortys couldn't have ruined it. The only one who wasn't charmed was Pick, who sniffed the around Leslie and backed up, making a throaty noise.

"You're in good hands, Miss Watts," he said, turning his spotlight on me.

"Who are you exactly?" I asked.

He smiled. "Leslie."

"Right. How do you know my dad? What did you do?"

"What makes you think I did something?"

"It's a given. I know my dad. If you were a cop, he'd have said so. That means you're on the other side of the coin."

Leslie leaned in, his breath caressed my cheek and a prickle of fear went through me, a reaction to I knew not what. "There are no sides. Only results."

"What do you—"

A guard stepped up. "Leslie, the limo is clear to leave."

Leslie nodded at Terrance, who hesitated by the driver's side door. He glanced at me with uncertainty and I felt another prickle of fear zip up my back.

"Goodbye, Terrance," said Leslie. "See you in four days."

"Yes, sir." Terrance gave me a meaningful look. "I'll be here right on time or early if you need me."

"Good to know," I said.

He got in and drove away. Very slowly to my mind.

A group of people walked around the side of the castle and a man with a greying crew cut said, "It is you."

"Yeah, it is," said a teenaged boy, obviously his son. They had the same broad cheekbones and thin lips.

"Who is she?" asked the woman with dark brown hair, curled and sprayed. She had extra-long fingernails that made me think of claws even though they were painted with blue orchids and had tiny jewels along the tips. She was one of the few women who could wear a jump-suit and made it look like a good idea.

"Mercy Watts." The other man wore a faded Cardinals' baseball cap and had the heavy look of an athlete who'd forgotten how to move.

"DBD's cover girl," said the boy. "She's hot."

"Quinn," said the woman.

"Mom. She knows she's hot."

Leslie extended his arm to bring them closer. It was a good thing, too. I felt a bit like I was in a zoo. "Mercy Watts, this is Nicole, Cory, Quinn, and Bill. They're with the Steel Vipers."

"Steel Vipers?" I asked.

"Baseball. Best traveling team out there," said Cory, the one with the crew cut.

"Dad," said Quinn. "The Grizzlies are good, too."

Cory snorted. "Enrique is good."

"Speak of the devil," said Nicole, looking down the drive as a couple of Cadillac Escalades came into view.

"Prepare to be dazzled." Bill whipped off his cap, slapped it against his beefy thigh, and then settled it back on his head.

"I'll be dazzled by Enrique," said Cory.

"That's a guarantee. That kid's got it together. He's in another league."

Nicole elbowed Cory. "Quinn is a serious contender."

Cory nodded and slung his arm over his son's shoulders. "He is, but we got our work cut out for us. Remember, son, you've got the potential to be another Bob Feller." Cory spouted off a mind-boggling amount of statistics comparing his kid to everyone from Oliver Jakes to Tom Terrific, whoever that was. Quinn disappointed his father by not being able to remember Sandy Koufax's ERA in 1963. Who would? What a freak.

Nicole leaned over to me. "Quinn is competing for the Pickford Prize."

"What's that?" I asked.

All three of the adults gaped at me. Quinn gave me a perfect teenager look. Adults. What idiots.

"It's the top scholarship in baseball. It's a full ride and you can take it to any school," said Cory.

"Huge opportunity," said Nicole. "The winner is always picked up by the majors. Always."

I glanced at Quinn. He couldn't have been less interested in baseball or his prospects.

"You look different," he said to me.

"She lost weight," said Nicole with an approving smile.

"Why?" Quinn asked.

I don't know.

"I went on a diet," I said.

"Why?"

"Quinn," said Nicole. "She just did."

Everyone's eyes were on me, searching up and down my form, looking for the differences. I wanted to melt into the ground and disappear.

Leslie took my elbow. "A chill wind is blowing in. I have hot drinks waiting inside. Shall we go in?"

I smiled at him and he turned me toward the door. I went toward it with Pick, but nobody followed. When I glanced back, the baseball parents were glaring at the Escalades rolling up. Only Quinn was starting after me. His mother snagged his arm and shook her head. His broad shoulders slumped and I winked at him, just to bother her. I could tell she thought there was a possibility that I wanted Quinn to follow me. Like I'd go after a senior in high school. Gross.

Leslie grabbed the long iron door handle and put everything he had into opening the door that Morty had whipped open. I raised an eyebrow at Leslie and he said, "Sometimes it sticks." At the word 'sticks' the door jerked closed and nearly yanked him off his feet. He then used two hands and heaved the door open. It gave out a screeching nails-on-the-chalkboard sound and we both winced.

"There we go," said Leslie.

I frowned at him and crossed my arms. "I've never seen a door stick like that before."

"There are a lot of unique aspects to Cairngorms Castle."

"So I've heard," I said.

Leslie waved me in. "Reception is to the left. John is waiting for you."

"Thank you."

"Anytime." He meant it. I was almost sure or maybe he was just charming me like he did everyone else.

I walked out of the cool morning air into the surprisingly warm interior of the great hall. The ceiling mimicked the cathedral ceilings I'd seen in Europe, only done in dark wood instead of stone. Lots of graceful arches and interlocking beams. The stone floor was dotted with dark red Turkish carpets and the walls were covered in enormous tapestries and paintings of 17th century gentry.

To the right was an ornate staircase zigzagging up the multiple floors in carved splendor. I went left through an archway into reception. That room wasn't on Dad's tour and it should've been. It was a library, two stories high, floor to ceiling books and golden oak paneling.

I bounced over a super thick rug to the desk, a chest-high counter that matched the woodwork. A man stood behind it, wearing a dark blue suit and zero expression. John was bland as Leslie was stunning. His dark hair was parted on the left and smoothed back from his average face. If I had to describe him to someone, I don't know what I would say. He wasn't anything in particular, but something felt off about him. Before John saw me, he shot a glance into the air and waved something away. I didn't see anything.

"Welcome, Miss Watts," John said in a flat voice.

"What was that?" I asked.

"I don't know what you're talking about."

I put my elbows on the desk. "You waved something away."

"Miss Watts, you must be seeing things," he said.

"I'm not the one seeing things."

"Of course. The guest is always right." John pulled out a ledger and I leaned in to take a closer look. He snuck a peek at me, raising an oddly slim eyebrow, looking for something, probably surgical scars or expert makeup, which wasn't there, I have to say. I have my mother's face and all that comes with it. I grimaced and obligingly tilted my head to the side so he could check out my jawline. My skin was smooth and unblemished, but I could tell from his expression that he was not buying it. John himself probably had some work done. His nose was too small to be believed. You only get that from a scalpel. I'd never seen a man so indistinct. He had absolutely no defining features. His face sort of disappeared. If I closed my eyes, I couldn't remember what he looked like. He was young. He was old. He was handsome. He was plain. He was John and it was creepy weird.

"What are you doing?" he asked.

"Nothing."

"Clearly that is untrue."

"Just wondering where I've seen you before," I said.

"Nowhere. You've never seen me," said John with total confidence and I was sure he was right, but only because I'd never remember him if I had.

"You seem pretty sure about that."

He smiled and even that was bland. "I would remember you."

"I suppose so."

"That doesn't please you?"

"Not hardly."

We looked at each other for a second and I got the strangest feeling. Deja vu. Had this happened before? Had I stood across from John at some other time and had this conversation? Something flickered on his smooth features, a reaction but one that was tightly controlled. He saw that I saw it and quickly spun the ledger around on the desk.

"Sign here."

"I guess there's no point in asking you who you really are."

"I'm John."

"And..."

"I'm John."

"Right."

John leafed through his brand new but made to look old ledger. The Castle was old school. No computers in sight. I didn't even see a phone. A neat stack of brochures sat on the edge of the desk, printed on expensive vellum. I opened the thick trifold. Inside contained what I feared. There were no TVs, phones, or movies at the Castle. What there was was relaxation, happiness, comfort, and excellent conversation or so they promised. Who this excellent conversation was going to be with wasn't so clear. I knew me. It wasn't coming from me.

"There you are," he said, checking something in the ledger.

"Has the rest of my group checked in?" I asked.

"Yes. They've gone up to their rooms."

"Including Morton Van Der Hoof?"

"Mr. Van Der Hoof has gone to his tower."

"Like Quasimodo." I smiled, breaking out the charm that melted the pants off a few men.

It didn't melt John's anything. If I hadn't been standing right in front of him, I would've thought he didn't see me and men always see me, for better or worse.

"Yes," he said.

"Um...okay. Where's my room?" I asked.

"We've put you in the South tower."

I was in a tower, too? It was okay for Uncle Quasimodo, but who was I? Mary, Queen of Scots? Off with her head. After the last couple of months I'd had, a tower sounded appropriate but less than inviting, a little too Rapunzel.

Oh, I get it. Lock Mercy in the tower. No doubt this was Dad's idea. He was full of ideas, full of ideas for me, that is.

"Let me guess. My tower room is on the top floor, isolated, small, has few windows, high and non-accessible."

John's face contained zero interest, but he asked, "How did you know that?"

"Because I know my father. I'm not on vacation. I'm a having a small stint in jail."

"I don't understand what you mean."

He totally understood what I meant. I could tell. I could smell it through the indifference.

"The Castle is the ultimate destination," said John. "We have everything you could possibly need or desire."

Twelve heads of lettuce? Chuck. A memory-deleting thingy?

"Except for TVs, phones, or escape routes," I said.

He plucked the brochure out of my hand, neatly folded it, and placed it back in the holder. "Why would you ever need any of that?"

"I can think of a million reasons why I need it," I said.

"After 20 minutes here you won't want any of those things, least of all a TV. This weekend has been specially designed by your mother to make it perfectly comfortable in every perfect way."

"Comfort is a matter of opinion."

"Not here." John stared at me and he looked like he wanted to have an expression but was holding it back. He leaned down and rummaged behind the desk and came up with a silver key attached to a large crystal dangling from a gold chain. The key was elegant, but big and bulky, not made to fit into a pocket.

"Shall I show you to your room?" asked John.

"I think I'll find my own way." I dropped the key in my purse. It was instantly five pounds heavier.

"I think you won't," said John. "The Castle is bigger than you think."

That was saying something since it looked huge.

"I'll chance it."

John gave me a keycard and explained that it would swipe me in and out of my room.

"A key and a keycard?" I asked.

"Yes."

"Alrighty."

He took a castle business card from under the desk and wrote something on it. "This is your personal code."

"Oh for crying out loud." I threw up my hands as the Steel Vipers crew came in, oohing and aahing over the interior.

"This beats the Motel Six," said Bill.

"This beats the Hyatt," said Nicole, extending her fingers and admiring her nail art.

Cory waved to John. "We're the Vipers, checking in for the camp. We sent the rest of our boys out to the carriage house."

"Very good," said John. Then he refocused on me. "All doors lock automatically at midnight for security. Your code will get you in and out of the building, if necessary. Memorize the code and flush the card when you get in your room."

"Seriously?"

"Yes. And keep your keycard on your person at all times. We chipped it," said John.

"Like a credit card?" I asked.

"Like a tracking system. Your father wants you surveilled."

I paled and got queasy. "You're going to have cameras on me."

"No cameras, except at the fence line, gates, and certain areas. We give our guests their privacy."

"Except for me." I glared, but he didn't react.

"You're a special case." He gave me my card and did an impression of smiling. He hadn't mastered the expression yet. It was more like queasy.

Cory joined me at the desk and winked. "I'll say she's special."

Nicole gave me the stink eye from the wingback chair she'd plopped down in.

Calm down, woman. It's a reflex. He doesn't mean it. I can tell.

I scooted away and looked at my card. Oh dear lord. Memorize that? Good luck, Mercy. This was no simple four-digit debit card code. My security code had letters, upper and lower case, numbers and flipping punctuation marks. Groan.

So I would not be leaving the building after midnight. No problem. Where would I go? I stuffed the card in my pocket as laughter erupted outside. Nicole sneered and I went to the bank of windows inset into the thick bookshelves. Through the leaded glass, I spied the Escalades unloading. Smiling people in white baseball jerseys with gold piping got out. The shirts proclaimed them to be the MVP Grizzlies and they looked like MVPs, every one of them. I recognized the look, self-confidence mixed with entitlement. It came from success. I grew up with that look in the form of a charming redhead. The world told them they were special and they believed it. The rules didn't apply to the Grizzlies and they'd be surprised if anyone thought they should.

Nicole came up beside me. "Look at them. They think they have it all sewn up."

A blond boy with messy hair got out with a smaller boy with brown hair and flashing dark eyes.

"Enrique?" I asked.

Nicole grumbled. "Yes."

The blond said something to Enrique and both boys started looking around. Enrique shrugged and the blond walked off looking for something.

"The prize is decided this weekend?" I asked.

"For all intents and purposes. Four of the judges are here. They're coaches for the camp."

"Is this camp always here?"

"No. This is the third year. It used to be at spring training in Florida, but somehow it was changed to here. I hear the owners are huge baseball fans. They host camps year around, but this is the one that counts." She leaned over to me. "The cost is outrageous, but it's worth it."

I was about to agree, but a prickle went up my neck and a feeling of discomfort that was so familiar came over me. I should've felt it before. I should've known. I don't know why I didn't. Maybe the lettuce was dulling my senses, which, of course, was the intent.

"What's wrong?" Nicole wrinkled her nose. "And what's that smell?"

That's when the smell of hot dogs came wafting over me and not just any hot dogs. Not Ballpark Franks. Not some kosher hot dog from New York. This was a special hot dog smell. That smell only came with one person on earth, Aaron, the partner my father had assigned to me because he decided that I was too incompetent to handle things on my own during a murder case. I had proved to be incompetent several times, in fact, but it was still a little galling to need Aaron. And I did need the little weirdo. For chocolate, if nothing else.

"Hotdogs." I turned slowly and saw them. Yes them, the two of them. Aaron was there, of course, looking rumpled and out of place as he always did. That day he had chosen for some reason to wear an ancient T-shirt from the Ron Jon surf shop, a place I'm sure he'd never been and would never be. Aaron wasn't much of a surfer or athlete of any kind, for that matter. I glared at him, but he wasn't looking at me. He wasn't looking at anything as far as I could tell but staring off to the left. He was probably thinking about recipes. Food was his passion. I suppose I sort of expected Aaron to be there, despite all of Dad's promises. His promises meant nothing. I'd learned that from the earliest days of my childhood. Or rather, Dad's promises meant what they meant to him, not what they meant to me. There was always a way around what he promised, a different interpretation if you like. Take my eleventh birthday party, for instance. Swearing he'd be there didn't actually mean Dad would be at my birthday party. It meant that he'd be at a party somewhere in the city where there might be a kid. On my birthday, Dad was at a bar mitzvah brawl, not my party, but he thought it counted. I did not agree.

The other person with Aaron was looking at me and he was the last person I expected. I wasn't expecting plenty of people so that's saying something. Tiny Plaskett, my cousin from New Orleans, gave me a little wave and a sheepish grin to go with it. I'd only discovered Tiny's existence two months before on my trip to New Orleans. We were something like first cousins twenty times removed. It was crazy to think Tiny would just show up at Cairngorms Castle out of the blue, but there he was, filling up reception like nobody else could. Tiny wasn't tiny at all. He was huge by linebacker standards. The last time I'd seen him, I'd been afraid he'd drop dead on me he was so unhealthy, but Tiny had transformed in the last two months. He'd dropped about a hundred pounds so his breathing wasn't as labored and his limp no longer obvious. I didn't need to take his pressure to know it was almost in the safe zone.

Tiny didn't move. He became rather shamefaced but still smiling. Tiny was always smiling. A very pleasant fellow indeed. But I wasn't going to be bought off by a winning personality. No way. No how.

"What are you two doing here?" I asked.

Tiny darted a look at Aaron, who didn't respond, of course, and then he settled his dark brown eyes back on me. "Aaron is giving a healthy cooking class and I'm taking it."

"Really? You're taking a healthy cooking class from him? He puts butter in everything, even things that don't get butter. He loves cream and cheese and salt. Don't try to sell me that crap. Aaron is not giving a cooking class of any kind, especially not healthy. He can't even spell it."

"He's giving a class and I'm taking it." Tiny's plump lips pursed and shifted to the side. Tiny had a tell and that was it. Liar!

"Okay. Fine. What are you doing in Missouri? There's no way you came all the way here to take a cooking class from Aaron. Spill it," I said.

"I work for your dad now," said Tiny, reaching down to pet Pick who was leaning on him. It was love at first sight for the poodle.

I pointed at him. "I knew it. Wait. What?"

"I work for your dad. He offered me a job and I took it."

"You're a private investigator?" I asked.

Tiny blushed a little. "Not yet. I'm more of an assistant."

Yes! You can do the scut work and I can do...something not that.

I gave him a big hug and tried to kiss his cheek, but I couldn't reach it and hit his collarbone.

"There were a few stipulations," said Tiny.

"Like what? You have to stalk me on bridesmaids' weekends?" I asked.

"Well..."

I rolled my eyes. "Were there other conditions?"

"I had to drop some weight. Can't really chase down a suspect at this point."

"You lost a lot already."

"Not enough, but I'm working on it," he said.

"By taking a cooking class from Aaron, the butter king."

He nodded vigorously. "Uh huh, but it's a healthy class. I'm eating healthy and Aaron's helping me. That's why we're here."

"That's your story?" I asked.

"And I'm sticking to it."

"Have fun with that." I saluted him, grabbed Pick's leash, and went for the door. The hotdog smell stuck with me out into the great hall to the foot of the stairs. I spun around and put my hand up. "No way. You two go to the kitchen or wherever."

Then I jogged up the first flight and there was a tremendous creaking behind me. Aaron and Tiny were coming up, single-minded and puffing like chain smokers.

"What the hell? Knock it off," I said.

"Gotta go to our rooms," said Aaron, speaking for the first time. I'm surprised he recognized me through his filthy glasses. He looked like he rode the entire two hours to the castle on his decrepit scooter.

"Where are your rooms?" I asked.

"The South tower."

"Of course they are. Fourth floor?"

Tiny hefted his bag onto his shoulder. "Is there any other floor?"

"Not for you I would guess. Fine. Follow me. I don't care. By the time this is over, you'll be sick of the sight of me and smell like nail polish and therapy candles. Serves you right for bodyguarding me."

Tiny jutted a thumb at Aaron. "He's going to smell like a hotdog. I think it's the only scent he comes in."

"Huh?" asked Aaron.

I flipped my hair back. "Never mind. Get ready for boredom boys. It's your lucky weekend."

CHAPTER SEVEN

John was right. Cairngorms Castle was bigger than I thought. A lot bigger and crazy confusing. I lost Tiny and Aaron on the third floor. It wasn't intentional. I just kept walking and, at some point, they weren't behind me. I used my compass app to make my way south toward the South Tower. I'd show John. How hard could it be? Sure I got lost rather often in my native St. Louis, but this was a castle. The South Tower had to be in the South, right? Wrong. To make matters worse, whoever designed the castle must've been related to the guy who designed the Winchester Mystery House. Stairs led nowhere. Corridors were dead ends. I swear three times I went upstairs only to wind up on the first floor. How does that happen? I would've asked directions, but I didn't see another soul for an hour and ten minutes. Somehow, I kept finding myself in the kitchens. It wasn't until the third time that I realized there were two different identical kitchens. The pots were different. That's how I knew. One had all copper pots hanging from racks suspended from the ceiling and the second kitchen had stainless steel. But they had the same enormous fireplace outfitted with a spit large enough to roast a pig and, oddly enough, had the same calico cat sitting next to the La Cornue range. It was a six foot long thing of beauty in pale blue. I'm not that into cooking, but even I had to touch it and open the ovens. The cat ignored me in both kitchens, cleaning its tail and sneezing at Pick. On closer inspection, it wasn't the same cat. One had more orange than the other and that was a relief. I'd had a cat encounter in New Orleans that left me nervous about whether all cats were actually cats or possibly something else entirely. The calicos were cats but completely unhelpful as all cats are.

After my third time in the copper pot kitchen, I stomped out and ran headlong into a broad hard chest, wearing a dusty baseball jersey.

"I'm so sorry," I said, momentarily winded.

A man with shaggy blond hair smiled down at me. His cheekbones were chiseled and had a deep tan with a hint of a recent sunburn. "No problem. Lost?"

"How'd you guess?"

"Everyone gets lost in the castle, including me." He stuck out his hand. "Oliver Jakes, camp director."

His hand was warm and covered with thick calluses. "Mercy Watts." I frowned. "Oliver Jakes, the ballplayer?"

"I was hoping you hadn't heard of me."

"That's a stretch. You're a legend in St. Louis."

"That makes two of us," he smiled and leaned on the wall between signed photos of Alain Ducasse and Eric Ripert, my favorite French chef. I'd never had his food. I just liked to look at him.

Oliver's smile deepened and I had the sense that he knew quite a bit about me. Very disconcerting. I only knew the headlines about him, but there were quite a few.

"So we're both notorious," I said, attempting to conceal my feelings.

"Me more than you."

"I don't know about that."

"How many times have you been arrested?" he asked.

"I lost count," I said.

His eyebrows shot up, creasing his rather leathery forehead. "Really. I never heard that."

"Well, it's been a while and my father is Tommy Watts."

"Right. You have connections. I could've used a few of those," he said.

"Even my dad doesn't have that much pull."

He laughed, deep and raspy. "You mean the great Tommy Watts couldn't conceal a few minor possession incidents?"

"Minor?" I asked.

"Okay. So maybe trying to take cocaine through the Hong Kong airport wasn't my best idea."

I laughed at the 'wasn't my best idea.'

"What can I say? I was an addict," said Oliver without a hint of regret or concealment. I guess when you're Oliver Jakes, Cy Young award winner, baseball's most winning pitcher, and drug addict, you just have to own it. Kind of like being my dad's daughter. There's no escape. Deal with the infamous.

"*Was?*" I asked.

"Was. I've been clean for three years, four months, two weeks, and one day."

"You're still counting the days?"

"It helps keep down the crazy. What are you counting?"

Heads of lettuce.

"Nothing. I'm not in recovery from anything," I said.

There was a slight eyebrow raise, but Oliver didn't cross-examine me on that point. "So what are you doing here? Has there been a crime that I'm not aware of?"

"I wish. It's a bridesmaid weekend."

He frowned slightly. "Really? I'm surprised John and Leslie would book anyone outside of baseball this weekend."

"Why?" I asked.

"The award is being decided. They don't like distractions."

I glanced down at my phone as it belted out *The Wrath of Khan* theme song, not the stirring heroic tones of Kirk's song but Khan's relentless superiority instead. Dad. Just who I didn't want to talk to. I turned my phone to vibrate. "We won't distract you."

"I'm distracted already. I'm supposed to be picking up snacks, instead of talking to you." Oliver reminded me so much of Chuck.

Oliver was much more rugged and well-worn, but the confidence was the same.

I stepped back. "I better be going now."

He laughed. "Just what I was thinking. You're what always gets me in trouble. I like trouble."

"I'm not trouble," I said, feeling a blush sizzle my cheeks.

"Trust me. You are." He whipped a piece of paper out of his back pocket and unfolded it. His cologne mixed with a musky athletic smell wafted over me. "I have a map. Where's your room?"

"South Tower on the fourth floor. Where's yours?"

Wait. What did I just do?

Oliver tilted his head and cocked an eyebrow at me. "Out in the carriage house. Why?"

I don't know. Quick. Change the subject.

"Do you have a bathroom?" I asked. God help me. I don't know why.

"Yes."

"With a toilet?"

Now Oliver was just confused. So was I. Where was I going with this? I know. Straight to hell.

"Yes, my bathroom has a toilet." He frowned. "Are you...sick?"

Oh my god! He thinks I've got...diarrhea.

"No, no," I said quickly. "Not sick. Totally fine. I just wanted to make sure you had a bathroom. It's a nurse thing. I'm a nurse."

"Why does it matter?" he asked.

"You have a lot of boys out there and they might get sick."

"We have plenty of bathrooms." He grinned at me. "You're welcome to come down and see my place."

"Okay."

What the hell? I'm not seeing his anything.

"Great. I look forward to it," said Oliver. "What about tonight? Nine?"

No, thank you.

"Sure," I said.

Dammit, Mercy, you idiot. What about Chuck? You love him, sort of.

Oliver pointed to the carriage house on the map. "I'll be there.

Waiting."

"Great." I yanked on Pick's leash. "Gotta go get lost again."

"You're not going to get lost."

"Want to bet? I go south and upstairs, but I keep ending up down here in the kitchen."

"Maybe somebody's trying to tell you something." He asked me for a pen and drew a line through a maze of passages to the tower.

"The castle's trying to tell me something?" I asked with a smile.

Oliver shrugged. "When I get lost, I end up in the wine cellar."

"Seriously?"

"Happens all the time."

"Maybe it's one of those subconscious drive things," I said.

"Except I don't like wine. It was only liquor and drugs."

"The castle is confused."

"I think *the castle* knows exactly what it's doing. How long were you lost?" he asked.

"Over an hour."

Oliver gave me the map. "Consider yourself lucky. We've had people wander around for over six, only to find them asleep in the armory."

"There's an armory?" I couldn't find it on the map.

"Oh, yeah and people are attracted to it. Big time." He turned the map for me. "Follow my directions and you'll get there."

"Thank you." I squinted at the tower. What the heck? "Why is the tower called the South Tower if it isn't in the South?"

"Miranda South was the architect."

"Of course. Why didn't I think of that?"

"Because you were using common sense. That doesn't help in Cairngorms Castle."

Oliver said goodbye and I tugged on Pick's leash. No reaction. The poodle had gone to sleep on the cold stone floor with his jaws clamped on my ankle and wasn't inclined to wake up.

I nudged him with my foot. "You're useless. Now I have a date and it's not with your master. You could've at least peed on my foot or bit him. What's Chuck going to think of you sleeping through that debacle?"

Nothing. Not even an eyelash flicker.

"Come on, you crazy mutt. We have a map."

Nothing.

"Sausage."

Pick's eyes popped open and he was on his feet in a flash.

"Sucker. There's no sausage. You get lettuce, just like me."

Pick yawned, showing some very impressive teeth that he only used for gnawing on my leg. Nothing useful like biting handsome ball players or preventing dating disasters.

"I bet they have a dog spa here," I said. "You could get that lovely show cut you love so much."

Another yawn. Pick could be calm about it, but I had a feeling in the next four days we were both going to have some stuff done to us that wasn't going to look good.

With the help of Oliver's map, Pick and I made it to our room in ten minutes. No kitchens or dead ends. We climbed the spiral stone staircase and found two curved oak doors on the small circular landing. There weren't any numbers or letters. For a second, I wasn't sure what door was mine until I noticed the door on the right had a crystal identical to one on my key, dangling from the heavy brass doorknob.

I unlocked the lock and swiped my keycard.

"Welcome, Mercy Watts," said the door. "Your itinerary is on your bed. Enjoy your stay."

Pick scratched at the door and whined. I opened it and found the cell Dad chose for me was better than I imagined, right out of a storybook. Or rather it was straight out of Chenonceau, Diane de Poitier's graceful chateau in the Loire Valley in France or Catherine de Medici's chateau, if you prefer. I thought of it as Diane's. She had it first and now I had Diane's bedroom, at least for four days.

The room was a half-moon shape, taking up half the tower. Other than the shape, I had everything Diane had, the blue canopy bed, the Flemish tapestries, and the huge stone fireplace with the gold initials of Diane and Henry II, her lover. The fireplace reached all the way to the inlaid wood ceiling. There was only one thing that I had that Diane didn't have and that was two dudes sitting in her embossed leather chairs in front of the fireplace.

"Hey, Mercy," said Tiny.

"You hungry?" asked Aaron.

"Oh my god. What are you two doing here?" I asked.

"Waiting for you," said Tiny.

"How'd you get in?"

"What do you mean?"

I held up my keycard and big key. "I have to use these to get here."

"We have whatever you have." Tiny tried to heave himself out of his chair and failed. The arms of the chair were not letting go.

"You hungry?" asked Aaron again.

"No, I'm not hungry," I said. "So you have access to my room?"

"Of course," said Tiny.

"Why of course?"

He stood up and the chair stuck to his butt for crying out loud. I dropped Pick's leash and pried it off. Aaron didn't move, not that I expected him to. I recognized the look. He was plotting food.

"We got to be able to get in here and help you if something happens," said Tiny.

"You're going to save me from a contract killer if he or she makes it onto the grounds through the castle to break into my room."

"That's the plan."

I'd never heard of a worse plan. I knew Aaron. He could stab somebody with a fork if they positioned the fork and ran into it. As for Tiny, he was a powerful guy, but I doubted the Costillas would send somebody that couldn't outrun my four-hundred-pound keeper.

Tiny must've read my mind. "I got skills," he said.

"I'm sure you do."

"Why you say it like that?"

Tiny had worked airport security so he had to be weapons qualified, but that wasn't going to help if he didn't have a gun. And what made Dad think Tiny was prepared to shoot someone? Firing at a range was different than real life. I should know.

"They used bomb sniffing equipment on the limo and x-rayed our luggage for weapons. What are you going to do? Smack the guy to death?"

Tiny cracked his knuckles in a way that made me think that was a possibility. Then he lifted his shirt and revealed a .22 stuck in his waistband under a roll of skin. "I'm packing."

"How come you get a gun? Where's my gun?" I asked.

"You don't need no gun. You got me takin' care of you. You're a bridesmaid, remember?"

"I'd rather have a gun."

"You get pedicures."

"That sucks. People are trying to kill me, not you."

"Yeah, well. Your dad said it ain't safe for you to have a gun on this trip," said Tiny.

My hands went automatically to my hips. "And why is that?"

"He thinks ya might shoot your cousins."

I can see that.

"I wouldn't shoot them dead. I'd wing them."

"So ya can see why I got the gun."

I climbed on the bed and sank into the velvety softness. Sweet. Just what I needed.

Tiny stuck the dreaded itinerary in my face. "You got a list of stuff."

"I'm sleeping. You're welcome to watch, but I warn you it's not exciting."

Tiny crossed the room and wedged his butt right back in the chair. I couldn't believe it. They were going to watch me sleep. How freaking weird is that?

"Fine," I said. "I don't care. I'm sleeping. I was meant to sleep." I burrowed under the covers and closed my eyes. Maybe I could sleep for the whole four days. I was pretty tired and the cousins didn't have a map to my room, I hoped. I could just sleep and sleep and...

Knock. Knock.

No! No! No!

Knock. Knock.

This is not happening. I refuse to believe it.

"Mercy! It's Bridget. Time for our pedicures. Are you in there?"

I sat up. "Don't answer that."

Too late. Aaron opened the door and stepped back to let the Troublesome Trio in. I never hated them more, not even when they duct taped me and put me in Grandpa's taxidermy shed on *my* birthday.

"Are you ready?" asked Sorcha, eyeing Tiny.

"For what?"

"Our pedicures. It's hot stone and totally lux."

I will harm you.

I took a calming breath and said, "Don't you want to nap first. We were up at O dark thirty as my dad would say."

Jilly ran her long fingers through her silky smooth bob. "We already took naps. What were you doing?"

"Not sleeping."

"Great," said Bridget. "So you're ready."

Groan.

Tiny stood up and once again the chair stuck to his rump. My cousins stared at him but didn't make a move to help as he struggled. I slid out of bed and popped the chair off.

Tiny straightened up with considerable dignity. "I'm ready."

"For what?" asked Sorcha. She was looking at him like she'd never seen a human before. She probably hadn't seen anyone like Tiny. The Watts family had tall genes, but Tiny took tall to the extreme.

"Pedicures," I said.

"Um...we're *all* getting pedicures?" asked Bridget.

I glanced at Tiny and he gave me a slight nod.

"Apparently so. Tiny has been ordered to guard me."

The trio looked at Aaron and Bridget asked, "They call you Tiny now?"

"No," said Aaron.

"I'm Tiny," said Tiny with a little wave.

"You're Tiny?" asked Jilly.

"Makes sense, don't it?"

"Not really."

"It's ironic." I opened my luggage and found a pair of flip-flops, probably for pedicures specifically. Shocking. Mom hated flip-flops. She thought they were cheap. The beauty of cheap was completely lost on my mother.

"How come you have to watch Mercy?" asked Bridget.

"Cause the Costillas put a hit on her," said Tiny.

"I get that, but why you?"

"He's my cousin," I said.

"Of course we're cousins," said Sorcha

"No." I gestured between Tiny and myself. "We're cousins."

"But I'm your cousin, so Tiny must be my cousin."

"He's on my mom's side. You're all Watts."

"Oh. So *we're* not cousins," said Jilly. "But Uncle Tommy is our dad's brother."

Head slap.

"I'm your cousin. He's not."

"Oh," they said in chorus.

I picked up our schedule. It was packed. I don't think there was a beauty treatment invented that we weren't having. My phone vibrated. It was Mom telling me that we were late for our pedicures in all caps. Fantastic. My mother had planned the weekend and was going to micromanage it from afar. Remind me never to get married. This was only Bridget. My wedding would be insane.

Sorcha, Bridget, and Jilly's phones then rang. The ring had the sound of Mom and I was right.

"We're late," they said and everyone looked at me, even Aaron. At least he was facing me. He could've been looking at the ceiling.

I texted Mom back. "Aaron and Tiny are here. What do I do with them?"

"Take them and hurry up."

When I looked back up, they were all still watching me. Now this was a bridesmaids' weekend. There were my Watts cousins, nearly identical and more Irish-looking than I ever realized, Tiny, my other cousin, the world's largest African-American man, Aaron, who fit into no category, except weirdo, and me, a Marilyn Monroe look-a-like, dressed in clothes two sizes too big and smelling like poodle. As Lillian said in *Bridesmaids*, we were a stone cold pack of weirdos.

"Pedicures it is," I said.

CHAPTER EIGHT

"Mercy!"

My eyes slid open a few millimeters. All I could see through my lashes were my toes, hot pink and hand-painted with white orchids. My feet were fancy. "Huh?"

"Were you asleep?" asked Sorcha.

"No, no. I was totally listening."

I totally wasn't listening. I'd discovered in the last three hours that I had no opinion on bouquets, corsages, boutonnieres, tablescapes, or seating arrangements. I'd also learned I could fake it while being half asleep. It was a useful skill since the last three hours had been some of the most boring of my life and of Tiny's life, if I went by the snoring. The only interesting thing was when Tiny stopped breathing. I had to hobble over with sponge toe-spreaders on and crack him on the back to get him going. Sleep apnea was definitely more interesting than what color the mother of the groom should wear.

So far, we'd had pedicures and massages. Now we were on to mud baths, my favorite by far. Each of us had our own bin full of special Italian mud. I have no clue why Italian mud was better, but the mud ladies swore it was. Tiny was the only one not in mud. He didn't fit in their largest bin so they wrapped him in hot towels like a ginormous burrito. He was snoring again, which was good since I couldn't get out of the mud to whack him and would have to get one of the mud ladies to do it.

I closed my eyes again and Bridget asked, "So what do you think?"

"It could go either way." I'd discovered that answer worked well when you didn't know what they were talking about.

"Don't you care?" asked Jilly.

"Of course I care." Also a safe answer.

"But you're saying it's okay?"

"You should do whatever feels right." Damn, I was good.

Bridget, who was on my right, moved and made a sucking sound in her mud. "You've got the go ahead. I'd go for it."

"Absolutely," I said.

"Wow," said Sorcha. "I never thought you'd say that, Mercy."

"Me, either, but what're you gonna do." Eyes closed. So warm. So comfortable.

"I'm so happy," said Jilly. "I've had a crush on him forever."

Crush?

"So you've had a crush forever, huh?" I asked.

"Couldn't you tell? When he comes back, I'm going to ask him out."

Sorcha smacked her mud. "I should get him. I'm closer to his age."

"Forget it," said Jilly. "I have dibs."

"You can't call dibs on a person," said Sorcha.

Jilly made a purring noise. "Chuck is so hot. I can't believe you don't mind me asking him out. Thanks, Mercy."

What now?

My eyes were wide open and I struggled in my warm mud. Jilly was asking Chuck out? My Chuck? Hell, no!

The door to the spa opened and my mud lady, Joanie, said, "Right this way, ladies."

Two women walked in, wearing what Sorcha called mom suits, swimming suits that had skirts and tummy control. I recognized them from the Escalades. They were the MVP Grizzlies that Nicole thought were overconfident. I'd say that was a fair opinion and one I shared.

Joanie helped them into tubs across from us and I tried to block out my cousins discussion of Chuck's fabulous abs and butt. Apparently, I'd given permission for Jilly to date Chuck and she was relishing the possibilities. I was queasy and the stink of the Italian mud wasn't helping. No. It would be fine. Chuck had never shown any interest in Jilly. He'd say no. Of course, he would. Then again, he'd said yes to pretty much every friend I had. Why not Jilly? And what could I say about it? I had a date with Oliver that night. I didn't do it intentionally but still it was a date. Chuck had been gone for a long time. He could be dating someone. He could be in bed with someone right then.

I'm going to be sick.

The door to the spa opened again and Aaron trotted in, carrying his brand of spa food. He had prosecco in champagne flutes, strawberries, and mounds of rough-cut chocolate on a silver tray. "You hungry?"

"Champagne!" exclaimed Bridget as she held out a mud-covered hand.

"Prosecco," said Aaron.

"Same thing."

"No."

She tilted her chin down into the mud. "Can I have some *prosecco* then?"

"Huh?"

I sighed. I was the one who needed prosecco. People trying to date Chuck. I would hurt someone. "Please give Bridget some prosecco, Aaron. She knows the difference, I swear."

"Well," said Bridget.

"Quiet. I need wine."

"So does Chuck like wine?" asked Jilly. "I know this great bar—"

"Wine now!"

Sorcha snuffled. "Me, too. I'm never going to get a boyfriend."

"Stop crying. That'll be a good start," said Bridget.

"Stop calling me Weepy all the time." Tears dripped into the mud. Jilly and Bridget rolled their eyes at each other.

Aaron dropped a sugar cube in each flute and then filled them with bubbly joy. My cousins, with the exception of Tiny, went on to swill prosecco and talk about the aphrodisiac qualities of wine and strawberries and whether they would work on Chuck. Sorcha sniffled while

I threw back two glasses and had some strawberries. No chocolate. I didn't want it. I tried to want it for Aaron, who stood there, waiting for me to scarf it down. I told him I wasn't in the mood, but he acted like he didn't hear me. There was nothing to be done. He didn't get it and neither did I so I proceeded to block him, and the escalating talk of Chuck's bod, out by concentrating on the Grizzly moms chatting away across from me. They were in full makeup for mud baths and had a pile of jewelry on the tables beside their tubs. Why bother?

"Where were you?" asked the dark-haired one, still wearing dangling diamond earrings. They were gorgeous and at least three carats. I wouldn't get them near mud.

The blond shrugged and slurred her words slightly, "I got lost again."

"Again, Deanna? Where did you end up this time?"

"The distillery again," said Deanna.

The brunette frowned. "Did you have a tasting?"

"I wish. It smelled fabulous. I wouldn't mind getting locked in there with Coach Oliver."

"Did you see him in those pants?" asked the dark-haired one. She was pretty and what my mom would call well maintained.

"Do you think I should ask him out?" asked her blond friend.

"Deanna, if you don't, I will."

"What about Tim, your husband?" asked Deanna.

The dark-haired one lifted a cucumber slice off her eye. "Tim? He looks like he ate a watermelon. Whole."

Deanna laughed. "You married him, Robin. For better or worse."

"Yeah and he's looking worse next to Oliver. I can't believe he's not married."

"I can't believe the Lions are here. They can't afford this."

"Something's fishy," said Robin.

"I don't care why they're here. If they want to be out-classed, they're in the right place."

Robin got quiet and bit her lower lip.

"What's wrong?" asked Deanna.

"Nothing. I was just thinking about the Vipers. They've never been here before either."

"This is really weird. Did Tim know they'd be here?"

"No. I don't think so," said Robin.

"Well, the Vipers and the Lions will both just have to suck it. Enrique was meant to have the prize. I don't know why they even bothered to come," said Deanna.

Aaron offered the Grizzly ladies prosecco and they accepted with many thanks, especially Deanna. Before they started up about Oliver's hot butt or the husband Tim's big gut, Joanie came over to me. "Time's up. Would you like me to help you out?"

Like? Yes, I would like it because I was never getting out if I didn't have help. Italian mud is heavy, so heavy I nearly lost my bikini bottoms to the stuff. Luckily, Tiny was still asleep and the Troublesome Trio averted their eyes.

I managed to get my bottoms to cover the important bits and said, "What now?"

Please say nap. Please say nap.

"Vichy showers," said Bridget. "I've been looking forward to this all week."

"Sounds like something the Nazis did in occupied France," I said.

My cousins stared at me and Tiny snorted under his towels. At least he got the reference.

"It's a special shower that increases circulation and lymphatic flow, relieving the body of toxins," said Joanie.

I seriously doubt that.

"How about you all take the Vichy thing and I take a regular shower and a nap?" I asked.

Bridget's lip trembled. "But we were going to decide on the favors."

"I vote for goldfish," said Jilly. "It's original."

"You want to give people live goldfish as a wedding favor?" This was worse than the exploding invites that spewed glitter all over the recipient's house.

"It'll be so cute," said Sorcha. "Beautiful goldfish with those long lacy tails. Whenever your guests look at them, they'll think of your wedding."

"Exactly," I said. "When they're flushing their dead fish, they'll think of your wedding."

"Ew," said Jilly.

"No goldfish," said Bridget. "How about Lovebirds?"

Oh my god.

I didn't answer that. I didn't trust myself not to use words that Uncle Morty would use. I helped Joanie unwrap Tiny, who could barely contain himself. "I wanna go to this wedding."

"You can be my date for the madness," I said.

"Deal."

The Vichy shower turned out to be pretty relaxing or it would've been if Bridget hadn't kept going on about Lovebird life expectancy while we laid on our tables and got sprayed. The worst part was the green smoothies they gave us for lunch. I'd been juicing since New Orleans, but my juices didn't taste like dirt and ginger. I drank it because I figured it was my punishment for hoping Joanie would aim the shower nozzles at Bridget's face.

After the Vichy shower, I figured we were done. What the heck could be left? As it turned out, quite a bit. We got our hair done. I said no Marilyn curls and the stylist promptly ignored me. Then we got our hands dipped in wax. That was weird and, I suspect, pointless. It was almost five o'clock and I was so done when Bridget said, "Let's do yoga before dinner."

Tiny and I looked at each other. I don't know who was more afraid, but it would almost be worth it to see Tiny do yoga. He'd need two mats or possibly three.

"Do we have to?" he asked.

"You got a pedicure, but you won't do yoga."

"I can't do that stuff." Tiny attempted to touch his toes. Let's just say it didn't go well.

The Troublesome Trio were discussing downward-facing dog when I stretched in my squashy armchair and said, "I think we'll skip the yoga. That wasn't on the schedule, was it?"

Bridget gasped. "Oh, no. You have to go. We haven't really talked yet."

Who talks during yoga? Wait. Think about who you're talking to, Mercy. Hello.

"There's plenty of time for that." I stood up and realized I didn't have my map or a clue where I was in the castle. Fantastic.

"But yoga is relaxing," said Sorcha. "You need to relax with the whole people trying to kill you thing."

"I'm plenty relaxed. An hour long shower massage will do that," I said.

"Let's just hang out," said Jilly. "I want to hear all about Chuck and New Orleans."

That's a hard pass.

"You're supposed to relax," said Sorcha. "Aunt Carolina told us to make you relax."

"Consider it done," I said.

"And eat," said Jilly.

"Huh?"

"You're supposed to eat." Bridget clapped her hands. "Perfect timing."

Aaron came in, carrying a wide silver tray. No prosecco and chocolate this time. Something much worse. Individual soufflés.

"I can't eat that," Tiny and I said together.

Bridget narrowed her eyes at me, shockingly similar to my mother's look of disapproval. "Why not?"

Tiny hastily said, "I'm on a diet. I got to lose another hundred pounds."

The trio nodded and turned to me.

"Um..." My heart was pounding. The soufflés were Grand Marnier, tall and crusty. They filled the spa lounge with a wonderful orangey smell and made my mouth water in spite of myself. Aaron placed one in front of each of us and rubbed his hands together, rocking up and down on the balls of his feet.

"I think we have to eat it," whispered Tiny.

"I can't." I needed lettuce, nice clean guilt-free lettuce.

"You can't," he said. "I shouldn't."

"We're quite a pair," I said.

Sorcha, Bridget, and Jilly broke the crusty tops of their soufflés and groaned with pleasure at their first bites. Tiny and I held our spoons like weapons, trying to fight off the ultimate temptation. Tiny was flushed and glassy-eyed. I was nauseous.

Aaron kept bobbing up and down, going faster and faster. He looked like he had springs in his heels.

"Looks fantastic," I said.

"Great," said Tiny.

My spoon broke through the top and a wisp of steam swirled up. The dish was hot in my hands like my Mauser in New Orleans.

"I can't." I shoved my soufflé into Aaron's hands and dashed out the door with echoes of "Mercy!" ringing out behind me.

I got lost, naturally, and found myself in the copper pot kitchen again. There was no one there, but traces of Aaron's Grand Marnier soufflés remained in scattered mixing bowls beside the La Cornue stove. I looked at those bowls and bit my lip. Aaron would be so hurt that I didn't eat what he made. How could I explain it to him? I couldn't even explain it to myself. The days of eating his food were over. I hadn't had one of his burgers since before New Orleans and I couldn't imagine a time when I could sit in Kronos and order like I used to.

I heard voices in the hall and dashed for the door. It was the right door, for once, and I was outside. The sun was still up but getting ready to tuck behind the rolling hills in an hour or so. I was in the castle's kitchen garden. Rows of herbs and vegetables grew in neat rows, all tagged and ready for the summer growing season to start. A gardener came out of a door in the base of the nearest tower with a double tank contraption strapped to his back. He saw me and waved. I waved back and watched him head out into the formal garden to spray something on the rosebushes.

The formal gardens, beyond the kitchen garden, were done in the French style. They reminded me of Villandry in the Loire Valley. Villandry had Myrtle and Millicent's favorite gardens in France and we'd been there many times to walk through the maze and flower beds. They'd take notes and I'd explore the love gardens. Cairngorms had the same setup in their ornamental garden, tender, passionate, flighty, and tragic love sections separated by hedges with a fountain in the center. I wandered through each square, admiring the details. The Girls would be impressed.

The castle loomed over me but no one came out and I had time to calm myself and get a grip. The castle was easier to understand from the back. It was built in a hook shape with the hook part curving around the kitchen garden. My tower was easy to spot. The other towers had stained glass windows, but mine had leaded glass in an intricate design. I'd opened my window so my room must be on the other side.

I left the love gardens and followed a trail around the last tower to find a rock garden that extended around the whole other side of the hook. The red and black gravel was carefully raked in concentric circles. Beyond it was a large stone building with five sets of wide doors. That must be the carriage house where the ball players were staying. Farther away was the stable, just as large as the carriage house but with white-fenced paddocks.

"Do you ride?"

I jumped and John was at my side. "You scared me."

"I apologize. You were looking at the stables. Would you like to take a horse out?"

"No. That's okay. I was just getting the lay of the land."

John nodded. "Your cousins are coming this way. Perhaps you should stay here."

"A ride sounds great," I said and John nearly had an expression or maybe it was wishful thinking on my part.

He walked me down to the stable and introduced me to Jamie, the groom, and suggested I ride down to the ball fields. John pointed at a trail through the thick trees.

"Where are the Shut-ins?" I asked.

"Johnson Shut-ins are beyond the ball fields."

"Do we have access?"

"With your code," he said. "But they're officially closed. The water's at a record high. Swimming is extremely hazardous."

"Who would want to swim now? The water would be freezing."

"You're not supposed to leave the grounds in any case."

It wouldn't be hard to forget Dad's orders and I fingered the code card in my pocket.

"You need to destroy that card immediately," said John.

"How do you know I didn't?" I asked.

He watched me without blinking, very robotic.

"I will."

"Good." John left without another word and Jamie came out with a tall chestnut gelding, who was dancing on the end of his lead.

"My notes say you've got experience," said Jamie.

"You have notes on me?" I asked.

"Of course. John and Leslie are very thorough. What's your level?"

"No clue."

"Lessons?"

"Yes. My godmothers think riding is part of a well-rounded education, but I'm wearing flip-flops."

Jamie smiled. "If you don't think you can handle it..."

"Oh, I can handle it. What's his name?" I asked.

"Sly dog."

That's not a good sign.

"Good name."

"His real name is Out of the Frying Pan," he said.

"Weird."

Jamie shrugged. "It's a thoroughbred thing. His sire is Cast Iron."

"That sounds familiar," I said.

"Third in the Preakness, but he had a biting problem. And there was kicking. You want Western or English?"

I kept a close eye on Son of Biter and took a step back. "English."

Jamie tied my ride to a post and got the tack. I was up on Sly Dog in five minutes and regretting it. There was something going on with that horse. He kept tossing his head and giving me the stink eye over his shoulder.

"Where're you headed?" asked Jamie.

"The ball fields, I guess."

"No. You don't want to spook him with all the cheering. Go toward the valley." Jamie pointed out the trail and told me never to give Sly his head. I promised I'd keep it at a trot and gave him a little kick. I expected a horse with so much energy while on a lead to take off, but I was sorely disappointed. I barely got a walk out of him. It took us fifteen minutes to get around the stables to the trail and he stopped when we got there.

"What are we doing?"

Sly blew out a breath.

"I thought you wanted to go. You were all excited," I said with a gentle kick.

Nothing.

"Do I have to get off and push?"

Another blow.

I looked up at the trees. This weekend was getting longer and longer. Even the horse was slow.

"Do you want me to—"

That's all I got out because Son of Biter took off. Full speed. Let's go. We're galloping. Off the trail. Through the brush.

"Oh shit!" I yelled.

I should've gone Western. There was nothing to hang on to and Sly knew it. He was jumping gullies and making hairpin turns. I thought I was a pretty good rider, but that was on regular horses. Ones without evil. I barely kept my seat. He tried everything, including bucking. I managed to stay on by grabbing his mane and I thought I'd worn him out. I should've known better when he slowed down and joined the trail again. Sly Dog wasn't a settling down kind of horse. I got myself back on the center of the saddle and took a deep breath just as he veered off the trail, ran through a thicket with his neck stretched out. Downhill. We're going downhill. Sliding. His haunches went down and my head went up.

Thwack.

I took a branch to the chest, tumbling off Sly's back and landing in a mess of muddy leaves. Sly whinnied as he cantered away down the hill. His haunches weren't down. He was under control. Out of the Frying Pan. Not such a weird name after all.

"You did that on purpose!"

Sly stopped about a hundred yards away, took a huge dump, whinnied, and took off.

"Well, that's just great." I'd lost a flip-flop. My rear felt like I'd landed on concrete and my horse was smarter than me. Not surprising but still. I hobbled through the woods, cursing his name and hoping he got bloat.

After walking for a half hour, I came to a clearing with seven batting cages and four full-sized baseball fields. The one closest to me had a game in full swing, but Jamie needn't have worried about the cheering. There was none. Not a chirp from the stands. I went over to watch from beside bleachers at first base. There were parents sitting there. Two guys. One did appear to have eaten a watermelon. On the other bleachers were Cherie and Anthony, the pair I'd seen in the gas station. They were the Lions and their pitcher, Taylor, was on the mound. He struck out the batter, but there was nothing than a polite hand tapping. The teams switched places and Oliver put his arm around Taylor's shoulders, giving him some cheerful feedback. The dark-haired boy nodded and worked his glove before running into the dugout.

Oliver spotted me and came around the chain-link fence. He was smiling, but then he became truly amused. "Went for a ride?"

"You could say that," I said with dignity.

"Sly Dog?"

"How'd you guess?"

"This isn't my first time."

"That horse is a menace," I said.

"Usually they give him to experienced riders," said Oliver.

I crossed my arms. "I am an experienced rider."

He bit back a laugh. "Sorry. Um...what else have you been doing?"

"Spa stuff. Why?"

"You're really shiny."

My arms were reflective. "They put some stuff on me."

"It's like you've been lacquered," said Oliver.

"They did put it on with a paintbrush."

"Nice.

"Not really," I said. "I have to tell you this is the quietest baseball game I've ever seen."

Oliver frowned at the boys taking the field. "I know. It's been like this all day. I'm hoping it's the drive down that's worn everyone out."

"Does this normally happen?"

"No. Never. They're usually wired with excitement."

"The parents aren't exactly bundles of joy then."

"They should be. Everyone's playing well." He nodded at the new pitcher on the mound. "Enrique's on. Nothing but strikes."

"He's the front runner?"

Oliver nodded. "The kid's got it."

We watched Enrique throw three strikes in quick succession and Oliver whistled softly. "Beautiful. Fucking beautiful. Have you seen Parker? He went to the bathroom and hasn't come back yet."

"What's he look like?" I asked.

"Six foot, messy blond hair. He usually sticks close to his brother, Enrique."

"Oh yeah. I remember him from when the Grizzlies arrived. Sorry. Haven't seen him."

Oliver glanced around and blew out a breath. "That kid is always disappearing. I've got to go. See you later."

I nodded and he yelled to the teams that it was the last inning before dinner. The parents and kids took it like they took all the strikes and triples. In silence. Really weird.

A blowing noise made me turn around and I saw Sly Dog walk out of the woods. He nickered at me all friendly. Yeah, right.

"Forget it, dirtbag. I've got feet and I'm gonna use them." I went up the trail to the castle and Sly followed, occasionally making nice noises. He probably hoped I wouldn't tell on him. I didn't have to. Jamie took one look and apologized to me before taking Sly into the stables, telling him he wasn't getting the good oats.

I walked back up to the castle, trying to ignore the phone vibrating like crazy in my pocket, but I saw the cousins, all four of them, searching the gardens for me and I answered just to delay the inevitable. It so wasn't worth it.

"What the hell do you think you're doing?" yelled Dad.

"Walking. Why?"

"Where's Tiny?"

I ducked behind a tree when the cousins turned my way. "In the garden. I'm fifty feet away. I thought I didn't have a babysitter this weekend."

"You don't," said Dad.

"Puhlease. Aaron and Tiny are here for one reason: to watch me and I don't get it."

"Get what?" Dad's voice got all cagey.

"You know a million guys who kick butt," I said. "Why not them?

"Aaron has saved your bacon more than once."

I peeked around the tree and Sorcha spotted me. Dammit. I stepped out and waved like I hadn't been hiding and asked Dad, "What about Tiny? Are you trying to kill him off or what?"

There was a pause and I could hear Dad tapping his blotter with a pen.

"Dad?" I asked.

"I wouldn't do anything to hurt Tiny. He's family and he's got a good mind. Get him in shape to work," he said.

"Me?"

"You're a nurse."

"He doesn't need wound care."

"Then you're not looking close enough. Get out of your head."

Tiny jogged up and bent over with his hands on his knees. "Where you been?"

I held up the phone and covered the microphone with my thumb. "Talking to Dad."

"He knows I lost you," he wheezed, getting redder.

"I know. Thanks for that," I said, turning my attention back to the phone. "I'll look into that, Dad. How's Lester?"

"Circling the drain."

My body went cold. Lester. Poor old Lester. This could be my fault. If The Klinefeld Group found out I was investigating them...

"Can I come home?" I asked.

"Hell, no. We're at a critical juncture," said Dad.

"Yeah, Lester's dying."

Tiny's head jerked up and I wiped away a tear.

"Mercy, my girl, there's nothing you can do. Nothing. His family is with him and he's not even conscious. The Feds are going to make a move on the Costillas in the next couple of days. I want you well out of the way."

"But…"

"But nothing. You're staying with John and Leslie. They know what to do," said Dad.

"How do they know?" I asked.

"Enough. Now go have dinner and get your feet buffed."

I groaned. "I already did."

"Find something to occupy yourself."

"I will, but you probably won't like it."

"Mercy!"

I hung up on him. It felt great, but Tiny froze in fear. I looked him over. He seemed fine to me. What wound was I supposed to fix?

"Did you just hang up on your dad?" he asked.

"Had to be done."

"You're gonna get me fired, girl."

I took his arm. "Never. You're fine."

The Troublesome Trio walked up, glaring at me.

"Where did you go?" asked Sorcha.

"Where's your shoe?" asked Bridget.

"There's blood on your shirt," said Jilly.

I'll be damned. There was blood on my shirt. Sly Dog really nailed me with that branch. "I took a horseback ride. I needed to think."

"About people killing you?" asked Bridget.

"I'm trying not to think about that," I said.

Jilly hooked her arm through my free one. "Yes. Let's not talk about that. Let's talk about Chuck. You still haven't told me how he kisses."

Somebody shoot me. Anybody. Calling all Costillas.

"It's twenty minutes until dinner," said Sorcha. "And they're doing gourmet s'mores by the fire pit after. We'll have plenty of time to talk about Chuck and the wedding."

Tiny laughed and I began to understand the builder of Cairngorms Castle. Tossing myself off the parapet was starting to sound like a viable option.

CHAPTER NINE

"Can't I just have a salad?" I asked Leslie as he seated us in the grand dining room.

Leslie smiled, pulling out all the charm in his beautifully tailored navy suit. He was so elegant and stylish; you couldn't stop staring at him. "What do you think?"

"Yes," I said, hopefully.

"No. I have my orders."

"What about me?" asked Tiny.

"Aaron has prepared a special menu just for you," said Leslie.

"Can I have that?" I asked. Tiny's food was bound to be lettuce heavy.

"No," said Leslie. "Your menu is Northern Italian."

"So lots of rice and cheese."

"Correct." Leslie turned as the MVP Grizzly parents came in, dressed like they were attending a business lunch. "Excuse me."

Leslie sat them near us and Robin applied a thick coat of lip gloss and immediately started texting, getting her many disapproving looks.

Her husband, Tim, who did look like he swallowed a watermelon, reached over and pushed down the phone. "Stop worrying. Parker's fine."

"Enrique doesn't know where he is. Why doesn't he answer?"

Tim hid a smile, telling me he knew where his son was, but wasn't telling the mom. Good dad. "He's having fun. Lighten up." He raised his glass and they toasted each other and the team. "To everything working out the way it's meant to."

Then Nicole and the rest of the Vipers came in. Nicole wore a jersey wrap dress, but her hair hadn't changed a bit. It was pretty in a helmet kind of way. Maybe she used Aqua Net. That's what my mom used to achieve her enormous hair in high school. She kept a bottle in her bathroom for the sake of nostalgia. I tried it out once and my hair looked like yellow wire.

Nicole and Cory nodded to me as they walked by and sat at a table close by. Leslie left the dining room and waiters filed in, carrying trays with thick wooden bowls filled with salad. Yes!

"Is this balsamic dressing?" asked Sorcha.

"Yes, ma'am," said Shane, our waiter.

"I love balsamic," said Jilly.

Apparently, everyone else did, too. The Grizzlies and the Vipers smiled and the chatter increased for a few minutes until the Lions came in. It was just Cherie and Anthony, hardly an intimidating pair, but they stopped everyone cold. Unlike everyone else, Cherie and Anthony hadn't changed for the upscale dining room and remained in their travel clothes. Anthony straightened his shirt as glanced at the jackets and ties. Cherie's face became defiant, but she hesitated when she saw Nicole and Cory of the Vipers staring at her with malice. Cory rubbed his crew cut and grimaced before finally looking away. Nicole never took her eyes off Cherie. She dug her nails into the tablecloth so hard that one of her jewels popped off and pinged against her husband's wineglass.

Cherie lifted her chin, took a breath and then smiled smugly at the Grizzlies. The dining room got very quiet. The Grizzlies cast puzzled glances at Cherie and the Vipers were visibly pissed, except for Bill. He took off his Cardinal's cap and said loudly, "I heard that people get lost in the castle, but I haven't yet. What about you all?"

Robin brightened up at the distraction and leaned toward the Viper table. "Deanna keeps ending up in the distillery."

Tim snorted into his beer and patted his round belly. Robin elbowed him and shook her head, making her diamonds shimmer in the light as they bounced off her jaw.

"Don't you be so smug, Tim," said Deanna as she directed a waiter to fill her wine glass to the brim. "You spend half the day at the pool."

"The pool?" asked Robin. "Are you taking up swimming again?"

"No. I keep trying to go outside and somehow I'm at the indoor pool."

Bill raised an eyebrow at Tim. "Creepy. Isn't that where one of the owners was murdered?"

"He wasn't murdered," said Robin. "He did a speedball thing and drowned. It's on the website. Leslie and John are very upfront about all the incidents that have happened here."

"What's a speedball?" asked Tim before downing the rest of his beer.

"A mixture of heroin and cocaine apparently."

Tim shifted uneasily in his chair. "You'd have to be completely bonkers to do something like that."

They went on to discuss the owner who put her head in an oven. Nobody was sure if it was completely voluntarily. Her husband wasn't all that fond of her. There was a mistress who wandered off into the woods and was never seen again. That was pinned on the jealous wife. No conviction, only a divorce. Two owners, not one, jumped off the parapet and another got locked in one of the towers and nearly starved to death before anyone noticed he was missing. I was going to have to look at that website.

The other Vipers weren't listening to the tales of mysterious deaths. Nicole stabbed her lettuce and muttered to Cory, who rubbed his head every time his wife spoke to him. If no one thought Taylor Marin was a real contender for the prize, what was the big deal? Whatever the reason there was no more smiling, except at our table. Aaron was in rare form. My cousins were in raptures over the pesto, risotto, and creamy polenta. Tiny's food didn't look like diet food either. It was so beautiful, Sorcha kept stealing bites from him. I could've hugged Aaron. His food distracted Jilly from grilling me about Chuck.

Instead, I got to people watch. Leslie in particular. He worked the room, a real pro, and his charm was infectious. He'd stop at a table and have them all happy in seconds, but it didn't last. When he moved on, the baseball parents snapped back to uncomfortable.

John never came into the dining room. He lurked in the shadows by a display of Japanese armor. I saw him and he knew I did. I had the distinct impression that he was there for me, counting my bites, of which there were few. I glanced up to see if he was still watching and saw the heavy armor fall over toward John. There was no reason for it to fall. It just did. The innkeeper kept his eyes on me and neatly stepped out of the way as if he expected it to happen. The bamboo and leather plates thumped on the thick carpet and the winged iron helmet rolled away, bumping into a potted palm. It made less noise than you'd think, but the dining staff froze, their eyes going wide with fright. John snapped his fingers and two waiters rushed over the set the armor upright. I gave John a questioning look and he answered me with a shrug. I wouldn't get more than that. Armor? What armor?

I turned my attention back to my plate and sighed. Why did there have to be so much? My technique of moving food around on the plate fooled the waiter like it did Mom, but not Aaron. He kept coming out of the kitchen to check on me. I wouldn't be surprised if he weighed my plate before and after. Let him. I was doing the best I could.

After dinner, a two-hour affair, the Troublesome Trio extracted a promise from me that I would come right down to the fire pit after getting Pick from my room. They held on to the bag o'dogfood that Aaron had specially made for Pick, a hostage in case I decided to make another run for it. I wasn't going to do that. Pick might poop in the Diane bedroom. Besides, Tiny got energized by Aaron's food and was watching me, poised to run me down. For the first time, I thought he might be able to do it.

I considered Fiking him anyway. I hated being accompanied every-where like a toddler, just like Michael Fike, my dad's first partner, who hated him enough to ditch him at every opportunity. It was safe to say that Fike didn't consider my dad much of an asset. According to witnesses, Dad showed no signs of his future brilliance. He could belch the alphabet and drink a gallon of beer in one sitting. Tiny wasn't like my dad and he was an asset. He had a sense of direction that was spot on. Not one wrong turn to our tower. He couldn't explain how he did it and I couldn't even remember how many turns we made. It was somewhere in the neighborhood of twenty. Tiny was like a giant homing pigeon and showed up at my door in an astonishingly short amount of time. I let myself in and found Pick spread out on my bed, snout on pillow. He was drooling. Yuck.

"Come on, hair hound," I said.

He leapt to his feet and barked. His black fuzzy hair was standing on end and he seemed to have put on twenty pounds. He did not jump off the bed. Pick's rule was never leave your cushion unless there's food.

"Food."

Then he jumped off and set about sniffing us. Finding no food, he gnawed on my leg while I put on his leash.

"What's he doing?" asked Tiny.

"He has issues," I said.

"Dogs be weird. Aunt Willasteen's dog only pees in her houseplants." He pried Pick off my leg and we retraced our steps and went out to the fire pit. Three stone circles matching the castle sat to the left of the formal gardens. Adirondack chairs, piled with cushions and lap blankets, surrounded them. Sorcha, Bridget, and Jilly were there already and they had the bride book. I'd been hearing about it all day. It was a thick binder with every dream Bridget had for her wedding. By the look of it, she had plenty of dreams.

"I have a date," I said, checking my phone for the time. Quarter to nine.

"A date?" Tiny frowned at me. This date was clearly not on the schedule. "With who?"

"The head of the baseball camp, Oliver Jakes."

"Aren't you in love with your cousin?"

I stopped short. "First of all, he's not my cousin by blood. Second, I don't know what I am to him anymore."

"I can see that."

"What's that mean?"

"It means you don't know which end is up."

That sounded about right, but I still didn't like it.

"I'll give you a hundred bucks to distract the Troublesome Trio so I can book it out of here."

Tiny crossed his big arms. "You really got a date?"

John appeared at my shoulder. "Yes, she does."

I jumped and bumped into Tiny. "What the... How did you know?"

"He's cleared," said John.

"For what?" asked Tiny.

"For Mercy."

"You sure?"

John held Tiny's gaze until Tiny nodded. "I'll take the dog."

I looked at my cousins bent over the book, poised to talk wedding for the next three hours. "What are you going to tell them?"

Tiny shrugged.

"Mercy has diarrhea," said John, just as blank as ever.

Tiny grinned at me. "Yeah, yeah. She has to wash out her drawers."

"Oh my god," I said. "Do not say that."

John nodded. "And clean up the bathroom floor."

"That would take some time," said Tiny.

"It's down in the grout," said John.

"It was explosive like Ebola diarrhea."

"Are you sure you're not a Watts? You sound like a Watts," I said. "Do not say that!"

Tiny tapped his chin. "Maybe you got it on the stairs."

I slugged his shoulder. "Can you hear me? Do not say that!"

"You want to go on that date or not?" asked Tiny between guffaws.

Not really. But it's better than wedding talk.

"Yes."

"You got a better idea?"

"Anything's better than that," I said.

"Anything that would keep them from demanding your presence anytime soon?" asked John.

"Um..."

"That's our story then," said Tiny, taking Pick's leash and walking off to the fire pits.

John turned me around and took me back into the castle. "They'll see you if you go that way."

"You know that story's going to get around," I said.

"I have no objection."

"Nice."

John walked through the castle, passing through the armory with decorative displays of deadly weapons covering the walls and going out a door hidden in the heavy oak paneling. I took a deep breath of the clean country air and tried to get my bearings. As it turned out, I had no bearings to begin with. "Where are we?"

John pointed at a flagstone path lit by tiny flickering lights in the grass. "Follow the path around the castle to the carriage house. Oliver has finished his evening seminar with the players. He's waiting for you."

The path led away into the darkness and my chest tightened up. Dad's warnings about the Costillas rang in my ears and a chill went down my back. Me. In the dark. With a price on my head. Perhaps not a great idea.

"Maybe we should call Oliver and have—" I turned to John and he'd vanished. "You've got to be kidding me." I searched the wall. The door was there. I'd just come through it, but there wasn't a handle or a button or any sign that it was there. Crap.

There was a soft rustling over my head. I looked up at the parapet, lit by the gleaming moon, and saw a thin shadow against one of the towers. I swallowed hard. It was fine. John put me out here and Dad trusted John. You could count the number of people Dad trusted on two hands and a couple of them were dead. John must be okay. Better than okay. It was fine. Of course it was.

"Hello!" I called up at the shadow.

No response.

"I can see you there!"

Nothing.

Okay. Time to go. I darted away down the path. Once I was at the edge of the other tower, I looked back up at the parapet. He was still there, but he'd moved to my tower, his identity hidden by its shadow. I turned and ran down the path. It took a winding, inefficient way, looping out into the woods. I wasn't happy about that, but I dared not leave the path.

I slowed down when the parapet was obscured by the trees and spotted a light up ahead to the right. The path split. Great John. Thanks. The right went to the light and the left back in the direction of the castle. I went with the left.

My sandals made no sound on the flagstones so they didn't compete with the voices that echoed through the trees from the direction of the light. Voices raised in anger. Fast and furious so as to be indistinguishable from each other. My path curved sharply to the left and I was even with the light, which turned out to be a wide arched doorway in what looked like an adobe mound.

In the gloom, I could make out a thin pillar of smoke drifting out of a hole in the roof. There was a sweat lodge appointment on my schedule. That must be it. The scene was singularly peaceful, except for the angry words erupting from the golden glow in the doorway. Figures walked back and forth, momentarily blocking the light. A man and a woman from their sizes.

The woman stepped into the doorway and yelled, "You listen to me, you son of a bitch. You—" She turned to look out toward me. Cherie, the mom from the Lions, squinted into the darkness and I froze. "Is somebody there?"

I sucked in my lips. I wasn't about to reveal myself. Cherie hesitated and then turned away. When she did, I continued down the path, glancing back to see if they'd come out. They hadn't, but the whole thing gave me an uneasy feeling. Not like one of Dad's famous feelings. He was known for having a sense that something wasn't right. But this wasn't like that. It was more heavy and foreboding. I kept waiting for a gunshot or a scream to ring out behind me, but the woods were silent with only the frogs singing in the darkness.

After a few more turns, the carriage house appeared in front of me. I almost ran to it; my relief was so great. I'm proud to say I controlled myself and walked up to the open center door where a guy wearing a track suit stood smoking a cigarette. The red tip lit up the darkness with each deep breath and he smiled at my approach. "I thought Oliver was shitting me," he said after a last puff.

"About what?" I asked.

"A date with you, Miss Marilyn herself."

"The name's Mercy, not Marilyn."

He put up his hands in surrender. "Sorry. I'll get him."

A few minutes later, Oliver came out. He wore a pressed white polo and slim-fitting jeans. The effect was excellent. Unfortunately, it only reminded me of Chuck. Nobody wore jeans like Chuck.

"They're having s'mores up at the fire pits. I thought we'd go up there," said Oliver.

"Well...um...I"

"There's not really anything else to do around here at night."

I racked my brain for another idea and came up empty. Oliver held out his hand and I forced myself to take it. I was on a date. Dammit. How did this happen? I'd have to tell Chuck at some point, although I didn't know why. He'd taken off, not me. We had no understanding. I didn't know if we had anything anymore at all.

Oliver squeezed my hand and insisted on introducing me to his staff, a bunch of rugged retired pro players. They were polite about staring at me. The boys weren't so much. Oliver introduced me to all the players. He began with the Grizzlies and I wondered if that meant something. Enrique was the front runner for the prize, according to pretty much everyone. He was there with the rest of his team. He had a shy smile and firm handshake. Enrique didn't look much like a star athlete being small and wiry, but in his eyes was a solemn determination. His two brothers, Parker and Kellan, were both big blonds that resembled Robin, the woman from the mud baths, but they had their father's hair. Enrique must've been adopted. He didn't resemble anyone. Robin's boys and the rest of the team were extremely polite. Their eyes flicking to Oliver to check his responses to their behavior.

Next were the Lions. Taylor was adorable close up with freckles and dark auburn hair that matched Cherie's dye job. The blond, spiky-haired kid he'd been trading punches with was James. Their team was equally polite, but they weren't as concerned with Oliver.

The Vipers were last. Quinn was there, more polite than the last time I'd seen him. He also resembled his mother with her dark hair and calm demeanor. His catcher was Anders. I'd seen him get out of the Escalade with Quinn.

When pleasantries were done, the boys went back to foosball and video games and we walked up to the fire pits. Cherie was there with Anthony, who was introduced as the kid's grandfather. Lane sat on her other side cuddled up in her varsity jacket over a huge white jersey that nearly reached her knees. When she saw me looking at her, she zipped up her jacket and looked away.

Nicole, her husband, and the rest of the Viper parents showed up and sat as far from Cherie and Anthony as possible. Some of the Grizzly parents were there, sipping cocktails instead of beer and being well-bred. Tim drank Long Island ice teas. He had three empty glasses on the table in front of him and he slurred his words as he bragged about Parker's academic scholarship offers and Enrique's going pro in less than a year. Both boys had bright futures and he let everyone know between hiccups and unintelligible sentences. Robin came out and sat next to him, her face bright pink with matching lipstick. Deanna followed a young waiter around, flirting and having her wine glass continuously refilled.

My cousins spotted us at the edge of the crowd and I dropped Oliver's hand. I don't know why, but I felt oddly guilty.

"Mercy, what are you doing here?" asked Bridget.

"I told you I'd come," I said, cheerfully.

"But Tiny said..." Jilly looked at Tiny, who sipped a beer.

Don't say it. Don't say it.

"I thought you were ill," said Jilly.

Thank you.

"Never mind about that," I said. "I'm better."

"You were sick?" asked Oliver.

"Monumentally," said Sorcha, looking Oliver up and down.

"But it's over," I said.

"How could that be over so fast?" asked Bridget.

"What was wrong?" asked Oliver.

I wrinkled my nose and batted my eyes. I'm told it's distracting and it was. "I'm fine. How about some drinks."

"Okay," said Oliver, looking deep into my eyes. "What would you like?"

"Red wine. Pinot, if they have it."

Oliver didn't move.

"Oliver?" I asked.

"Huh?"

"Something wrong?"

He shook his head. "No, no. Pinot. Got it." Oliver went into the castle and I sat down.

"Wow," said Jilly. "Can you teach me how to do that?"

"What?" I asked.

"He was like a deer in the headlights."

"Oh, that. It's a gift, comes with the face."

Jilly frowned. "So you can't teach me."

"I can try."

"I can use it on Chuck," she said.

Ah crap!

Oliver came back with drinks for everyone and Aaron brought out the gourmet s'mores. Gourmet was right. He'd made the graham crackers and the marshmallows. The chocolate came from Peru and had gold flecks in it. Aaron also brought out thermoses of hot whole milk for hot chocolate. He had a tray of chocolate from the Chocolate House in Luxembourg City. The Chocolate House was my favorite when I was a kid, especially the hot chocolate. Nobody made hot chocolate fun like them. Wooden spoons stuck in chocolate blocks that you dipped into steaming mugs of milk. Aaron knew I loved about twenty flavors and it'd be hard to avoid drinking it. The s'mores were bad enough. Oliver made me a triple decker. It oozed chocolate on my fingers. The homemade marshmallows were super light and fluffy, not like store bought at all. Everyone licked their fingers and the mood lightened up. The baseball parents even laughed when Anthony's marshmallow fell off his stick and plopped into the fire, sending sparks up five feet. After the influx of sugar, we talked about baseball with the parents for a while. Oliver kept trying to hold my hand with Sorcha watching us covertly. She hardly said a word. Everyone except Sorcha and Lane were having a decent time. Lane looked more and more bored and excused herself early.

"Where are you going?" asked Cherie with an edge in her voice. It's only 9:20."

"To bed," said Lane. "I'm tired and I'm going for a ride in the morning."

She didn't look tired to me, but she left quick before her mother could stop her. Moms. Always so suspicious. In my case, it was justified. I didn't know about Lane.

There was probably something I didn't know because Cherie left a half hour later with a concerned frown. For heaven's sake, the kid was sixteen and Cairngorms Castle was a fortress. But the rest of us didn't last much longer. The air got misty and cold as clouds rolled in. The fire pit and blankets couldn't combat the chill. I shouldn't have worn a dress. My legs had goosebumps. I tucked the blanket tighter around my legs and did a jaw-cracking yawn. It's amazing how being pampered tires you out and the baseball parents had to get up early to hover over the players. Tiny was already asleep in his chair after his beer. The only ones that weren't tired were Sorcha, Bridget, and Jilly.

"Let's not go to bed," said Jilly.

"Slumber party!" exclaimed Bridget and Sorcha. They looked at me with big smiles.

Oliver laughed. "I know when I'm not wanted."

"Sorry," they said in chorus.

"Wait. Aren't we too old for slumber parties?" I was too everything for one of my cousins' slumber parties. They always included duct tape, permanent marker, and pillow fights where I was the only target. Pass on the so-called party.

"You're never too old to have fun," said Bridget.

"I am."

"Mercy," she whined. "It's my bridal weekend."

Oh dear lord.

"I'm sort of on a date here." It wasn't a date I wanted to be on, but a girl's gotta do what a girl's gotta do.

Oliver hauled me out of my chair and gave me a thankfully brief kiss on the lips. "It's okay. Lunch tomorrow? We can picnic at the Shut-ins."

"Um...they're closed. Flood waters or something."

"We'll stay on shore. I'm not crazy," Oliver gave me a rakish grin, "despite what the sportswriters say."

Sorcha grabbed my arm. "That sounds good. We'll picnic."

We?

Oliver frowned but agreed. He left, walking off down the path into the darkness. We all watched him, even me. I couldn't help it. Oliver had a great rear view. The walk was pretty slow so I suspect he knew it.

"I can't believe you got a date already," said Jilly. "We've been here five minutes."

"It's definitely been longer than five minutes."

Five months. Five years.

Bridget shook Tiny awake and announced we were having a slumber party and he was coming. For the first time, Tiny said no. He'd be around if I needed him. The big coward. All they were going to do was straighten his hair and mascara his long lashes. Now it was all me. Break out the duct tape. Thanks, bodyguard.

There was no duct tape, just wine. Lots of wine. And talk of Chuck and men and sex. All three made me uncomfortable so I drank plenty. I didn't manage to get out of Bridget's room until after midnight. My tower room was stuffy and hot when Pick and I got back to it. I opened the window wider, thinking the cool air would make me feel better. It made me cold and I ended up vomiting a little. I collapsed on my bed with Pick trampling all over me in an effort to get under the covers. I finally gave in just so he'd stop stepping on me. He burrowed underneath the coverlet and I fell asleep with my nose buried in his fuzzy neck.

Bark.

Bark. Bark.

Bark. Bark. Bark.

"What the hell?" I rolled over.

Bark. Bark. Bark. Bark.

"I will kill you!" I yelled at the empty bed. Pick was at the window with his front paws on the sill, barking his fool head off.

I stumbled out of bed, yanked him back by the collar, and closed the window. "Go to sleep, maniac."

Pick ignored me and paced in front of the window, growling, as I climbed back under the covers. He barked several more times and I threatened him with dismemberment. He finally jumped back on the bed, spun around seventeen times, and plunked down on the pillows. All the pillows. What was happening to my life? This wasn't even my dog. I grabbed my phone and texted Chuck. "I'm going to kill your dog. Come home and save him."

There was no response as usual, but I fell asleep staring at the screen, hoping.

CHAPTER TEN

I woke up six hours later with a pounding on my door and in my head. I was prepared to ignore both. Pick wasn't. He started barking and he wasn't going to stop until I got up.

Tiny charged in the room and jogged in place. "Let's go for a run."

I stared at him bleary-eyed and hunched over. "Are you serious? It's barely seven."

"It's like 7:15 and I slept like a drunk on Bourbon."

"Is that supposed to be a good thing?"

"Hell yeah," he said. "Get dressed and we can run before breakfast."

"What about your knees?" I asked.

Tiny's knees weren't built to take that level of pounding. Nobody's were.

"Feels good." He jogged out and Pick pranced in front of the door.

"I suppose you want to go."

Bark.

"I'll bark you right in the snout." I popped a couple of Tylenol, put on a yoga ensemble and a hoodie as slowly as possible and dragged my feet into the hall. Tiny was still jogging in place. The crazy bastard.

"Coffee first," I said.

"Coffee after. Don't wanna lose the go."

"I never had the go. I've got the stay and sit."

"Come on, girl. You gotta get me fit to fight."

"How about fit to sit?"

Tiny jogged down the stone steps and Pick yanked me along behind him. I tried to be slow, but neither of them would entertain the idea. Tiny led me through the castle and down to the copper pot kitchen where Aaron was up with a kitchen staff of three making long loaves of French bread and heavenly croissants. There was coffee. I could smell it.

Pick and Tiny went for the door and I dug my heels in. "I need coffee."

"No way, man," said Tiny, opening the door. "Hear them birds. Smell that morning dew."

"I'll beat you to death."

Tiny laughed, but I was never so serious. I grabbed Aaron's sleeve. "I'll eat a croissant if you make him let me have coffee."

Aaron squinted at me from behind his smudged lenses. "Huh?"

"I'll eat. Anything. A stick of butter. Anything. I need coffee."

Pick yanked me so hard he nearly pulled me off my feet and began sniffing at the open door. Then the barking began. Serious barking. Barking like he'd never barked before. No. That wasn't true. Pick once chased down a bigamist with me and that barking was similar.

"What's wrong with him?" asked one of the cooks, his hands covered in flour.

"I don't know. He hates me and coffee."

A harder yank and furious barking.

"He wants to run," said Tiny.

"You take him," I said.

Tiny was about to agree when Pick lunged, dragging me out the door and into the foggy kitchen garden. The dog was going bat shit crazy and he didn't stop there. He lunged with me pulling back with everything I had. His barks had turned into strangled gurgles, but he wasn't about to stop. "Tiny! Help!"

Tiny ran out the door, but he was too slow. Pick had me through the kitchen garden into the formal garden, heading for the tragic love section with its daggers and swords design.

"I'm coming!" yelled Tiny just as Pick took a flying leap over the closest three-foot-high hedge, dragging me face first into it.

"Son of a bitch!" I screamed and that wasn't the worst of it. I sounded like Uncle Morty when his rogue character got bested in Dungeons and Dragons. It wasn't pretty.

Tiny hauled me out of the hedge by the seat of my pants, took the leash, and yanked Pick back with ease. "What's wrong with this damn poodle?"

"I'll kill him, starting with the tail and working my way up!"

"There's no need for killing the dog," said Tiny.

I held up my deeply scratched arms. "You don't think?"

A head popped up on the other side of tragic love, Leslie with a tinge of pink on his cheeks. "I might've of known you'd be the first on the scene."

"Scene of what?" I asked.

He raised an eyebrow. "Homicide, of course."

Pick continued barking his brains out. Tiny and I stood there dumb with shock.

"Did you say homicide?" asked Tiny after a minute.

"Yes. Your dog isn't as stupid as he looks."

Pick did look pretty stupid at the moment, hurling himself at the hedge and slinging his head around as he strangled himself. Plus, he was a poodle. Nobody takes a giant poodle seriously.

I did an involuntary shake, reached over, and grabbed him by the snout. I clamped his jaws together and yelled in his berserk face, "No!"

Pick whined, dropped to the ground, and put his paws over his eyes.

"Very adorable," I said. "You are not forgiven."

Tiny poked me. "Mercy, he said homicide."

"I heard him."

"What're you gonna do?" he asked.

"Yes, Mercy," said Leslie. "What *are* you going to do?"

"Me? Nothing. Call the police," I said.

"I'd rather not."

I frowned and put pressure on a particularly deep cut on my forearm. Blood oozed between my fingers. That was going to leave a mark.

"Why not?" I asked.

"Let's just say I'd like to handle this in-house," said Leslie and he was completely serious. There was no such thing as handling a murder in-house unless you're the mafia. Ah crap. Leslie could be mafia. Maybe that was how Dad knew him. It wouldn't explain why he considered Leslie a friend though.

"What do you want me to do?" I asked.

"Only what you normally do."

"Stitches and pressure checks?"

"Solve the murder."

Tiny was sweating like crazy in the early morning chill and his hands were shaking, but he nudged me. "It is what you do."

"Not really. Not on purpose."

"Come on. I need the experience." He sounded a little shaky on that and I didn't blame him. I had as much experience as I wanted.

"Tiny," I said.

"Come on, girl. We're...professionals."

Groan.

"Fine, but we're calling the cops," I said. "Who is it?"

"Cherie Marin."

I checked my emotions and discovered I wasn't surprised. Cherie wasn't exactly Miss Popular, but still murder was a bit excessive. We walked around tragic love to the path between it and passionate love. The path was clean, the gravel was undisturbed, and there was no blood or signs of a struggle. I came to the center of the love garden. The fountain squirted away, lovely arcs of clear water. At the base of the fountain was Cherie, lying on her back. Her face was a hideous purplish red, her eyes were open, filled with burst capillaries and staring up at the sky. There was clear bruising in the shape of hands on her neck. The rest of her was where it got odd. She was stick straight, not a natural position at all. Her hands were folded over her stomach and her jeans were down around her knees. Her legs weren't spread though and her boxy t-shirt was pulled down to cover her pelvis. Her body was damp from the last night's rain. Forensics wouldn't be happy.

"Amateur," I said automatically.

"I'd say so," said Leslie and he put his hand over his mouth, turning away.

Tiny called over the tragic love hedge, "What happened to her?"

"Come and see for yourself," I said. "You're the one who wants to do this thing."

John walked out of the kitchen door, saw us, and came over. He was wearing a suit with a full Windsor knot in his tie. It was seven o'clock in the morning. Did this guy ever relax? Even Leslie wore sweats. They were tailored but still.

John came up to Tiny and took Pick's leash. The poodle sniffed frantically and snapped at something next to John's leg. He ignored the behavior and pointed to the path. Tiny took a breath and walked in. Every inch of him showed that he didn't want to do it, despite what he said, and it surprised me. He took a job with Dad. At the very least there'd be crime scene photos.

"Are you okay?" I asked before he reached the fountain.

"Yeah," he said as he looked down at Cherie. "Ah damn! Tommy's gonna flip. You gotta go. Now!" Tiny grabbed my arm and I winced as his fingers dug into my cuts. "Sorry. But you gotta go."

I peeled his fingers off my arm. "I'm not going anywhere. This has nothing to do with me. Call 911."

"No 911," said Leslie, turning back. His eyes dropped to Cherie and he grimaced. "Funding issues."

"Well, call the local cop shop then," I said.

"There hasn't been a murder around here in years, but go ahead. Give it a shot. Maybe they'll know what to do."

A prickly feeling went up my back. I shivered and turned around. No one was behind me, but, on the parapet, a shadow darkened the spaces between the gaps in the stone teeth high above us. It could be the murderer, gazing on the horror he'd wrought or it could be nothing, the kind of nothing that locked people in the distillery or got them lost for hours on end. I had the strongest feeling it was that kind of nothing.

Leslie gently turned me away and I squatted beside Cherie's body. "Tiny, call them."

"Ah damn. She was raped. This is a sex crime." Tiny pointed at Leslie. "I can't believe this shit. What the hell is wrong with you people? This place is supposed to be secure."

"It is." Leslie relaxed as if remembering who he was and a lazy smile came over his face. This clearly wasn't his first body.

"The hell it is."

I leaned in to look at Cherie's fingernails. Clean. No blood or tissue. She didn't get a piece of him. "Leslie means that the murderer is still on the grounds."

"Ah damn!" Tiny walked in a circle, throwing his hands in the air. "Ah damn!"

"Call the cops," I said. "It's fine."

"It ain't fine, but I'm callin'. This shit is unbelievable."

Leslie gave me a sidelong look. "Perhaps not. Mercy is said to garner trouble wherever she goes."

"Like this is my fault," I said. "You're a more likely cause."

"How do you come to that conclusion?"

"You're not who you say you are."

"Who did we say we were?" Leslie asked.

He had a point. He and John hadn't said anything about themselves. They were blanks. Witness protection program? Leslie smiled as I thought it over. He cared, but he wasn't scared or worried about this murder. Either it had nothing to do with them or he was one hell of an actor.

"Hey," said Tiny into the phone. "I got a murder out at Cairngorms Castle."

He paused.

"Nah, I didn't do it."

Another pause.

"Would I call ya if I'd done it?"

"Cause she ain't breathing," said Tiny, rolling his eyes at me. "And she's got hand marks around her neck."

Long pause.

"Look man, this woman is dead and it ain't no accident."

Leslie cocked an eyebrow at me. "See what I mean."

"Maybe that cop is the only incompetent one," I said.

"I'm sure that will be the case since the most they handle around here is theft at the state park."

Tiny held out the phone to me. "You wanna talk to this...cop?"

"No. You can handle it," I said with a smile.

"You're a pain in my ass," he said.

"In many asses if you believe what people say."

"Yeah, yeah," he said and spoke into the phone again. "Listen here. We need a medical examiner."

Yet another pause.

"Well, send whatever doc you got. She was raped. She needs one of them kits."

I shook my head. "She wasn't raped."

Tiny's eyes went to Cherie's hips and he frowned. "I don't know. Just get over here. Cairngorms Castle. I told you that already. Yes, they'll let you in. You're the cops." Tiny hung up. "That's an idiot right there."

Leslie nodded and said, "He's what you call unprepared."

"He's uneverything." Tiny turned his attention back to me. "How can you tell she wasn't raped?"

"Her pants and panties are down, but not far enough. And her shirt is pulled down to cover her area, and there's no bruising."

"Staged?"

"I think so. After she was strangled. Manually."

"Have you seen a lot of stranglings?" asked Leslie.

"I've seen a lot of crime scene photos," I said. "How far away is the station?"

"Twenty minutes at best."

I groaned. Great. I doubted the guy on the phone was sprinting out to the car. He was probably looking the procedure up in a manual and trying to figure out who to call for the medical aspect.

"Alright. I guess we'd better block off the scene. Do you have any rope?" I asked Leslie.

"I'm sure we do."

"Somebody's got to tell Anthony and her kids," I said and they looked at me.

Okay. I guess that'll be me. What a way to start the day.

Leslie's estimate of twenty minutes was a tad bit generous. Two deputies showed up forty minutes later with no sirens and driving so slow I thought they might be octogenarians. They weren't. The deputies were in their mid-twenties but lacked all the brashness I would've expected at their age. They parked in the lot just through trees between the formal gardens and the baseball field. They got out and conferred before heading up to us like they were heading to their own executions, slow with hunched shoulders.

"Any questions?" asked Leslie.

"So many questions I don't know where to start," I said.

"Not everyone can be Tommy Watts."

"I'm not expecting that, but a sense of urgency would be nice."

"This is the back end of nowhere. Life is slower here."

I supposed it didn't matter that much. Cherie was already dead. They couldn't change it, but the slow walk was making me want to scream.

When they finally reached the love garden, they stopped at passionate love. "Hey there," said the taller of the duo.

"Please come over, gentlemen," said Leslie. "She's here by the fountain."

They hesitated and then walked down the path slower than ever. When they reached us, they introduced themselves as Deputies Phelong and Gerry.

"What happened?" Phelong, a thin Asian-American with light acne on his cheeks, got out a pad and pen to take down the details, but when we told him what we knew he forgot to write it down. Gerry wasn't like his partner in looks at all. He resembled a lawn gnome in height and width but, like Phelong, he couldn't stop looking at Cherie's body. The color drained out of his pale face and his breathing went rapid.

"We've got a fainter," I said.

"Huh?" asked Phelong.

"Gerry's going to pass out."

"No, I'm not." Gerry lurched to the side and whacked his hip on the fountain.

Each of the individual love gardens had a stone bench at its entrance. I took Gerry by the arm and waist and led him over to tragic love to sit.

"First body?" I asked.

He wiped some spittle from the corner of his mouth. "Yeah. Who are you?"

"She's Mercy Watts, remember? The DBD girl," said Phelong. "Dude, you're making us look bad."

"It's fine," I said. "You don't get many murders out here, I assume?"

"Not since we've been on the force."

"How long is that?"

Phelong straightened up. "I graduated from the academy eighteen months ago."

"Five months," said Gerry, making an involuntary horking noise.

That explained it. These two weren't near ready for this.

I sat next to Gerry. "Where's your supervisor?"

Before he could answer, the baseball parents came out of the kitchen door. Anthony and Lane were among them. "Oh crap."

"Who's that?" asked Phelong.

"Other guests and the victim's family," said Leslie.

John headed the group off, but they didn't look like they'd be restrained for long. The Viper parents were a tall group and they were up on their tiptoes and Tim, Robin's husband, was ready to dodge John. His blond hair stood on end and his belly jiggled as he darted back and forth.

Lane and her grandfather, Anthony, went from person to person, asking them something, presumably about Cherie's whereabouts, and got only shakes of the head. I watched each person, but everyone seemed normal aside from the curiosity.

Lane dialed her phone, hung up, and then dialed again. She began to cry and Anthony took her by the shoulders. His eyes met mine and his shoulders sagged as I bit my lip.

Lane pulled away from Anthony and dashed to the edge of the love garden. "Leslie, have you seen my mom?"

I turned to Phelong and Gerry and mouthed, "Daughter." They began babbling about procedure. So helpful.

"Never mind. I'll tell her. Did you call the medical examiner?"

"We don't really have an official one. We can call the doc we've got."

"Good enough for now."

Lane darted past her grandpa and came walking down between the tragic and passionate love sections with her hands in fists. I headed her off. She was not going to see her mom that way.

"Hi, Lane," I said. "Let's go inside. It's cold out here and you only have on shorts."

Her voice went an octave higher and became squeaky. "Where's my mom?"

"We'll talk about it inside."

"Why are the cops here?" Everyone watched us, suddenly silent. I'd delivered the bad news a multitude of times, but never at the scene. Waiting rooms were my poison where the family already knew something terrible had happened. Lane knew, but she wasn't expecting it. Sixteen-year-old girls never expect their mothers to die, much less violently.

I took her by the shoulders and she looked at me with clear, frightened eyes.

Now it was my job to change her life. I had to do it right. She would remember the moment forever. I remembered when Dad told me that my boyfriend, David, was probably dead, and then quickly said he *was* dead so that I wouldn't hope. I remembered what Dad was wearing. What I was wearing. The stillness of the Morning Room in the Bled mansion. The smell of Myrtle's beloved French macaroons in the air and the feeling of my chest hardening in pain and disbelief. A hardness that never really went away.

"We called the cops," I said. "Did you know that they don't have 911 out here?"

"They don't?" she asked, looking over my shoulder toward the fountain.

I had to tell her inside where I could contain her. Otherwise, she might run to her mother, embedding that horrible image in her young mind forever, and ruining our scene.

"No, they don't. I'm not even sure they have a good doctor, but I'm a nurse. You don't look so good. How do you feel?"

Lane focused on my face. "You're a nurse? I thought you were a model."

"I'm both."

"You've got cuts all over you. What happened?"

"My poodle freaked out and dragged me into a hedge." I pointed at Pick. He sat at John's feet like he would never do such a thing.

"Oh my god. He's adorable. I didn't know we could bring dogs," said Lane.

"He's a special case. Why don't we take him inside and you can help me with these cuts? I can't do it by myself."

John quickly gave her the leash and I gently prodded her back into the kitchen. Aaron was in there and he guided us to the staff dining room. He closed the drapes, so we couldn't see out into the garden, and closed the door.

I sat Lane down and I told her. I don't remember what I said. I only remember the pain at causing the look of devastation to come over her face. I was never so glad to have a poodle. I couldn't comfort her. The loss was too immense. But Pick knew what to do. He licked her cheeks and she slid onto the floor to sob into his neck like she would never stop. Pick just sat still with the occasional lick. For the first time, that fuzzy leg biter was noble.

CHAPTER ELEVEN

Lane sobbed with Pick for ten minutes until Anthony came in. His eyes were glassy and he leaned on the door frame, arms wrapped around his waist as he watched Lane's grief. His Wrangler jeans had been cinched up another notch and almost looked like they were pleated. The man was wasting away, and Pick had to yip to get him going.

"Lane. Baby girl," he said softly before going to his granddaughter.

"We're orphans," said Lane between sobs. "Did you tell Taylor?"

Anthony shook his head. "He went for the run this morning with the team and they haven't come back yet." He took her wet face between his rough hands. "You're not orphans. You have me."

"Grandpa." Lane cried into his knee and I went out the door to find Tiny there. He was nearly as destroyed as Lane and Anthony. His cheeks were deep red and his eyes filled with tears.

"Are you okay?" I asked.

"I'm good. Why?"

"Um...just thought you looked upset."

"A woman's dead."

Yes. A woman was dead, but that didn't account for Tiny's expression. That was personal. Before I could inquire further, John came in the kitchen. "Reinforcements."

"The medical examiner?" I asked.

"Not yet. Coach Jakes. He'll handle the parents. You need to tell the son about his mother."

I need to tell him. Right. Of course. Nobody else could take on that special task.

John read my mind. "You don't want me to do it." He was as flat and expressionless as ever.

"Do you have any feelings?"

"Not that I'm aware of."

I nodded. "Yeah. You're probably not the right choice to break the news to an unsuspecting son."

He gestured to the door and we went out into the garden. It'd warmed up considerably in the few minutes I'd been inside. The sun reflected off the dew on the young plants in the kitchen garden and the air smelled of freshly turned over soil. I hadn't noticed before since I was being dragged out by a crazed poodle who smelled a body. Pick wasn't trained or particularly useful, but he had skills. Chuck must've rubbed off on his dog. It wasn't me. I didn't go looking for bodies, no matter what people thought.

Most of the time I didn't much care what people thought, except for Chuck, and he still wasn't talking. I texted him with yet another lame attempt to get a response. "Murder at the castle. Come help me." He did like a good crime. Maybe this time... No luck.

"Are you going to start your investigation?" asked John.

"Explain why this is my problem."

John nodded to Phelong and Gerry. "You know the answer to that."

"They'll get backup."

"Would you rather spend the day going over your cousin's bride book?"

"Good point," I said.

"I thought so."

I led the way into the formal garden. Oliver and the other coaches had herded the parents toward the carriage house. He caught my eye and jogged back.

"The boys are back from running," he said. "We have them in the training room. What should we do? I heard you're in charge."

How did this happen? Seriously. How?

"That's the word on the street. Taylor's with them?" I asked.

Oliver sighed. "He's there. Poor kid. His mother's the reason he's here and he knows it. Losing her will be a serious blow in more ways than one."

"How so?"

"Cherie was a single mother. Taylor's dad died a few years ago and he didn't leave them much. She worked three jobs to pay for travel teams, pitching coaches, equipment. It's not cheap at this level."

"So they were strapped. Were the Lions here on scholarship?" I asked.

"We don't have a scholarship that I know of."

We both looked at John and he remained blank. He wasn't giving anything up. Maybe I could get more out of Leslie.

"What else do you know about Cherie? She didn't seem very popular."

"Really? The boys love her. The team is devoted. She bakes, hosts sleepovers, all that stuff."

"How do you know that?" I asked.

"The Lions aren't a well-to-do team and the other teams know it. There was some razzing, typical boy stuff. The one thing the Lions had was Cherie. She talked them into major league games for free and got pros to come out to talk with them. She got things for the Lions that the others didn't get, even with their money. Her boys bragged about it."

"Maybe that's why the other teams' parents weren't crazy about her."

Oliver shrugged and glanced at the love garden. "They could've put the effort in. It certainly wasn't a reason to kill her."

"Someone had a reason," I said. "Baseball is a good place to start. Was Taylor in the lead for the prize?"

Oliver's eyebrows shot up under his cap. "You think they killed her over the prize?"

"I don't think anything yet. Was he in the lead?"

"He and Enrique were neck and neck. Enrique might've had a slight advantage."

"Why?"

"The kid's an old soul. Very calm and purposeful." Oliver grinned. "Taylor's still a kid. Focused one minute. Spastic the next."

"Let me guess which one you were," I said. "Spastic?"

"All the way."

"Can you think of anyone who would want Cherie dead?"

"Like I said, I thought she was popular. She was with her team."

One of the other coaches yelled, "Oliver! What's the holdup?"

"Be right there!" Oliver yelled back and then asked me, "What should I do with Taylor?"

"What would you normally do now?"

"Feed them and take them to the fields."

I rubbed my eyes. "Okay. Feed them and I'll be there in a minute to tell Taylor."

Oliver put an arm around me and drew me close. His warm breath blew against my cheek. He smelled like fresh cut grass and Listerine. The combo was oddly pleasant, but it made me miss Chuck's scent of beer and wintergreen gum. "I can tell him."

"It's okay," I said. "I already told Lane so what's one more shattered kid today."

He stepped back. "I'll do it. I've known Taylor for a couple years from different camps. It'd be better coming from me."

Oh thank god!

"If you think it's best," I said.

"I do."

"Okay."

Oliver took off for the carriage house and Tiny came up. "What now?"

"I'm not sure," I said. "I've never been in charge before."

A bunch of honking erupted in the distance beyond the ball fields. There must be another entrance for service vehicles. John's lip twitched at the sound and I stared at him for a second. I was beginning to think his facial muscles were incapable of moving à la Botox, but he didn't seem like the type. The honking continued, more and more insistent. John actually frowned. Shocking. Phelong and Gerry looked like a couple of hamsters trying to escape a cage, and Leslie ran his hands through his long grey hair repeatedly. Tiny was looking at his feet. Hmm. Interesting.

"Tiny?"

"Uh huh?" He snuck a quick peek at me.

Now that was a look of abject guilt.

"Who did you call?" I asked. "My dad?"

"He's out of town on the Costilla stuff," he said, still staring at those ginormous feet.

"Uncle Morty? Why would you bother? He's already here."

John crossed his arms as the horn went to one long blare.

"Your mom. I have to give updates," said Tiny.

Groan.

"Did you get any useful info? How's Lester? Have the police caught anyone yet?"

"Nothing yet. Lester's the same."

"So who's at the gate?" I could only think of a few candidates who'd be desperate to get at a crime scene.

Leslie walked out of the love garden. "I can answer that. It's Dr. Watts. I'd recognize that horn anywhere."

"Watts? Really? That's a coincidence. Who is he?"

"*She* is the closest thing we have to a medical examiner," said Leslie. All the muscles in his face were tight and he barely moved his lips.

"Not a friend then?" I asked.

"Dr. Watts has many friends."

But you're not one of them.

Leslie nodded to John. "Open it. She'll start ramming the fence in a minute."

"You say that like it's happened before," I said.

"It has," said John before he returned to the kitchen with Tiny to check on Lane and Anthony. The honking stopped immediately and Leslie did a sort of bracing yourself shake.

A couple of minutes later an old sage green Morris Minor drove in with an older lady behind the wheel. She had a shock of spiky silver hair standing straight up and touching the roof of the car.

She was driving at least fifty and screeched to a halt in the parking lot next the police cruiser. She got out, hip-checked the door shut, put her hands on her hips and scanned the scene. She wore baggy green scrubs and a lab coat that looked like it'd been purchased in the seventies. Huge collar. She whipped a black stethoscope off her neck and stuffed it in her pocket in the manner of someone who always knew exactly what she was doing. I was intimidated even at a distance.

"Wow," I said.

"You have no idea," said Leslie.

Dr. Watts' eyes settled on me and she nodded as she walked into the garden.

"Let's go," said Leslie and we met her before she reached the fountain.

"Well, it was only a matter of time, eh Leslie?" she said.

"I don't know what you're talking about," said Leslie without his usual charm.

Dr. Watts made a sneezing noise in the back of her throat. "You've got a body, don't you?"

Leslie's cheek twitched. "Yes."

"Who's dead?"

"Who called you?" he asked.

"Tommy Watts. We have what you might call a relationship."

I gasped and she turned to me. "At last we meet, Miss Marilyn."

"Are you..." I couldn't say the word fan out loud. Instinctively, I knew it wasn't right. The doctor didn't fit the profile of my fans.

"A fan?" she chuckled. "No. I've never been a fan of anything." Her eyes flicked a glance at Leslie, who did a micro flinch. If I hadn't really been looking, I wouldn't have seen it.

"May I introduce Dr. Watts? Doctor, this is Mercy Watts," said Leslie.

"Are we related?" I asked.

She smiled as she looked me over. Dr. Watts was in her seventies. She wore no makeup, but her face had the soft pleasing lines of a woman who'd aged into beauty. "Ace never mentioned me then. Stands to reason. I'm the biggest skeleton in that man's closet."

Ace? That was my grandpa's call sign from when he was a helicopter pilot in Vietnam.

"Do you know my grandpa?" I asked.

She made the sneezing noise again. "Only in the biblical sense. Dorothy Watts, your ex-grandmother."

Biblical? Ew.

"Did you say...grandmother?"

"I'm Ace's first wife. The one they don't talk about. You could've been my blood had he not dumped me for the luscious Janine." She leaned in and her eyes roved over my face. "You wouldn't be a looker, but you would be a doctor."

I think she just insulted me.

"I'm a nurse," I said.

"I know. Take me to your body."

"It's not my body."

"You think it belongs to Keystone and Cop over there. I don't think so. Sheriff Greer is up in St. Louis for another two days. His wife is having a hysterectomy and a bladder sling. We're not bothering the man."

"We're supposed to call Springfield," said Phelong aka Keystone.

"Forget it. We're not passing this off to Springfield like we can't handle it," said Dr. Watts.

Gerry aka Cop fiddled with his jacket zipper. "We can't handle it. We don't have a crime scene unit and you're retired."

"You're retired?" I asked.

"Technically. I'm the volunteer medical examiner. I like to keep my hand in for fun."

Fun?

"We have to call Springfield," I said.

"Are you questioning my abilities, my own almost granddaughter?"

"No, but I don't have any lift cards on me. Do you?"

She jerked a thumb at Gerry and Phelong. "They've got the full kit. They just don't want to use it without Greer. It's time to put on your big girl panties, boys, and glove up."

The boys didn't move.

Dr. Watts rolled her eyes at me and said, "Gerry, you go get the kit. Phelong, you're with me. Hop to it."

"But Springfield," said Gerry.

"You want to tell them that we're incompetent boobs?"

"No." Gerry didn't sound sure about that.

"Go get the kit. We'll have this wrapped up before Greer gets back."

"But who's the detective? I ticket illegal campers and Phelong handles speeders. There's never even been a murder around here."

"Wrong. Hal Jackson. 1993," said Dr. Watts. "Shotgun blast to the stomach. Solved it in six hours."

"That was like twenty years ago."

"Twenty-two and we handled it. We didn't call in Springfield. Go get the kit."

Gerry reluctantly went back to his cruiser. Phelong watched longingly.

"Phelong, go get the guest list from John. Mercy, show me the body."

I led her to the fountain and stopped at Cherie's feet.

"Tell me what you know," ordered Dr. Watts.

"It's Cherie Marin, mid-forties, manually strangled, the rape is fake," I said.

"Very good. Now, Leslie, go get my bag. It's in the backseat. I've got to get a liver temp ASAP."

Leslie scowled, but he did as she commanded. She could've brought the bag with her, but I got the feeling she enjoyed ordering Leslie around.

Dr. Watts squatted behind Cherie's head and she sniffed her face. I shuddered and she smiled up at me. "Not long. Six hours, maybe seven."

"You can tell that by smell?" I asked.

"Among other things. Lividity is fixed, for instance. I've been doing this for a long time. I know the dead better than the living. They reveal more."

Leslie came back with the doctor's bag and she set about her work, a seasoned pro all the way. She dictated notes into her phone with a headset, so I got to hear her every thought. Dr. Watts confirmed the time of death with liver temperature and a complicated calculation that took into account the outside temperature and gravel temperature with some sort of sliding scale I couldn't follow. She took pictures of every inch of Cherie's body before picking up her hand to bag it.

Dr. Watts exposed the palm to me and raised a scant eyebrow. "Interesting."

Cherie had gravel embedded into her palm, but it wasn't the white gravel of the love garden.

"Very interesting," I said. "Her wrist looks slightly swollen, too."

"Good catch."

I squatted next to the doctor. "So she fell backward and tried to catch herself in...in the rock garden. Part of that garden has red and black gravel like that."

Dr. Watts bagged Cherie's hands and I told her I was going to check out the rock garden.

"Take those two with you. I hate hovering. Can't stand it," she said with a glare at Phelong and Gerry, who'd returned and placed the crime scene kit and guest list next to her.

Gerry's lower lip jutted out. "We should probably help you."

"You think you're helping me?"

"We could help you if you tell us what to do," said Phelong. He had a lot of dignity for a guy with pants that were three inches too short.

Dr. Watts tossed him a pair of gloves and a flashlight. "Alright, Mr. Helpful. You can check her vagina for abrasions and tearing."

Phelong gasped and dropped the gloves and flashlight. Gerry said, "Where's that rock garden?"

I pointed to the winding path around my tower and they scurried away.

"Get out of here, you kids. Jesus Christ. They'll put anyone in uniform these days." She jumped up and yelled after them, "Don't touch anything! Or think about touching anything!"

"You weren't really going to have him do a pelvic, were you?"

"No. This lady doesn't deserve that. I'm a pro and they're morons," said Dr. Watts.

"They're just young," I said. "They have to start somewhere."

"Sheriff Greer had to cite Gerry for cow tipping last weekend. His own deputy for crying out loud."

"I take it back," I said and started to follow the young cops who didn't manage to find the path that was right in front of them and were wandering around aimlessly in the herbs.

I glanced back at Leslie, who said, "If they trample our basil, I'll sue."

Dr. Watts snorted and began taping the bottom of Cherie's shoes for trace evidence.

"Wait," I said. "Did he actually manage to tip over a cow?"

"Do you seriously think that kid could tip over a 1,500 pound Holstein?"

"Well..."

"You are so city. Tell your grandpa I said so. No, Gerry didn't tip over a cow, but he was pestering the hell out of them. That's not good for dairy cows. Those girls need their sleep." She shooed me away. "You better go lead those two by the nose or they'll never get there."

I booked it out of the love garden, not feeling much smarter than Phelong who was now trying to open a door at the bottom of my tower. Did that look like a path? In what universe?

I gathered Phelong and Gerry and took them down the path and around to my side of the castle. At first glance, the rock garden was undisturbed. The path led through the middle of it. My window was right above, now with the window closed. I crossed my arms and kept looking up at it.

"What?" asked Phelong. "Do you see something?"

"No, but that's my window and it was open last night."

"So?"

"So my dog went bat shit crazy in the middle of the night. He must've heard something. You two stay here."

"But we're suppose—"

"Stay." I went into the garden section under my window and I saw it. The mulch around some freshly planted lavender was messed up, scraped away from the dirt and showing what were footprints before the water system had run.

Damn. I could use some footprints.

"What is it?" asked Gerry.

"Ground is disturbed. Looks like what happened to Cherie started here. Give me a second." I tiptoed around to get an idea of how big an area we were dealing with and spotted a larger area of messed up gravel next to three granite boulders. The left boulder had a smear of blood on it and, unless I was mistaken, a few hairs. I took some pictures with my phone and backed out carefully.

"This is the crime scene?" asked Phelong.

"It's the first of two." I checked my phone for my texts to Chuck. I'd sent one at 2:02 am. That's when it happened exactly and the poodle knew it. We went back to Dr. Watts who was talking to someone on her phone. She'd packed up and had stripped off her gloves.

"Get a move on. Time's a wasting," she said and hung up.

"Who was that?" I asked.

"Flincher, the local ghoul, he'll pick up Cherie, and I'll do the autopsy at the funeral home. What'd you find?"

"Cherie or somebody took a blow to the head at 2:02 am."

"Why so specific?"

I told her about Pick and my text to Chuck. Dr. Watts got quiet and tapped her foot while staring down at Cherie. Phelong and Gerry edged toward the path to the parking lot like there was a possibility of escape. Puhlease. They weren't going anywhere. Dr. Watts snapped her fingers at them without looking up. They might've been considering running for it and I kind of hoped they would. I had no doubt that my ex-grandma would chase them down and pummel them. It would make a great video for Dad. He collected funny cop videos. An old lady beating the crap out of a couple of deputies would be right up his alley, but the deputies didn't make a move. Cowards.

Leslie elbowed me. "How much you want to bet that one of them quits before the weekend's over."

"A hundred bucks says neither quits," I said.

"The cover girl's a gambler. I'll take that bet but make it two hundred."

I stuck out my hand. "Deal."

"Just out of curiosity, why are you so sure they won't quit?" asked Leslie.

"The worst part is over. Dr. Watts will pack off the body and do the autopsy. All they have to do is follow orders and keep everyone from leaving the property."

He smiled and pushed up his glasses. "We'll see."

That doesn't bode well.

There was a crunching of gravel behind us and Aaron walked into the garden with a big coffee mug. Finally. Coffee, my sweet friend.

I held out my hands so ready for my first sip, but Aaron skirted me and gave the doctor my coffee. Dr. Watts took a drink. "That's just what I needed."

"That's what I need, too," I told Aaron.

"Huh?"

"Coffee. How come that coffee isn't mine?"

"It's a vanilla cappuccino," he said.

Dr. Watts sighed. "Exactly how I like it, too."

Exactly how you like them? WTF?

"You know her?" I asked.

"Yeah."

My hands went to my hips. "Who is she then?"

"Ace's ex-wife," said Aaron.

"How come nobody ever told me?"

Aaron was looking past me, far off into the distance. If it'd been anyone else, I'd have thought he was avoiding looking at the body, but that was just Aaron. "Tell you what?"

I groaned. "Never mind. Can I please have some coffee?"

"No."

"No? Are you serious?"

"You didn't eat yet."

"What's that got to do with it?"

"You got to eat."

"Says who."

"Your mom."

Leslie was smiling. "You'll have to eat."

"I eat," I said.

"I estimate that you consumed less than 800 calories yesterday."

"It had to be more than that."

"Why?"

I didn't know. Mostly, I didn't want to eat whatever Aaron was cooking up. It was bound to have lard and guilt mixed in.

"It just had to be."

"Very logical," said Leslie.

"Bite me."

He smiled, showing me his super white teeth in a carnal way. "Gladly."

I had the strongest feeling that biting was not off the table with Leslie.

"No biting," said Dr. Watts and she threw back the rest of the cappuccino. "We've got work to do and you, Miss Mercy, will eat if for no other reason than I don't want to have to hear about you eating. Two a.m., was it?"

"Yes. 2:02 exactly."

She gave Aaron the coffee cup and squatted. "Let's see, shall we?"

Dr. Watts put on a fresh set of gloves, rolled Cherie's head to the side, and revealed a small amount of blood. "Well, I'll be damned." Then she gently manipulated a spot on the back of Cherie's head and nodded. "Hmm. Feels like a fracture, but I won't know until I open her up."

"Know what?" asked Gerry, getting a little paler.

"Whether this blow was fatal."

"But I thought she was strangled."

"She was," she said

"But..."

I leaned on Aaron, breathed in the coffee scent that he was cloaked in. I didn't even mind the hot dog stink that came with it. "It looks like she was attacked in the rock garden, she got away, ran and he caught up with her here. Then he strangled her. The head wound might've been fatal, given enough time."

"Oh," said Phelong.

"He?" asked Dr. Watts. "Are you sure?"

"Takes serious hand strength to manually strangle someone," I said.

"I could do it." Dr. Watts held up a larger than average hand with strong blunt fingers."

"You probably could, but I'm guessing you're not the average woman."

"There's the head wound to consider. She may have been incapacitated. That changes things."

"I didn't see any fibers or skin under her nails, did you?" I asked.

"No. They appear to be clean."

"If so, she didn't fight and he or she was right up in her face when he strangled her. That's pretty up close and brutal."

Dr. Watts shrugged. "Plenty of rage, but, if she was impaired, a child could've done it."

I glanced in the direction of the carriage house. A child. We had no children, but we had plenty of teenaged boys, well-muscled and strong.

"Will you be able to tell how big the hands are?" I asked.

"I'll get a pretty good idea."

"So you could tell if it's an adult or a teenager?"

She glanced past me in the direction of the baseball fields. "Most of those boys are men. At least in size."

"Oh." I really wanted to rule out the boys. "Leslie, what about the security system for the carriage house. Is it like the castle? Do they have to use codes after midnight?"

"Yes, but that's John's area of expertise. He'll be able to tell you who left or keyed themselves in after midnight."

"If anyone," I said.

Leslie smiled and Dr. Watts said, "What do you mean? We know it was after midnight. Your text and the dog barking proves it circumstantially"

"They could've just stayed outside and then come back in when the castle opened."

Dr. Watts grumped and muttered, "Naturally."

"How good is your security system?" I asked.

"The best or you wouldn't be here," said Leslie.

"And the property is completely fenced?"

"It is."

"Would you know if someone breached the fence?"

"We would," said Leslie.

I stepped closer to him and saw his biceps bunch under his shirt. Hmm. "Well, was it?"

"You'll have to ask John." His eyes flicked to the left. It was a micro expression. Telling if you could catch it. There was a breach last night.

"I will," I said. "Maybe Phelong and Gerry should walk the fence line and look for disturbances in the brush or cut wires, something like that."

"If you wish." Leslie was all laissez-faire about it, but there was something in the way he shifted his feet and the fixed smile on his handsome face.

"Great. I think they will."

"What?" asked Gerry. "Us? You mean us?"

"Are there other Phelong and Gerrys?" I asked.

"Our dads live in town," said Phelong.

"I've got two uncles," said Gerry.

I slapped my forehead. "I'm talking about you. You're going to walk the property and see if you can find anything."

"But...but this property is huge," said Gerry.

"And I haven't had breakfast." Phelong made a sad face.

I glanced over my shoulder. "Aaron."

Aaron took off in what passed for a run in my weirdo partner.

"He'll get you something," I said. "Do you have a camera to document the area?"

Dr. Watts was already ahead of me. She gave Gerry a bulky Nikon digital. "Cover everything and no wandering off."

Leslie's stance had loosened. Either his self-control had taken over or he'd realized what a couple of morons I had working for me. I'd show him. I had at least one non-moron at the ready.

I dialed Tiny and told him I had an assignment for him and to come right out. I watched Leslie during my brief conversation and he showed nothing. Maybe that wasn't it or he was too good for me to spot his tells.

Tiny jogged out of the kitchen, saw us still at the fountain, and came over, red in the face and breathing way too hard. That weight had to go if he was going to keep up with Dad or me, for that matter.

After he stopped huffing and puffing, I told him what I wanted him to do. He agreed. "Inside or out?"

Leslie blinked rapidly. Damn if that wasn't the one thing he was worried about, the fence had two sides. He didn't think I'd think about it and he was right.

Thank you, Tiny. Inside or out? Inside or out? What don't you want, Leslie?

"Outside," I said, sounding much more certain than I felt.

More blinking from Mr. Charming Host. Nice.

"Aaron's making you some food to go and as—" Before I could finish my sentence, Aaron came jogging out, carrying four paper bags and to go cups.

Let the fourth be for me. Let the fourth be for me.

Aaron handed out a bag and cup each to Phelong, Gerry, and Tiny. They opened their bags and the best smells came out. Crusty bread, sausage, cheese, and something healthy, maybe spinach. It all mixed with the heady smell of fresh hot coffee. I started drooling and lunged for the last cup. Aaron showed some surprising reflexes and moved the cup away from my grasping.

"Who's it for then?" I demanded.

"You."

"Then gimme."

He held out the bag. "Eat."

"No. You wouldn't keep me from coffee. Do you have a death wish?"

"Orders."

"From my mother, I suppose," I said.

Aaron blinked and I came close to whisper in his ear, "I can't."

"You will."

"Please, Aaron. You don't understand. I can't eat that."

"My food is good," he said.

"It's not that," I said, my eyes filling. "How about a salad or a green smoothie with lots of kale and ginger.

"That tastes gross."

"I know."

He put the bag under my nose. "Four bites and you get coffee."

I narrowed my eyes at him. "My mother agreed to four bites?"

"No."

"Oh."

Aaron was breaking the rules as set down by my mother and that was quite something. Aaron didn't go against Carolina Watts. Nobody did. Not even me usually.

Aaron shook the bag and I was filled with gratitude. Maybe he did get it.

Dr. Watts marched over, ripped the bag from Aaron's hand, opened it and sniffed. "Smells good. I'll take some of that. Now you," she pointed a blunt finger at me, "eat."

"I'd rather have—"

"Nobody cares what you'd rather," she said. "I've got fifteen blond devil nephews and eleven blond devil great nephews. I can get you to eat."

I looked at Tiny. He had half a small whole wheat bagel in his mouth. Aaron was nice enough to give him a filling with cheese, spinach, and egg. Tiny's eyes were closed, chin tipped up in bliss. There might've been moaning. No help there. I turned to Leslie.

"Don't look at me," he said. "I'd eat it."

"Fine." I took the four bites, chewing as fast as possible and getting it down quick. If you hardly taste, it doesn't count, right?

"Mercy," said Dr. Watts.

I wobbled around and bumped into the fountain.

"Okay. Okay," she said in a soothing voice. "Sit here."

I sat on the edge and felt a light spray of water on my neck. Better.

"When was the last time you ate?" she asked.

"Last night," I said.

"Less than a thousand calories is not enough. You've got a job to do and I'm not losing this to Springfield. You're eating the rest of that."

"But I can't," I whispered.

"I believe that you can. You've just forgotten who you are. Soon you'll remember, but not without sausage. Eat it."

I ate. I'd like to say it was easy, but it wasn't. It was hard.

"Stop thinking about it," said Dr. Watts.

"I'm not," I lied.

She made her sneezing noise and waved the coffee under my nose. "You lie all the time. It's part of the profession."

"Nursing?"

"At times, but that's not what I mean and you know it. Eat and then coffee."

I groaned. "When's that funeral director going to be here?"

"He's driving through the gate right now," said Leslie, looking at his phone.

"Excellent. We can get this show on the road."

"Eat those last two bites," said Dr. Watts.

I stuffed them in my mouth and grabbed the coffee. "Happy?"

"Delirious." She turned to look through the trees at a hearse coming up the road even slower than the cops had. It was an old school hearse, probably from the sixties. It had lots of chrome, fins, and was super long. It reminded me of the old batmobile from the TV show. Uncle Morty had a model of it next to the Death Star in his living room.

"That is one old hearse," said Tiny.

"Wait until you see Flincher," said Dr. Watts.

"Did you call him a ghoul earlier?" I asked.

"Yes," she said. "And you're about to see why."

CHAPTER TWELVE

The hearse pulled into the parking lot and the door creaked open. Yes, I could hear it, even at a distance. The oldest man I'd ever seen got out in slow motion and that's saying something. I know a lot of old people. He had a ring of snow-white hair, a large hooked nose, and a hump, for crying out loud. Flincher was exactly the person you'd expect to get out of *that* hearse.

"Abacus B. Flincher," said Dr. Watts. "Our local ghoul."

"Because...he so old?" I asked.

"No."

"Because he's a funeral director?" asked Tiny.

"I wish."

"Okay," I said. "I give up. What is it?"

"If you're a decent detective, you'll figure it out," said Dr. Watts. "We better help him or we'll be here all day."

Nobody moved.

"You two," she pointed at Phelong and Gerry, "Go help Flincher."

Gerry shuddered. "I don't want to. I thought we were searching the fence line."

"You will. After you help Flincher," I said.

"I'd rather stay with her," said Phelong, looking at Cherie on the ground. "By myself. At midnight."

"Go!"

The cops gave Aaron their empty bags and he trotted back to the kitchen. Then they went to help Flincher, giving the man the widest berth possible. They got a gurney out of the hearse and practically ran back to us. Flincher hobbled along behind, peering at us under bushy eyebrows.

"I've seen that guy before," said Tiny.

"Really? Where?" I asked.

"Scooby Doo."

Dr. Watts and Leslie laughed, but it was nervous laughter.

Phelong leaned over to me. "Don't get too close. He'll like you."

"Good to know," I said.

"What was that smell?" asked Gerry.

"I don't want to know," said Phelong.

"What smell?" I asked.

Dr. Watts nudged me as Flincher entered the love garden. "It's possum. Shush." She took the neatly folded heavy duty body bag off the gurney and opened it on the ground next to Cherie.

Flincher entered the center of the love garden on the other side of the fountain and I got a whiff of the smell Gerry was talking about. If that was possum, I'd like to know what had been done to the animal because it was stank or rank or both combined if that's possible to imagine.

Flincher walked around the fountain, heavily stooped and completely silent. That's not easy to do on gravel, but he managed it. He was incredibly thin or emaciated, depending on how you looked at it. Maybe he didn't have enough weight to move the gravel, but he was able to move us. We all, including Leslie, took a step back when he got close. It was a completely involuntary reaction.

"Well, well, well, what have we got here?" asked Flincher in a raspy oddly high voice that made the hairs on my arms stand up. He smiled at us, showing yellowed teeth with big gaps.

"A murder, Flincher," said Dr. Watts. "Try not to look so happy about it."

"Death is my business. Why shouldn't I be happy?"

"It's unseemly for one thing."

Flincher came closer and the smell made me wish I'd thought of a way to get out of eating Aaron's food. That sausage wasn't sitting well. He saw me, cocked his head and smiled wider, revealing all his ghastly teeth and reddened, blotchy gums. "Yes, I've always been concerned with appearances."

"Obviously," said Dr. Watts. "Back up. You're going to make *my* ex-granddaughter vomit and I can't have that."

She emphasized the 'my' quite strongly and Flincher's faded green eyes settled on me. Now I know what a mouse feels like when the cat spots him.

"Yours," he said.

"Mine," said Dr. Watts, watching him with intensity.

"I'll keep that in mind."

"Do." She waved at Phelong and Gerry. "Come on, you two."

They stepped back again. "Why? What? What? Why?" they asked, rapid fire.

"She has to go in the bag. It's not a one-person job."

"Oh, no. Not me," said Gerry.

"What about...him?" asked Phelong with a head bob at Flincher.

"I'm too old to be moving bodies," said Flincher.

No kidding. You look like you're made of tinder.

"And my assistant has the day off."

Dr. Watts tossed gloves at Phelong and Gerry. They bounced off their chests and fell on the gravel.

"I can't," said Phelong. "I have a condition."

"Cowardice?" asked Leslie.

"Yeah, sure. I'm not touching her. I'm not doing it."

I rolled my eyes. "I'll do it, you wussies."

Dr. Watts gave me clean gloves and Leslie took some, too. He didn't hesitate to pick up Cherie by the shoulders, despite the fact that she wasn't completely in rigor and her head lolled a bit. It was unpleasant for me and I'd seen plenty of bodies. Curious that it didn't bother a spa owner one bit.

I took one of Cherie's feet and Dr. Watts the other one. We got

Cherie in the bag and zipped it up quickly. The three of us lifted her onto the gurney and ratcheted it up to waist height.

While we were doing that, the smell got considerably stronger and my nose got runny. Something brushed against my back and Dr. Watts yelled, "Flincher!"

I bumped into the gurney and spun around. Flincher was up on me, six inches away. He looked even worse close up, and the smell was unbearable. Gag.

Dr. Watts dragged me away and pushed me behind her. "It's time you get going, Flincher."

"Yes. I'll be seeing you later, Miss..."

"Watts," I said.

"Ah yes, so she said." He turned to Phelong and Gerry. "Who will be pushing?"

Neither moved. No surprise there.

"I'll do it." Leslie cracked his knuckles and stretched, revealing a taut belly with a greying treasure trail. He caught me looking, winked, and pushed the gurney out of the love garden in front of Flincher as it began to drizzle.

Phelong sniffed his uniform sleeve. "Is that going to come out?"

"I use OxiClean," said Dr. Watts. "Go help Leslie."

Phelong and Gerry reluctantly followed, their feet kicking up the gravel.

"Was that really possum?" I asked.

She waited until the cops were out of earshot and then said, "Partially."

"It smelled like decomp. What is he? I've met plenty of weirdos but he's beyond weird."

"Take a guess."

"Some sort of predator. Has he killed anyone?" I asked.

"They couldn't prove it in court," said Dr. Watts.

"Who was it?"

"His parents. Murder-suicide. But nobody really believed that theory."

Leslie had the gurney at the back of the hearse about to put Cherie in and I had a wave of guilt for subjecting that woman to Flincher.

"He won't do anything to her," Dr. Watts said quickly. "I'll make sure."

"Otherwise…"

She shrugged. "Nobody knows for sure what he's up to."

"How old was he when the parents died?" I asked.

"Seventeen."

"Before you're time here then."

"Right, but he's only fifty-eight," she said.

"Holy crap. That's fifty-eight? What happened to him?"

"I don't know, but there are some theories floating around."

"Like what? He was cursed?"

"That's one." She smiled at me and packed up her equipment.

I gathered up the cops' kit and asked, "How does he stay in business?"

"He's very cheap and the only mortician for fifty miles."

"Still."

"People around here are just getting by, and nothing's been proven."

"They said that about Robert Durst."

"Yes, they did." She gave me her phone. "Put yourself in. I'll call you when I finish the autopsy."

I put myself in Dr. Watts' phone as 'Mercy the ex-granddaughter' and dropped it in her lab coat pocket. Leslie, Phelong, and Gerry came back and she ordered the cops to document the rock garden and tape everything off before searching the fence line. Tiny took charge like he knew what he was doing and I slipped away as Dr. Watts went down her long to do list.

The kitchen door closed behind me and I leaned back against it, heaving a big sigh. Aaron was bustling around the La Cornue stove, tossing herbs in the different pots and somehow directing the staff without saying more than three words together. It smelled like Thanksgiving, complete with pumpkin pie. That weirdo was an evil genius. I loved Thanksgiving food best of all. Stuffing! How could I not eat stuffing? Easy. I didn't deserve stuffing. There. Problem solved.

One of the cooks made me a latte without my asking and I thanked him before taking a heavenly sip and thinking over what to do next.

Aaron gave a few more minimalist orders and came over to stand silently in front of me.

"What?" I asked after scraping the last of the foam out of my mug.

"I'm ready," he said, bouncing on the balls of his feet.

"So now you're helping me instead of force-feeding me."

"Huh?"

I gave him my mug. "Let's find John and get the security data from last night. Maybe we'll get lucky and our killer keyed himself out at 1:50 and when confronted will confess in a river of tears," I said.

"Ya think?"

"No, but I always hope." I tapped one of the cooks on the shoulder and asked where John's office was. He gave me a set of directions I had no hope of following. To be fair, he lost me after the second right at the first set of armor and I stopped listening. Aaron appeared to be following it just fine or at least he was facing the general direction of the cook while he talked so I texted Chuck. "Scary mortician. He likes me in a bad way. Don't you want to come back?"

I waited and got the usual silence. Maybe I should get Flincher to attack me. That might spur Chuck into action. I pondered it for a moment. I was pretty sure I could take Flincher in a fair fight or even an unfair one, but him touching me was totally out. I'd have to come up with something else. Non-gross peril. Chuck was a detective. He couldn't resist a good mystery, plus the camera loved him. I tried again. "Big case. Possible serial killer mortician. Woman strangled at exclusive castle. Competitive baseball. Very newsworthy."

Nothing.

The cook finished and Aaron faced me, waiting without a word. It would've been unnerving if I hadn't been so used to it.

"Do you know where we're going?" I asked.

"Uh huh."

Aaron led the way out and we went through a maze of corridors. We turned at some suits of armor and not others. How could he tell the difference? I had no idea. Eventually, we passed the great hall and ran smack into Robin and Deanna from the Grizzlies. A wave of flowery perfume washed over us and instantly took me back to high school, a place where certain girls wore so much perfume that it cleared a path through the halls for them. That wasn't me. Remembering deodorant during freshman year was a challenge, a fact that Miss Perkins, the gym teacher, felt compelled to point out. Daily.

"Miss Watts!" Robin grabbed my arm before we could race away. "I heard you're a detective."

"Er...not exactly," I said, trying to loosen her grip. Robin was wearing Miss Perkins' favorite fuchsia lipstick and, you guessed it, I forgot deodorant and I might've had vomit in my hair.

"Don't you want to interview us?" asked Deanna, wrinkling her nose and breathing in my face. Lots of mouthwash, but it didn't quite cover the sour alcohol smell.

I sighed and gave in. "You heard what happened then."

The women got solemn. It wasn't grief for Cherie certainly, but something else.

"Yes. Coach Jakes told us. How did they get in?" asked Robin, fiddling with her big diamond earrings. Did she sleep in those things?

"Do you think the murderer's still here?" asked Deanna.

Ah. They think they're in danger.

"They?" I asked.

"Whoever did it."

"Of course. I'll be interviewing everyone as soon as I talk to John." I went to pass them, but Robin let go of my arm and stepped in front of me.

"I know the time of death," she said.

2:02 or thereabouts.

She clasped her hands over her chest and quivered with excitement. "3:15 am."

"What?" I spat out.

"But that's not—" Aaron grunted when I elbowed him.

"I heard it happen," said Robin. "Of course I didn't know Cherie was being murdered, but I heard it. I would've helped her if I'd known. I hope you believe me."

The jury's still out on that one.

"Of course. What did you hear?" I asked.

"The shot. I heard a gunshot at 3:15. I just thought someone was hunting. Something's probably in season out here."

Who hunts in the middle of the night?

"You heard a gunshot?" I asked. "You're certain."

"I'm certain."

"Why were you awake?"

Robin checked her phone for messages while saying, "I don't know. I don't usually wake up in the middle of the night, but I was awake. Oh. Maybe there was more than one gunshot. Our window was open. It was so stuffy last night. Maybe the first shot woke me up. I looked at the clock. Then there was a second shot." She pumped her fist. "Yes. That's it."

"You are so *CSI*," said Deanna with a discreet burp.

"Miami or Las Vegas cast?"

"Miami, of course."

"Thanks."

I waved at them. "Hello. Ladies."

"Do you need something else?" asked Robin.

"Where were you at 2:02 am?"

"Asleep," they both said and Deanna gave Robin a questioning glance.

"What about your husband?" I asked Robin.

"Him, too."

Deanna put her hands on her hips. "Come on. Just tell her. She's going to find out anyway."

"Well..." I said.

Robin wrapped her arms around her slim waist. "You won't tell anyone what I say, will you?"

"I doubt it's as much of a secret as you think. Tim has a drinking problem?"

"No. Absolutely not. He's just been stressed lately and sometimes he has one too many."

I counted five too many last night.

"So you weren't sleeping," I said.

"No, I was, but Tim got sick. He vomited for a couple of hours," said Robin. "I'd just gotten to sleep when the gunshot woke me. It was a rough night."

The door to the office opened and John watched us silently.

"How well did you know Cherie?" I asked them.

"Not at all really," said Deanna. "Our boys aren't in the same school division. We're Class 5 and her son's Class 3."

"They didn't play each other ever?"

"Rarely," said Robin. "They couldn't afford the big traveling team tournaments."

"But the boys are in direct competition for the prize," I said.

Deanna sniffed. "Not really. Everyone knows Enrique's a shoo-in."

Robin beamed. "Let's not take it for granted."

"It's obvious. He's in a class by himself."

I cocked my head at her. "So if Enrique's sure to win, why was there so much tension last night?"

Robin frowned. "It was tense, but I don't know why."

"Yes, you do," said Deanna with scorn. "Cherie was pushy. She got on people's nerves. And I do not know how they afforded this place. It's totally out of the Lions' price range."

And nothing's worse than the sin of being poor. I get it.

"Can you think of why anyone would want to kill her?" I asked.

"No," said Robin. "Sure she was pushy, but that's no reason to kill her."

Deanna's hand fluttered over her chest. "You don't think anyone of us could've done it, do you? We're not *those* kind of people."

I had the impression that Deanna thought the Lions were *those* kind of people and it was not warming the cockles of my heart.

"In my experience, *those* kind of people are every kind of people," I said.

"Well, not us," said Deanna. "And not the Vipers."

"How do you know? They have a bit of money so they must be innocent?"

Robin had the good sense to blush, but Deanna plowed on. "They're not desperate like her."

"So Cherie was desperate?"

"How else is she going to pay for college," she said with a sniff.

Robin touched Deanna's shoulder. "Taylor will scholarship no matter what."

"It's not the same. The prize is the key to big money in the majors and you know she wanted that."

Deanna said it like they were above money, which she so obviously wasn't.

"None of this gives the Vipers alibis," I said. "Excuse me. John's waiting."

"I can give one of them an alibi," said Deanna.

"Really?"

She smiled. "Bill Wayling has sleep apnea. His breathing machine was on all night."

"So you heard that, but not the gunshot?"

"My window was closed and that machine is ridiculous. I was going to ask John for another room. I share a wall with Bill and I'll never get any sleep if I stay there."

John came out of his office. "I'll have you moved immediately."

Deanna beamed. "Do you have any tower rooms available?"

"I can put you in the West Tower, but you'll be far from the other parents."

"That's fine with me."

John told her to go to the front desk and they would take care of her. She and Robin took off and John watched me in quiet appraisal.

"What are you looking for?" I asked.

"A hint that you are capable of taking care of this for us."

"Thanks for the vote of confidence."

"How long will it take you? Sheriff Greer will be back in two days."

"I won't need that long."

"Are you certain?"

"If you show me your security logs from last night, I will be," I said, but he didn't move. "What now?"

"I was surprised to see you up so early. Your cousins ordered quite a few bottles last night."

"Tim wasn't the only vomiting one. I'm thankful I had apple juice in my mini fridge."

"Apple juice is a hangover cure?"

"It helps, if you drink it before you sleep. Speaking of drinking, has anyone besides his wife seen Tim this morning?" I asked.

"He's in his room. I can confirm the vomiting," said John.

"Whose vomiting? You better not have a camera in my room."

"Tim's. Robin called room service at one for ginger ale. He was seen lying on the floor, gagging into a towel."

"They're definitely off the list then, unless your system shows one of them leaving the building."

He gestured toward the office and I swept in ahead of him like I was wearing a ball gown, not yoga pants.

"This way," he said, pointing to one of two over-sized desks that could've belonged to Napoleon they were so ostentatious. There was a desktop computer with an extra-large monitor showing various live shots around the castle grounds, both driving entrances, the ball fields, several gates, and sections of the fence line. Tiny, Phelong, Gerry were outside the fence in section East 55 and finding nothing if I went by their bored expressions.

"Do you have the whole fence line visually available?" I asked.

"No. Our cameras keep getting taken out by wind and animals."

Convenient.

"There was a gunshot last night at 3:15. Can you show me the footage from that time period?"

John sat down in the enormous green leather swivel chair and typed until the screen was filled with around forty thumbnails of video. The time was in the lower right-hand corner of each and showed 3:12. John pressed a key and the videos ran simultaneously. I scanned them. There were no people in any of them. When they got to 3:15, I asked him to slow them way down and he did. Still nothing. Either Robin was lying, mistaken, or...

"How many of your cameras were out last night?" I asked.

"Eight."

"That doesn't sound like something you'd allow."

His gaze didn't waver. "You don't know me."

"I'm getting a pretty good idea of you."

"Miss Watts, the fence line wasn't breached."

I crossed my arms. "How do you know?"

John hit a few more keys. The thumbnails disappeared, replaced by reporting data on the fence. "It's electrified and there were no indications of an intruder."

"What about the gates? Anybody in or out?"

More typing and the gate logs came up. Nothing was accessed after 10:30 pm when the last employee let himself out after work.

"How many people were on the grounds overnight?" I asked.

He gave me a printout of employees and guests. Besides the baseball people and Bridget's bridal party, there were only ten employees on the property, not counting John and Leslie.

"Okay. Let's narrow it down," I said. "Did anyone code themselves out of the carriage house after midnight?"

John brought up the log for all the carriage house doors and the answer was no.

"How about the castle?"

He smiled. It was the first time and to say happiness did not sit well on his face was an understatement. "Only one."

"You're happy. That can't be good."

"You won't like it."

Oh my god! It can't be Tiny. Not Tiny. Or Aaron. Sorcha? Please. She could barely walk last night along with her sisters.

"Let me have it," I said.

A name appeared on the screen, keyed out at 1:29 and back in at 2:32.

"Me?" I yelled.

CHAPTER THIRTEEN

I jabbed the screen with my pink sparkly nail. "I did not leave the castle last night."

"I know," said John.

"What do you mean you know? How do you know? That thing implicates me in a murder."

He brought up another picture, the top of a spiral stair. The time stamp said 12:32.

"Is that...my tower?" I asked.

The video started running and there was me. How much did I drink? I dragged myself up the stairs by the handrail, fell over, and exposed my bum to the camera. And yes, I was wearing a thong. It was all cheek.

"How many times have you watched this video?"

John looked at me as blank as ever and I tried to detect something, anything in his eyes and failed. "Does it matter?"

"I don't know. You're really weird, not Flincher weird, but weird."

"You're not the first to say so."

The video kept going and there was me with my dress hiked up around my waist, taking eight tries to swipe my damn door open. My rear was hideous from that angle. Hideous, I tell you. And I spit on the wall. I couldn't say why. I had no memory of it.

Video-me finally got out the enormous key, unlocked the door, and fell through, once again landing on my face and kicking the door shut.

"I don't remember it like that at all," I said.

"Nobody ever does," said John.

"So what does this prove?"

He sped up the video and we saw Tiny and Aaron coming up the stairs a half hour after me. Tiny checked my door to make sure it was locked and then they went in their room. John skipped to 1:29 and my door didn't open. It didn't open at 2:32 either.

"We have the key card records for your room as well, but they can be tampered with. The video is definitive."

"Thank god for that." I glared at him. "Show this to no one or I'll kill you in your sleep."

"Doubtful."

"I know, but don't show it to anyone."

"Prove who did it and I won't have to."

"Are you threatening me?" I asked. Wasn't he Dad's friend? What the heck?

"The prosecutor will want it if you are a suspect in an unsolved homicide."

I got a little nauseous. "I have to solve this case. That's just the kind of thing that gets leaked to TMZ."

"They'd love it. So would the world given your celebrity."

I could see it now. My flabby, lost too much weight, butt on computer screens everywhere. If Chuck was considering coming back to me that would put him off me for good. Hell, I was put off me and it was my butt. My eyeballs hurt just looking at it.

"So let's see the other videos," I said.

"What other videos?" John asked.

"The ones showing everyone else's rooms? We'll have the murderer."

"No videos. Our guests deserve their privacy."

"Everybody but me?"

"Correct."

"Well, that's just swell. What about their keycards?" I asked.

He shook his head. "Only you needed a keycard for access to your room. I installed your system at Tommy's request."

I punched his shoulder. It was surprisingly firm. "You are useless."

"I proved your innocence."

"Besides that." I rubbed my eyes. "So we know Cherie left the castle before midnight because my code was the only one that was used after midnight."

Aaron nudged me and did a discreet little point at John.

Of course. I can't believe I didn't think of it.

"You have my code," I said to John.

"I do," he replied completely unperturbed.

"You could've done it."

"Yes."

"Well?"

"I didn't."

"Prove it," I said.

"I'm counting on you to do that."

"Are you serious?"

"Completely."

I sighed.

"Aren't you happy?" asked John, changing the screen to room service orders.

"No," I said. "Why would I be?"

"You'll be too busy for your sea salt scrub today. I'd make myself scarce."

"Oh really. Why?"

"Your cousins are awake and have just ordered breakfast."

"Right."

I went to leave, but John's hand darted out and grabbed my wrist. "Miss Watts, I want this done quickly."

"I get it."

He tugged me down closer to him so that we were nose to nose. "Do you?"

"I get that you didn't move to nowhere Missouri because you wanted to be noticed."

"Excellent deduction. If cameras show up outside our gate, we will be...displeased." John let go, but my heart was pounding. There was a threat in there somewhere. He didn't just want privacy. It was more than that. Much more.

Aaron led me back to the copper pot kitchen where we found Lane still in the staff dining room cuddled up with Pick and on the phone, crying.

Anthony sat at the table with his arms around Taylor, who was practically howling with grief. I didn't know a boy could sound like that. His friend, James, sat on the fireplace surround, pale and shaking.

I hesitated before I went through the door. It was so personal. So raw. I didn't know how to intrude to ask my questions.

Anthony looked up, his teeth bared in a grimace of pain. It was so visceral I had to remind myself that he was a suspect. He'd fought with Cherie at the gas station. "Yes," he managed to force out.

"I'm so sorry. I have to ask you a few questions," I said, regretting every word.

"You?"

"Leslie and John have asked me to investigate on their behalf."

"The cops were here."

"Yes. They're out gathering evidence now," I said. "I'm trying to get a picture of where everyone was at 2:02 this morning."

Taylor's howling came to a slow shuddering end and he looked at me with streaming eyes. "Where's my mom?"

Flincher appeared in my mind and I shoved him right back out.

"She's at the local funeral home."

He jolted to his feet. "I don't want her there. Her funeral has to be at home."

Anthony put his head in his hands and shook once. I came over and took Taylor by the shoulders. Sometimes you need to be touched. I learned that when David disappeared. Taylor gazed down at me—he was quite a bit taller—and then fell into my arms. "I have to take her home."

I rubbed his back. "I know and you will. I promise."

"Why does she have to be there?" he asked between soft sobs.

"For the investigation," I said.

He jerked back. "Are they doing something to her?"

I squeezed his shoulders. "It won't take long."

"I don't want them to do anything to her. What are they doing?"

I took a slow breath, feeling a tear slip down my own cheek. "There has to be an autopsy in the case of a suspicious death."

He got stock still. "Suspicious death?"

"Didn't Coach Jakes tell you?" I asked.

"I did," Oliver said behind me.

He came over and gave Taylor a mug of hot chocolate that I recognized as Aaron-made. It had a distinct super chocolate smell and was so thick a spoon could've stood straight up in it. Taylor sat and stared down into the mug and a muscle quivered in his tan cheek. "You didn't say what happened to her."

Oliver sat down with the boy and placed a big hand on his back. "Because I don't know and I'm not sure you should ever know."

Lane put her phone away and pulled a quilt around her shoulders. "I want to know. I keep thinking she was...you know."

"She wasn't," I said.

Both kids looked at me with doubt and fear radiating off of them.

"I'm sure, but the doctor will confirm shortly."

Lane began to cry again. This time in relief that her mother hadn't been violated.

"I'm sorry, but I do need to ask you a few questions," I said.

"Now?" Oliver's eyes grew hard.

Anthony stood up and walked to the window. "Let's get it over with."

"Where were you all at 2:02 a.m.?" I asked.

"In bed," Anthony said. "Alone. That doesn't help, I guess."

"It's just a fact and they do help. What about you, Taylor?"

The boy glanced at Oliver.

"It's fine," said his coach. "I don't care what you were up to, just tell her."

"Quinn stole some of his dad's whiskey. We got up after you went to bed and went up into the attic to drink it," said Taylor.

"Who was there? All of you?" I asked.

Taylor thought about it. "No. Not everybody. The Grizzlies were too good for us. They had their own bottle. That's how they are. The Vipers were there and my team."

"How big was that bottle?" asked Oliver.

"Pretty big. Quinn said his dad got it at Costco. The Grizzlies had more than us."

"So you were drunk," I said, rubbing my eyes. "None of you are going to remember who was where. Great."

A blush lit up Taylor's cheeks.

"What time did you start drinking?"

He shrugged. "I don't know. Maybe eleven."

Oliver nodded. "I went to bed at eleven fifteen."

"All the coaches went to bed by then?" I asked.

"They were in bed before I got back from the fire pit. It was a long day."

So any of the Grizzlies or the coaches could've slipped out after 11:15.

"Was everyone present this morning when you got up?" I asked Oliver.

He thought about it for a second and then nodded. "Yes. All the boys and my coaches were there when we got them up at five."

"I assume you didn't hear or see anything unusual?" I asked them.

They all shook their heads, but Lane got out her phone and fiddled with it.

Interesting.

"Lane?"

Her head jerked up, but she avoided my eyes.

"Where were you at 2:02 this morning?" I asked.

"In bed, of course," she said.

Taylor frowned. "Didn't you notice Mom was gone?"

"I was asleep, Taylor." She began to cry again. "It's not my fault."

Anthony knelt by her side. "Nobody thinks it's your fault."

"Absolutely not," I said.

I got Lane's version of the timeline and Lane wasn't being truthful.

She never met my eyes and cried whenever I pushed her to be specific. Lane's story was simple. She was in bed when her mother came up to their room. Cherie got in bed and went to sleep immediately and when Lane woke up that morning her mother was gone. She didn't think anything of it. Cherie was an early riser. Lane thought she'd gone down for coffee.

This smells like boy.

"Your mother was out of the castle before midnight when the lockdown happened. Can you think of anything that would get her to go outside?"

Lane's lip trembled. She had a pretty good idea, but she wasn't going to tell me. At least, not until I backed her into a corner, and I *would* back her into a corner. I darted a knowing glance at her and she ducked her head, burrowing down into the quilt.

"Do you have the key to your room on you?" I asked Lane and she nodded. "Can I have it?"

Lane gave me the key without looking up.

Yeah, girl. If you don't look at me, I won't know that you've got something to hide. Puhlease.

"What are you going to do?" asked Taylor, wiping his cheeks dry.

"I'm going to search the room and see if anything turns up."

"Like what? My mom didn't do anything bad."

"I know, but maybe someone threatened her. Did she have a laptop?"

Taylor gave me his mother's password for her computer and her email password. I was briefly taken aback. If Cherie gave that info to her kids, she had nothing to hide or she thought she'd hidden it so well that her kids wouldn't find it even with the passwords.

"How good was your mom with technology?" I asked.

Anthony gave a little laugh. "Terrible. I'm bad and she was worse than me. She told us her passwords because she could never remember them."

So it's nothing to hide.

"She told you everything then?"

A shadow passed over Anthony's face. "Not everything."

"How about how she paid for this trip?"

The kids' both frowned and Anthony said, "I don't know what you mean."

"I heard you arguing at the gas station yesterday."

Anthony picked at a jagged fingernail. "Oh, that was you behind the rack."

"I was heating up a burrito. What were you arguing about?"

"This place," Anthony gestured out the window, "this camp. We couldn't afford it. That money should've been spent on personal coaching. Taylor needed that, not this."

"What about the prize?" I asked.

He scoffed, "The prize? You mean the one they give out to the shiniest pitcher, not the most talented."

"Shiniest?"

"That Enrique, he's had the best of everything. New uniforms every year, every tournament, and the best specialized coaching money can buy. He makes a good story. Poor kid from Ecuador gets adopted by wealthy family and they turn him into a winner. That kid's been buffed until he gleams. We shouldn't have bothered with this place."

"I have a chance," said Taylor, bowing his head. "Mom believed I could get it."

Anthony instantly turned bright red. "I'm sorry, boy. You shouldn't have just a chance. You should win hands down, but that junker will take it because he's the story. You're just another poor white kid."

"Enrique's got a rifle."

"I'm not saying he can't throw, but you're better and more consistent."

Taylor stood up and walked out of the room, saying over his shoulder, "I don't care who wins anymore. I just don't give a fuck."

Anthony watched him go. "His mother cared. Cherie would've done anything to help him. It would...break her heart to see him give up."

"Mom just got killed, Grandpa," said Lane, standing up and following her brother. "Who cares about stupid baseball? It's just a game."

She left and Anthony said, "Just a game? Baseball's never been just a game to this family."

I patted his shoulder. "Maybe that was the problem."

"You think someone killed Cherie over baseball? No. It's…"

"Just a game?"

Anthony turned away and leaned on the windowsill. Unless I was completely off, baseball was much more than just a game to someone at Cairngorms Castle."

Cherie and Lane's room was in the South Wing. I never would've found it if Aaron hadn't been there, trotting along ahead of me. His sense of direction was spot on even when I told him I wanted to interview Nicole and Cory first. Instead, of taking me to their tower or the ball fields, he took me to a staircase modeled on a flying buttress. At the top of the buttress were arched cathedral doors. Aaron opened a door and we emerged onto the parapet, the parapet where more than one Cairngorms owner decided to end it all. I stopped. I can't say why I didn't want to go through those doors, but I couldn't stop staring at the low wall ahead with its crenelated stonework like bad dental work. How could anyone climb over that rough stone?

Aaron touched my arm and the smell of hotdogs washed over me, bringing me to my senses with a wrinkled nose. "Listen."

I stepped out onto the parapet and heard Nicole say, "Why did you bring us up here? You know I hate heights."

"Me?" asked Cory. "You were leading."

"No, I wasn't," said Nicole.

"You've been up here at least six times."

"Not on purpose."

"How do you climb all those stairs on accident?" asked Cory.

"I don't know. How do you keep ending up in the armory? I hate it up here. It makes me think about Quinn and then I think about Cherie. I hated her, but she was so young."

"She wasn't that young," said Cory.

"Thanks. She was my age."

"You're always angry. I thought you didn't—"

"You called me old."

"No, I didn't. I meant Cherie seemed older. Older than you."

"Don't you know exactly how old she is? You've memorized every other fact in the world."

"Nothing I do makes you happy," said Cory.

Somebody blew their nose and Nicole said in a strangled voice, "I don't know what to do."

"Come here," said Cory.

"Get off me," said Nicole.

"There's nothing to do. She's dead. Don't think about her anymore."

Nicole cried softly. "I think we should go. The murderer could get back in."

"Whatever you want. Come on."

They walked around the corner. Nicole's hair hung around her face in limp waves, no more Aqua Net, but Cory's crew cut was just as pointy as ever. They looked like they dressed in the dark with mismatched workout gear. They stopped short when they saw us, and Nicole started peeling off the paint on her nails.

"Were you spying on us?" asked Cory, his cheeks going red to match his wife's eyes.

"Yes," I said.

Nicole wiped her eyes with a very used tissue. "You admit it."

"Absolutely," I said, smiling. "I'm supposed to find out who killed Cherie."

"You think we did it?" Cory rubbed his head and Nicole pulled his arm down to stop him.

"Not necessarily, but I have to ask you some questions," I said.

Nicole tried to push past me. "Forget it. That was unforgivably rude."

It was, but I didn't care. Dad considered eavesdropping a high art and if I told him I missed an opportunity because I was honest, he would chase me around with a rubber spatula, a stick, or a handful of lemon curd. I know because all three of those have happened, the curd more than once.

I blocked her path. "It won't take a moment. Where were you at 2:02 and 3:15 this morning?"

Cory tried to lift me out of the way, but Aaron said, "John won't like that." Cory stopped instantly. "What time did you say?"

"2:02 and 3:15."

"We were asleep," said Nicole. "That's the middle of the night."

"We're heavy sleepers," said Cory.

"You didn't hear a gunshot?"

"Gunshot? Was she shot?" asked Nicole. "Who would shoot Cherie? She was...annoying but..."

Cory edged around me, careful not to touch. "We have to go. The boys are going down to the field."

"I'm surprised you aren't with them," I said.

Nicole trotted out behind Cory and said over her shoulder, "The coaches wanted to talk to the boys about what happened before practice."

I watched them hustle down the buttress stairs. "Sleeping. Everybody's going to say they were sleeping."

"I was," said Aaron, staring off into space.

"Well, I don't think you strangled Cherie," I said.

"Oh."

I rolled my eyes. "Let's go to Cherie and Lane's room."

"Where is it?"

"I thought you knew."

"Do I?"

"I hope so because if you don't, we may as well call for help right now," I said.

Aaron didn't answer. He trotted down the stairs like he knew something and I followed with crossed fingers. Ten minutes later, we were standing in front of a door with a green crystal embedded into the knob. Since Aaron didn't offer up any information, I used Lane's big brass key with a dangling green crystal to open it, but we didn't go inside.

I stopped on the threshold and looked in at the destruction. The room had been torn apart. In the mess, I recognized some of the clothes Lane and Cherie had worn. We had the right room.

Aaron looked around my shoulder. "What?"

"It's been searched. Thoroughly."

"Huh?"

Well, to me it had been torn apart. To others, perhaps not. The others, in this case, was Aaron. He was wearing his favorite Bat signal tee. It'd been washed to grey and had shrunk up to reveal the hairy belly protruding over his formerly navy sweatpants. I could only imagine what his apartment looked like. Probably like Cherie's room without the girly clothes. The drawers were open. Panties and bras strewn on the floor. Women don't throw our lacy bras on the floor. We just don't. The closet was open and Cherie's good dresses were off their hangers and lying in silky heaps where her shoes should've been. The shoes weren't paired but were tossed at the foot of one of the double beds. Both beds were slept in but not seriously. The covers had been neatly drawn back in a triangle as if someone slid in to read a book for a bit, not for a full night's sleep.

Most importantly, Cherie's laptop was nowhere to be seen. Even the bag was gone. Either she took it with her or someone helped themselves. I didn't see her phone and it wasn't on her body. Lane told me she had a Kindle Fire. It was gone, too.

"I didn't expect this," I said.

"I did," said Aaron.

I eyed the little weirdo, who appeared even less with-it than usual. He was staring at a random point on the wall and scratching his chest. "You expected this?"

"She got murdered."

"Obviously, but who would steal her stuff and why? Can't be for profit. Everyone here had better stuff than Cherie."

"Evidence?" asked Aaron, flashing a piercing look that was usually aimed at food.

I pulled out my phone. "Yes. Evidence. I assumed this was about rage. Maybe an argument about the prize. It wasn't. Or, at least, that's not all it was. She left the safety of the castle in the middle of the night. She could've been lured by the killer."

I hated to think Lane was a part of that, but the girl was hiding something. Daughters did kill mothers. It happened. Did it happen here? I shivered and Aaron put a warm hand on my shoulder. I had the strongest urge to call my interfering I-know-what's-best-for-you mother, but I resisted. She'd probably ask why I wasn't sitting in bed eating French toast with my cousins.

Uncle Morty got my call instead. He couldn't care less about my cousins or the wedding.

"What?" he yelled. "I'm working."

"You're working? Now? Right now?"

He growled. "I'm pulling an all-nighter. Got to get it out. It's flowing.

"It's after ten in the morning. Time for a break."

"To work for you?"

"Yes."

Click.

"He's working," said Aaron.

"So I gathered." I dialed again and got his voice mail. Angry bastard.

"It's me," I said. "I'll call Spidermonkey."

Then we waited. Spidermonkey was Uncle Morty's main competition and, even if he was working, I didn't see him letting Spidermonkey get one over on him.

My phone rang and his water buffalo voice burst out of it, "Make it quick!"

"One of the guests has been murdered. If you came up for air once in a while, you'd know that."

"Why the fuck do I care?" he yelled.

"Because Dr. Watts put me in charge of the investigation and, let's just say, John made it clear that it behooves me to do a good job."

"John who?"

"The owner. Leslie's partner of some sort."

His voice lowered and got gravelly. "Oh, that one."

"Yeah, that one. Do I need to call Spidermonkey or what?" I asked.

"I'll freaking do it. What do you want?"

"Cherie Marin got strangled. I want you to look at her financials and email. I have her passwords."

He growled, "Don't insult me."

"Fine. Fine."

"What's your theory?"

I had a theory? It was news to me. "Well, the other baseball parents didn't like her and I can't figure out how she paid for this place."

"That's it? How long you been on this?"

"Like an hour. Give me a break."

"Screw that. Get me something else. I got work to do. The fans are waiting for this book."

With bated breath, I'm sure.

Actually, they probably were. Uncle Morty was a famous novelist. People dressed up as his characters at Comic-Con. Even though I knew it was true, I still had a hard time reconciling fame with the lumpy grump currently holed up in a tower.

"The daughter lied," I said.

"Nice. How?"

I told him about the barely mussed up bed and Lane's demeanor.

"Could she kill her mom?" he asked, his voice deep and throaty. If there was one thing I knew about Uncle Morty, he loved his mom. Minnie and Moms in general were revered. He'd drop work to nail Lane if she had a hand in it.

"I doubt it. She's small and Cherie outweighed her by a good twenty pounds." I told him about the head wound and he growled again. "I didn't get the feeling that Lane did it, just that she was lying about something."

"She's protecting the man that murdered her mother."

Oh no. I've poked the bear.

"Not necessarily. If you get into her phone, I'm sure there'll be a text record."

"If?"

"When. I meant when."

"Anything else?"

There was, but I feared bringing it up. Uncle Morty didn't seem to care for John and Leslie already, but, on the other hand, he did enjoy besting people. Me included. "I think we have two crimes."

"Well, that's just fan fucking tastic!"

"Don't yell at me. I didn't do it," I said.

"Give it to me!"

"There was a gunshot at 3:15 this morning."

"She was strangled!"

I kicked the wall and yelled back, "I know! I told you!"

Uncle Morty lowered his voice. "Who's the vic?"

"I haven't found one yet, but John and Leslie are hiding something."

He was silent, a rare occurrence in my experience.

"Uncle Morty?"

"You could tell that they were hiding something?"

"That's what I said."

"Maybe they're losing their touch," he said.

I kicked the wall again and Aaron jumped.

"Or maybe I'm just that good."

He gave out a long juicy snort. "Yeah, that's it."

"So what's the deal with those two? They're not really spa owners, are they?"

"They are now," he said.

"What were they before?" I asked in my most innocent voice. I don't know why I thought it would work. Nothing worked on Morty. He was impervious to feminine wiles or any kind of wiles as far as I could tell.

"Forget it, sister. They're spa owners. I'll send you their backgrounds," he said.

"You will? For free?"

He growled. "Yeah, what of it?"

"Well, if that isn't suspicious, I don't know what is."

"End of discussion. You got anything else to screw up my day."

I sighed and my phone vibrated. "No. I've got to go. Tiny's calling me."

"He's not with you?" He yelled again, "He's supposed to watch you."

"He's searching the fence line with the cops and I've got Aaron."

Uncle Morty grumped about security and hung up on me. Next time I'd call Spidermonkey just to spite him.

Tiny had given up so I called him.

"Mercy?" he asked, tremendously out of breath. "Are you okay? You didn't answer. I'm not there. Where are you? Where are you?"

"I'm fine. Calm down. Your heart can't take this. I was on the phone with Morty," I said.

"Thank god." He took a few deep breaths and then said, "We found something, but you won't like it."

I squeezed my eyes shut. "What?"

"Blood, a trail of it. Outside the fence near the service entrance."

"Take some pictures and send them."

Sure enough. Blood. Not a huge amount. There were spots on some leaves, a bigger patch on a trunk a few feet away like someone had put their hand there, and a few broken branches. Not exactly a smoking gun but something happened there.

I called back. "No body?"

"Nope. You want to come out here?" asked Tiny.

"I guess I have to."

"You better hurry 'cause it's starting to rain. I think there was a lot more blood but that drizzle last night washed it away. We almost walked by this stuff."

"What caught your eye?" I asked.

Tiny chuckled. "Phelong falling down the embankment. It's pretty wet by the fence and there's only a little space to walk. He slipped and landed right next to a drop. It was the first picture I sent you. Lucky, huh?"

"Maybe."

"What do you mean maybe? If he didn't fall, I wouldn't have looked down in this here gully."

"Why'd he slip?" I asked.

"I told you it's wet. Why what are you thinking?"

I wasn't thinking. I was feeling. That was a whole lot of luck, especially for me, and it was barely a drizzle last night. I had to see the spot. "I'll be right out. Oh, and send in Gerry. I need him to finger-print Cherie's room."

"How come?"

"It's been searched and her laptop, phone, and her daughter's Fire is missing."

Tiny told me exactly where he was so that even I could find them and hung up. There really was a second crime. I sent Uncle Morty the pictures and he responded with texted cursing, which came across more funny than he intended and I told him so.

Aaron was bouncing up and down on the balls of his feet. He was so excited he cleaned his glasses on the hem of his tee. "Where are we going?"

"I'm going to look at some blood. You're staying here to protect this room. Gerry's coming to fingerprint it and I don't want anyone getting in and mucking it up.

"No."

"Yes."

"No. You'll get lost."

"Good point." I couldn't take Aaron and leave the room. The murderer might come back. Everybody else was a suspect, except my cousins. Mainly because they were drunker than I was last night. But I couldn't ask them. It was a bridal weekend, not a crime-solving weekend.

I called Tiny back. "Tell Phelong to take samples. I have to wait until Gerry gets here."

"Samples of what?" he asked.

"The blood."

"Okay. How do we do that?"

"Just tell Phelong to do it. He has the stuff, right?" I asked.

Tiny asked Phelong if he had it. The reply was muffled, but I didn't have a good feeling about it. It took a couple of minutes.

"Um...what does it look like?" asked Tiny.

"A tube with a Q-tip thing in it and a security seal."

"No."

"Give Phelong the phone!" I yelled.

After a short argument, Phelong said, "Hey there. How you doing?"

"Not good! I sent you to look for evidence and you didn't take the kit?"

"I didn't think we'd find anything," he said.

"There was a gunshot," I said.

"Eh, there's gunshots around here all the time. Maybe somebody was rabbit hunting."

I kicked the wall again. "Do rabbits climb trees?"

"Probably not."

"Probably? Did you say probably?"

"It's raining more. Can we come in? I'm getting really wet and my mom says I have a weak constitution."

"You've got a weak brain. You've got to take a sample of that blood now. Do you have some clean paper or tissue?" I asked.

"Nope."

"Oh my god. Okay. There are leaves with blood, right? Break off the leaves and hold them under your hat until I get there."

Phelong whined, "I might get blood on my hands or my hat. I can't get blood on my hat. It's my uniform. Sheriff Greer is always talking about respecting the uniform."

"If you don't protect that blood, I will tell Dr. Watts. Do you want me to tell Dr. Watts?" I asked.

"God, no. She kicked me once," said Phelong.

"I'm going to kick you. In the wiener. Do it!"

Did I say wiener? What am I? Five.

"Are you doing it?" I yelled.

Tiny came back on the phone. "He's breaking off the largest leaves."

"Good."

"Mercy?"

"Yeah?"

"Did you say wiener?" asked Tiny. "Big girls can say penis, ya know."

"Clearly I'm not a big girl. Now just stay there until I come with collection bags. Okay?"

"Phelong isn't going to like it."

"Fine. If he tries to leave, kick him in the *penis*."

Tiny hung up laughing. Wiener. My god.

Aaron raised an eyebrow.

"No," I said. "Don't even start."

We waited twenty minutes before Gerry moseyed down the hall with the fingerprint kit. I would've lectured him, but it was pointless. I told him to tape off the room and dust all the surfaces. He was very damp and even more reluctant. Aaron promised a bunch of sausages and he got moving.

I watched Gerry for a couple of minutes, afraid to leave and afraid to stay. Anything I did seemed like a bad idea.

Aaron nudged me. "Raining."

I groaned and called Tiny, telling him we were on our way. He asked me to hurry. The rain was getting worse. I told him we'd run.

"Okay, Aaron. Let's go get us some bloody leaves."

CHAPTER FOURTEEN

It took us thirteen minutes to find Tiny and Phelong. Having cousins yelling your name is very motivating. So are the words wax, pluck, and hot yoga. The Troublesome Trio yelled them all and I discovered I had a sense of direction when being pursued. I think it's castle specific though.

Tiny and Phelong were still down in the gully when we arrived at the section of fence where the cameras were broken. There were two cameras perched on high poles above the fence to give a wide view, and their green lights were out. There were plenty of old apple trees in the area. Some of the big branches extended over the electric fence, an ideal place to go over if you could avoid being shocked to death. But it certainly wouldn't be easy by a long shot.

"Can we go now?" Phelong yelled up the hill at us.

"Just a minute!"

I scanned the area. No footprints. The grass was thick and uncut on the outside, but it was trampled down quite a bit. I could see where Phelong had taken his tumble. He had taken out a track of undergrowth and he wasn't the only one. There was a second track beside it. I took several pictures and crept along the edge of the fence. The spot where Phelong had lost his footing was slightly narrower and extremely wet.

I looked up at the trees. They gave good cover and it wasn't so wet a few steps back.

"What are you doing?" yelled Phelong.

"Looking for why you slipped."

"I slipped."

I groaned and squatted. No. He didn't just slip. While it was damp everywhere, the ground was completely saturated where Phelong slipped. Leaves from last fall covered the ground and slope, except where he fell. They'd been washed down the hill in a torrent of water so that the area was extra slick and muddy. This didn't come from any drizzle. Someone had washed it. I got down on my hands and knees, my palms sinking into the goopy muck, and I sniffed.

Something. Faint. Chemical. They treated the area. I wondered just what that gardener had been spraying on the rosebushes. Probably fertilizer, but it hardly mattered. The rain was washing the area clean as I looked at it, and fertilizer was hardly a smoking gun on a lush estate anyway. I couldn't think what to do. What would Dad do? Something brilliant while I was just getting wet. The rain soaked my back even though Aaron was holding an umbrella over me.

"Miss Watts!"

"I'm coming."

Aaron helped me up and my eyes roved over the black metal bars of the fence. "There!"

"Huh?"

I sloshed over and pointed to a dent in the metal and several scrapes. "We'd be able to see it better from the other side. The other side. The shots came from the other side. See?"

Aaron peered at the marks and agreed. To be fair, he probably would've agreed with anything I said. All I got was a nod.

"They were standing here," I said, "and someone shot them through the fence. They fell down the hill just like Phelong and whoever did it cleaned up the blood, except they missed a few spots. Our suspect is someone on the inside." I did a happy dance. "Yes!"

"Okay," said Aaron.

"Aren't you intrigued?"

Nothing. I guess shots fired in the middle of the night, blood evidence, and a trail weren't all that interesting to a guy obsessed with hotdogs.

"Miss Watts, come on!" yelled Phelong. "I'm all yuck."

"Fine!" We walked a little ways to where the hill wasn't so steep and trotted down to them. Both were soaked and Phelong was yuck. Mud coated him from head to toe. He had a stick in his hair and a small leaf plastered to the side of his face. I pulled out a couple of evidence bags and opened one. "Okay. I'm ready."

Tiny and Phelong ducked their heads and that's when I realized Phelong was holding his hat and he certainly wasn't protecting anything from the rain.

"Tell me you didn't let the leaves get wet," I said.

A furious red blush crept up Tiny's neck and lit up his ears. Phelong stuck out his pointy chin. "I didn't."

"Oh, really. Where are they then?"

"You see there was this accident," he said.

"Accident? How could you have an accident? You were supposed to stand here and do nothing."

He ducked his head again and stared at his formally shiny shoes that were now caked with fresh mud. Very fresh. "What did you do?"

Phelong reached up and peeled something off his chest. I flipped a lock of dripping hair back and leaned in. "Tell me those aren't the leaves."

"They aren't the leaves," he said in an unnaturally high voice. "Except they are."

"You wrecked them? How? How? You were just standing here?"

Tiny raised his head. It looked painful. "It's my fault. I should've stopped him. He got tired of waiting."

"It took thirteen minutes!" I didn't know my voice could get that high. Impressive, even for a girl.

"It's raining and I thought I could do it," said Phelong.

I raised an eyebrow.

"He was going to meet you halfway," said Tiny.

"How far did you get?" I asked.

"Five feet. I slipped."

"And landed on the evidence, I presume."

"Little bit."

Breathe, Mercy.

"Okay. What about that spot on the tree trunk? Where's that?" I asked.

Tiny pointed to a tree with nothing on the bark. "Rain."

I grabbed a fallen tree branch. "That was our blood evidence. Our only evidence that somebody got shot out here." I hauled back the branch, aiming at Phelong's crotch. "Stand still!"

Aaron grabbed the branch and wrenched it out of my hand. He tossed the branch away into the trees. "You're hungry. Let's go."

"You always think people are hungry. This isn't hungry. This is mad. Mad beyond measure." I went into a stream of consciousness rant. I used every cuss word Uncle Morty ever used, including the ones that didn't make sense.

When I was done, I fell over into the mud, panting.

"Wow," said Tiny.

"Don't get me started again," I hissed at him.

"Believe me I won't."

"We still have the pictures," said Phelong, brightening up, "and the trail. There are bullet things on the fence. How about that?"

"Did you find a body?" I asked.

"No."

"Then we don't have a crime without the blood." I flopped back onto the wet leaves and let the rain wash over me. "Dad's gonna kill me."

Tiny squatted. "He doesn't have to know."

Phelong nodded like crazy. "I won't tell."

"Like you said, there's no evidence, there's no crime. We can't fail if nothing happened."

That was interesting. You can't do the time if there was no crime. I liked it. Then the trail on the hill caught my eye and I flung my arm over my face. "No. There was a crime. You know there was." I sat up. "Somebody out here got killed by someone in there."

Tiny and Phelong just looked at me.

"And we have to go back in there."

"Uh huh," said Tiny.

"Just because we can't prove a crime happened doesn't mean there's not a murderer in there among the guests. Two murderers most likely. And we have to spend the night three more times," I said.

Tiny ran his big hand over his face, wiping away the rain. "I don't think we should stay here."

"No kidding. But where do you suggest we go? Costillas are looking for me. We're stuck for three more days. I'm not even supposed to be outside the fence."

"Who are the Costillas?" asked Phelong.

"We should tell your dad," said Tiny. "I'll do it."

"No, you won't," I said. "He'll just say, 'So what? Figure it out.'"

"Who are the Costillas?" asked Phelong.

Tiny hauled me to my feet and pointed me up the hill. "But there's been two murders."

"I wasn't the target." The tree overhead showed no sign that it'd been used to get in or out, but I wasn't sure if it would. John said no one got in, but I wasn't sure I trusted him. "Maybe whoever killed Cherie escaped over the fence but got shot before they got out of range."

"That's complicated," said Tiny. "Why's she worth all that?"

"We'll have to figure it out." I climbed back up the hill, not falling once. Phelong fell three more times. I had serious concerns about his inner ear.

We rang the bell at the service gate to be let back in after trying our codes and John answered, "Cairngorms Castle. How can I help you?"

"You can let me back in," I said into the tiny black microphone.

"Miss Watts. Whatever are you doing out there?" John's voice was as flat as ever, but I still thought he was smug.

I squinted up at the camera perched on the post beside the gate. "You know what I was doing."

"I assure you I don't," he said.

"You don't seem to mind that I'm out here."

"It's your life, Miss Watts. If you choose to risk it, who am I to stop you?"

Tiny frowned at me and I shrugged. "My father's friend."

"Friendship only goes so far. You are technically an adult."

"Whatever. My code isn't working," I said.

"We just changed them all."

"Why? Oh, never mind. I swear I don't care. Just let us in."

"Of course."

There was a click and the gate rolled back a scant two feet.

"Very funny," I said. "Open it!"

"It is open."

I wanted to flip off that camera. That's not something I normally do, but he deserved it. Instead, I grabbed Tiny and pulled him in front of the camera. The gate opened another three feet, wide enough for Tiny to get through.

"I didn't know Mr. Plaskett was with you," said John.

"Yeah, right."

"Come through and we'll give you tea. Perhaps you'll find a clue somewhere."

He was just so smug. I had another stream of consciousness moment. Well, not so much a moment since it lasted all the way back to the copper pot kitchen. Tiny and Phelong gave me a wide berth. I would've given me a wide berth, too. But I couldn't escape me or the weekend from hell.

I thought I could make it back to my tower without being noticed. I was quiet, but I was wrong.

"Mercy!" called out Sorcha. "Where have you been?"

I had one foot on the bottom step of my tower. For a brief moment, I considered running for it, but what was my plan? The tower was a dead end. I'd have to face Sorcha and her sisters sooner or later. I took a breath and tried to think of what to say. Nothing useful came to mind. How was I going to explain what had happened and that I was supposed to do something about it?

Tiny put a heavy hand on my shoulder and manually turned me. "Just say it."

"Just say what?" asked Sorcha, dripping with tears. "You've been avoiding us, your own cousins." Weepy's eyes screwed shut and she wailed, "It's like you don't love us."

Love? Let's just work on like.

"I'm not avoiding you. There's been a complication," I said.

"I knew you'd come up with some excuse to Fike us."

I rolled my eyes. "Look at me."

Sorcha opened one red-rimmed eye and blew her nose on an embroidered hankie. She had a huge supply of them. "Ew. What have you been doing, Mercy?"

"You see, there's...out in the garden...someone—"

She waved her hankie in my face. "Oh my god. Did you have a treatment without us? I can't believe this. It's Bridget's weekend." Her pouty lower lip trembled and then she lived up to her name with full force. Tears streamed out with amazing speed. Nobody could compete with Sorcha's crying on speed or sheer volume. "I thought we were getting so close. We didn't even duct tape you once," she wailed.

What spa included getting soppy wet and having mud-encrusted shoes? She must not have been wearing her contacts.

"You think I've had a treatment?" I asked.

"Obviously." Sorcha covered her streaming eyes with her hands.

"Look at me. What treatment would this be?"

She peeked through her fingers. "That tropical rain shower. Did you have the eucalyptus scent or the pomegranate?"

"Neither. Look at Aaron and Tiny. Do you think we took a tropical rain shower together?" I asked.

"It said it could be for couples in the brochure."

"There are three of us and our clothes are wet."

Sorcha sniffed and dabbed at her eyes with her fingertips. "Well, I would hope you wouldn't do it naked with your cousin and Aaron."

"We didn't do it at all." I straightened up and ran my fingers through my hair. "Sorcha, there's been a murder."

"Uh huh."

I braced myself for the inevitable freak out. "Here. At the castle."

She clapped her hands. "Like a murder mystery? Oh my god. That'll be so much fun." She hooked her arm through mine. "Let's go tell Bridget. You're a genius."

What's happening?

"Did you hear me? I said a murder and I've been appointed to solve it before the sheriff gets back in town. It'll take up most of my time," I said.

"That's okay. Will there be clues?"

"I hope so."

"How many?"

"How would I know?" I asked.

She pulled me closer. "That's right. You have to find them and we'll help you. It'll be great."

Tiny's mouth hung open and Aaron chewed on a fingernail. No help was coming from those two.

"I don't think you really want to help me," I said.

"Of course we want to help. You're so good at this. Mom says you shouldn't get involved in the things you get involved in, but this is fine. We're at the castle. Hello."

"Uh...one of the guests was murdered last night. You understand murdered as in dead?"

"Which guest?" she whispered, her big brown eyes darting around.

"Cherie, one of the Moms. She was strangled."

"That's nasty. We have to tell Bridget and Jilly. They won't want to miss anything. Oh! I can take notes. You need to take notes, right?"

"I guess."

"Great. I'll be your secretary." She tugged on my arm. "Let's go."

"I have to go to my room and take a bath. I'm soaked. I was out looking for evidence of a shooting," I said.

"Two crimes? That's even better. Wait until I tell Mom. This is *the* most unique bridal weekend ever. Everyone said we should go to Vegas, but everybody goes to Vegas. Who else gets to do this? Nobody. That's who. Okay. You go take a bath and I'll fill in Bridget and Jilly. Do you have a dossier or something?"

"Um...no."

"That's okay. We'll figure it out in record time. Uncle Tommy will be so impressed." With that, Sorcha took off down the hall practically skipping.

I turned to Tiny. "I said murder, didn't I?"

"Yeah, but I don't think she gets it."

"You hungry?" asked Aaron. "I'll make crepes."

"No crepes."

"Galettes?"

"No. I'm having a bath and that's it." I trudged up the stairs, listening to Tiny's strained breathing and Aaron mumbling about mincing sausage up for galettes.

By the time we reached the top of the stairs, Tiny was bright red and wheezing. Even Aaron noticed and moved out of the way in case he collapsed. Tiny wasn't going to collapse. He'd looked worse. Much worse.

"I gotta drop this weight," he said between ragged breaths.

"You're getting there," I said.

He staggered across the landing and bumped into my door, setting off furious barking inside.

"Quiet down, Pick!" I yelled as I unlocked the door.

He didn't quiet down. If anything, it got crazier. I could hear him running around and bumping into things. I didn't have the strength for this. I really didn't.

"Tiny, I need a break from that dog. Can you take him for a while?" I asked.

Before he could say yes, my door swung open and he never got any farther.

"Oh my god!" I couldn't move. I'm rarely shocked, but Pick managed it all by his curly self.

"Wow," said Tiny as we stood in the doorway and watched something the size of Pick race around the room in a maelstrom of white. There was a storm in my room, a tempest, a blizzard beyond anything I'd ever seen.

Aaron squeezed in beside me. "He's hungry."

"I'm not sure that's Pick. He was black this morning," I said.

Tiny snatched some of the white stuff out of the air. "Feathers. Millions of feathers."

"Pick!" I yelled.

At the sound of his name, the white-encrusted creature leapt onto the bed and began barking his head off. I walked in, batting feathers away from my face. It was a mess. No, not a mess. Mess didn't cover it. I had no words for it and I always did well with vocabulary. Everything was coated. The fireplace, dresser, bookcase, everything. Even the walls were white.

"How?" I squeaked out.

"Do you want me to call for a maid?" asked Tiny.

"You better call a vet because I'm going to kill that dog." I darted for the bed, but Tiny caught me by the back of my dripping hoodie.

"Chuck wouldn't like you killing his dog."

"You don't know. Maybe that's why he left him with me. He knew the dog had to die and he was setting me up."

"You lost it, girl."

"I never had it. Never!"

Tiny picked me up and set me in front of Aaron. "Hold on to her."

Aaron grabbed my arm and Tiny went for Pick, snagging his collar. Maybe it wasn't his collar. I couldn't tell under the fluffy feather shroud.

"He's got something on him," said Tiny. "It's sticky, but it smells good."

I dragged Aaron with me to the bathroom, the scene of the crime. Pick had lost his pea brain in there. My shampoo and conditioner bottles lay in shreds on the floor along with my lotion and every cosmetic I had. Aaron picked up the only intact bottle. "He didn't get this."

Baby oil. I used it on my feet, but not anymore. The bottle was empty.

There was a bizarre rumbling and squeaking out in the bedroom.

"What the hell?" yelled Tiny.

I dodged Aaron and ran back in. Tiny held Pick at arm's length.

"What now?" I asked.

"He's got something wrong with him."

"You think?"

"No, I mean, really wrong."

"Drag him in here," I said.

Tiny reluctantly carried Pick into the bathroom and put him in the tub. He resembled The Bumble from Rudolph the Red-nosed Reindeer but with nicer teeth.

"What's wrong with him?" I asked. "Besides the obvious."

Before Tiny could answer, a wet flappy squelchy noise came from Chuck's dog, the rear end of Chuck's dog to be specific. Without a word, Aaron left. He just up and left. Oh, how I envied him.

"Where's he going?" asked Tiny.

"It's every weirdo for himself," I said. "What do you think that is?"

Tiny let go of Pick and stepped back. "I don't know, but it ain't good."

Pick sat down in the tub and panted. His little black button eyes gleamed. He was pleased with himself. The dog was happy.

I tentatively sniffed him. "Well, the smell is my shampoo and conditioner. And the sound, I guess he ate some."

Pick tried to jump out of the tub when I turned on the water, but Tiny blocked him and stuffed him back in. I washed the snow beast while Tiny called housekeeping and told them what happened. From his end of the conversation, I think they had a hard time believing the extent of the mess.

"Just bring a bunch of vacuum bags," he said and hung up.

"Are they coming?" I asked.

"Yeah, but they ain't happy about it."

"They can join the club."

Pick was the only happy one. He liked baths, although he never remembered that until he was getting washed. He trampled around the tub, smiling his dog smile and shaking every chance he got. I thought I looked bad before. Adding feathers, shampoo foam, and a bunch of curly black poodle hairs made it so much worse. And the operation took forever. The feathers kept clogging up the drain and Pick ran around like a crazy nut whenever his rear made that bizarre noise. It wasn't until I got him washed off that I was brave enough to take a look. His rear seemed okay, except the fur was weird, all gloppy and shiny.

"What's up with that?" asked Tiny.

"I don't know. Touch it and tell me."

"I'm not touching that."

"Come on. You're a giant manly dude," I said, batting my eyes.

"That mighta worked if ya didn't have dog hair all over your face," said Tiny.

I wiped my face frantically. "Better?"

"Na. You gonna need two or three showers. Go ahead and touch it. Can't get any worse."

I was going to touch it, but I didn't have to. I pulled up Pick's stumpy tail and the noise happened and it was action packed, complete with spray and smell.

"Oh my god. He ate the baby oil. He ate it!"

"It won't kill him, will it?" asked Tiny.

"I'm not that lucky." I pointed at Pick's snout. "You are disgusting. What is wrong with you? You ate the bed and then you ate baby oil. That cannot taste good."

"Maybe it does to dogs," said Tiny.

"I don't put meat on my feet. It doesn't taste good. He's an idiot, a poodle and an idiot. They're supposed to be smart."

My phone vibrated in my pocket and I asked Tiny to get it.

"It's Dr. Watts," he said.

"Answer it, please," I said as I began to spray off Pick's oily butt. That stuff wasn't going to come off easy.

"She wants to talk to you."

"I'm a bit occupied." Pick shook again and I was resoaked. "Ask what she wants."

I washed Pick with the only thing left intact in my bathroom, a bar of exfoliating soap. I guess that didn't look tasty with all the grit. It did take off the oil, but, since he kept spraying, it was a losing battle.

Tiny listened for a minute and then hung up. "She wants you to come to the funeral home. There's something she wants to show you." He hesitated and then said, "You think it's something on the body?"

Pick whacked me in the face with his tail. Yuck. Now I had oil. Butt oil. "What else could it be?" I asked.

Tiny went quiet and I rinsed off Pick. His rear was hopeless. I washed it five times, but he kept spraying. I'd have to figure out a diaper or he'd have to live outside.

I toweled off Sir Sprays-a-lot and he gave me a big slurp on the other side of my face. Since he'd just been licking his nether regions, I didn't consider it to be a gesture of love. He jumped out of the tub and gave a humungous shake and danced around like he was about to be given a prize. He wasn't. I didn't even want to feed him for fear of what might come out.

There was a knock on the door and I asked Tiny to get it since I was plucking more feathers out of the drain. After a couple of minutes, I got curious when I didn't hear any conversation.

"Tiny, is it housekeeping?" I called out.

"No. It is not," said John. I think I caught a hint of emotion. Anger.

I came out of the bathroom and found him still standing in the doorway with a red-faced Tiny, trying to look like wallpaper.

"What happened?" asked John.

"Dog," I said.

"Do you need this dog alive?" He said it exactly the way he told me my security code, factual and utterly disinterested.

"Need is a strong word, but my parents will want him back in one piece." I got a bit nervous and my stomach twisted at the way he was looking at me. Men look at me in a variety of ways. Most of them weren't so nice, especially the ones that proceeded an attempt to kill me, but John was a different animal altogether. He was cold. That question should've come with visceral anger, but it didn't. It came with nothing and nothing was so much scarier than something. John was totally capable of killing Pick and making it look like an accident or making it look like he never existed at all. That bothered me way more than the idea that he may have shot someone through the fence and done away with the body. Pick was a dog. You don't kill dogs, not even destructive, spraying ones. "He's really my cousin Chuck's dog. You know my dad. Do you know Chuck?"

The coldness continued. I'm not completely certain John was breathing. Finally, he said, "We've not met, but I hear he's good."

"He is."

"And he's fond of you."

"He is," I lied. I had no idea if Chuck's weakness for me continued or not. I could tell my lie was the right thing to say though. Never say you're unloved. The unloved are more likely to disappear.

Pick sauntered out of the bathroom and growled in John's direction. I pushed him back in with my leg. "So about that housekeeping."

John switched his icy gaze from Pick to me. "You'll be moving rooms. This one will take time to restore."

"I'm very sorry about this. I don't know what got into him," I said.

Pick chose that moment to spray, a nice long flappy one and I swear the temperature dropped five degrees in the room.

"I'll have you moved directly," he said and stepped backward without taking his gaze off me.

I wanted to shrink back, but the crazy Watts inside of me wouldn't let that happen. "Excellent. I appreciate it. So when will that be?"

"Are you in a hurry?" he asked.

"You are. Dr. Watts wants to see me and we have a deadline."

"Yes, the return of the prodigal sheriff." He got a tablet out of his pocket and searched for something. "It's difficult. This tower is the most secure."

"Meaning no cameras elsewhere?" I asked.

"Yes, but another tower will do."

"How many towers have you got?" asked Tiny.

"Eight. I'll put you with your uncle." There was a slight narrowing of the eyes on the word 'uncle' and I instantly knew this was punishment.

"Fine. He likes me," I said.

Sort of.

"I was not aware that Morty liked people," said John.

"He's not aware of it either," I said. "So where am I going?"

"The Tudor Tower. Are you ready?"

I shot him my own icy stare and gathered some unsullied clothes out of the closet hidden in the wall. "I'm ready."

Pick ran out of the bathroom, spun in a circle, kicking up feathers galore.

"No. Not the dog," said John.

"He's with me," I said. Pick was many things, including an incorri-gible barker. Considering my decreased security, I could use all the help I could get. Plus, I was not leaving the dog alone. If the last twenty-four hours had proved anything, bad things happened at Cairn-gorms Castle.

CHAPTER FIFTEEN

The Tudor Tower lived up to its name. Every wall and ceiling was paneled in dark wood. The carved furniture was ornate and sturdy. I'd probably get a hernia if I tried to lift a chair. John took me through the small hall on the first floor. The walls were lined with portraits of Henry VIII between panels of *The Lady and the Unicorn* tapestries. I wanted to take a closer look at the reproductions. They weren't from the Tudor period, but that hardly mattered when they were so beautiful.

It would have to wait. We passed by and went up the narrow stairs to the fifth floor instead. It got darker with every step. The dim lighting couldn't compete with the dark wood so it didn't even try.

"Where's Morty's room?" I asked.

"Second floor." John produced a large metal ring with keys of every size and shape. He removed a black iron key with a simple cross in the bow. The lock made a grinding clank that reminded me of the cell doors at Hunt Hospital for the Criminally Insane, not reassuring in the least. But the room wasn't what I expected, no dark wood and minimal furniture. It was all cold stone arches and small windows. The bed was a single and looked comfortable enough, but there was a distinct unpleasantness about the room.

"Whose room is this supposed to be?" I asked.

"Anne Boleyn's apartment in the Tower of London."

"That explains it."

"What?"

"It feels like a punishment. I assume that's what you were going for. What else have you got?"

John stared into empty space. It was just he and I. Aaron and Tiny were packing up their stuff for the move to morbid and Pick was outside in the castle kennel, spraying away. "It's the most secure room available."

"Pass."

"I have Lady Jane Grey's cell."

"Why would you have that?" I asked.

"The castle was designed this way," he said.

We left and went down to the fourth floor to another room that was much more pleasant but resembled a dorm with several simple beds and plain walls.

"Alright. Whose room is this?"

"Catherine Howard. Lambeth Palace, her grandmother's home."

"Of course it is," I said. "Next."

We went across the hall to a sumptuous room. I loved the full tester bed with flowered fabric hangings, a beautiful wood ceiling, tapestries, and a big window. I was ready to move in. Until I thought about it.

"You approve?" asked John.

"It depends. Whose is it?"

"Mary, Queen of Scots. Holyroodhouse."

"I'm sensing a theme."

"It wasn't my idea."

"It was your idea to put me in this tower. Gee, I wonder why," I said. "Could it have something to do with the blood and bullets out by the service entrance?"

"It has to do with your dog destroying your last room."

"And that's it? You don't know anything about what happened out there in the woods."

"I don't and I fail to see why you're so interested since there's no body," he said, his voice flat as ever.

"Maybe there is a body and I just haven't found it yet."

John just gazed at me. I wasn't going to find a body. He'd made sure of that. I'd never know what happened. Whatever John was, he was a professional at it.

"Fine. Let's save some time. What other rooms are in this tower?"

"I have the Duke of Norfolk's room."

"Finally, a man," I said, all ready to go for it, but John almost looked pleased. It's hard to describe how. There was the smallest pinch by the right eye. "Wait. Is this the Duke that Elizabeth executed?"

"Naturally."

"Oh, come on. Haven't you got any rooms of non-executed people?"

"Anne of Cleves."

"I'll take it."

We went down to the third floor and Anne's room gave off no weird vibe. It was a Tudor bedroom with all the trappings but had a lightness to it with pale green hangings on the bed and wide leaded-glass windows. I heaved my armful of clothing onto the bed.

"Excellent," I said.

"I had no idea that you'd be such a difficult guest."

"Nothing's easy when it comes to me. I'm here because people are trying to kill me. That doesn't happen to Miss Congeniality. Also, there's been two murders in the past twelve hours."

"One murder."

I rolled my eyes. "Oh, right. One murder."

John didn't react and I didn't expect him to. He gave me a simple brass key with a green ribbon from his ring and said he'd put Tiny and Aaron in Catherine Howard's dormitory room on the fourth floor. It wasn't ideal but nothing that weekend was.

An hour later, I'd showered hard and gotten dressed. By hard I mean I washed everything multiple times, including my brain. When I finished, the memory of Pick's butt oil on the side of my face was completely gone.

I texted Dr. Watts and said I'd be over soon. First, I had to hitch a ride. I had no clue where Phelong and Gerry were. The rain was coming down in sheets so I assumed they were in the castle somewhere. But they might be hiding from me and my yelling until the storm passed so they could escape, not that I blamed them. If they were hiding, I'd never find them. I'd be lucky to find my way outside. Tiny and Aaron could help, but they were showering upstairs. I plopped down on the bed and looked for nonexistent messages from Chuck. Mom had sent updates on Lester. He was holding steady for now. I asked her why Tiny got a gun and I didn't. She texted back that she feared I'd shoot the cousins, so Tiny had that right. I wanted to know why they thought Tiny was up to dealing with the Costillas. Mom replied that Tiny was a sight more fit than me, considering that he was Special Ops in the Marines. He'd served in Iraq and Afghanistan and could kill people with his thumbs. Tiny didn't seem much like a thumb killer, but I promised not to ditch him and went on to Uncle Morty's texts. He'd sent me backgrounds on Leslie and John. I couldn't have been more surprised. There was no bill attached and the backgrounds were detailed as well as complete crap. Almost nothing rang true. So frustrating, but everything that weekend was. The waiting didn't help.

I grabbed my purse and whipped open my door, jumping back a foot and nearly falling over. Tiny and Aaron filled the doorway.

"Don't do that," I said.

"Huh?"

"You scared me, standing out there like vultures." I squeezed between them and locked my door.

"Sorry," said Tiny. "I was gonna knock, but you beat me to it."

I jogged down the stairs. "It's fine. Do you know where the cops are?"

"Why?"

"I need a ride to the funeral home."

"They might've left. You were pretty pissed and they were wet."

The hall at the foot of the stairs was still gloomy and getting worse.

The ominous clouds kept getting darker and darker and that room needed sunshine in a huge way. Dimness wasn't helping my sense of direction. I thought I'd recognize the door that I came in with John, but there were four doors and they were identical.

"Where are we going?" asked Tiny.

"Kitchen," said Aaron.

"You're going to the kitchen," I said. "We're going to the funeral home."

"I got to stick with you."

"That's what Tiny's for and you're making dinner."

The little weirdo didn't move. Okay. Whatever.

"Which way to the office?"

Tiny led the way and, at some point, Aaron peeled off, presumably to go to the kitchen. I felt a little bad about it. He'd been replaced, to some extent, by Tiny and most people would be stung by such a thing. But with Aaron it was hard to tell what he thought if anything at all.

We found Phelong and Gerry holed up in reception. They were wrapped in blankets and holding steaming cups of tea. Their hands shook so much they sloshed tea all over their knees.

"What are you doing here?" I asked. "I expected you to high tail it home."

Phelong shrunk down into his blanket. That tea was mighty interesting. "You didn't say we could leave and Dr. Watts is scarier than you. She'd get mad if we left."

"Is that why you're shaking? You should've warmed up by now."

They glanced at each other and said nothing.

"What?" I asked.

"You'll say we're stupid," said Phelong.

"Likely. What happened?"

"We got locked in the big walk-in fridge."

I rolled my eyes and asked the obvious, "What were you doing in the fridge?"

The young cops shook their heads and shrugged.

"I don't know," said Gerry.

"We went looking for hot tea and then we were in there." Phelong flushed at the absurdity of it.

"That kind of thing happens around here. The safety latch didn't work?"

"Safety latch?"

I rolled my eyes. "How'd you get out?"

"One of the cooks found us, but he didn't lock us in."

"No kidding."

Gerry became less abashed and actually got up the nerve to smile tentatively at me. "I did everything I was supposed to before the bad rain hit."

"Is that it?" I pointed to a plastic bin filled with evidence bags and Dr. Watts' camera.

"Yeah and guess what?"

"I give up."

"I found her phone," he said.

"Cherie's phone?"

"Uh huh and it wasn't broken or anything."

I went through the bags and found Cherie's phone bagged up nicely with a cracked screen. "I thought you said it wasn't broken?"

"It still works."

"Good job, Gerry. Where'd you find it?"

"Under a stone bench next to the rock garden."

I'd seen that bench. It was directly between the site of the first scene where she got her head bashed and the second where the strangling took place. I took the camera and scrolled through the pictures. Gerry'd done a good job documenting every inch of the place. Even my dad would've been pleased. There was hope for him yet.

The bench pictures showed the phone next to the left leg of the bench, partially concealed by the leg and some irises that were beginning to sprout. There was a smear of blood on the back of the bench. The phone wasn't really hidden. It looked to me like Cherie dropped it on her way to the second scene. Did she rest with her hand on the bench and drop the phone or did she hit the bench while being chased? I couldn't tell, but both ways made me feel unbelievably sad for her. No one helped her. Somebody should've helped her. She must've cried out. Pick heard her. Why not anyone else? Why not me?

"Miss Watts?" asked Gerry. "Did I do good?"

"Very well indeed. I was just thinking. Are you two ready to take off?"

"Where would we go?" asked Phelong. "I'm never gonna live that leaf thing down and Dr. Watts is going to kill me a lot."

"She'll only kill you a little, I promise. Besides, I need a ride," I said.

They perked up. "To where?" asked Phelong. I suspect he was hoping I'd say to a burger joint or a bar. "To the funeral home. Dr. Watts wants me to look at something."

Their shoulders slumped. "Do we have to go?" asked Gerry.

"You want me to drive your squad car?" I asked.

They thought it over when Leslie came out of the office. We were to his left and he didn't see us at first. Before I could call out to him, his stride faltered and he swept something away from his face like there was a spiderweb hanging in midair and then he continued walking.

"Leslie," I said and a micro-expression flitted across his features when he realized he'd been seen acting odd. The expression vanished and I saw no point in asking the obvious question. He wouldn't acknowledge anything.

"You're trying to leave the grounds again?" he asked.

"It's necessary. Dr. Watts wants me over at Flincher's."

Leslie ran his fingers through his silver hair and it fell back into place perfectly. "You must see...the body then?"

I caught the hesitation and he saw me catching it. We stood there, eyeing each other and waiting for someone to say something. Tiny did the deed. "Are we going or not?"

"You are," said Leslie. "But Mercy will lay down in the back of the squad car and the car will be driven into Flincher's garage so no one will see her."

"You're letting me go?" I asked.

"How would I win the bet otherwise? The last thing Phelong and Gerry want to do is go to Flincher's. I'm counting your money already."

That was easy. Hm.

"You're not going to win, but I will try to be inconspicuous."

"Good." He retrieved an enormous golfing umbrella from the office and gave it to Tiny. "You're to protect her at all costs. Life and limb."

"That's a bit overly dramatic," I said.

"No, it ain't," said Tiny. "It's my job."

"You've got it?" asked Leslie.

Tiny patted his waistband where there was the distinct outline of a gun. It did make me feel better although I'd rather have had it in my waistband.

"We're all set then." I went to leave and Leslie caught up to me.

"How far have you gotten with this?" he asked me. "Remember, we expect results."

"You'll get results. Can I go now?"

"What've you got so far?"

I gave him a brief rundown, but it was too long. The Troublesome Trio came through the archway into reception, all smiles and dressed like they were going to a garden party, hats and all.

"Finally!" exclaimed Bridget. "We've been looking for you everywhere. Is your phone not working?"

Oh, it was working alright and I was working at ignoring it.

"Sorry," I said. "I turned it off when I took a shower. Where are you going?"

"Wherever you're going?" said Jilly. "I'm totally ready for this."

Leslie straightened his vest. "You've missed your hot yoga class, ladies. What are you ready for?"

"To investigate," said Sorcha. "It's going to be awesome. Now we didn't tell our parents about the extra activities this weekend. We're going to surprise them when we solve it."

"*You're* going to solve it?"

Bridget put her hands on her hips. "We are Watts, you know? We can detect things."

"Of course," said Leslie. "I was only surprised that you wanted to interrupt your bridal weekend."

"Well, this is part of it after all."

"Part of it? The murder is part of your weekend?"

"Of course," said Sorcha. "Mercy told me everything and we're ready to go. What do you think of my hat? Is it too much?"

I had no words. None. Sorcha's hat was huge, a hat you'd see at a royal wedding.

"Your hat's nice," said Tiny after we all just stood there and looked at the hat.

"Good. Where are you going?"

There was nothing for it, but to tell her and hope she wouldn't want to go. "To the funeral home to view the body," I said.

"Oh my god. Really?" asked Jilly. "That is so detailed. I want to go."

What the hell?

"Unfortunately, ladies, Mercy has other plans for you," said Leslie.

My mouth fell open and I had to think about shutting it. "I do? Oh yeah yeah. I do."

Plans. Plans. What plans? Oh my god. Think of something, you idiot. They can't see the body. Mom will kill you.

"Interviews!"

My cousins jerked back. That came out louder than I expected. Then Sorcha rubbed her hands together. "Ooh, we get to interview the suspects. Yes!"

Yeah. Interview away. I have no suspects. I don't even have a motive.

"Actually, I'm hoping you will find me a suspect. I'm fresh out," I said.

"Really?" asked Jilly. "This is like your thing."

"Well, you know, I'm not quite at my best. Stress or something. Can you three interview the staff?"

"Absolutely," said Bridget. "We'll do it."

"What do we ask?" Sorcha picked some lint off her sleeve and then admired the crease.

I gave them a few things to ask. It was pretty simple and it would keep them out of my way. Best of all, it had to be done.

"Do you have a list of staff for them?" I asked Leslie.

"I do. Right this way." He led my cousins into the office. There was much flipping of hair and dimple popping. Leslie had *it* in spades. John did not. He came into the shadows of the far door and watched me leave. Something about him made me never want to return.

CHAPTER SIXTEEN

Flincher Funerals and Crematoria sat on the edge of Lesterville, a quaint little town of less than 1000 people. The former mining town was now dedicated to tourism with plenty of canoeing and camping in the summer. Now, in the spring, it was dead quiet and even quieter where Flincher Funerals sat. As if the rest of the buildings sensed something amiss, they were built far away. There was plenty of good Main St. property available, but nobody was getting close to Flincher. And I could see why. The building wasn't at all what I expected in a funeral home. There were no columns evoking the South or some bygone era. There were no flower beds or well-manicured anything. Flincher Funerals was in an industrial building with corrugated metal siding. The lime green paint had peeled off in spots and rust ringed the main door. It looked more like a place that people got killed in than a place for sending off loved ones.

"That is the worst funeral home in the world," I said.

"Mercy!" Tiny grabbed my arm and tried to force me to hide for about the thousandth time. I didn't want to hide and he couldn't make me. I kept popping up. Sometimes it wasn't even of my own accord. It just happened. Instinct, I guess. I had to see where I was going.

"Give it up. We're here."

"What's Tommy going to say?"

"Nothing if you don't tell him."

He groaned. "If you get shot because I couldn't do my job, I'll never recover. I'll have to throw my damn self off a bridge."

I rolled my eyes and plopped over. "Fine, but only so you don't jump off a bridge."

"I should've said that earlier."

"You should've."

Phelong told Gerry to turn right in a low, tense voice. I could see their heads over the back of the seat and little beads of sweat were forming at their hairlines. I felt bad for making them go into the bowels of Flincher Funerals. I thought about saying that I should be the one who was worried since someone tried to murder me in a funeral home once, but it probably wouldn't be helpful.

To distract them from the sense of impending doom, I said, "So how does he stay in business? Who would want a funeral here?"

Phelong glanced back at me. He was all flushed and jittery. "Flincher's cheap, fast, and he doesn't ask any questions."

That has a bad ring to it.

"Like what kind of questions?"

"Last year, Callie Bacon's husband fell into their cistern and died," said Gerry.

"So?"

Phelong shifted in his seat as Gerry parked, took a deep breath, and got out.

"It happened two days after he smacked the crap out of their six-year-old in the Quik Mart," said Phelong.

"Stuff happens. It doesn't mean anything," said Tiny.

"Sheriff Greer was having his annual family camping trip down at Taum Sauk. Harry fell down the cistern early in the morning and Callie had the funeral and cremation before five o'clock. They never even called us."

"That's crazy fast," I said.

"She killed him," said Tiny.

"Yeah, she did and Flincher just burnt up the evidence. No problem."

"So everybody knows about Callie and Harry?" I asked.

"And everybody knows about Flincher. Callie sold Harry's truck for 5000 dollars at noon. We all know who got that money."

"Callie sounds like a woman who gets things done."

"She was reading that Stephen King book, *Dolores Claiborne*, at the time. Her sister told me," said Phelong.

"What did the sheriff say when he got back?" asked Tiny.

Phelong shrugged. "It was a done deal and everybody hated Harry anyway."

A grinding noise erupted in front of the squad car and Gerry got back in. "Somebody owes me something."

"What happened?" asked Phelong.

"I don't want to talk about it." Gerry pulled the car into a darkened garage and left it idling.

"Ya think he's gonna turn on the lights?" asked Tiny.

"Probably not," said Phelong.

I sat up and blinked in the gloom. We were parked next to the old hearse and two more stalls filled with packing crates the shape of coffins. I did not want to get out.

A door at the back opened with a sickly yellow light outlining Flincher's hump, and everyone sucked in a breath.

"We have to get out," I said.

"Do we?" asked Tiny.

"Yes, we definitely do." Somehow, I didn't move. I wasn't much troubled by my previous funeral incident. It happened and I survived, thanks to Aaron, and I hadn't relived it since. I'd let it go until seeing Flincher in that doorway. He was so much scarier than my would-be murderer was.

Just when I was about to say, 'Screw it. Let's go', someone came into the light and pushed Flincher aside. The spiky hair said it was Dr. Watts, and we all started breathing again.

She stomped down the stairs into the garage and flung open Gerry's door. "What are you waiting for? Time's a wasting."

"Well, I, um..." muttered Gerry.

She chuckled. "It's just the bogeyman. Don't be such a scaredy-cat."

"Please don't call him the 'bogeyman,'" said Phelong.

"Like Flincher's any better. Come on." She leaned in. "Mercy, you're as bad as these nincompoops. A fine thing for my ex-granddaughter to pull."

"Puhlease." I scoffed and got out.

Flincher pushed a button and the garage door closed, bathing us in darkness.

"Flincher!" yelled Dr. Watts.

A light flickered on in response.

"Better?" she asked me.

"I'm fine," I said, coming around the car and heading for Flincher, despite every instinct in my body saying don't do it, don't go in there.

"Miss Watts, a pleasure to see you again," said Flincher.

"Yeah, it's swell. Where's the body?" I asked.

"In the basement."

Of course it is.

"Lead the way."

I followed Flincher through a warren of small rooms filled with funeral paraphernalia, fake flowers arranged in the shape of hearts, stacks of chairs, and coffin pedestals. Each room had a unique smell, ranging from the rot of narcissus to formaldehyde to wiener schnitzel. At the end of the wiener schnitzel room, Flincher stopped and I nearly ran into him. The smell of possum emanating off him, combined with the wiener schnitzel and decomp, caused me to involuntarily hork. Flincher slowly turned and glanced past my shoulder. The room was empty, except for us, and I stepped back. Distance was a good thing. A weapon would've been better.

Flincher looked me up and down. "You appear to be healthy."

"Er...yeah," I said. "How much farther?"

"Are you hungry?" he asked and it was totally different than when Aaron asked. Aaron wanted to feed me, make me happy. Flincher was up to something else entirely.

"No. Not at all."

Disappointment briefly flitted over his features. "Will you be getting your hair cut at the castle?"

"What? No. Take me to the body," I said.

He raised his craggy eyebrows. "Have you had your blood drawn recently?"

"What the hell? No, I haven't."

"I have a little lunch prepared." Flincher reached for my hand and I recoiled. "Your skin is so lovely."

"Flincher!" yelled Dr. Watts as she entered the room. "I might've known you'd take the long way round."

"It's a direct route."

"Only if you want a few minutes alone with Miss Watts."

He lifted one shoulder and eyed me like a science experiment. "Shall we?"

"We shall." Dr. Watts brushed past him and opened the door, revealing a rickety metal staircase with a naked lightbulb hanging down from the ceiling on a frayed cord. "Mercy, let's go."

Flincher went to follow and she held up her hand. "Not you. Just Miss Watts and her bodyguard."

Tiny came into the room. He had one hand on his weapon and the other one in a fist. "You shouldn't have left me."

"I didn't know I had," I said.

We went down the stairs into the bowels of the funeral home. How anyone could send their loved ones to that place was a mystery to me. I'd have to be desperately broke to do it.

Dr. Watts told me to go all the way down and take the second door to the left. Like every other door in Flincher's domain, it was unmarked. I opened the door slowly for Tiny's benefit. His breathing was rapid, more rapid than it should've been for a flight of stairs. The funeral home was getting to me and it was definitely getting to him.

I was afraid Cherie's naked body would be exposed on a slab, but it was covered with a sheet in the only well-lit room in the place. Dr. Watts' equipment was shiny and clean and there was no smell, which was a relief. She had very nice equipment and a small but complete lab. It was a sweet setup for a town that hadn't had a murder to investigate in forever. The Callie and Harry situation didn't count and the equipment was spanking new.

"How did Lesterville afford this?" I asked. "You don't even have a Wal-Mart."

"Grants. I can be very persuasive."

I imagined by persuasive she meant she bothered people until they gave her money. That's what my mother would've done. It worked for the Widows and Orphans Fund.

Dr. Watts closed the door behind us. "Sorry about Flincher. You shouldn't be alone with him. Nobody should, including me, I suppose. Before we go any further, never accept anything to eat or drink in this place. Never."

"No problem," I said. "Why?"

"There have been incidents."

"Like..."

"Severe vomiting and hallucinations to name two."

"He's poisoning people. Why doesn't the sheriff do something about him?"

She shrugged. "It's eater beware around here. Besides, he couldn't prove it was Flincher and nobody died. Did he ask you for blood?"

"He asked if I'd had blood drawn."

"Figures. He'll probably ask if he can buy some off you."

"He buys people's blood. What the hell for?" asked Tiny.

She walked over to the lone table in the middle of the room and stood by Cherie's shoulder. "I don't think he drinks it."

"That's comforting," I said.

"I think so. He'll definitely want yours, beautiful, healthy, and smart. You're everything he likes. There're a select few townspeople who will sell to him, but new blood is always of interest to the man."

"You're kinda freaking me out."

"Sorry, but you need to know. The man is devious and not as frail as he looks."

"You think he'd attack her?" asked Tiny.

She shook her head. "No, no. He doesn't attack humans. He finds other ways to get what he wants." She picked up the edge of the sheet. "Now on to the reason you're here." She pulled back the sheet and exposed Cherie's head and shoulders. There was a faint squeak behind me and I turned just in time to see Tiny go down. It was like watching a tree fall in the woods, very slow and surprisingly quiet.

"First body?" asked Dr. Watts.

I knelt beside Tiny and I checked his vitals. "I doubt it. He was in Iraq and Afghanistan."

Tiny groaned and we rolled him onto his side, in case he threw up.

"War is different," she said. "I saw plenty of bodies when I was a nurse in Vietnam, but I barfed in Gross Anatomy."

"Really?"

"Oh yeah. Real *Exorcist* barfing. I was also the only girl. The boys took bets on how long I would last. I made it through medical school just to bug them."

"Sticking it to the man."

"Many times. Don't bother poor Tiny. He's better off down there."

We went back to the table and I blew out a breath. Twenty-four hours ago this had been a live woman, beloved by her children with a long way to go in life. Now she was here and every plan she had was over.

"Mercy?"

"Go ahead. I'm fine."

She showed me Cherie's neck and the finger marks. "They have an odd pattern to them."

"Gloves?" I asked.

"Yes, but they're unusual."

The measurements proved the fingermarks to be from a large person, at least six feet with thick fingers. I hadn't seen any women tall or beefy enough to make those marks. I'd have to see about the staff, but I thought we could safely say it was a man. Dr. Watts touched a computer keyboard at the desk and an x-ray lit up on the screen. She used a pointer to show me the head wound.

"Do you see it?" Dr. Watts asked.

I wanted to say yes and seem like I knew what I was doing, but her sharp eyes were on me and Dr. Watts wasn't a woman easily fooled. "I see the bleed, but I don't know what it means."

She nodded approvingly. "It's a slow bleed. It took one to three hours to get to what we're seeing here." She waited as the information sank in. I turned and paced back and forth beside Cherie's body.

"So there was a huge gap between the head injury and the strangling that killed her," I said finally.

"Yes."

"Could it have been before midnight?"

"When anyone could've left the castle? Yes," said Dr. Watts.

"Would the head injury alone have killed her?"

"Hard to say. If she'd gotten help, she would've lived, in my opinion."

This change made my head hurt. I'd assumed both injuries happened in rapid succession. Cherie had definitely left the building before the alarms were set, so it sounded like she'd been lying in the rock garden for at least an hour, perhaps longer. This was a fact I hadn't expected. Would the person who gave her the head injury in the rock garden come back later, using my code, to make sure she was dead? Maybe, but I didn't think so. If they were so set on killing Cherie, why not just finish her off in the rock garden? And what was she doing for the rest of the time before the head injury? Or did she get clobbered immediately upon leaving the castle?

"This changes everything," I said. "And it's much worse."

"I'm afraid so," she said.

"Why wouldn't it be? I'm here after all."

Dr. Watts made her sneezing noise. "You do have a track record. I particularly liked your stint in New Orleans. How many crimes were there in the end?"

"Depends on how you count." I went over to Tiny and helped him sit up.

"What happened?" he asked.

"You fainted."

"Nah. I don't faint. Men don't faint."

I punched him in his beefy shoulder. "But women do?"

"Didn't mean that."

"Whatever."

Dr. Watts gave him a bottled water and called Phelong, asking where the rest of her evidence was. I gathered it was still in the car with them, and they had no intention of moving. She ordered them to bring it in or she would tell Gerry's mom about the cow tipping he'd been up to.

"They're coming. Idiots." She gently pushed Tiny back down from his attempt to stand. "I have more evidence for Mercy to see. I don't recommend it."

"I'm better," he said.

"I know," she said softly. "I know."

I stood up, but I didn't want to. Usually, more evidence was a good thing. This time I wasn't so sure it would be.

Dr. Watts and I returned to the table and I ran the possibilities through. Maybe Cherie was raped after all or dying of some dreadful disease.

"Your victim was in excellent health, for the most part," she said.

"For the most part?" I asked.

"Are you familiar with cutting?"

It took me a second because it was so unexpected. "A little. Why?"

She pulled down the sheet to Cherie's waist and rolled over her right arm. Thin white scars marred her skin from her forearm nearly to her armpit. "It's the same on the other side."

I almost reached out and touched the delicate skin she'd slit open. "I wonder why."

"It's your job to find out," said Dr. Watts.

My eyes jerked up to meet hers. "What's this got to do with her murder? These are old."

"They are old. I would guess she began cutting in her teens, but these," she pulled down the sheet farther, "are new, done in the last 24 hours."

Cherie's thighs were crisscrossed with angry red slits, fresh with no signs of healing. I forced myself to look closer. Some of them were quite deep, right down into the muscle. So painful. What would cause a person to do that to themselves? I remembered one of my teachers in nursing school talking about cutting. She said something about the pain being a release. Cherie must've needed a big release.

"She started cutting again while at the castle. I wonder if it's common to start up at her age."

Dr. Watts fingered the edge of the sheet. "In my experience, cutting starts for a specific reason. If the reason isn't resolved, they can start again when certain triggers occur."

"Your experience?" I asked. "Since when do pathologists handle cutters?"

"What are you talking about?" asked Tiny, still seated on the floor.

Dr. Watts looked at me in a way that said she wanted to say something that she'd rather Tiny didn't hear.

"Nothing," I said. "Just trying to nail down the timeline."

"Oh. Okay." He didn't make a move to stand.

Dr. Watts smoothed the sheet. "Your grandfather doesn't know."

"Know what exactly?"

She glanced over at Tiny then lifted the hem of her scrub top. Pale scars like spider webs spoiled her smooth skin. They covered her entire abdomen. I didn't know what to say and, for once, I stayed silent.

"You see I had nice arms and legs. The stomach was much easier to conceal."

Now silence was wrong. I knew that, but what do you say to such a revelation. It was so painful, so private, I found it hard to bear. "Why?" I managed to squeak out.

"When I went to Vietnam as a nurse, I had no fear. I thought I knew what I was getting into. I didn't. I wasn't prepared. No one was, but it was especially hard on me. I was a pampered only child. Even my nursing school protected me from the harsher side of medicine. I didn't do an ER rotation. It wasn't required. Over there, people were dying every day in hideous, unspeakable ways. I made mistakes I couldn't take back. No place was safe. There were times I thought I wouldn't make it out alive, but I was never injured. I was lucky. So many weren't."

"You were punishing yourself for living?"

She shrugged. "I don't know what I was doing."

"How'd you hide it from my grandpa?" I asked.

"We got married on leave in Hawaii in a whirlwind. It didn't last long and we hardly saw each other what with the war. I convinced him I was shy and always kept a top on. When we were together, it was better anyway. Ace had a way of making me forget all the bad things. I stopped when I got back to the States and began med school," she said.

"Did you ever start again?"

"No, but I'm sure I would have if I'd ever been in a war zone again. Mayhem was my trigger. That's why I ended up out here after years of practicing in Kansas City. It's very quiet."

"I can see that, but why in the world did you become a pathologist. Every day is death."

"The patients are already dead and they certainly can't suffer if they're already gone."

"Oh." I counted the scars on Cherie's arms. There were a lot, criss-crossing and some on top of each other. "This went on for a long time."

"Looks like it." She pointed to the fresh cuts on Cherie's leg. "No hesitation marks. She went headlong back into it. She needed the release. What went on over there at the castle?"

"Nothing that I know of."

"Exactly."

Tiny tried to get up. "What did you decide?"

I helped him as Dr. Watts covered the body. "Nothing yet."

"Are we getting closer?"

"Not really. It just got a whole lot more complicated."

Tiny glanced at Cherie's shrouded body and swallowed hard. "How?"

"Cherie was attacked twice. Once possibly before the lockdown and once after.

"You mean the guy attacked once and came back to strangle her. Why? She looked like an ordinary mom to me."

"I don't think he did," I said.

"She's definitely dead," said Dr. Watts with a wane smile. "I notice these things."

Tiny clutched his stomach. "Yeah, she is."

"I mean, I don't think he came back. It was two people. Two sepa-rate attacks."

"I like it," said Dr. Watts.

"But why two? The guy who cracked her on the head probably just came back to get rid of the body and discovered she was still alive," said Tiny.

"That makes sense, except he didn't."

"Didn't what?"

"Get rid of the body. We found her in the love garden."

"Oh yeah. Well...maybe he just wanted to finish her off."

Dr. Watts crossed her arms. "Maybe, but if he wanted to kill her, the rock garden was the time to do it. She would've been unconscious for a period of time. Easy as pie then. Why wait so long to do the deed? She could've gotten up and alerted the staff."

I shook my head. "It doesn't make sense. This was a crime of passion complete with regret."

"Because of her clothes?" asked Tiny.

"Exactly. If you planned to go back and kill her, you wouldn't regret it and cover her up. You dump her in the river and hope for the best."

"So it is two," said Dr. Watts. "This isn't so hard. The Castle has a code system. Who left after the lockdown?"

"Me," I said.

"You?" asked Tiny, his eyes going wide.

"My code anyway."

"Did you give someone your code?" asked Dr. Watts.

"Of course not. I don't even know it. I flushed it like John said. I wasn't planning on going out or letting anyone in."

"So who would know it?"

"John and Leslie, I presume, but they know my dad. There's no way they'd involve me if they wanted to kill someone."

Dr. Watts made her sneezing noise. "Those two. They wouldn't make such a mistake. Certainly not."

"What do you know about them?" I asked.

"Nothing that concerns you."

"That's not comforting."

"I'm a pathologist. I don't do comfort."

"You might be interested to know that there was a shooting out at Cairngorms last night," I said, nice and casual.

Her brow wrinkled and her eyes went back to Cherie's body. I could see her having a moment of doubt about the cause of death and then shaking it off. "Why wasn't I called?"

"Because there's no victim." I told her what happened and Tiny looked longingly at the door.

"Where are those idiots?" she exploded and called the deputies.

There was a faint ringing outside the room. Dr. Watts stalked over and flung open the door. "What are you doing?"

Gerry dropped his phone that they had both been looking at. "Nothing."

"What are you waiting for? Get in here."

Phelong picked up the phone and they shuffled their feet, glancing at Cherie's shrouded body.

Dr. Watts pointed at them. "Let me remind you that she's dead and can't hurt you. Flincher's alive and there's a good chance that he would."

They were in the room in two seconds flat. Flincher was definitely scarier than a body in pretty much everyone's opinion. Dr. Watts took the evidence box and sorted through the various bags. Some she'd send off to bigger labs and others she'd handle herself.

"So," she said to Phelong and Gerry, "you mucked up the other murder."

"There's no body," said Gerry.

"And you think you're off the hook."

"What are we supposed to do without a body?" asked Phelong.

"What are we supposed to do without the blood?"

Phelong had the good sense to blush and stutter. Dr. Watts whacked him on the shoulder. "Don't be too hard on yourself. This is what I call a blessing in disguise."

"What?" I gasped. "There was a crime. I know there was."

"I don't doubt it. But no one from around here has been reported missing. Your victim was from out of town."

"That makes it okay?"

"Think about it, Mercy."

I thought about it and came up empty. Murders went unsolved. It happened.

"My dad would never let this go," I said.

"You're wrong about that. Tommy Watts knows what's what. You weren't sent to John and Leslie by accident."

"You suspect them."

"I didn't say that." She clapped her hands together and gave them a furious rub. "Alright now. Who wants to help with organ weighing?"

Phelong and Gerry didn't hesitate. They ran out and slammed the door. Dr. Watts burst into laughter and slapped her knee. "Gets them every time."

It looked to me like the autopsy was done, but I was still nervous. "Is there any other evidence I should know about?"

"Sadly, no," she said. "Cherie's nails were clean and the only blood was hers. She wasn't raped. Good call on that. I'd say you're looking for a man six feet or over."

"Nothing else?" I asked.

"Afraid not. I swabbed her neck and face, but, unless he spit on her, we're going to get bupkiss." She smiled at Tiny, who wasn't looking so good since the mention of organ weighing. "You can go. I just wanted to impress upon you Cherie's mental condition at the time of her death."

"I get it," I said.

She narrowed her eyes at me. "What do you get?"

"That she had a history with someone at the castle and they killed her."

She nodded. "I've got to sort out this evidence. What there is of it."

"What's next?" asked Tiny as he edged toward the door.

"I'm going to visit Uncle Morty in his lair and then talk to Lane," I said.

"Lane, the daughter," said Dr. Watts, tapping her chin. "The hands aren't big enough."

"I don't think she did it. But Cherie might've been able to hide those scars from her son, but not her daughter. They were close and it's hard to hide something like that for sixteen years. Plus, they shared the same room, the same bathroom this weekend. And while we're on the subject, Lane claims to have been in their room all night. How is it that she didn't know her mother got up in the middle of the night? They slept five feet apart and Lane's bed was the closest to the door. Cherie got up and got dressed, all without her knowing? And why did Cherie go out at all. Clearly she wasn't well liked by more than one person and by the state of her leg she knew it."

"She must've been scared," said Tiny softly.

"I think she was and there's only one thing that would make my mother go out in the middle of the night if she was scared," I said.

"What?" asked Dr. Watts.

"Me. Cherie was looking for Lane."

Dr. Watts gave us detailed directions on how to get out of Flincher's domain and I was determined to follow them, but then I didn't. Tiny led the way. He actually remembered the directions. I had to put them in my phone. We went up the stairs, took a right and a left, went through more storage rooms, all with questionable smells and found the exit. It didn't lead into the garage but outside into the continuing downpour.

Tiny grabbed the doorknob and I snagged his sleeve. "Do you hear that?"

"What?"

"That racket?"

We both stopped and listened. There was definitely a racket coming from a room behind us, a metallic banging and grinding.

"What do you suppose that is?" I asked.

Tiny shook his head. "I really don't want to know. We got to follow orders and go through this door now."

"They weren't orders," I said. "They were directions. It's not the same thing."

"In this case, it is. We got to get out of here."

"Puhlease." I rolled my eyes. "I'm pretty sure you can take Flincher."

"Flincher, yeah, but who knows whatall that old ghoul has hidden in this place."

"Aren't you the least bit curious?" I asked.

"Are you kidding me, girl?"

I slipped past his bulk so fast he wasn't able to catch hold of me. "Come on. Just a peek."

The noise was easy to follow, even over Tiny's muttering about ghouls and tempting fate. Normally, I would say I was tempting fate but that time, no. I had a feeling that noise was important. It was a Tommy Watts kind of feeling, the first one I'd had since getting to the castle. Something wasn't right. I had to find out what was making that noise.

I followed the trail to a set of double doors, once painted a sickly lime green but now half the paint had chipped off leaving bare metal. The noise was coming from inside and it was louder, not loud but just louder.

"Ladies first," I said, turning the grimy knob.

Tiny grabbed my arm, but I opened the door anyway. A rush of hot air flooded out with the faint smell of something burning. Tiny needn't have bothered. Flincher wasn't in there. The room was a large open area with a concrete floor and various types of equipment. In the center of the room was a metal box about seven feet tall and six feet wide. It had a door in the center and a control panel on the side. It reminded me of a pizza oven, except it wasn't pizza that Flincher was cooking in there.

The noise came from another piece of equipment off to the side, a weird stainless steel contraption. I had no clue what it was so I took pictures of the room. "We need to get the hell out of here."

"Thank god," said Tiny and we hoofed it back to the exit.

I ran out into the rain and around the building to the garage. Phelong and Gerry were in the squad car with the motor running. I hesitated when I touched the rear door handle.

"What?" asked Tiny, flinging open his door.

"We're leaving Dr. Watts here alone with him."

"She does it all the time." He got in and so did I but not without feeling bad about it.

Phelong peeled out of the garage and I caught a glimpse of Flincher in the doorway watching and a shiver went down my back as I laid down.

"What's wrong?" asked Gerry, turning in his seat.

I bit my lip. "This is a small town so you'd know if anyone died recently, right?"

"Sure."

"Did anyone? Die, I mean."

"No. Why?"

I looked at the pictures on my phone with my hands shaking a bit. "Because Flincher cremated someone today."

CHAPTER SEVENTEEN

I called Dr. Watts to tell her about Flincher and the cremation. I wanted her to get out of the funeral home. She didn't. I knew she wouldn't. My ex-grandmother wasn't a woman to abandon her work for anything less than a tsunami.

We drove back to the castle in silence. Phelong and Gerry were visibly shaken. When we stopped in front of the great hall, Phelong asked softly over his shoulder, "What should we do now?"

"Go home and sleep," I said. "I'll need you tomorrow."

Both sets of the cops' shoulders relaxed.

"Okay," said Gerry. "We'll call you if we hear anything about that body of Flincher's."

I said that would be a good idea although we all knew they wouldn't hear anything. That body was the body from the woods and we all knew it.

My phone vibrated. It was Dr. Watts texting me that she'd confronted Flincher. My stomach flipped over while I waited for the next text.

Confront Flincher? No! Terrible idea! Run away!

She finally texted again, "Claimed dog found dead in the woods. Testing equipment. Liar."

"No kidding," I said and sent her the equipment picture, asking what it was.

"What is it?" asked Tiny.

"Hold on."

Dr. Watts sent another text. "Processor. Crushes bones."

Sorry I asked.

Dr. Watts texted again. "F made call. Don't know to who."

I texted back that she should get out of there. She sent me an emoticon of tongue sticking out so I guess not.

Tiny poked me. "What?"

The arched black walnut doors opened and John walked out, his eyes on me and I knew. I knew like I knew my name. He did it.

"Mercy?"

"It's fine." I got out and went to John before Tiny could follow.

"I assume you have the cause of death," said John.

"Who was it?" I hissed.

"Your investigation is going slower than I'd hoped. Your victim is Cherie Marin, mother of two, mid-forties."

"Not her. The person Flincher cremated this morning."

His eyes fluttered in mock surprise. "Someone else died. I wasn't aware."

"Yes you were because you killed them."

"Why would you ever say such a thing? I'm just a spa owner, a friend of your father."

Tiny came up behind me and I stomped by John, saying under my breath, "Like hell."

I charged through the door, hung a right and was lost in three minutes flat, a new record.

"Mercy!" Tiny jogged up behind me, huffing and puffing. "What did John say?"

"Nothing," I said, spinning around. It's amazing how a place so unique could be without landmarks. All the armor looked alike to me, not to mention the paintings of aristocrats looking down their long noses. "Which way?"

"To where." He bent over, putting his hands on his knees, and I felt instantly guilty.

"I'm sorry. I shouldn't have run." I rubbed his broad back.

"It's...okay."

"I need to see Uncle Morty about a phone call."

Tiny groaned as he straightened up. "What phone call?"

I told him what Dr. Watts said and he reflexively grabbed my arm. "I'm fine," I said.

"Now Flincher knows that you know what he did. I got to call your dad."

"Flincher won't do anything. The evidence is gone. You can't get a cause of death or DNA after a cremation. I don't think you can even tell if the remains are human. It's over." The words hurt my throat to say them.

"It ain't over," said Tiny.

"How do you figure that? We've got no body and we're never going to."

"Somebody's gonna notice their loved one is missing."

"Do you know how many people are reported missing each year?" I asked.

Tiny shrugged. "Nah. Do you?"

"No, but I bet Uncle Morty does. He's weird that way."

"He's weird in many ways."

"Agreed but he's useful. First, we need to know for sure who Flincher called. If it's John, that cinches it."

Tiny directed me down a hall filled with still lifes of fruit and dead birds. I knew I'd never been down it before. How many ways were there to get to the Tudor Tower?

We went through a maze of halls and ended up at the foot of the Tudor stairs right where we should be. I put a foot on the bottom step and touched the oversized newel post. The top sported a carved globe with the world as Henry VIII would've seen it, including all the little details. There were borders and dots with the capitals like London and Paris. The details were amazing. They told you what time period you were looking at if you took the time to notice.

"You know," I said, "we can still figure it out."

"What?" asked Tiny.

"Who was cremated?"

"By looking at missing reports?"

"No. By looking at us," I said.

"Us? What did we do?" he asked.

"Nothing, but we're here. John and Leslie are here. The teams are here. "Whoever it was was trying to get in. They were shot through the fence and disposed of. It's not someone local, like some kid pulling a prank, so they were from away. Who would be trying to get in here and why would John kill them? This joint is pretty secure. Why bother?"

"It wasn't secure that night," said Tiny. "All those cameras were broken."

I smiled and crossed my arms. "Do you really think they'd let multiple cameras be down? I don't think so. John saw them on camera, trying to shimmy up a tree. Then he went out and shot them. It's almost like they were set up with those tree branches left hanging over. That's like an invitation to try and breach the fence."

"What about Cherie?" Tiny asked.

"What about her? I doubt our new victim would've climbed over the fence, attacked Cherie, and then waited around to strangle her before going back over. It's totally separate. Dr. Watts knows something about John and Leslie. They are not on the up and up. Cherie wasn't Leslie's first body."

"Cherie's the victim you're supposed to be working on."

I waved him off. "I will. That's why we're going to see Morty. That and the phone call Flincher made."

I found Morty's door all by myself. Not difficult since there were only two on the floor. But still, if anyone could've gotten lost it would be me. I knocked on the extra wide door. No answer. More knocking and still no answer.

"Let me." Tiny banged on the door as only a giant can and twenty seconds later Uncle Morty opened the door, red-faced and yelling, "What the hell are you bothering me for? Idiots! I'm working!"

"On my case, I hope," I said, plenty loud to get his attention.

"What case? I got a dragon battle going on." He pointed to his temple. "I'm gonna lose it."

I pushed my way past him. "Oh please. You can write a dragon battle in your sleep. It's your thing."

Uncle Morty preened, smoothing his stained and rather smelly sweats. "I'm good, but you got to work at it."

"You make it look easy," I said, smiling to myself. He was such a diva.

"It flows outta me sometimes."

Just like the smell of onion pizza. Gross.

"Well, you weren't the number one fantasy author the last five years in a row for nothing." I winked at Tiny from behind Uncle Morty's back and he smiled.

"I kicked that Martin's ass," said Uncle Morty and the preening got worse.

"Yeah, you did." I plopped down on the enormous carved bed and scanned the luxury Uncle Morty had rated. The room was nicer than any of the others I'd seen. It was completely paneled in gleaming wood, including the ceiling. An Italian marble fireplace took up half of one of the walls and there was a small chapel in a corner, adorned with gold crosses. "This room is fit for a king."

"Henry VIII. His room from one of them palaces," said Uncle Morty.

Henry VIII. Of course.

Uncle Morty fit perfectly in that room. All he needed were royal robes and red hair. He had the gout and obesity covered, not to mention the surly nature.

"Nice. So…I went to the funeral home and the mortician, who is super creepy by the way, cremated a body today. A body we can't account for."

I told Uncle Morty everything that happened at Flincher Funerals and he straightened up. I knew that would get him, especially after the flattery. I ran it down for him as he wedged himself into the chair at the desk by the little chapel. "Let me see." He typed more rapidly than I would've thought was humanly possible and thirty seconds later he said, "No one in a fifty-mile radius has been reported missing that stayed missing. No deaths. It ain't local."

"That's good to know," I said like I hadn't figured that out already. "How many people go missing on an annual basis?"

"Somewhere in the neighborhood of 600,000 countrywide."

I gasped. "That many?"

"Most show up. Ya got about 2,000 per year that stay missing. The missing ain't gonna help you though."

"No kidding. Can you break into Flincher's phone records?"

After another thirty seconds, he nodded, "You're right. He called the office line here at the castle. Call took all of two seconds."

"Two seconds? What can you say in that amount of time?" I asked.

"You can't say shit. He called a cellphone immediately after."

"Oh."

Tiny sat next to me on the bed. "Oh, what?"

"Flincher made a mistake. He called the castle line. I'm guessing John hung up on him and he remembered to call an untraceable cell," I said.

Uncle Morty nodded. "I'm gonna look into that Flincher. I don't like him."

"You've never met him."

"He wants your blood. I don't have to meet him," he growled. "You want the Cherie stuff?"

"Did you have time?"

"Hell yeah. I can do anything."

"I know. I know," I said quickly. Dear lord that man was testy when he was writing. Dad said he once tried an anti-anxiety drug when it got too bad, but all it did was make him sleep. Personally, I thought some more sleep couldn't hurt, but no one cared what I thought.

"It'll cost you," he said with a sly grin.

I rolled my eyes. "Are you going to charge me extra for interrupting your work?"

"Nope. I want you to eat."

"Huh?"

Tiny sucked in his lips and picked at the ornate tapestry bed cover. He was in on it. The giant was probably texting my mom, calorie counts and all. Traitor.

Uncle Morty spun around in his chair and pointed at me. "Eat. I want you to eat. You're worrying Carolina and that sucks. Eat for info. That's the deal."

I raised an eyebrow. "How will you know if I ate?"

"Aaron and Tiny. John and Leslie."

Groan.

I flopped over and sneered at him. "Fine, you old buzzard."

"Don't pretend like you don't like me. I'm a second father to you," he said with conviction.

"You're a deadbeat dad to me. Happy?"

"Hell, yeah. It's the closest I'll ever come to fatherhood. Call me when you've had your first course."

"Can't I just get it all over in one go?"

"Nope. It's one at a time or nothing. And no barfing. You got to get this shit under control with a quickness."

"I'm not an anorexic," I said.

"You're something. Eat and we'll talk."

I sat up. "No way. I need information now. We have a timeline."

"You can have dinner."

"Dinner?"

"It's five o'clock, fool. You're gonna eat or I'm not giving you a damn thing."

"I'll just call Spidermonkey and pay him to do it." I crossed my arms.

"I called that bastard already," said Uncle Morty.

Now that was unexpected. Uncle Morty hated Spidermonkey like herpes. He either pretended he didn't exist or was very colorful in his descriptions.

"What for? You hate him."

"I threatened the smug son of a bitch. If he helps you, I'll jam him up good. Eat!"

"You are an enormous pain in the ass. You know that?" I asked.

"Yeah, but you're gonna eat." He looked at Tiny. "Take this girl to dinner and keep track."

"There's no dinner for another two hours," said Tiny.

"Figure it out!" Uncle Morty spun back around and that was the end of that.

I had to have that information and Aaron was happy to oblige. The Thanksgiving dinner was all prepped and ready. I sat down in the copper pot kitchen and braced myself for more food than I'd eaten in two months. Aaron served it up on a platter. I'm not kidding. He served me on a platter and I ate it, turkey, mashed potatoes, cranberry chutney, the works.

When I was done, I couldn't sit up straight. Hell, I could barely breathe. I gave Tiny my phone and whispered, "Get info."

Tiny managed to get Uncle Morty to answer on the third try. I could hear his complaining over my own groaning. My stomach wasn't used to food anymore and it was not happy about the influx.

"I'm gonna put you on speaker," said Tiny.

"What's that noise?" Uncle Morty bellowed.

"Me," I said. "Sick. Your fault."

"You ate then."

"Yes. Happy?"

"Ya damn skippy. Tiny, how much did she eat?" asked Uncle Morty.

Tiny gave him every little detail. It was nauseating to hear. I slumped over and braced my head on the table. "Info!"

"Don't get your panties in a twist," said Uncle Morty. "I got it. Lane loved her mom. I went through her texts and emails. They were good. Normal mother daughter shit but the kid didn't want her dead."

"Good," I said. "That's a relief."

"Nobody's used any of Cherie's accounts since last night. She started texting the daughter at 11:13 and kept it up until 11:40. All texts stop after that."

I sat up and suppressed a belch. "That must be when she met up with someone in the rock garden. Did Lane get her texts?"

"Nope. The kid's phone was off until this morning. That's when she read them. She didn't know her mom was looking for her."

"Did someone lure Cherie outside?" I asked. "Where there any other communications?"

"She texted the son a few times asking about Lane, but his phone was off, too," said Morty.

Tiny sat down next to me and made the bench jump. "So she wasn't lured outside."

"She went outside to look for Lane. Somebody saw their opportunity and took it," I said.

"Two somebodies."

Uncle Morty began to type and we listened to the clicking for a minute.

"What else did you find out?" I asked. "How did she pay for this trip?"

"She didn't," he said.

"Come again?"

"Not a freaking dime for any kid on the Lions. Everybody else paid out the wazoo. She had 2500 to her name."

"Did any of the other teams pay for them by chance?"

"Nope. I checked. None of them had any contact with the woman, period."

"Can you get into John and Leslie's finances?" I asked.

"No," Uncle Morty said with an edge in his voice.

"What do you mean 'no?'"

"I mean I can't do it. Is that okay with your highness?"

Tiny and I exchanged a look. What the hell? Uncle Morty couldn't get into their accounts? I couldn't comprehend it.

"Okay. What about the backgrounds?" I asked after a minute of digesting that information and the giant lump of turkey in my stomach.

"Backgrounds? What the hell are you talking about? I got to get back to work. Those dragons won't wait forever," he growled.

"Yes, they will. You're the writer."

"Shows what you freaking know."

"Whatever," I said with a sigh. "Can you just give me the backgrounds?"

"Whose?" he asked.

"Everybody's. Two people attacked Cherie last night. I have to know the guests."

More typing.

"I got it," said Uncle Morty, but his voice had become suspiciously pleased.

"Well?" I asked.

"It'll cost you extra."

I banged my fist on the table. "I ate like 5000 calories."

"That's good for the financials. Backgrounds will cost you a reasonable breakfast."

"Define reasonable?"

"Aaron'll make it."

My head hit the table with a thump. Aaron's breakfasts were the bomb but eating one of his sausage hash brown concoctions would make me crazy. There wouldn't be a lettuce leaf in sight.

"Oh, come on," I pleaded. "How about a smoothie with kale. I can eat kale."

"You'll eat sausage and you'll like it," said Uncle Morty. He couldn't have been more satisfied with his blackmail.

"No. I can't. I won't."

"That's the deal. If you don't like it, solve it without me."

"Fine. Maybe I will."

Uncle Morty gave out a big juicy snort and hung up. Aaron had come over and was hovering, bouncing up and down and rubbing his hands together like the evil food genius he was. "What do you want to have?"

"Nothing."

"You got to eat."

"That's debatable."

Tiny shook his head. "It really isn't. Morty won't tell you if you don't eat."

"Fine." I pointed at Aaron. "Nothing too heavy. I can't feel like this tomorrow."

Oliver walked in with a furrowed brow. "Feel like what? Are you sick?"

"Not exactly." I attempted to straighten up and failed.

"Does it have to do with the investigation?"

"I guess it does." I told him about Uncle Morty's food for info deal.

"So you don't normally eat?" Oliver asked.

Normally? Has the last two months been normal? Hmm. No.

"That's hard to say. I've been on a...diet," I said. "What's up?"

"I wanted to see how the investigation is going. The boys are distracted. They think there's a murderer on the loose here."

"There is," I said.

That stopped him in his tracks and he sat down opposite me. "You really think whoever did it is still here?"

"Without a doubt."

Oliver ran a hand over his morning stubble. "I think we have to cancel the camp. I can't keep the boys here with this going on. I assumed..."

"That someone broke into the castle grounds and strangled one of the moms randomly?" I asked.

"It sounds stupid when you say it like that."

I laughed. "It's easier to think it was some stranger than someone you know."

"And it is someone I know," he said, softly.

We had a moment of silence that Aaron filled with pumpkin pie and dollops of rich whipped cream. I said no, but he persuaded me with putting in a good word with Uncle Morty. I barely managed to stuff the slender piece in my gullet without barfing. He didn't make me eat the decorative crust with pastry leaves and pumpkins. They were a marvel. How Aaron's stumpy little hands formed those tiny perfect images in the dough was a mystery.

"So," I said after several groans, "how is Taylor doing?"

"Not well. He came down to practice for a while, but he didn't get on the field."

"Understandable."

Oliver nodded, but he was tense and fiddled with his fork.

"Can he still take the prize?" asked Tiny. "He needs that scholarship."

"He does," said Oliver. "But I don't know. We've never faced anything like this before. There's always been a clear winner. This year it was a dead heat before his mom got killed."

"It could go either way," I said.

"Before it happened, yeah, but now Taylor can't perform. The kid's destroyed."

Tiny glanced at me and I nodded. "That's a pretty strong motive."

Oliver's broad shoulders twitched. "No. Nobody would do that."

"It's happened before. Think about that cheerleader mom in Texas," I said. "If Taylor can't compete, Enrique takes the prize by default."

He shook his head. "These people aren't like that. It's not win at all costs. Robin and Tim want Enrique to win because he deserves it. You almost want to give it to him after what the kid's been through."

"What's he been through?"

"He was adopted out of an orphanage in Ecuador." Oliver went on to tell me how Robin had met Enrique through her church group six years ago. He'd been seriously ill with malaria and needed medical help the orphanage couldn't provide. Robin and Tim paid for the treatment and eventually adopted him. He still had brothers and sisters in Ecuador. Oliver thought that Robin and Tim were supporting them in some way.

"This sounds like a movie plot," I said. "Poverty-stricken kid is saved by well-to-do family and goes on to rock whatever sport."

Oliver smiled. "It is a Cinderella story. Enrique would probably be dead without them. I'd hate to think you'd suspect them."

"I don't suspect Robin or any of the women really. Their hands are too small."

Oliver grimaced. "He strangled her with his bare hands?"

"He wore gloves but yes. I overheard Cherie arguing with a man the night of the murder before we all got to the fire pit for s'mores. Any idea who that was?" I asked.

"I have no idea." He looked into my eyes. "It wasn't me."

"I didn't think it was. You were at the carriage house. I suppose you could've run ahead and beat me there, but you weren't winded. The argument was quite heated."

"That's him then."

"Not necessarily but I'd sure like to know who it was."

"I can ask around," said Oliver.

"Please do. If you get a weird vibe from anyone, let me know," I said.

"I'm not sure I'd know a weird vibe if it was sitting right in front of me."

I laughed and barely held back a seriously unladylike belch that was bubbling away in my chest. "You would, trust me."

"Are you sure it wasn't a woman in the sweat lodge with Cherie?" he asked.

"Definitely."

"I heard from one of the cops that she was pushed and hit her head on a rock. A woman could've done that."

I drummed my fingertips on the table just like my dad. He said it helped him think and it helped me, too. "You're right. That could've been a woman and it was much earlier.

"How do you know?"

"Autopsy. The head wound bled—"

Oliver stood up. "I'll take your word for it. Dinner tonight? Smells like Aaron made Thanksgiving."

"I know. I just ate it." I put my hand over my mouth and did a mock vomit.

He laughed. "You can watch me eat."

And my suspects will all be in one room. Sweet.

"Your cousins will want you there."

I groaned. "Those three."

"What's wrong with your cousins?" he asked.

"Nothing, I suppose. On the other hand, everything."

"Everything is wrong with your beautiful red-headed cousins?"

Bridget sashayed in, carrying a heap of files. "Our ears are burning."

They were, too. Bright pink and glowing. My cousins were like Beetlejuice, say their names three times and they showed up out of nowhere. Then they taped your legs together and poured lemonade on your head if it was available. I would say that was kid stuff, but it'd happened as recently as Jilly's college graduation last year after she remembered that I graduated with honors and she didn't. There's always plenty of lemonade at graduations and I had just shaved my legs. I will never forgive that one. Never.

None of the Troublesome Trio carried any duct tape so I relaxed. "I was just wondering where you were."

"Completing our mission, of course," said Sorcha, smiling at Oliver but speaking to me.

"Your mission?" I asked.

"Interviewing the staff." She squeezed in next to Oliver. "We interviewed you, didn't we?"

"You did. I was very well interviewed." He smiled, looking rather rakish despite the baseball attire.

"We're all done," said Jilly. "Where do you want it?"

"It?"

"The stuff."

"You have stuff?"

Bridget plunked down her files and spread them out on the table like a fan. She pointed to each one in turn. "Kitchen staff. Housekeeping. Stables. Spa. Baseball. And reception. That's everybody."

"Wow," said Tiny.

"Wow is right." I opened the kitchen staff folder. Neatly written on yellow legal paper was each staff member's name, their whereabouts at the time of the murder, and a short section on their relationship to the victim. "This is impressive. How did you do this so quickly?"

"Mom's a party planner," said Jilly as if that explained it. She placed a three-foot-long roll of heavy paper on the table. "And here's the map."

"You made a map? You're kidding."

"Of course we made a map. This whole castle is a crime scene. You need a map." She rolled out the map and I'll be damned if it wasn't awesome. It looked like a copy of the original architectural plan of the property, showing the castle and its grounds. My detail-oriented cousins had color-coded the staff. The kitchen staff was red for instance. There was a red dot marking where every member of the kitchen staff was at the time of the murder and when the body was found. It was the same with each section of staff. They went above and beyond labeling the rooms of all the guests.

I poured over the dots and the different sections of the castle. Nobody admitted being anywhere near the rock garden or the love garden. Most of the staff was off the property overnight anyway, but there was a multi-colored line leading from the staff parking lot through the gardens to split off to different entrances.

"What's this?" I asked.

Jilly beamed. "My idea. Those are the routes the staff took to get into the building this morning." She pointed to tiny blocks on the lot. "Here are their names and arrival times. We cross-checked with John."

Holy crap!

"You rock, Jilly. All three of you rock. Dad will be seriously impressed."

My cousins grinned like crazy, popping out the Watts dimples and looking ready for more. Oliver was staring and I didn't blame him. The Troublesome Trio were seriously shiny. It was hard for me to stop looking at the happiness glow.

I forced my attention down to the map and traced the parking lot paths. "So nobody went into the love garden?"

"That's what they say," said Sorcha.

"Do you believe them?" I asked.

She tipped her chin down and became seriously adorable. I did that all the time, but I'd never gotten a view of it before. No wonder it was so effective when I was interviewing men. Oliver was glazed over.

"Do you really want my opinion?" she asked.

"Of course."

"You trust me?"

I considered it. "I do. What do you think?"

All three of my cousins nodded their heads.

"The staff knows nothing," said Bridget.

"But..." said Jilly.

"But?"

Sorcha leaned over the table. "They're afraid of John and Leslie."

"And the castle," said Bridget.

"Seriously?" That's what I said, but I wasn't surprised. Something was off about those two in a huge way and the castle was pretty unsettling.

"Oh, yeah. Weird things are always happening like the armor falling over or the pots being rearranged in the kitchens. The Smoking Room changed color overnight."

I wrinkled my nose. "What do you mean?"

"It was green when staff left on a Tuesday and it was blue the next morning."

"Somebody painted it."

The Troublesome Trio shook their pretty heads in unison. "Nobody painted. It didn't even smell like fresh paint," said Jilly. "It was just blue."

"That's...pretty strange," I said.

"You want strange?" asked Sorcha. "There were gunshots last night and it's not the first time. Laurie the head housekeeper said that John and Leslie always act like nothing happened, but she can tell they know all about it."

Jilly elbowed Sorcha. "We don't care about any other gunshots. The ones last night had nothing to do with the mystery we're working on."

I was intrigued. They were my cousins. Not stupid girls by a long shot but always more interested in purses than police work. "How do you know?"

"You said she was strangled and the gunshots were later," said Sorcha.

"It is a separate issue," I said. "So why's the staff afraid of John and Leslie exactly?"

My cousins took a long time to tell me that the staff wouldn't say anything about their employers except that they paid very well. The staff fidgeted when questioned about the security measures and they all had to pass background checks before being hired. You'd have to be an idiot not to think that was weird for a job at a spa. The staff thought John and Leslie were afraid of something.

"They think somebody got killed in the woods, but they don't have a clue who or why," concluded Bridget.

Jilly wrinkled her nose. "That's not helpful, is it?"

"It gives me a better picture of John and Leslie," I said.

"Do you think someone died out in the woods?" asked Oliver.

"Yes and I think Flincher was in on it."

"Flincher? The mortician?"

I told them about the funeral home and they were suitably creeped out. Bridget checked her watch. "It's almost time for dinner. We should change."

We all stood up. Oliver touched my elbow and said, "See you in the dining room." He left and Sorcha teared up as she watched him go. Oh, for the love of god. I could not handle any tears.

"What should we do next?" asked Bridget.

"You did a stellar job with the staff so how about doing the same with the guests?" I asked.

Bridget and Jilly high-fived. "We'll do it tonight."

We took off in different directions. The Troublesome Trio to their rooms, and Tiny and I toward our tower. I let Tiny lead me as I ran all the evidence through my head over and over again. None of the pieces fit. Everything felt so far apart. The body in the woods. Two separate attacks on Cherie. A nervous staff and a high-stakes baseball scholarship. Nothing really went together. Maybe Dad could've seen the connection, but they were eluding me completely and that thought made me tired. I did not want to go watch my suspects eat Thanksgiving dinner. I didn't want them to be suspects. It would be so much easier if it had been someone from the outside. As usual, I wasn't that lucky.

After ten minutes of walking through the warren of halls and rooms, I realized Tiny hadn't said a word. His brow was furrowed and his sharp eyes barely looked up.

"What's wrong?" I asked as we entered an armory. Weaponry covered walls and filled display cases. The castle must've cornered the market on the stuff.

"This weekend is off the hook crazy. I was supposed to watch you. None of this shit was supposed to happen."

"You've watched me just fine. And nobody plans a weekend full of murder except maybe the murderers."

"Somebody's gonna try to kill you," he said with a flush of anger.

I stopped short. "What makes you say that, I mean, other than the obvious? The Costillas don't know where I am."

"Don't people always try to kill you?"

"Not always."

"Name one time."

I couldn't think of an example off the top of my head. Richard Costilla in New Orleans was too imprinted on my brain. There were times. There had to be.

"Thought so," said Tiny. "I'm gonna sleep in your room tonight."

I cocked an eyebrow at him and his eyes went wide. "What're you thinking, girl?" Then slugged me in the shoulder and I went flying, crashing into a suit of armor. Metal flew every which way.

"Ow! Ow! Ow!" I yelled.

Tiny's mouth hung open and he just stood there.

"Tiny!"

He woke up and ran over, lifting me to my feet with one hand. "I didn't mean to do that."

"Oh yeah? Have you seen you? Have you seen me?"

"I don't punch people much anymore."

"Thank god for that. I honestly don't see how we can be related. Look at us. People think fee-fi-fo-fum when you come into a room. I'm practically a midget."

"You ain't that small and my dad was bigger than me."

"Holy crap. Tell him never to punch me, please."

Tiny kicked some of the armor away from my feet and didn't meet my eyes. "He died when I was ten."

I hugged him without thinking about it. "I'm so sorry. That's how you related to Lane so well."

"Yeah." He hesitated, holding something else back.

"Was he murdered?" I asked softly.

"Nah. Industrial accident. A crane fell on him."

I can't even think about that.

"That's terrible, worse than terrible. I'm so sorry."

He kicked more of the metal. "I was in the Marines."

"I know. My mom told me."

"I got discharged."

Silence. I wasn't sure if I should speak or let him go. Since it was me, silence wasn't so much an option. "Do you have PTSD?"

"Yeah, but it was a medical for shrapnel in my hip, not the PTSD."

That explains the lurching walk.

"When was that?"

"Three years ago. They put me on some stuff to help but..." He made a motion to his body. "I was always a big guy but not like this."

"What medications are you on," I asked softly.

"I don't want to talk about it."

Tiny walked away. I followed and elbowed him in the hip. "You can sleep in my room, but don't get any ideas."

He grinned at me and the sadness vanished from his face. "I don't know. You're pretty damn irresistible."

"Are you making fun of me?"

"Would I do that?" He laughed, big and hearty.

"Well, you better not snore," I said.

"You're lookin' at a man who loves fried everything. You think I don't snore?"

"God help me."

"He won't. My mom prayed on it and I still snore."

"That's not encouraging but tell me about her."

We walked to the Tudor Tower and I got to hear all about Tiny's mom. She was a woman of strength, conviction, and hearing impairment, thanks to years of his snoring.

Tiny and I made it to dinner exactly on time and it's a good thing. Either everyone else was starving or they were hoping to get in and out without being seen. From the number of downturned faces and fast-moving forks, I'm going with both.

Tiny went in to sit with my cousins. I hung back to watch from the shadow of a potted palm. I thought I might be able to spot some signs of guilt, but everyone looked the same. If I went by the hunched shoulders and furtive looks, they were all guilty, every single one. The Grizzlies sat together at the window and when they did look up, it was outside. The Vipers were closer to me and had no window but kept up a running dialog about the woodwork. There wasn't much I could do with that.

Tiny and my cousins laughed and went over their plan of attack for the next day. There were charts and graphs. I have no clue what they planned on charting, but the more power to 'em. They were out of my hair.

Deanna came lurching in, using the backs of chairs to stay upright until she plopped down next to Robin who frowned. "Where have you been?"

"Got," burp, "locked in the distillery," said Deanna loudly.

That broke up some of the tension as a nervous twitter went around the room.

A hand touched my shoulder. "See something interesting?" asked Oliver in my ear.

"Not really."

"They all look depressed."

"Or guilty," I said.

"That, too." Oliver drew closer and put a light hand on my waist. "Shall we?"

"Oliver?"

"Uh huh."

"Did anyone get killed in the distillery?" I asked.

"Martha Sweet, fifth owner, one of the stills burst and scalded her to death," said Oliver while wrapping one of my curls around his thick finger.

"Deanna keeps finding herself in the distillery."

"Like I said somebody has a sense of humor." He came in to kiss my cheek.

I pushed him back into the hall. "We need to talk."

He leaned against the wall and crossed his arms. They bulged underneath his polo and I was momentarily transfixed. "That's never the start of a good conversation."

"Depends on how you look at it."

"I doubt that." He took my hand and stroked it softly. "I know what you're going to say."

"No, you don't."

"Yeah, I do because I've heard it before. I'm a drug addict. You can't get involved with someone like me. I have a history and it's not great. I get that. But I've turned it around." He smiled and it was extremely winning. "My parents are speaking to me. John hired me for the camp and we both know if I did anything wrong, I'd be in Flincher's oven. So what do you say? You and me. It could work. If it doesn't, you could have Tiny squash me."

I laughed and squeezed his hand. "I could do that. Or my dad could have you shot. He knows people."

"He knows John in some other life, which frankly scares the crap out of me. I'm willing to risk all that."

"But…"

He groaned. "Not the but. There's always a but."

"But I'm not the one you want," I said.

"Huh?"

"See you didn't know." I pulled him by the sleeve and we peeked around the palm. "That's the one for you."

Oliver pulled me back. "Tiny? I must've given you the wrong impression."

I whacked his shoulder. "Not Tiny, dufus. Sorcha."

"Sorcha?"

"You said she was beautiful."

"I guess."

"You don't like red-heads? She's too smart, too educated, too organized." A flush came over my cheeks. What did he mean with that 'I guess'? I guess he'd killed too many brain cells to see that my cousin was perfect.

"Don't be mad. You said she duct tapes your legs together."

"She won't duct tape you. You're bigger than her."

"That's not as comforting as you seem to think."

"Don't be stupid. You just want me because of my face," I said.

"It's a hell of a face."

I whacked him again. "Hers is just as good. It's just not famous and that's a good thing. I have baggage. Lots of baggage. Do you really want the media on you again because it will happen."

He gently pushed me back against the wall, cupped my cheeks in his callused hands, and kissed me. He was into it and very good I must say.

I pushed him back. "I'm in love."

Where the hell did that come from?

His eyes went all bedroomy. "With me."

"Uh...no. I'm in love with Chuck." I slapped my hand over my mouth. "Oh my god."

Oliver dropped his hands and stepped back. "You sound surprised."

I threw my arms around his neck and hugged the hell out of him. "I didn't know for sure until you kissed me. I felt nothing."

"That answers a lot of questions in my life. I kiss women and they fall in love with someone else."

"Your lips didn't do it. You are, let me just say, a great kisser. Like crazy good. If I didn't love someone else, I'd be all about it," I said.

"Go on." He gave me a look of such utter seriousness that I burst into laughter and he joined me. We laughed until we fell against the wall, clutching our stomachs.

"I hope he's worth it," Oliver managed to wheeze out.

"He's not speaking to me actually," I said.

That made us laugh more.

"I think we might be pathetic," he said.

"I know we are."

Tiny came out of the dining room. "What're ya doing out here?"

"We repulse people," said Oliver.

I wiped my eyes. "We do."

"I don't know why that's funny," said Tiny.

"Me either."

"Are you going in?"

"There's another woman in there to repulse. Hell yeah," said Oliver and he walked through the archway still quaking with laughter but with his head high.

"You get weirder all the time," said Tiny.

"Tell me about it." I spun him around and we went in. Oliver was seated next to Sorcha and he did not repulse her. Dinner took over two hours and by the end, they were sitting so close their noses were touching. Can I matchmake or what?

"Alright," I said. "I can see my work here is done."

Oliver and Sorcha didn't look up. They were discussing burger joints in Brooklyn. They each had a top five list and they didn't match.

That topic could take until midnight. The merits of Pho took forty-five minutes.

"Where're you going?" asked Tiny. He was slumped in his chair, dejected after his healthy Thanksgiving dinner. His green beans were steamed, not sautéed with bacon and shallots. No gravy. No stuffing. The big man was sad, but he practically licked the plate.

"Pick needs a walk," I said. "John texted me that he's back from the kennel."

"Alright." He got up slowly, casting longing looks at Sorcha's untouched pumpkin pie.

I told him he didn't have to come, but that only got me a scornful look and a pat on the bulge in his waistband. He did let me run up the stairs and leash up Pick all by myself. I had a feeling that Tiny's protection had gone into overdrive and I'd be lucky to go to the bathroom alone.

We walked out of the castle and followed a path around the side toward our tower. This might've been Cherie's path and the thought gave me the creeps, but the night was beautiful. Pick sniffed every rock and then attempted to pee on them. He ran out of fluid after the first three, but that didn't stop him from lifting his leg.

We made it to the back of the castle and saw the yellow crime scene tape fluttering in the breeze. I stopped on the edge of the rock garden. Most of the windows that overlooked the garden were dark, but a few notable ones were bright yellow.

"They're all here," I said.

"Who?"

"Our suspects. On the map, they were all here in rooms overlooking the first crime scene."

"You think that it was dumb luck that got Cherie killed?"

"Not exactly. It was dumb luck that the killer had a room overlooking this area. I think he looked out, saw her, and came out to kill her. He made a decision. That wasn't luck."

"How can we tell which room it was?" asked Tiny.

"We can't. But there are still interviews to do. We haven't talked to the men yet and we can only cross one off our list so far."

Tiny readjusted his weapon and stared up at those ominous yellow lights. "Who?"

"Bill. Deanna alibied him by hearing the breathing machine going all night," I said.

"That woman's a drinker. How would she even remember?"

"She doesn't have any reason to lie so I'm going with it for now." I tugged on Pick's leash. He stopped his latest attempt to wee on a rock and ran back to me, wagging his fuzzy tail. "We'll find out tomorrow anyway. It all comes down to tomorrow."

"Why tomorrow?"

"The sheriff comes back the day after. It's tomorrow or we're the losers who had to turn it over to Springfield."

Tiny shook his head. "Failure is not an option."

I took his offered arm and we strolled back to the copper pot kitchen. John stood in the shadows by a tree sculpted into a square, reminding me of what was expected. No. He reminded me of what was required. Tiny was right. Failure was not an option.

CHAPTER EIGHTEEN

I woke up the next morning with a crick in my neck, my back, and both my feet. I didn't know you could get a crick in your feet, but I'm here to tell you it happens.

Tiny did sleep in my room. He took the bed because, let's face it, he couldn't fit anywhere else. I took the settee, which seemed like a good idea until I laid down on it. Tiny offered to take the settee but, since he'd have to sleep bolt upright, I said no. Now regret was imprinted on my every muscle. It wasn't long enough even for me. I slept with my head up on one hard wooden arm and my feet up on the other. Actually, slept was a bit too generous. Dozed maybe. To go along with my night on the rack, I had Pick and Tiny's snoring, the music of severely deviated septums. By the morning I was ready to crack Tiny in the nose with an iron skillet to force him into a surgical repair. He competed with Uncle Morty and that's saying something.

I was so happy when Tiny went back to his room and I showered in silence. Then we met in the hall and headed down to breakfast. Tiny led me, talking about how great my bed was. Pick sniffed every inch of the stairs, getting under foot and annoying me.

Tiny took the leash and made Pick heal, something I'd never accomplished. "I slept great," he said. "How're you feeling?"

"I don't want to talk about it," I said.

"Did you sleep?" He asked.

"Do you think Aaron has an iron skillet I can use?" I asked.

"Why you need an iron skillet?"

We entered the kitchen to find Aaron hovering over multiple pots. "I'll show you later."

When you least expect it.

"Hi, Aaron," I said. "What tortures have you prepared for me today?"

He didn't even turn around but began tasting several pots and muttering.

"Okay. We'll just have coffee."

Aaron stopped with a spoon halfway to his lips. "You hungry."

"For lettuce, but I'm probably going to need some more info from Uncle Morty so I'll eat your food for credit."

"I made biscuits and gravy."

Shudder.

"Bring it on. Where's the coffee?" I asked.

Aaron pointed past me to the fireplace. There was a deluxe commercial espresso machine built into the wall. Next to it in the corner was Lane, wrapped in a quilt and hunched over a mug. It was too early to face such overwhelming grief.

Why? Can't we just have a Mr. Coffee? Pour and go. Pour and go.

Before I could attempt to make something with that monstrosity, one of Aaron's assistants ran over and whipped up a cappuccino for me and straight espresso for Tiny. He gave me my cup topped with lovely foam and whispered, "Can I have your autograph?"

I smiled. "Let's see how the cappuccino is first." I sipped and, oh my god, I could've been in Rome. The foam was so thick I'd have to eat it with a spoon. "You're a genius. What do you want me to say?"

I signed his apron with, "Emil, you're my favorite baker. Love, Mercy Watts." He was embarrassed, but I was happy to do it, especially after he showed me his escargot pastries. Chocolate pistachio has always been my favorite and I'd never gotten a good one outside of Paris. Emil's looked so good I almost wanted to eat it.

"Please eat that," said Tiny. "Cuz I can't."

Emil smiled with an eagerness that reminded me of a cocker spaniel, and Aaron was watching from the stove, no doubt taking note. What the hell? I had to eat something and nothing in Aaron's pots was going to resemble lettuce so I took a pair of chocolate pistachios over to Lane and sat on the hearth next to her. "Want one?"

She didn't glance up. "I'm not hungry."

"Me, either."

"Then why are you eating?"

"A girl's gotta do what a girl's gotta do." I took a bite. Heaven but not a bit like lettuce and the guilt settled in around my heart. I shouldn't be eating and enjoying.

Lane peeked at me from under her thick lashes. "Why do you have to eat?"

"It's a long story, but it has to do with your mom's case. I need information and eating is how I get it."

"That's weird."

"You haven't met my father's best friend. He's the devil to deal with."

"Is he the writer? My brother said there was some writer in one of the towers."

"That's him. He's helping me with the case. Have you thought of anything new to help me?" I asked.

Lane's eyes snapped back to her mug. "No."

"I found some things out about your mom yesterday."

"Like what?"

I glanced around the kitchen. Everyone was well away, letting us talk in private. I scooted closer. "She had a problem with cutting."

A tear fell onto the edge of Lane's mug.

"It was something she dealt with as a teen and she'd started up again here at the castle, right?"

Lane produced a ratty tissue from the depths of her quilt. "How do you know all that?"

"The doctor told me."

"She's doing an..."

"Yes, she is," I said quickly to avoid the word autopsy. In my experience, it's best that way. "Just procedure and it's being handled respectfully. Dr. Watts is very good at this."

"Okay." Lane blew her nose and sniffed.

"Why do you think she was cutting again?"

"I don't know. She tried to hide it, but I saw the bloody towels. She had them soaking in the tub."

"Did you ask her?" I asked.

"Yeah, but she said she was fine. She said everything was fine. Yeah, right."

"Do you think the cutting had to do with your brother and the prize? She worked hard to get Taylor here and it might not work out. "

She looked me in the eye for the first time. "No way. She said it was in the bag."

"The prize was in the bag?"

"Uh huh. Taylor was going to win for sure. She said so."

Weird. Cherie *knew* Taylor would win? She was the only one.

"How come? Enrique's a strong contender."

"That's what I said, but Mom said don't worry about him."

"That's interesting," I said. "Lane, I figured some other things out, too."

She shredded the tissue and Aaron brought her a new box and a little trash can. "What else is there?"

"The timeline."

"Timeline?" she squeaked out.

I took her moist hand in mine. "You might as well confirm it. I already know you weren't asleep in your room."

"I was too."

"No, you weren't." I gave her the timeline, point by point. I didn't want to hurt the girl, but I needed to know where she was, who she was with, and if she'd seen anyone up and about at the time of her mother's death.

Lane held it in for a good two minutes before she admitted to going out of the castle to meet one of the players, Parker from the Grizzlies. They'd had a thing for about a year, mostly long distance.

"He didn't do anything to my mom," she said. "He wouldn't. He loves me."

"You were with him all night?"

"Yeah. All night. We were in the stables. I didn't think Mom would wake up. She took a Trazadone. I thought she was totally out."

"Were you drinking?" I asked.

"Parker had a bottle of vodka. It was gross and I just go to sleep when I drink." She teared up again and whispered, "Do you think Mom was outside looking for me and that's why she got killed?"

I squeezed her hand. "That's not why she got killed."

"It's my fault then. I did it. I killed Mom." She burst into a full-fledged ugly cry.

Well done, Mercy.

"No, no. It's the person who hurt your mother who's at fault. Nobody else."

"You don't understand."

David crossed my mind and then the guilt that plagued me afterwards. I didn't like to talk about what happened, but Lane needed it. I did understand. Sort of. David disappeared with two friends when I was sixteen. Maybe if I'd been with him. Maybe if I hadn't gotten myself grounded.

"I lost someone when I was your age. My boyfriend disappeared. They think he was murdered."

The squished up lines of her face straightened. "Oh my god. Really?"

"It wasn't my fault or my responsibility." I didn't exactly believe that but I sold it well.

"Did they catch the guy who did it?"

Probably not.

"Yes and he's in prison. He confessed." I didn't go further into it. She didn't need any doubts.

"Did it help?"

No. Lie. Lie. Lie.

"No."

Dammit.

"It didn't? How come? I want you to catch him."

I smiled. "It's complicated. I had to mourn David. His killer didn't have much to do with that."

"I'll feel better," Lane said, suddenly fierce.

I hugged her. "Then we'll catch him."

"Soon?"

"Very soon. Are you sure you don't know why the scholarship was in the bag?"

Her eyes shifted to the left. "No. She didn't tell me everything."

Aaron came over with a plate heaping with his homemade corned beef hash, over easy eggs, and biscuits and gravy. My mouth watered, but I couldn't eat it. I couldn't. I ate the pastry. That was bad enough.

"Morty said you want this," said Aaron.

"He did, did he?" I asked.

Blink.

"Eat it, Mercy," said Tiny, walking over. "If you don't, I'll have to. We're gonna need more information."

"I ate the pastry. I can't eat anything else. I can't."

Emil came and gave Tiny a large glass of green gunk. He groaned. I would gladly have traded.

"Don't be getting any ideas," said Tiny. "This glass of healthy, delicious kale, turmeric, and ginger is mine."

"There's apple," said Aaron as if that changed the whole thing.

"And apple." Tiny gulped it down and coughed. "Too...much...ginger."

"It's good for you," I said with a grin.

"Eat your happiness." He slumped onto the hearth and belched so juicily I could smell it. Gross.

He wavered back and forth. "I got a kale high."

Lane wiped her eyes and took the platter of calories from Aaron. "I'll eat it. You need information so I'll do it." She waggled her finger with its painted heart on the nail at Aaron. "Don't tell."

Aaron gazed over her head for a second and then went back to the stove.

"Is he going to tell?" Lane asked me.

"Who knows? You need the calories anyway. Eat it. I'll handle Morty."

Tiny leaned over me and sniffed. "I remember breakfast."

Lane forked up a big piece of biscuits and gravy. "I'll give you some. They're mean. That green stuff was yuck."

He pulled back and fixed a patently false cheerful expression on his face. "No. Go on with you. I've got to lose weight or I'm gonna have a heart attack."

"Are you a vegetarian?" she asked. "My mom was a vegetarian for a while after we got back."

Emil made me a fresh latte and I stretched out my thighs. "I'm trying to be. Tiny's not. Back from where?"

"Um…Ecuador. Mom and I went for two weeks of service. It was a church thing. That's why we could afford it."

"That's right. I saw the airline tags on your luggage. When did you go?"

"January," said Lane.

"Isn't Enrique from Ecuador?"

She shrugged and didn't look up. "I don't know. I wish I could go down to the Shut-ins. Mom loved them. She always took us every summer." She teared up and began shoveling in Aaron's food, going on autopilot eating.

Cherie went to Ecuador. How many people went to Ecuador? And Enrique was from there. Could be a coincidence. The US has people from everywhere. But…Enrique was special and Taylor's rival for the scholarship.

Lane finished half the plate and gave it to me. "I can't do anymore. That's a stink load of food."

Aaron was watching from the stove. I knew from the nervous jitter that he thought she didn't like it. "It's okay. I'll finish it for you."

"I'm gonna go see Taylor. He wants to leave, but Grandpa says Mom wouldn't want that. I don't know what to do," said Lane.

"Don't decide anything for now. But do me a favor and tell Aaron his food is the best thing you ever ate. He probably won't respond, but say it anyway."

"I like Aaron. He's so nice. He made me French hot chocolate." The tears began in earnest again.

"That's his specialty."

Lane spoke to Aaron and went out the door into the kitchen

garden. Tiny got me a fresh fork and I ate her leftovers as promised. My stomach rebelled, but I got it down.

As I scraped up the last bit of egg, I said, "That could be our first connection. Ecuador. What are the chances?"

Aaron gave Tiny a cup of green tea, no sugar. He choked it down. "I miss cream."

"Aaron, what do you think?" I asked.

"I like cream."

"Not that. About Ecuador."

Aaron stared over my head.

"I would kill for cream," said Tiny.

"You're hopeless. Both of you." I got up. "Tell Morty I ate and I want everything he can find on Cherie's trip to Ecuador and Enrique."

"Where are you going?" asked Tiny.

"To question Taylor. You stay here and mourn the death of your cream-filled life."

"This is hell. You don't know."

"Actually, I do. And when this is over, we're going to discuss that medication of yours," I said, standing up and doing a quick toe touch.

"I don't wanna talk about it."

"Well, then you shouldn't have told me," I said, grabbing Pick's leash. "Back in a bit."

I didn't find Taylor. Pick did. We looked in the carriage house, the castle, and the stables until Pick's nose brought us to the sweat lodge. Taylor sat inside, wearing his baseball gear and staring blankly at the center fire pit. There wasn't a fire, just cold ashes.

Taylor didn't notice us in the doorway even though Pick was sniffing like mad. Taylor was so still he could've been a statue.

"Taylor," I said softly.

No response. The boy didn't even blink.

Pick lost what little patience he had and yipped, dragging me through the door. Taylor jerked to attention. "What're you doing?"

"Looking for you," I said. "Sorry to interrupt."

"Whatever."

I gestured to a spot next to him on the curved bench along the wall. "May I?"

He shrugged, but he didn't want me there and I didn't blame him.

"I'm sorry, but I have to ask you a few questions."

"About Mom?"

"In part."

Pick sniffed the fire pit like it was made of meat.

"What's he doing?" asked Taylor.

"It's a mystery to me. He probably doesn't know," I said.

That got a slight smile. "He's a nut."

"He is. Are you up to a few questions?"

"Go ahead. At least you have a reason for asking," said Taylor, back to staring at the pit.

Pick pulled harder and nearly dislodged me from the bench. "For god's sake, knock it off, freak dog."

Freak dog did not knock it off. He barked. And then he barked again. I ended up dragging him back to the bench, clamping his squirmy body between my knees and holding his jaw. "Dogs are so not worth it."

Taylor laughed a little. "Maybe it's just poodles."

"It's pugs, too. Or maybe it's me. That's a possibility," I said, struggling with Pick's drooling jaws. "Are other people asking you questions?"

"Try everybody. They act like they have a right to know about us."

"Who's asking?"

"The Vipers and the Grizzlies. My team won't say anything."

"Is it the parents or the players?" I asked.

"Both. The Moms act like they give a crap about how I feel and the guys are just weird. I think they just want to know if I'm dropping out of the competition."

Pick broke away and frantically sniffed at the pit, now jumping up and trying to get inside.

"Fine, you idiot." I let go of the leash. "Are you? Dropping out, I mean."

He bent over and put his face in his hands. "I can't. Mom would hate that and Grandpa would go fucking nuts. Sorry."

"Don't worry about it. If anyone has the right to cuss, it's you. Have you talked to your sister this morning?"

"Yeah. She told me what Mom was doing." Taylor looked up and his eyes were watery. "Is it true?"

"It is. Do you know any reason why she started up again after you got here?"

"Stress, I guess." He buried his face again. "She wanted me to win so bad and the other parents were kinda dicks to her."

"What's the deal with that?" I asked.

"I don't know. Sometimes people would say stuff."

"Like what?"

"We're white trash. Stupid shit like that. We don't have any money, but I'm just as good as Enrique."

Pick went absolutely nuts clawing and barking at the pit and I had to yank him back and wrestle him outside, slamming the door. I expected him to run off, but he didn't. He clawed at the door and barked. I would question what I'd done to deserve this, but I already knew.

I sat back next to Taylor, gazed up at the stream of light coming in through the smoke hole in the ceiling, and brushed a sweaty lock off my forehead. "How well do you know Enrique?"

"Just from around tournaments. He's okay."

"Does he say anything nasty to you?"

"No. It's more the parents from other teams. The Grizzlies and the Vipers aren't that bad. They just act like Mom's not good enough, but she never did anything wrong.

She did something to somebody.

"Did you go down to Ecuador with your mom and Lane on that church trip?" I asked.

Taylor jerked to attention. "Why're you asking about that?"

"Because it's an interesting coincidence. Enrique is from there."

"I didn't go. I had training."

Pick banged against the door. I had to wrap it up or that fool would injure his tiny brain.

"Where did they go?" I asked.

"I don't remember. Some orphanage. They dug wells and stuff."

An orphanage. Ding. Ding. Ding.

"Did your mom say anything about Enrique when she came back?" I asked.

He shrugged. "No. Why would she?"

"I don't know yet. I have a feeling that this is the key."

"To what?" asked Taylor. "To who did it?"

I nodded. "Do you know how this trip was paid for?"

"Mom paid for it."

"Did she tell you she paid for it?" I asked.

He shrugged again. "I don't know."

Pick went batshit crazy, ramming himself against the door.

"I have to go," I said. "He's berserk." I braced myself and opened the door an inch so I could hopefully snag his leash. No hope. One inch was enough for Pick to shoot through. He charged past me and hurled himself at the fire pit.

"What the hell!" I yelled.

Pick leapt onto the pit and dove into the ashes. The lodge instantly filled with soot. I dove across the room, grabbed Taylor, and dragged him out. We fell out the door, gagging.

After I hacked up a lung, I asked, "Are you okay?"

"Yeah." Taylor sat up and looked at his formally white uniform. "Mom would be pissed."

"We look like chimney sweeps," I said.

"Hey, your dog stopped barking."

He had stopped and the sudden silence was weird. I'd gotten used the torrent of noise. "If he's dead, Chuck's going to kill me."

"The guy in the video?" asked Taylor.

"You saw that?"

"Everybody saw that. My friend Cassie has it as wallpaper on her phone. Is that him?"

"Yes," I groaned as I went to the door with Taylor at my elbow.

"Do you hear anything?" he asked.

"Not really."

The inside of the sweat lodge wasn't bright normally. Now it was dark and murky with all the soot in the air.

I squinted into the darkness. "Pick?"

There was a scrambling of nails on adobe and then a muffled sneeze.

"Oh thank god. Get out here, you nut."

Muffled bark.

"I'm not going in there to get you. I already look like a coal miner."

Muffled bark.

Taylor pushed past me. "I'll get him."

I snagged his jersey. "I'll do it. Stupid dog."

Taylor followed me in. The soot settled and a beam of dim sunlight spotlighted Pick. He stood on the fire pit with his four paws spread apart on the rim.

"What are you doing?" I asked. "Get down."

Muffled bark.

"He's got something in his mouth," said Taylor.

I held out my hand. "Drop it."

Pick dropped something both crispy and soft in my hand.

Please don't be a dead rabbit.

"What is it?" asked Taylor.

"I don't know. Grab his leash, will you?" I asked.

In response, Pick shot through the door and shook, letting off another cloud of soot.

Taylor and I followed him out into the sunlight slanting down in beams through the tree branches. Taylor grabbed Pick's leash and peered into my hands. "Are those gloves?"

They were gloves or at least I thought they were. But they weren't normal gloves made of leather or cloth. Those gloves were made of a woven plastic material that had been half melted in a fire.

"They're mechanic's gloves," I said, examining the pattern. It matched the marks on Cherie's neck.

"Mechanic's gloves?"

"People used them for other stuff. My godmother's used them for trimming their rose bushes because they're tougher than ordinary gardening gloves."

A flake of something broke off and fluttered to the ground.

"There's some paper in-between them," I said. "But it's mostly burnt."

"Can you read anything?" asked Taylor.

I knelt down and peeled apart the plastic. I shouldn't have. Dad would be pissed, but I had to know what was in there.

"It's a newspaper."

A piece of intact newsprint fell into my lap. It wasn't large, about three square inches.

"What does it say?"

I held it up. "It's about a band and some fairgrounds."

"What band?"

"The Charlie Daniels Band."

Taylor wrinkled his nose. "Who's that?"

"I think they're country. My grandpa likes them," I said.

"What fairgrounds?"

"I don't know. It just says the concert was a benefit for flood victims and had record attendance."

Taylor paced with a panting Pick at his side. "Do you think this has something to do with my mom?"

Cherie was strangled with those gloves, but I wasn't about to tell her son that.

"Maybe. They didn't burn them for no reason. The gloves look to be in good condition, but this newspaper is old."

"How old?" He turned to face me, his young face somber and sadder with the layer of soot decorating it.

I got to my feet. I can't tell, but it's pretty yellowed. I'll figure it out."

"How?"

"My uncle's pretty good at gathering information. I'll get him on it right away." I took Pick's leash back.

"Did you eat enough?" asked Taylor.

"Lane told you about that, huh?"

"Did you?"

I hooked my arm through his. "If I didn't, I'll eat more. My partner,

Aaron, makes an incredible hot chocolate. That ought to buy me something. You should have some, too. I'm guessing you didn't eat."

"Not very hungry."

"I thought so." I tugged on his arm.

"I'd rather stay here."

"You need a shower and we need information."

Taylor agreed reluctantly and we walked back to the castle.

"Don't tell anyone about the gloves or newspaper," I said.

"What about Lane?" he asked.

"You can tell her, but we don't want anyone else to know we have it."

Taylor frowned. "What do you think the…murderer would do if he knew we had it?"

"I don't want to find out and while we're at it no need to mention the mess in the sweat lodge to John and Leslie. It wouldn't be healthy for Pick."

"I won't tell them anything and I'll drink your hot chocolate if it helps," he said.

"I'll take my own medicine. You just keep your ears open and your mouth shut."

We approached the love garden and saw the police tape. Taylor fell silent and his body tensed. I squeezed his arm as I scanned the building. All those windows, anyone could see us. And anyone with half a brain could figure out where we'd been.

CHAPTER NINETEEN

An hour later, Uncle Morty bent over the scrap of newspaper with a magnifying glass he'd found in a drawer. It was a real Sherlock Holmes special and made me want to go creeping around moors at night in a deerstalker cap.

"It's about the Charlie Daniels Band and a flood benefit," he said.

"Elementary, my dear Watson," I said with a grin after I flopped on the bed. I'd showered in Uncle Morty's bathroom and was swathed in the fluffy bathrobe that luckily he hadn't used.

"Shut it, smart ass."

"Well, I already knew that and I didn't need a magnifying glass to figure it out."

"There's a tampon ad on the other side," he said.

"Also not so useful."

Uncle Morty growled at me. "I don't need any freaking criticism from the likes of you. There's soot all over my room and you washed that damn dog in my tub. I gotta work in here."

At the word dog, Pick put his head on Uncle Morty's pillow and sneezed. I'm not going to lie. It was gross. Black stuff sprayed out.

"He found a clue and, let's face it, you're not using the shower."

"You don't know."

"I can smell the evidence. Take a shower. That's gross."

He growled at me. "You're not creative. It's flowing here. I can't wreck it."

"And soap wrecks it? You're nuts."

"You're a nurse. What's creative about that?"

"Good care includes creativity."

"Bullshit. Get out."

"I will not." I poked Pick. "Sneeze. A big juicy one."

Uncle Morty stood up and winced. "What'll it take to get you the hell outta here?"

"Promise to get me more information about that newspaper," I said.

"How'd you expect me to do that?"

"That newspaper's important to Cherie's case. I need to know why."

"Hell. It could be about your disappearing body in the woods." He pointed to the scrap. "The shooter could've burnt the gloves and newspaper to hide gunpowder residue."

I slid off the bed and loosened my belt. "It's not the shooter's stuff."

"How the hell do you know that?"

"Because John is the shooter and he wouldn't make that mistake."

Uncle Morty's mouth fell open. I'd astonished him. At least I thought he was astonished. He might've been having a stroke.

"Uncle Morty? Are you okay?" I asked.

His mouth snapped closed. Then he grabbed his chair and wedged himself in with a grimace. Thank god. It really looked like a stroke for a second. "You think it was John?"

"I know it was."

"How?"

"The cameras for that section were conveniently out and that's his area. He wasn't remotely surprised or worried about blood in the woods. Most of the staff wasn't here that night and I'm guessing they don't have the kind of money it takes to bribe Flincher to cremate the body. It's John, and Leslie knows."

"Still got no idea who it was?"

"Nope, but this isn't the first time there have been gunshots in those woods. Right now, I'm more interested in Cherie. Are you going to research that paper or what?"

He raised a bushy eyebrow. "What do you suggest? That I find out how many newspapers ran this particular tampon ad and go from there?"

"You could or you could go with a flood benefit, The Charlie Daniels Band, and record attendance," I said.

He smiled, revealing what I feared was a two-day old piece of onion between his teeth. "You ain't as dumb as you look."

I snapped my fingers and Pick leapt off the bed. "Right back at you. And what about the rest of those backgrounds."

"Go have some brunch and we'll talk," he said, showing me his onion again.

"I ate like 3000 calories this morning," I said.

"And that was good for the newspaper."

"That sucks. I'll do it myself."

He snorted. "Yeah, right."

"See ya. I've got people to see, crimes to solve." With that, I flounced out with my super fluffy poodle and ran smack into John, who was standing on the landing.

I jumped back. Pick growled, crouching low and baring his teeth.

"Are you following me?" I asked, backing up and dragging Pick with me.

John ignored Pick and said, "Yes."

"Yes? What the hell? Who are you? I can find out, you know. I do have connections."

"Not the kind you'd need. Your father expects you to be returned to him safe, and there's a murderer on the loose."

"So you're watching me like a three-year-old."

"Like a prize possession, which I'm told you are...to some."

"Who told you that? Not my dad. He usually says I'm a prize idiot."

John didn't answer. "Call the doctor. She says you're not answering your phone."

Anything to avoid the blank stare. I had missed a bunch of calls. I'd turned off the phone when I went into Uncle Morty's room. He hated interruptions.

I turned away and texted Dr. Watts. She told me that she was done with the autopsy and I said I had an idea. Could she come out to the castle with some fancy equipment? She agreed and didn't question my idea. I had the feeling she was ready for anything.

"What have you found out?" John asked.

"Nothing. Information is a two-way street." I went around him and headed for the stairs.

"Not in my experience," he called after me.

I jogged up the stairs. Pick ran beside me, making a low throaty noise.

"Miss Watts?"

I stopped. "What?"

"Leslie would like to see you."

"Oh really. What for?"

"I wouldn't hazard a guess."

Pick and I turned around though I almost put the dog in my room but thought better of it after I saw the way John was looking at him. If that man could get rid of a human, he could certainly get rid of a dog.

We followed John to the armory, one of three from what I gathered. Leslie was waiting in the center of the room, which was more like a hall. The second we entered, Pick began growling and my stomach went into a knot. It didn't help that the walls were covered with decorative displays of swords and knives arranged in circular patterns. Leslie bent over a display case with an open glass top and for a moment there was a second shadow, belonging to no one, on the knives inside. I sucked in a breath and it was gone.

"Miss Watts," he said, charming as always. "How are you doing?"

"I think I saw something," I squeaked out.

John took my arm and squeezed my bicep. "It's better if you didn't."

"But..."

"But," said Leslie, "you'll never be the owner of Cairngorms Castle, right?"

"Right," I said with plenty of hesitation.

John squeezed again. "So you saw nothing because there's nothing for *you* to see."

"I say again, Miss Watts," said Leslie. "How are you doing?"

I peeled John's hard fingers off my arm. "I've been better. You wanted to see me."

"John and I would like a real update on your progress." He looked down into the case.

"In here?" I asked.

"It's as good a place as any."

As good a place as any? Right.

"I would've thought your office would be more appropriate."

John came around the other side of the table and opened that side's top. "It's my favorite room."

"I believe it." I was surrounded by weapons. John and Leslie were two of them unless I was very wrong about them. "I'm not prepared to tell you anything at this point."

"We're the clients," John said.

"I'm doing you a favor."

"And we're doing your father one by keeping you hidden and alive," said Leslie.

"I'll tell you whatever I know if you start telling me what I want to know."

John pulled out a slim piece of metal from the case. "This is my favorite piece, a Brown Bess bayonet used by the Black Watch."

"Fascinating," I said. "Are you going to answer my questions or not?"

John cocked his head at me and smiled. I was so startled my mouth fell open. The smile was natural but rusty.

"Now you're just trying to freak me out. Don't bother. I've been freaked out since I got here. It's not going to change anything," I said.

The smile dropped off his face like it had never been there and that was way more creepy. He reminded me of a mannequin.

"Don't mind him," said Leslie. "He has an enthusiasm for the Napoleonic Wars."

"Among other things," I said.

"What would you like to know?"

I went over, tightening my grip on Pick's leash, and took the bayonet out of John's hand. "Who paid for the Lions to come here?"

"You're very comfortable with weaponry," said John.

"I'm Tommy Watts's daughter. It was required. Now about the Lions?"

Leslie shrugged. "Our guest's finances aren't our concern."

We went around and around for ten minutes, but they weren't going to say a thing.

I placed the bayonet back in the case. There were three rows of the nasty things lined up and tagged with their particulars and provenance. There was a whole lot of death in that case and standing beside me in the form of John.

I closed the case rather forcefully. "Do you want me to solve this or not?"

"Of course. But, if you don't, we'll make other arrangements," said Leslie.

That sounds ominous.

"Good luck with that. If *I* don't solve it, you're going to be getting lots of attention. Springfield will be crawling all over this place. Right now, nobody knows I'm here. The minute the real cops arrive, my presence is no longer a secret and you aren't either."

"Are you threatening us?" asked Leslie with a smile. Clearly, it wasn't his first time.

"Hello. I'm here. There's been a murder. You think the press isn't going to notice?"

"I see your point." Leslie tapped his strong chin and glanced at John.

"She is Tommy's daughter," said John.

Leslie nodded. "Cherie didn't pay. We comped it."

"Why would you do that?" I asked.

"The team is talented. Taylor is talented. He shouldn't lose the scholarship because of where he's from."

"That's very generous," I said.

And a lie.

"If you won't tell me the real reason you comped this very expensive weekend, then maybe you'll tell me something else."

"What's that?" asked John.

"Are you missing any gloves?"

For the first time, they looked surprised.

"Not that I know of," said Leslie. "Should we be?"

I told them about the gloves in the fire pit, but it somehow slipped my mind to mention Pick's part in it. The poodle lay at my feet, making throaty growling noises. Despite the threat that Leslie and John so obviously posed to me and pretty much everybody else, I felt calm with a fierce poodle beside me. If nothing else, Pick could do some damage before John shanked him.

Leslie called the staff, asking about the gloves and I turned to John.

"Did the other teams know the Lions would be here? I had the impression they didn't."

"We don't let the teams choose their companions. They pick their week and that's it."

"But Cherie knew who would be here."

John merely stared at me. That line of inquiry was over.

Leslie slipped his phone into his vest pocket. "Our head gardener reports that a pair of mechanic's gloves are missing."

"From where?" I asked.

"His workroom in the Crystal Tower."

"Where's that?"

"It's the tower next to your original tower," said Leslie.

"Overlooking the rock garden?"

"Naturally. It's the one with the arched stained glass windows."

My chest got tight. "Everyone had access to the workroom?"

Leslie nodded. "The door wasn't locked and it's next to the exit to the rock garden."

"Alright. I'm going to call Phelong and have them come out to dust," I said.

"Of course."

"I want to know exactly how Cherie ended up with these particular teams."

John and Leslie remained silent. Something in the way they gazed at me said I wouldn't get another thing out of them and they sure weren't getting anything out of me.

"I see," I said.

I didn't really see. There was something about those teams. Something about them being at the castle together. That wasn't an accident. They could've told me more. One thing was clear. Leslie and John wanted the Lions there enough to pay for it. Why? Because they knew Cherie would get killed? No, Leslie was upset. He didn't expect it. I was sure of that. John, on the other hand, was blank. He didn't care one way or the other.

The other teams cared about Cherie being there and about her death, at least as how it related to them. They cared a lot. No. That wasn't right. Not at first anyway. It was only the Vipers who cared at that first dinner. Robin and the Grizzlies showed surprise and discomfort. But the Vipers? That was something else.

I found the Troublesome Trio in the library, collating data and working on the map.

"There you are," said Sorcha. "Do you have some new clues?"

"I do. Can I use your laptop?" I asked.

"Of course."

"Do we get to know what you're going to do with it?" asked Jilly, twirling a colored pencil between her fingers.

"Sure. I want to do a background on Cherie," I said, taking Sorcha's laptop to a cushy green leather sofa.

"Didn't Morty do that?" asked Bridget.

"No. He said he would and then he didn't. He wants me to eat more for it." I opened the laptop and went to a background investigation site I'd seen Dad use.

"Eating wouldn't be a bad thing."

"It's a bad thing. Trust me."

My cousins exchanged looks and Sorcha said, "You're awfully thin."

"You should talk." The Troublesome Trio were much thinner than me. Okay. Maybe not much thinner but my cousins were straight up skinny.

"But we're built this way," said Jilly. "You're not."

"You just want me to be flubbery again."

"We want you to be you again."

"Whatever." I put in what little I knew about Cherie. I had her license plate number and that was gold. Ten minutes later, Cherie's life was emailed to me in a nutshell, and it wasn't interesting in the slightest. No arrests. She was an LPN at a nursing home, did home care on the side, and delivered newspapers in the middle of the night. No wonder her kids loved her. The woman had no life. Worse than no life. Her husband died in a drunk driving accident. Car vs tree. Anthony wasn't her father as I had assumed. He was her husband's father, a retired Chrysler worker.

Cherie had a mortgage, which she mostly paid on time, and the minivan was their sole vehicle. None of this was helpful. It certainly didn't connect Cherie to the Vipers. What had Dr. Watts said? The cutting was from a long time ago. Maybe if I went farther back. Cherie graduated from St. Sebastian Senior High School in St. Sebastian, MO. I knew St. Seb better than I wanted to, having found a body there once.

I paid to get Cherie's school records and got them in another ten minutes. Her life was completely available. Nobody had any privacy. It was just a matter of money and interest.

Cherie's school records were no more revealing. She never got in trouble and graduated with a 3.3. She was seeing the school counselor for the last three months before graduation. That was odd. There weren't any records of her going before that.

I quickly paid for her medical records and they were pretty thin. She'd been healthy or at least healthy enough. Her parents didn't have health insurance. They used credit cards for a couple of ear infections, strep, and a yeast infection treatment. It wasn't until she was in college that there were records of depression and the meds that went with it. I couldn't see any details of her situation. Thank goodness for that. I needed to know, but it wasn't right that anyone with a credit card could know her most intimate secrets.

Jilly plopped down next to me and Pick jumped in her lap, making her squeal about his toenails before asking. "What did you find out?"

"Nothing. She had an ordinary life."

"That can't be right. How are you supposed to figure it out?"

"I'll have to be creative," I said.

"Then get to it."

"Thanks for the motivation. Let me think."

Cherie was depressed in college and all her adult life, taking a variety of meds to cope with it. But she went to the school counselor in 1987. Okay. 1987, it is. I found the online site of the St. Sebastian Herald and poked around their records. For a tiny town, the Herald had it going on. They had their editions on file back to 1980. Excellent. Not so excellent was the search engine or lack thereof. I had to go through the editions one by one, starting with the week Cherie had her first meeting with the counselor. Nothing. The big excitement that week was some kids vandalized both of the town's gas stations and I didn't think that would throw Cherie into counseling. I went back a week, another week, and then a third. That's when I found it in black and white, a front page article next to the article about The Charlie Daniels Band. The article I wanted was about a high school senior who'd fallen to his death off a railway trestle. Cherie was one of three witnesses. The kid was drunk. They all were. The article said that there would be a police investigation, but it was thought to be an accident. The boy's name was Quinn Hasselback. He didn't go to school with Cherie. He went to the catholic high school. Quinn. That was an unusual name. The Vipers had a Quinn, Nicole's son.

"I'll be right back." I jumped up and tugged Pick off Jilly's lap.

"Where are you going?" asked Bridget.

"To the parking lot, if I can find it." I wasn't even sure which door I'd come in, much less which one to go out.

"I'll take you," said Sorcha. "I have an excellent sense of direction, plus I've been studying the map."

"Thank god," I said. "Lead on."

We went through a maze of hallways and ended up in the copper pot kitchen. All roads led to food and it was not a good thing.

"Oh my god," said Sorcha. "What is that smell?"

Aaron was hard at work, stirring a huge stockpot with a wooden paddle. One of his assistants was slipping a white tube over what looked like a broom handle in the sink.

Pick went crazy, sniffing and wagging. I gagged. "Aaron! Why? Why would you do it?"

He turned and there was a white tube hanging off his paddle. It kinda looked like a ginormous condom. It wasn't a condom, but I would've sooner eaten a condom than what he had in that pot.

"Huh?" he asked.

Sorcha's shoulders heaved. "What is it? What is it? Oh my god. It's like something died but worse."

"He's making andouillettes," I said.

"What's that?"

"A French sausage made of intestines." Another gag. Myrtle and Millicent forced me to tour an andouillette factory in Troyes, France. That place should've made up another circle of hell for Dante. One entitled 'Smell.' After the tour, during which I utilized not one but two trash cans, they made me try a sausage during lunch. Myrtle said I must not dismiss things before trying them. Myrtle is usually right about everything. In that case, she was dead wrong. It was perfectly okay to dismiss intestine sausage out of hand.

"Don't sausages have intestines normally?" Sorcha waved her free arm frantically in front of her nose. "What is that smell?"

"Normal sausages use intestines as the casing. Andouillette is made up of intestines. On the inside." The memory of biting into that rubbery sausage and how it bounced off my teeth in a most unpleasant way still haunted me. During our lunch in Troyes, the chef kept a beady eye on me to see if the little American could swallow and smile. I did swallow, dammit, and I smiled at him. When he turned his back, I told Myrtle and Millicent I saw a cockroach on the ceiling and tossed the rest out the window. It seemed like such a good idea. Everybody was happy. The sausage, if you really insist on calling it that, was gone and they thought I ate it. But like most things in my life, it backfired. The owner was so pleased, he brought me another sausage on the house. I wanted to stab myself in the throat with my fork.

"Why would anyone want that?" asked Sorcha.

"It's an acquired taste."

"Who would want to acquire it?"

"The French."

"Of course, it's French," she sneered.

I grabbed her hand and dragged her and the drooling Pick toward the door. "Don't judge. Your dad likes pickled pig's feet."

She made a horking noise as I pushed her out the door and pointed at Aaron. "I'm not eating that."

"I trained in Troyes," he said, his glasses fogged up with intestine steam.

"Nobody's going to eat that."

"Morty."

"Morty requested this atrocity?"

"No."

"Who asked for it?"

"Morty said he'll eat it."

"But who...oh never mind. Tell Morty I'd rather this case go unsolved than eat one bite of that sausage."

"Huh?"

I shrieked in frustration and slammed the door. Sorcha was leaning on the wall, taking deep breaths. "Is that really what that sausage is supposed to smell like?"

"Unfortunately, yes." I pulled her off the wall and we skirted the love garden.

"How do you know?"

I told her the story of the factory tour and she laughed until tears overflowed. "I always thought your trips with The Girls were magical. I wanted to go so bad. Now I feel better. You had to eat intestines."

"Remind me to tell you about the lutefisk in Norway."

"That sounds pretty bad."

"There are no words bad enough for it." I hooked my arm through hers. "I didn't know you wanted to go on those trips."

"Of course, I did. We all did. You were so special and we were just us."

"I wasn't special."

Sorcha snorted a delicate little snort. "Yes, you were. It's like you belong to them like you were part of the Bled family. We could never figure out why."

I thought about the photo album I'd found in New Orleans and the link between me and the Bleds that it contained. I nearly told her about it while we walked out to the parking lot. Only the memory of the duct tape Sorcha certainly had in her suitcase held me back. I was starting to like my cousins, but they were still my cousins. Not to be entirely trusted.

We found the Vipers' van in the center of the parking lot. I went around to the back and the memorial was as I remembered it.

Rest in Peace
Beloved
Q
March 3, 1987

"That's it," I said.

"What's it?" asked Sorcha.

"The link between the teams and the reason the Lions and the Vipers are here together."

"Who's Q?"

I took the laptop bag from her. We headed to a nearby tree and sat in the shade beneath the branches. I opened the laptop and showed her the article.

"Wow," she said. "I can't believe the detail."

"It's a standard newspaper article."

"But still."

Okay.

I clicked on the background investigation site and paid for an investigation of Nicole. Ten minutes later, the connection was secured. Nicole was Quinn Hasselback's younger sister. It could not be a coincidence that she and Cherie ended up at the castle together, but I doubted either of them was the one behind it. The Vipers hadn't been happy to see Cherie and she started cutting again after she got here. Someone put them together, but why? To get Cherie killed? Revenge? That was pretty evil so naturally I thought of John. I was sure he killed whoever was in the woods, but what did he have to do with Cherie and Nicole? Why would he care about them? He didn't seem to care about much.

I went back to the article and looked at the other names. Carl Cox and Shaun Simmons were the boys who'd been there that day on the bridge. Carl went to school with Cherie. Shaun went to Immaculate Heart with Quinn. They were on the baseball team together. Quinn was the star pitcher and Shaun was his catcher. Immaculate Heart was the same school Nicole's son, Quinn, went to according to the bumper sticker on the van.

"Who are these people?" asked Sorcha.

"Nicole is the dead boy's sister," I said.

"Which one is Nicole?"

My eyes stayed on the screen. "The one with the long nails."

Sorcha wrinkled her nose. "Those are over the top." Then she lost interest and lay down in the grass. "I wonder what Oliver's doing right now."

"I'm guessing something to do with baseball."

"Did you know he was a major league pitcher?"

"Uh huh." I focused on the Herald and let Sorcha rattle on about Oliver and how smart he was, etc. I found the articles over the next few months more interesting. The three survivors from the bridge were exonerated. Quinn had been drinking and lost his balance. Case closed, except it wasn't. The Hasselback family raised a stink, not about the boys but about Cherie. They wanted her charged with everything from criminal mischief to murder because they said she brought the alcohol to the bridge so it was her fault. The police declined to charge her with anything. There was some noise about a lawsuit, but the judge threw the case out, citing that Quinn was eighteen at the time and Cherie was seventeen. No one made Quinn drink and nobody pushed him. It was an accident and that should've been the end of it. The memorial on the back of Nicole's van told me it wasn't.

Carl and Shaun had an easier time of it. Nobody blamed them and I gathered it was because they had prominent families. Carl was the son of the town dentist and Shaun's father was a retired Army colonel.

Cherie's family was deemed white trash. The Herald didn't come out and say it, but it wasn't hard to figure out how people saw her.

I ran background checks on Carl and Shaun and their good fortune ended with graduation. Carl died after he fell out of his dorm window during his sophomore year in college. His blood alcohol was twice the legal limit. Shaun was a star pitcher with a full ride to Mizzou. He did go to Mizzou but blew out his knee his junior year and left school. He joined the army, served one enlistment, and disappeared. And I mean disappeared. Shaun went backpacking alone in Estes Park, Colorado and was never seen again. He was declared dead seven years later. Cherie was the sole survivor and somebody had a bone to pick.

I pulled up the pictures of the four kids that were on that bridge in March 1987. Their senior pictures showed nothing of the terrible fates that were coming. Their smiles made me hurt all over. Shaun, in particular, was so much like David, not in looks, but in hope and promise. The world lay before them, but they'd never get to see it.

Pick jumped to his feet and barked. I looked up to find Tiny weaving through the parked cars.

Before he could open his mouth, I said, "You ate cream."

"No, I didn't," he said.

"You have a milk mustache."

"It's skim."

I closed the laptop. "You are a terrible liar. We have to work on that."

"What're you doing?"

"Finding a motive." I pointed to Nicole's back window.

"So?"

I told him what I'd found out. "Quinn Hasselback is the Q on the back of the Vipers van."

"No shit?"

"Has to be and it says here that the family tried to get Cherie charged, but the police refused. She was the one who bought the vodka. They blamed her for giving it to Quinn."

"Ya think Nicole'd kill her now. That was a long time ago and he drank it."

"I think you don't put a memorial on your brand new vehicle over two decades later because you're over it."

"Nicole was in The Castle when it happened," he said.

"Someone used my code to get out, but her hands are too small," I said.

"She could've pushed her so she hit that rock."

I shrugged. Her and everyone else in the castle.

"What else ya got?"

I told him about the trip being comped. "Leslie said the teams didn't know who would be here, but I heard Cherie at the gas station. She knew somebody was going to be here. She was surprised by the Vipers."

"But not by the Grizzlies."

"She knew about them and she picked this week specifically."

"Maybe a chance for her kid to psych out their kid."

"I don't think so. Taylor likes Enrique. There's something else going on. She went to Ecuador but so what? It was a church mission," I said.

"When did they go?"

"January. I wonder when the Lions signed up for this week."

"Ask Leslie," said Tiny. "God I'm hungry."

"You just drank cream."

His face went blank à la John. "I didn't say nothing about no cream."

"Yeah, right. You drank skim," I said.

"Skim's the bomb."

"Sure it is. Everybody loves skim. My dad calls it white water." I shook Sorcha's shoulder. She'd flipped over and was snoozing face-down like my cat, Skanky. I don't know how either of them could breathe like that.

Sorcha snorted and looked up. "I wasn't sleeping."

"I know. Just like how Tiny didn't drink cream."

"What?"

"Nothing. Come on. We've got stuff to do."

Sorcha jumped to her feet and frantically began finger combing her perfect locks. Oliver walked up from the direction of the fields, smiling and looking rugged in the best way possible. He gave Sorcha a light kiss on the lips and she blushed to match her hair.

"I thought you might like to have lunch together today?" he asked her.

"Okay. What time?"

"Noon."

"Sorcha might be busy," I said. "We've got a murder to solve."

She wrinkled her nose and said, "Please. That can wait."

What the...

"It really can't. We have a deadline."

"Oh, that. I was thinking of extending our trip by a couple of days." Sorcha looked deep into Oliver's eyes.

"That would be great," he said.

"Great. Fantastic," I said. "But that won't help with our deadline."

"Uh huh," said Sorcha.

I groaned. "Come on, Tiny. Let's go look at the map."

Tiny didn't move. He stood frozen with the funniest look on his face.

"Tiny?"

"I think I'm going to..." He ran around the tree and barfed like I've never heard barfing before. It was like tyrannosaurus rex barfing, huge and tremendously loud. He tried to hide behind the trunk but missed the mark and I could see the steady stream of white spewing from his mouth. Gross and double gross.

I made a face and then put on my big nurse pants. It was my job to go around that tree, but I so didn't want to. "Tiny?" I rubbed his back as he gagged.

"When you, uh, finish. I want you to lie down for a while," I said.

"Got to watch you." Another spew.

"John'll watch me and I have Pick. Your body can't take a fat influx anymore. You're going to feel rotten for a while."

He waved me away. "Go. Got to barf."

"Er...okay. I'm going to the copper pot kitchen."

He waved frantically and a bunch more came out. I told Sorcha and Oliver that Tiny would catch up to us later. They nodded and would've agreed to anything. I rolled my eyes and headed for the kitchen with Pick, who liked the smell of vomit even less than I did.

When we came to the love garden, Uncle Morty walked out the door of the kitchen, squinting and shielding his eyes. He reminded me of a bear coming out of hibernation.

"You're out," I said. "Did someone set fire to your room?"

"Smart ass."

"You know it."

"I got the answer on your damn newspaper."

I narrowed my eyes at him. "You could've called me."

"Yeah, well, my ass hurts. I think I got a boil." Uncle Morty turned and tugged on his sweatpants.

Oh my god no!

"What are you doing? What are you doing?"

"You want to see it, right?" he asked.

"Wrong. So so wrong. Why would I want to see your rear?" I asked.

He growled at me. "You're a nurse, ain't you? I went to your graduation."

"I'm not your nurse."

"You are today. Look at this bastard." He turned and tugged again.

I should've gone to law school. Nobody asks a lawyer to look at their butt boils. Sorcha was the smart one. I was an idiot.

Oliver and Sorcha, two people who chose their careers wisely, dashed around Uncle Morty and went in the kitchen. Uncle Morty glared after them. "Squeamish bastards." With that he exposed one of the largest hairiest rears I ever had the misfortune to see.

I shuddered. "That's not a boil."

"What the hell do you mean?"

"That's a bedsore."

"I ain't hardly been in bed."

"You've been in a chair for forty years. Paraplegics sit less than you."

He glared at me over his shoulder. "Fix it."

"Or you'll be what? Super crabby?" I asked. "I fail to see the difference."

"Fix it."

"With what? All I've got is a poodle and, by the way, pull up your pants. You're scaring the birds and wilting the flowers."

"Bite me."

"No thanks."

"Fix it or I won't give you shit on that newspaper."

I crossed my arms. "I don't need it. I already put it together."

"The hell you did."

I put my nose in the air and went past him into the kitchen which was filled with an incredible stench so thick I swear I could see it.

Aaron looked up from stuffing his casings. "You hungry."

"I may never be hungry again." I rushed through the kitchen and into the hall, bumping into Leslie and John huddled together in the hall. Leslie frowned as John explained something. I caught the name Flincher and my name before they saw me. I raised an eyebrow. "Making new arrangements?"

"Arrangements?" Leslie smiled. "What would we be arranging?"

"Another convenient vanishing perhaps."

"I don't know what you're talking about, but..." Leslie came closer, "perhaps you should remember who you are and why you're here."

That stopped me and I took a step back. "Me? What's it got to do with me?"

John said to Leslie, "Didn't Tommy say she was bright?"

"He did and she is," said Leslie. "She's just not thinking."

Pick growled and strained at his leash. I pulled him back to my side. "I'm thinking about the task *you* asked me to perform."

Leslie straightened his vest and ran a hand through his long grey hair. "And how's that coming?"

"It'd be better if you'd be more forthcoming," I said, walking past them to see if they'd follow. They did. I had no clue where I was going, but they followed me anyway.

I took a right and ended up in a billiards room all dark wood and covered in animal heads. Pick began sniffing at a stuffed grizzly bear and I picked up a pool cue, twirling it between my fingers. "I want to know how Cherie came to be here this particular weekend."

"Not who was in the woods?" asked John.

"If that has to do with me, I'll find out eventually. When did Cherie request this weekend?"

Leslie walked off while waving something away from his ear that I couldn't see. John watched him for a split second and then said, "Why?"

"Can't you just answer the question? When did she contact you?" I could barely contain my rage. Somebody freaking tell the truth.

"January," said Leslie without turning around.

"When in January?"

"The twenty-seventh."

That would've been after she and Lane came back from Ecuador. Something happened on that trip. "She contacted you?"

"Yes."

"Did she ask you about the Grizzlies?"

"I told you—"

"You told me lies. She wanted to know when the Grizzlies would be here and she wanted the same weekend, didn't she?"

Leslie hesitated and then turned around to meet my eyes. "Yes."

"Did she give you a clue as to why she wanted to be here with them?"

John racked the pool balls and chalked a cue he'd plucked off the wall. "We assumed she wanted her son to go head to head with Enrique. The prize is decided here."

"A reasonable idea, but that's not why."

John took his first shot, scattering the balls. The shot was casual. His eyes were actually on me when he took it, but he sank six balls. I didn't know crap about pool, but that looked pretty good. "Why did she pick this weekend then?" he asked.

"I don't know. It's something to do with Enrique and the orphanage she and Lane worked at in January. It looks like she got off the plane and called you."

"I suppose so," said Leslie.

"Something happened on that trip. How did she plan on paying for this camp if you hadn't comped it?"

"I didn't ask."

"But you comped it?"

John sank another ball. "Yes. What has this got to do with the murder?"

"I don't know. It's all mixed up together. Why she wanted to come. What she found out in Ecuador. The first Quinn, Nicole's brother, died in 1987. I think Lane knows something, but she's not ready to say."

"You think she will tell you?" asked Leslie, drumming his fingers on the edge of the billiards table.

"I do. She's protecting someone, but it won't last. It can't. She'll have to say what happened in Ecuador."

Sorcha and Oliver walked in. Her lipstick was smeared and he was smiling way too much.

"Did you say something about Ecuador?" asked Sorcha.

I told her about Enrique's adoption and Cherie's visit to the orphanage. "I think she found something out about the adoption."

She shook her head. "That can't be."

"Why not?"

"Because Enrique can't be from Ecuador."

Oliver held up his hand. "He's definitely from Ecuador. I've seen his paperwork."

"No. He might be adopted, but it's not from Ecuador." Sorcha never looked this sure about anything, except maybe the bridesmaid dresses.

"How do you know?" I asked.

"Because I interned with Valerie Fimmel, the big adoption lawyer in my second year. Adopting out of Ecuador is extremely difficult."

"But they did. Enrique's here," said Oliver.

"I'm just telling you what Valerie said. Ecuador says they allow international adoptions, but they don't want Ecuadorian children to leave the country."

Leslie walked across the room, took off his glasses and cleaned them with a handkerchief. His face was different without them. Familiar. I stared and he hastily put them back on. "That must be it. There was something fishy about the adoption and Cherie found out."

Sorcha nodded. "Sure. She would've heard about the difficulties in the orphanage. They struggle to care for children and they can't place them."

I shook my head. "I don't know. If the adoption was illegal, would it preclude Enrique from the prize?"

Oliver paced next to the pool table. "I can check but I don't think there's anything that says he even has to be a citizen. We had a Japanese kid win five years ago."

"Then that's not it. Cherie had something." I went for the door but Leslie headed me off. "Where are you going?"

"To see a man about a bedsore."

"What?"

"I need information and, for once, I don't have to eat anything for it," I said.

Leslie put a hand on my shoulder. "What should we do?"

What would Poirot do?

"Gather the suspects," I said.

"Who are the suspects?" asked John.

"All the men who were in the castle that night, but bring in the women, too. I'll meet you in the library."

Leslie and John said they would take care of gathering my suspects and left.

"Can you find the library?" asked Oliver.

"Sorcha, you're with me." I grabbed her by the hand, but then dropped it and ran to watch John and Leslie walk away. "That is freaky."

Oliver and Sorcha came up behind me. "What?" she asked.

"Them."

"John makes me nervous," said Oliver.

"Me, too," said Sorcha. "He's so...I don't know..."

"Nothing?"

I nodded. "He is nothing, but there's something in his nothingness."

John turned a corner, leaving Leslie. Even after having spoken to him not a minute before, I couldn't picture John's face. It was nothing. Completely forgettable. Who would want that? Where would that be an asset?

"Mercy?" asked Sorcha.

"Just a minute."

"Something about the case?" asked Oliver.

"Let me think." But the truth was I could think all day long and not get anywhere. John was a blank and when I tried to picture either John or Leslie, I couldn't. Not really. I could see Leslie's glasses, his gray hair swooping back, his vest, but I couldn't see him. His face was obscured by the rest of him. Leslie was showy like me and, like me, our veneer concealed much. That was it. Veneer.

"Okay," I said. "I got it."

"What did you get," asked Oliver. "Because I got nothing."

"That's exactly the way they want it and why I have to solve this pronto."

CHAPTER TWENTY

Uncle Morty wouldn't open the door.

"I know you're in there!" I yelled through the keyhole. "I've come to fix your rear."

There was a couple of minutes of silence and then he bellowed, "What're you gonna do?"

"I have to take a look before I decide."

"You already looked."

And my eyeballs are still burning.

"That wasn't an evaluation. I don't know if the wound is infected," I said. "Just let me in."

He cursed a blue streak and then yelled, "It's freaking open, genius."

I had considered trying the knob, but the thought that I might catch Uncle Morty naked was enough to nip that idea in the bud.

I opened the door and found Uncle Morty sitting at the desk, working on one of the incredibly detailed maps he put in his books. "Why are you sitting?"

"Working. What the hell does it look like?" he asked without looking up.

I groaned and went to the bed with my supplies. Mom had packed my kit. I always traveled with the basics, especially after my trip to Honduras. It pays to be prepared, but I didn't have the right antibiotics if Uncle Morty was bad. Mine were broad spectrum and bedsores were specific. I gloved up. "Come on, Pus Butt. I've got stuff to do."

"Pus Butt?"

"It's your new nickname, short for He Who Sits Too Much."

Uncle Morty glared at me and then went back to his map. "You want something."

"Yeah, I do. And I'm not the only one. That's got to be painful. Let's work on it."

He grumbled and then pried himself out of the chair, slow and in obvious pain. When he got close, I caught a whiff of pus. The Henry VIII comparison was getting a little too close for comfort. I don't know how I missed it before, but the onion pizza stink that enveloped him was pretty strong.

"Alright. Lay on the bed face down and we'll get this done," I said.

Uncle Morty crossed his arms. "What do you want for fixing my butt?"

"First of all, I can't *fix* it. This is a time and treatment thing. There's no magic wand."

"And second?"

"I want you to look into Enrique's adoption." I told him what Sorcha said and his eyes lit up. "Maybe the adoption was illegal, but I think it's something more. She was out to help her son. The adoption wasn't enough."

He nodded. "How many times are you gonna fix me?"

"Hello," I said. "Just the one time."

Once is so much more than enough.

"You'll have to see your primary care when we get back."

"I hate that guy. He tells me stuff," he said.

"I can imagine," I said. "I'm going to tell you stuff, too."

"Screw that."

"You've got a giant ulcer on your butt." I pointed at his chair. "This lifestyle isn't working out for you."

"I like sitting."

"Obviously. Lay down."

Uncle Morty lay on the bed, protesting my evaluation of his sedentary lifestyle as if crabbing changed it. "I want you to treat my sore until it's better and I'll do that adoption thing."

"I'm not a doctor."

"I don't need a damn doctor. Tommy'll want you to do it."

Dad would want me to do it. You do for family, no matter how gross. That's all there was to that. I grabbed his waistband and mentally prepared.

Not Uncle Morty. Just another butt belonging to some guy you do not know.

I pulled down his sweats and got to business. It was worse than I originally thought, nearly a Stage III. How he stood the pain was beyond me. I cleaned and dressed the wound and, in the process, discovered two more sores in Stage I so I cleaned them and applied some barrier cream.

Uncle Morty wasn't happy, but I ignored the cursing and the insults to my character and did my job. It wasn't easy, but at least he didn't need debridement. I can't imagine what he would've said or rather yelled.

"Am I done?" he asked, his face contorted in pain.

I pulled up his sweats, grimacing at the griminess. "For now. They're not too bad, but that Stage II will require a dressing change once a day. You need to take a sponge bath and have fresh clothing, including underwear." I unplugged his laptop.

"What're you doing? Don't touch that," he bellowed, rolling over and gasping in pain.

I rolled him back on his stomach. "No sitting. On your belly for now." I put the laptop in front of him and got out my phone.

"Who you calling? You ain't telling nobody about this."

Hmm. This could be useful in the future.

"I'm telling Dr. Watts, so she can bring some more dressings."

"I'll kill you if you tell her about my sores. I'll kill you good."

I whacked him on the shoulder. "I'm real worried. You can't even sit. Get on that adoption stuff or I'll tell her you cried like a girl."

"You're evil."

"Whatever it takes, buddy." I texted Dr. Watts and she said she'd bring out fresh supplies. Which, of course, meant that I'd have to look at Uncle Morty's hairy rear repeatedly. My life was not working out for me. "Okay. You stay here and I'm going to the library to corner a killer."

"Wait. Wait. Where's Tiny? Why isn't he here?" he asked.

"You wanted Tiny to see this?"

"Hell, no, but he's supposed to be watching you."

I packed up my stuff and put it on his desk. "He's sick."

"What'd you do to that kid?" he asked.

"Nothing. Honestly, you and Dad are doing more to him than me."

He began typing, going to some international adoption site. "What'd you mean by that? He wants a career. Tommy wants to give him one."

"I'm not sure it's the right career. How much background did you do on Tiny?"

"I do good work. You're pushing it with this butt blackmail thing."

"You did it to yourself. Take a walk for heaven's sake. And you have to change your diet or this will just keep happening."

He hissed at me like one of his dragon characters and I rolled my eyes before checking my phone. Phelong and Gerry were in the castle, fingerprinting the gardening room door. Good. We could use all the evidence we could get.

"If I change my diet, I won't have to give you anything," said Uncle Morty with a satisfied smirk.

I smirked back. "But you're stuck for now. Wasn't there anything in Tiny's medical records from the Marines?"

"Like what?"

"He has PTSD. He told me."

Uncle Morty rolled on his side. "There ain't nothing on that in his file. He'd tell us if it was a problem."

"Would he?" I asked. "Or would he try to gut through it."

"How's he gutting through then?"

"He got all sweaty when he first saw Cherie in the Love Garden and he passed out when Dr. Watts showed him the body during autopsy."

"That ain't good. What'd he say about it?"

"I didn't ask. He's been through a lot and he's trying. I'm just saying we've got to be careful. I want you to call him off me. The case and the diet are too much for now. I'll keep Pick with me. I'm good."

"The damn dog? Screw that. Tiny can kill people with his thumbs."

"I'll keep John or Leslie with me. Happy?"

"The innkeepers?" His eyes went back to the screen. "Yeah, they're pretty tough."

I went for the door. "I know you think I'm an idiot, but Dad sent me here for a reason and it's them."

Uncle Morty wouldn't look up. "Could be." His voice got cagey. "So you got an idea about them?"

"Well, they aren't former cops and if they were friends, I would've heard about them before now."

"Yeah."

"They're using assumed names," I said.

Uncle Morty's head jerked up. "How do you know that?"

I shrugged. "The backgrounds you gave me. They're very neat and tidy. You might've composed them for all I know."

"I don't compose nothing but books," he said.

"Well, someone did a great job."

"How'd you know the names are fake?"

"Because I know Leslie's real name."

He frowned and I knew from that look that Uncle Morty didn't know it. It was nice to be the one who knew something he didn't for a change. "What is it?" he asked.

"Shaun Simmons."

Shaun Simmons aka Leslie stood at the bottom of the stairs looking like a Ralph Lauren commercial, the kind they put in front of *Downton Abbey*. Pick wasn't impressed. He chased his tail and then started biting the air.

"Your bodyguard is sick," he said. "And the other one is...dizzy."

"I know. Where's Tiny?"

"The yoga room. We rolled him in there."

"You rolled him. Seriously?" I asked.

"There aren't enough people in the castle to pick him up."

"Good point. Are the suspects assembled?"

Leslie checked his watch. "Should be. You're enjoying this, aren't you?"

"Little bit. Usually, I have to chase people down in a bikini and have lewd pictures taken of me and put on the internet. This is much better. Quiet library. Ooh. We should serve wine. Can we serve wine?"

"Champagne?"

"That might be going a little too far."

Leslie laughed and texted someone. "I'm surprised anything is too far for you."

I smiled and looked down at my breasts in the mother of all push-up bras. "You know what, me too."

He shook his head and went for the hall, I assumed the one that led to the library, but I couldn't follow. I had to say it. I couldn't hold it in anymore. "You're Shaun. You were on the bridge with Cherie when Nicole's brother died."

Pick barked in agreement and started trying to dig a hole in the carpet. Leslie watched him for a moment and put his hand on the ornate trim of the arched doorway. He said nothing, but I could see his breathing. His vest strained with each intake, a controlled panic.

"It's why you brought them here and comped it for Cherie. What did you think was going to happen?" I asked.

He held up a finger and then moved to the right, stopping beside the third panel of *The Lady and the Unicorn*. He felt under the tapestry and there was a loud click. The tapestry swung out as the wall opened, revealing a dimly lit passage. Leslie stepped back and took off his glasses. Once you knew who he was, it was obvious. All the showiness was to distract and it did its job well. "This is how John and I get around the castle so quickly."

I did love a good secret passage, but this felt a whole lot like when I isolated myself at a funeral home with a murderer on the prowl. Mom never let me live that one down. This time there were several killers on the loose in the castle and Leslie was probably one of them.

"I can't go in there with you," I said.

"Tell your father where you're going if you're worried. I won't harm you. But if you don't go in, I'll never speak to you about this again."

He meant it and, honestly, I wanted to go. Maybe it was his level gaze. Maybe it's because I'm nosy like my mother. Or maybe I just couldn't help doing the wrong thing, the exact thing Dad warned me about. Like drinking and being in backseats with boys. I had to do it.

Now I wasn't a total idiot, despite my family's assertions. I texted Dad and Chuck so, at least, they'd know where to look for the body. Then I stepped inside, tugging Pick in with me. The dog wasn't thrilled with the idea. He tucked his tail and whimpered.

"Some bodyguard you are."

Bark.

"Whatever. Come on."

Leslie closed the panel and I had a mini panic attack. The passage was smaller when you were inside it and I'd never been so close to Leslie. He smelled like expensive cologne and saddle soap. It was a nice combo.

"How did you know?" he asked.

"I saw the pictures of you, Cherie, Carl, and Quinn in the St. Seb Herald."

He leaned against the wall. "You recognized me. You're the first. Cherie and Nicole didn't. What do you want to know? I didn't kill Cherie if that's what you're thinking."

I looked at him and knew he concealed much but killing Cherie? No. He was much too smart for that. He wouldn't bring her onto his own turf and kill her. Above all, Leslie wanted to remain concealed. Killing people on his property was the worst way to do that.

"I don't think you did, not that you couldn't kill people. I'm sure you could, that you have, just not Cherie."

He smiled down at me. "You're sure."

"Yep. I can tell."

"Tommy said it was obvious that you're his daughter. He was right."

"Don't tell him that."

"I won't. I know him, too, remember?" Leslie walked away down the passage and took several turns with me in tow. I don't know how long we walked. It probably felt longer than it actually was.

"Are you going to talk to me?" I asked.

He stopped and pointed to several tiny beams of light jutting in from the left side of the passage. "That's the library where they're waiting for you. Are you sure you want to delay? It's not important to the task I set you to."

"I want to know for me. I won't tell anyone ever. I'm Tommy's kid. I can keep a secret."

"Very well then. Ask away."

"Did you hate Cherie? Did you blame her like Nicole did?"

He turned away and I thought he wouldn't tell me. I thought that after so many years of hiding and lying he wouldn't be capable of revealing anything, but I was wrong.

Leslie turned back to me. "I didn't hate her. Of course, I didn't hate her. She blamed herself. She brought the bottle. But I was there and it wasn't her fault."

"Because Quinn wanted to drink the vodka?"

"Yes, but Cherie bought it for me and I gave it to him, even though I knew he had a problem. Quinn was a drinker from early on. I met him when we were twelve. He was already sneaking his father's Scotch. He'd had a few that day before we left school. He had a little silver flask he kept in his backpack. Quinn was my pitcher. We were a team. He asked me for the vodka and I gave it to him. I couldn't say no. It was my fault, not Cherie's."

"You didn't say that to the police."

"I tried to, but no one wanted to hear it. I thought Quinn's family knew. I'd had dinner with them when he was hammered. I thought they were putting up a front."

"But they really didn't know?"

"Apparently, not. He was the star of the family. I guess they saw what they wanted to see. They couldn't hear what I said about Quinn. It hurt them and I shut up. I didn't think they'd blame Cherie."

"But why didn't you tell the cops after they did?"

"Pure selfishness. Cherie blamed herself for buying it and she said it didn't matter what they said about her anyway. I had a scholarship to lose. I didn't want to ruin my life by stepping up. My parents put so much into my career, but then I ruined it anyway. Cherie didn't have any of that to deal with. She was generous. I was a shit.

"Why did you bring Nicole and Cherie together this weekend? How was that supposed to go well?"

He ran a manicured hand over his face. "It was so long ago. I thought...I thought we could talk about it."

"You were going to tell them who you are?" I asked.

He laughed. "No. I can't. There are legal issues. I was going to say I was a friend of Shaun's in the Army and that he told me about what happened on the bridge. I was going to say that I wanted to make it right for him. I thought they could finally let Quinn go."

"But you didn't tell them," I said.

"I saw that memorial to Quinn on the back of Nicole's van and I knew it wasn't so long ago for her. I hesitated and then it was too late."

Raised voices came through the panel, angry voices asking to leave.

"The natives are getting restless," said Leslie. "Do you have a plan?"

"Sort of. Whatever I say, just go with it?" I went for the panel and Leslie grabbed my arm, squeezing but not hurting me.

"I want this finished, but you can't use me. I'm not Shaun."

I patted his hand. "I know. Even if I wanted to out you, I couldn't prove it."

"No, you couldn't." Leslie pulled me to him and went in for a kiss. Pick growled and snapped at him and Leslie let go.

"What the hell?" I asked.

Leslie smiled wanly and cleaned his glasses. "I wanted to see what it would be like, but your poodle isn't keen on the idea."

"Kissing me isn't any different. I'm just regular. Don't let this face fool you. I'm not some sexpot."

"I didn't think you were. I wanted to kiss someone who knows my name."

I couldn't say anything for a minute. What would it be like to hide for over twenty years? I couldn't imagine.

"Don't mention this to Tommy. He won't take it well," he said.

"No problem." Then I kissed him. Not a big one. Just a soft kiss on the lips. I don't know what made me do it or why Pick didn't growl. Maybe he knew I wasn't serious or maybe the spot he was licking on his paw was too distracting. Either way, the kiss only lasted a second and then I stepped back. "Well?"

He chuckled and put his glasses back on, becoming Leslie once more. "Other than the fact that you have lovely lips, it was the same."

"You're Leslie now. Shaun's gone."

"He is."

"Exactly how did you turn into Leslie?" I asked.

Voices erupted through the panel again. "What the hell are we waiting for?" yelled a man. I couldn't tell who it was. Leslie went to the panel, pushed a button, and it creaked open. The shouting ceased instantly as light flooded into the passage.

"That is so cool," said Jilly.

"This is the perfect place for a murder mystery caper," said Bridget.

Caper? My cousins are so weird.

Leslie crooked a finger at me and swung the panel open. Pick leapt into the library followed by us, squinting at the light.

"Mercy! What were you doing in there?" asked Sorcha, cuddled up on the sofa with Oliver.

"It's a shortcut," I said. "I see we're all here."

"Why are we here?" Bill's face was red to match his Cardinals cap. He'd been the one yelling.

Dr. Watts came in through the arched library doors. "To discover who killed Cherie, of course."

Everyone went silent.

"Please," I said. "Take a seat."

Nobody moved. Nicole and Cory stood by the windows overlooking part of the formal garden. They'd changed into matching attire and Nicole's hair was curled back into its helmet shape, but she'd ripped off her nails and left them ragged. They saw me, and Cory began rubbing his crew cut furiously.

Bill adjusted his cap and checked his Fitbit, walking in place to keep his heart rate up. He looked like the only one who slept well, thanks to his breathing machine. Robin and Tim stood at the library table where Sorcha's map was spread out. Robin twisted her earring and Tim rubbed his watermelon belly. Deanna was hovering at a small liquor cabinet, eyeing the decanters. Grandpa Anthony, Oliver, and my cousins were the only ones who were seated on the green leather sofas. Anthony's eyes were baggy and showed red rims. "You still don't know who did it?" he asked hoarsely.

"I will in a minute."

John walked in carrying a silver tray with wine glasses and two bottles of Nuits-Saint-Georges Premier Cru, the good stuff. No Boulogne Rouge for our little experiment. "Mercy said sit."

That's all it took. My suspects dropped into seats with a quickness, such was the power of John's intensity. He set the tray next to the map, uncorked a bottle and poured a generous glug in each of the glasses.

Nicole accepted her glass saying, "It's the middle of the afternoon."

"Even so," said Leslie, taking a glass himself. "There's no reason we can't be civilized about this."

"Hand it over," said Dr. Watts. She did the expert swirl and sniff before taking a sip. "Not cheaping out on us. I like it."

"No, Dr. Watts, I haven't served you cheap wine."

"Good, because I'm busy."

Deanna downed her glass and said, "What exactly are you going to do?"

"Run some tests to determine the murderer," said Dr. Watts.

Robin's hand shook slightly. "Tests on us?"

"Who else? The murderer is in this room."

Robin's wine sloshed and dripped onto her white capri pants. "Dammit."

John handed her a napkin and took the glass. There wasn't an expression on his face, but I could tell that to him spilling a Premier Cru was a greater crime than murder.

Dr. Watts took another sip, made a small humming sound of pleasure, and put the glass on a bookshelf. She clapped her hands once. "Who's going to help with my equipment?"

"That'll be me," I said before anyone could offer.

I went out into the hall and nearly screamed. Flincher stood by the door with his bony fingers steepled.

"What the hell are you doing here?" I asked.

"Good question," said Dr. Watts. "He insisted on coming."

"Yes," said Flincher. "I wanted to see Miss Watts at work."

Nobody in history has ever made 'at work' sound so creepy.

"Yeah, well, great." I closed the library door behind Dr. Watts and looked at the stack of equipment Dr. Watts had bungee corded to a dolly. "What did you bring?"

"Everything portable."

"Got any luminol?"

"Always. What do you have in mind?" she asked.

"I want you to tell them that you've got conclusive fingerprint evidence off of these." I pulled the half-burnt gloves out of my pocket. Dr. Watts took the baggie and shook her head. "I can't get fingerprints out of these. It's impossible."

"Yeah, but they don't know that. You have your magic spray." I grinned at her.

"How stupid do you think they are?"

"They're not stupid at all, but Robin and Deanna watch *CSI*. Maybe the others do, too. The *CSI* effect could help us out here. None of our suspects are scientists. How do they know that the technology they see on TV isn't real? They carry around amazing technology in their back pockets. Doesn't *CSI* have a magic spray that illuminates pretty much anything at any time?"

Dr. Watts scowled. "I hate that show. I never carried a gun or interrogated a suspect."

"Now's your chance. It's funny when you think about it."

"No, it's not."

"Fine," I said, suppressing a grin. "Let's just go in there, you talk about the unique characteristics of the hands that were in these gloves, and we'll see what happens."

Dr. Watts held up the baggie. "I might get some DNA out of these. Sweat, skin cells. They were in a fire though."

"Yes," I said. "DNA is good. People love DNA. Tell them you got samples and sent them to Springfield. They'll have the results within an hour."

"It's not that fast," she said.

"Lie. Lying works. My dad does it all the time."

"This isn't what my profession does, but I can lie with the best of them."

I turned to Flincher, who'd crept up on me and was stinking so bad I got nauseous. "And you?"

"Me?" he asked.

"I want you in there, creeping around and looking at them. You know, what you usually do."

"Why?" asked Dr. Watts.

"Because he scares people. I want you hitting them with your science and him being him."

She grabbed her dolly. "That is a winning combination. Your father will be proud."

I fluffed my hair. "Scheming is a family trait."

Phelong and Gerry ambled up carrying their fingerprinting kit.

"Perfect. We'll fingerprint them, too."

"Who?" asked Phelong.

"Our suspects," I said.

"We have suspects?" asked Gerry.

"Yes, we do and with any luck we'll have a murderer in a minute. Grab that dolly."

We went back in. I was pleased to see the wine glasses were empty and there was plenty of fidgeting going on.

"What took so long?" demanded Bill.

"This isn't *CSI: Miami*," said Dr. Watts. "Proper science takes time."

Nice one, doctor.

"Who's first?" I asked.

"For what?" asked Tim, taking Robin's shaking hand.

Dr. Watts directed Phelong to take the dolly to the table. I rolled up Sorcha's map and gave it to her. She whispered to me, "This is so cool."

Er...okay.

I helped Dr. Watts unpack her autopsy equipment. We obviously weren't going to need a rib spreader, but everyone's eyes were trained on that thing. There was some serious frowning going on, and I suppressed a smile. The frowning got worse when Flincher started circling the room. He'd look at everyone's hands, make a phlegmy noise, and move on. Gross and effective. The men's brows shown with sweat and Nicole cleared her throat every couple of minutes. The only problem was that they all looked guilty and not just a little bit. They looked super guilty and they all didn't do it. It only takes one to strangle.

"Here." Dr. Watts gave Gerry the cord to a portable scanner and he plugged it in. It was a regular HP scanner, but everyone shifted in their seats. Dr. Watts opened a fat metal packing case and pulled out a can of luminol. She tossed it in the air, caught it like a juggler without looking, and popped off the top, aiming the nozzle at the suspects in a broad sweep. "Who's first?"

They froze. Phelong and Gerry retreated to the door and appeared just as nervous as my suspects. I hadn't told them anything about the plan and it was working out for me. The cops were clueless and it made them fearful. My suspects were watching them. If the cops were scared, they should be, too.

"It won't hurt." Dr. Watts lifted one shoulder. "Not much anyway. A little stinging."

Nicole jolted to her feet and pointed at me. "She did it."

"Me?" I asked. "What's my motive?"

She wagged her finger. "You...you...I don't know, but you did it. Confess."

"I confess you're an idiot. I never met Cherie before this weekend whereas you knew her well, didn't you?"

Nicole gasped. "I didn't. No, no. You snuck out. The front desk guy told me. He said you used your code in the middle of the night and you did it."

"Mercy is cleared," said Dr. Watts.

"By who?" asked Bill.

"By me. Tell them how it happened, Mercy."

I ticked off the series of events. I got nice and detailed about the brutality and the times. Their windows all overlooked the rock garden and they knew it.

"So you were in your room during love garden part. So what?" Bill pointed at me. "You could've been the one in the rock garden."

I yawned. "Drinking with my cousins and Aaron."

"Maybe your family faked the video time and John went along with it."

John stared at Bill and the big man swallowed hard, but he wasn't backing down. "They're your family. They'd lie. I heard you say that your father knows Leslie and John."

"We wouldn't lie and alter evidence," exclaimed Sorcha, waking up and taking her attention off Oliver. "That's a crime. Accessory after the fact."

"Well, maybe she wasn't that drunk," said Robin. "Maybe she was faking. They probably have her all wrong on the news. She could be a sick lunatic that strangles women."

"No, she isn't," said Dr. Watts. "Would you like to see why?"

The women crossed their arms.

"Yes, I would," said Deanna. "She looks like the type."

Hey now. Slut I can see, but crazed murderer? Come on.

Bill stood up. "She's trying to pin it on us and you're helping her. She killed those kids' mother. Their only parent left."

Anthony stood up and, without a word, sucker punched Bill in his gut. "I'm left, you smelly bag of cat barf."

Bill keeled over and gagged on the floor. Everyone jumped up and started yelling about evidence and justice and me, of course. Pick pranced around, barking and growling, nearly pulling me off my feet.

He snapped at Bill, and Anthony yelled while hitching up his jeans, "Get up and I'll punch you again, asshole!"

John walked over, real casual, and put Anthony back in his seat with minimum effort. "You," he nudged the groaning Bill, "shut up. Mercy's cleared."

"I don't believe it," said Cory, rubbing his head so hard it was jerking the skin up and down on his forehead. "She knows everything about what happened."

Dr. Watts pulled out the autopsy photos of Cherie's neck. Anthony buried his face in his hands. "She was such a good woman."

Nicole shot him a look of hate. "No, she wasn't. She was the bitch who killed my brother."

"Shut up," said Cory.

"It's alright," I said. "I already know all about it." I told them what happened on the bridge. Nicole and Cory looked stunned. Anthony wept and said over and over again, "It wasn't her fault."

"Yes, it was," hissed Nicole. "She did it. She did it on purpose. I hated her. I hated that she got to keep on breathing when my brother was dead."

"Shut up, Nicky." Cory had gone pale and jittery. "Stop being so angry. I'm so sick of you being angry."

"I didn't do it so who cares what I say?" she yelled. "I'm glad she's dead. Now I can be happy. And Mercy probably did it. Everybody hated that bitch. Who knows what Cherie did to her."

Dr. Watts held up the photo. "See here. The fingers that did this were blunt and thick."

"So what?" asked Tim.

"It was a male of good size." She held up my arm. "Her hands are too small."

"So what are we here for?" asked Deanna, holding up her glass for a refill. "What do you want to do to us?"

Dr. Watts held up the luminol can in one hand and the glove baggy in the other. "I'm going to match the very unique fingerprints in these gloves to—"

She didn't even get to the DNA part. Cory bolted off the sofa and darted across the library past the cops and out the door. Phelong and Gerry actually stepped aside to make room for him.

"Get him!" I yelled and John responded. I should've known he'd be the one. He pulled a .22 from his waistband and ran out after Cory. Pick yanked the leash out of my hand and darted after them.

"Pick!" I'm ashamed to say that was my first thought. Not catch the murderer but catch the dog, Chuck's dog. If that poodle got shot, Chuck would never forgive me. I'd never forgive me and John was totally capable of shooting him.

I ran over paintings, over tapestries, and scattered pieces of armor. Cory had a plan and it was pulling stuff off the walls. What else can you do when you're a murderous idiot. Cory's plan didn't stop John and they

were his paintings. He ran right over the Duchess of Devonshire with his Italian loafers. Pick jumped over everything gaining speed so that I barely got a glimpse of his puffy tail as he went around a corner. I jumped over an intact suit of armor and caught up with John. "Do not shoot my dog!"

John put on speed and turned into a long hall lined with bookcases. Cory was hauling ass down the middle with Pick attached to his rear. The poodle dragged down his workout pants, exposing his pale flabby rump. He smacked Pick's snout. There was a rip. He lost half his pants and Pick fell to the floor. John assumed a firing position.

"No!" I yelled.

Cory juked to the right toward the Japanese armory and Pick leapt at him. John fired just one shot. Cory screamed and Pick hit him in the back, knocking him to the floor. Pick had him by the hoodie, snarling and tossing his head back and forth.

"Pick!"

The poodle jerked his head up and looked at me. He was fine. Cory wasn't. The murderer rolled around, howling and clutching his rear. "I've been shot. My ass. My ass."

"You could've killed him!" I yelled, referring to Pick not Cory. He could kill Cory, an eye for an eye and all that. Pick was another story.

"No," said John not blinking at my outburst.

I poked him in his breast pocket. "What do you mean 'No'?"

John whipped out a crisp handkerchief and cleaned the gun in it. "No, I couldn't have killed him."

"You're that good?"

"Yes."

"You could've killed the dog."

"Collateral damage," said John, disinterested at best.

I punched him in the shoulder with everything I had and it was a pathetic effort since John didn't appear to notice. "We would've caught Cory eventually."

"Chasing is for amateurs."

That cinches it. I'm an amateur.

Cory rolled around yelling, "I'm going to bleed to death. I'm dying. Help me!"

"Shut up," John and I said together.

"But he shot me!"

"It's just a .22, you wuss. It's barely bleeding," I said and turned back to John. "What are we going to do now? You just shot Cory. People are going to notice. You'll be arrested. How is that hiding?"

John pressed the gun into my hands. I screeched and dropped it. "What the hell?"

He pushed me against a bookcase and Pick ran over growling. John pointed at the dog and said, "Quiet."

Pick dropped to the floor and whined.

"You're a young woman," said John. "Daughter of a famous well-connected man. You panicked and fired a warning shot, winging him in the butt."

"No!"

"Yes."

"When did you know that Cory did it?" asked John, loosening his grip.

I glared up at him. "When he ran."

His grip tightened. "When?"

"Nicole reminded me earlier that Cory's very good at memorizing facts and figures, but I didn't know why he'd kill Cherie until I found out about Nicole's brother."

"Ah, yes. Cory knows a million baseball stats."

"And he was standing next to me when I was holding my card with my code on it."

He nodded. "That's not enough for a slam dunk."

"I was hoping for a confession," I said.

"Consider it done." John let go of me and stalked over to the writhing Cory, whose hollering had gone up in pitch. He kicked him over, knelt, pried off his hand and grabbed his rear.

I followed and grabbed John's arm. "What're you doing?"

John squeezed. "Why did you kill Cherie?"

Cory screamed, a piercing howl that hurt my ears.

"Stop! Stop!" I yelled.

John looked at me.

"They never confess," I said. "I should've known better than to try."

"You've been listening to the wrong people or should I say the good people. He squeezed again. "Answer me, Cory. I haven't got much patience and you're not accustomed to pain."

Cory gasped. "I...I..."

John squeezed and was answered with a scream.

I yanked on John's arm, but he didn't budge. "Did you work at Abu Ghraib or what?"

"I only offered some tips," he said.

"Are you kidding?"

"I have no sense of humor." John dug his fingers in and Cory answered with, "I wanted her to confess."

"To?"

"To killing Quinn. Nicole never got over it. She obsesses. If Cherie went to jail..."

"But she wouldn't confess," I said.

"No." Anger flashed across his face. "She said she didn't give the vodka to him. Lying bitch. She ruined Nicole. She ruined my life."

"So you strangled her."

"I didn't mean to. It just happened. If she would've agreed, I would've stopped."

"It's all her fault. She made you kill her," I said.

"Yeah, yeah. It's not my fault."

I tapped John's arm and he squeezed, not one of my proudest moments, but damn did it feel good to watch Cory writhe in pain, a man who blamed his victim.

"She didn't give it to him," I hissed in Cory's ear. "You killed an innocent woman."

John glanced at me. "Leslie told you."

"He did." I removed John's hand and took the handkerchief from his pocket, pressing it to Cory's rear. There was a small amount of blood, not nearly as much as he deserved to lose. I felt around and discovered entry and exit wounds. It was clean and through the muscle, the perfect shot with minimal damage. .22s could take some pretty interesting paths in the body. I'd seen one enter the buttocks, spiral down, and exit out the knee. Much more painful. I wish that had happened to this scumbag.

Cory howled as I pressed the handkerchief to the exit wound and John smacked him in the jaw, not a light smack but a full on brain rattler.

"Enough," said John and he got to his feet as Tiny and Dr. Watts ran around the corner. Tiny was feeling around his waist and stopped short at where I'd dropped the weapon.

"My gun," he said, looking at it on the carpet.

"I borrowed it," said John. "Mercy accidentally shot him."

Dr. Watts knelt beside me. "Oh really. I seem to remember that *you* didn't have that gun."

"Um..."

She glanced at John and narrowed her eyes. "I see."

Everyone else came up behind her with wide eyes. Nicole screamed and ran to Cory, cradling his head. "What did you do?" she hissed at me.

I couldn't answer. It was confess to John's crime or out him. My fingerprints were on the gun. I was me and he was a supposedly gentile innkeeper with a well-laundered past.

John straightened his tie. "It was an accident. Mercy was only firing a warning shot. He darted into it."

"Mercy?" asked Tiny with a furrowed brow and I shrugged as the rest of my former suspects ran up. They saw Cory caterwauling on the floor and the questions came, fast and furious.

The Troublesome Trio pushed through the gathering crowd.

"That blood looks so real," said Sorcha, hanging onto Oliver's arm.

Tiny wavered on his feet as he stared at Cory's blood. Dr. Watts stood up and steered Tiny around Cory and into the armory. She waved Oliver in after him. He obeyed without question.

Bridget shook her head. "It's too watery. They could've done better."

I stared at her.

"But it's very well done," said Jilly quickly.

"It's real blood," I said, holding up the stained handkerchief.

My cousins laughed.

"You are so good at this," said Bridget.

"Good at what? This is blood coming out of a gunshot wound. A .22 but still."

Dr. Watts pointed at Phelong, who was hovering at the back of the crowd. "Go get my bag. It's in the hearse."

"You brought the hearse?" I asked.

"Convenient, huh?"

Nicole burst into tears.

"Oh hush up," said Dr. Watts. "He won't die. This is a measly flesh wound."

Nicole screamed at Gerry, pointing to me, "Arrest her! She shot my husband."

"Nobody is arresting anybody but your husband," I said.

"What? Cory didn't do anything," said Nicole.

Dr. Watts raised an eyebrow at me. "He confessed, didn't he?"

"Oh, yeah," I said.

Leslie gave John a fresh handkerchief and he wiped the smear of blood off his hands. "Cory strangled Cherie in an ill-fated attempt to get her to confess to killing Nicole's brother in high school."

Nicole stared at John and then switched her gaze to her husband. He wouldn't meet her eyes. "Did you?" she asked.

Cory didn't answer.

"Did you?" She dropped his head to the carpet with a thump and pummeled him with clenched fists. Nobody made a move to stop her. She could beat him bloody as far as I was concerned.

Phelong ran in with Dr. Watts' medical bag, an old school black leather one. She opened it slowly and began organizing her equipment on a sterile pad in no hurry. Phelong thought about it for a moment and pulled a screaming Nicole off her husband and got a fist in the throat for his trouble. Gerry grabbed her and it took the two of them to control her.

I stood up and Dr. Watts ripped open an alcohol wipe. "You're not done."

"We got him," I said, pointing at the sobbing Cory. "He confessed."

She got out an extra-large syringe and loaded it with saline. "Did you attack Cherie in the rock garden?" she asked Cory.

He stared at the needle as Dr. Watts tapped the barrel.

"This is morphine," she said with a wink at me. "You want it?"

"Yes," he said.

She used the wipe on his thigh. "Did you attack her in the rock garden?"

"No. I don't know who did that. I couldn't sleep. I saw Cherie out there and I went down to talk to her. I wasn't going to hurt her. I swear I didn't plan to hurt her."

"You stopped to get a pair of gloves," I said.

Cory averted his eyes. "I thought it was cold out."

"Yeah, right."

Dr. Watts shoved the needle into Cory's rump, none to gently. "He wasn't in the rock garden. Get back on task."

I groaned and texted Chuck. "Caught murderer. Pick almost shot BTW."

Nothing. I wanted to shatter my uncooperative phone against the wall and stomp on it, but everyone was watching to see what I'd do next. I couldn't be acting like a brat when, as Dr. Watts pointed out, I had a job to do. So I just stood there until Pick came over to give me a slurp on the knee and then clamped his slobbery jaws on my leg. Just what I needed. Slobber. It might not be over, but I was so done.

CHAPTER TWENTY-ONE

Aaron pushed through the crowd and pressed a mug of hot chocolate into my hands. "You earned it."

No. That kid's still dead in New Orleans. Cherie's dead.

"Okay." I managed to get down a sip for Aaron's benefit and then felt lightheadedness come over me. Sugar rush. I'd almost forgotten how that felt. The sense of well-being, of straight up joy.

I pulled out my phone and called Uncle Morty.

"Whaddaya want? My ass hurts," he said.

Joy over.

"Answers, please," I said, leaning on the wall's dark paneling.

"You gonna change my dressing soon? I think it's wet."

Ew.

"Of course I will. I solved the murder by the way."

If I expected congratulations, I was sorely disappointed.

"Whaddya want? A freaking trophy? It's your damn job. I need some pain killers," he yelled.

I rolled my eyes at Dr. Watts and she grinned at me, waving the saline bottle.

"That can be arranged. What have you got on Enrique?" I asked.

Robin dashed forward. "What was that? What about Enrique?"

Bill grabbed her and pulled her back.

"You're gonna like this." Uncle Morty cleared his phlegmy throat, groused about his butt, and complained about his book being longer than expected. Anything to draw out the suspense. I commiserated because I was supposed to, not because I gave a rat's ass.

"You don't care. You don't even read my work," he said in a petulant tone. He sounded like he was my wife and I forgot our anniversary.

"Er...of course I care."

"Wouldn't hurt you to show it."

What the...oh right...Mom and Dad are busy and not telling you you're a special special boy. So needy. Groan.

"I do care." I went on to name important plot points from the last book and soothed the savage writer.

"All right then," he said.

I was afraid to ask, but I had to. Everyone was looking at me and it wasn't over. Not yet. "So do you have anything on the adoption?"

Robin wriggled out of Bill's grasp and tried to snatch my phone out of my hands. "Give me that."

I smacked her, a good crack across the jowls that snapped her head back. It was instinct, a good one as it turned out.

Uncle Morty said something I couldn't make out over Robin's freak-out.

"What?"

"It's freaking fake."

"Fake?" I asked.

Robin was stunned for a second, but her eyes refocused and she lunged at me. Dr. Watts stuck out a foot and tripped her. She went down with a screech and Bill grabbed her again before she could come at me a second time.

"What's wrong with you?" he asked.

"Get that phone!" she yelled.

Leslie stepped in front of her and in an ultra-soothing voice said, "Her uncle knows. Getting the phone won't stop it."

Robin bit her lip and then went into the ugly cry. "Don't listen to him. Don't. Don't."

What have you done, woman?

"Uncle Morty?" I asked.

"Gonna pay attention to me now, eh?"

"Sorry. We've got a couple of situations here. What did you say?"

He did the phlegmy throat thing again and then told me the secret Robin had been so desperate to hide. The adoption was illegal, obtained through some serious money changing hands. Enrique had been in the Hope Refuge Orphanage, not Mission of Hope. At first, I didn't get it. So what? It was an orphanage. He was an orphan. But there was a difference, a big difference. There were five kids in Enrique's family. He was the oldest. His siblings had been in Mission of Hope because they were younger. That was Morty's first clue. The separation. Mission of Hope was for kids fifteen and under. Hope Refuge was for kids sixteen and up. Robin and Tim had adopted Enrique four years ago and his birth certificate said he was eighteen. If so, why was he in Hope Refuge? Were they too full for him? Uncle Morty didn't buy it. He found the siblings' birth certificates. At the time of Enrique's adoption, they were fourteen, ten, nine, and four. If you believed Enrique's birth certificate, he and his sister, Maria, were born two months apart.

"Oliver," I called out.

He came into the doorway and I caught a glimpse of Tiny sitting on the floor doing some deep breathing. "Yeah?"

"What's the cutoff for the prize?" I asked.

"What do you mean?" Oliver asked.

"What's the age cutoff?"

"It's for high school seniors," he said, his brow wrinkling under his baseball cap.

Sorcha's eyes went wide and she tugged on his sleeve. "Of course. But you can't be twenty-eight and win, right?"

"No. Nineteen is the age cutoff. Oh." His eyes went to Robin, who began shaking. "How old is Enrique?"

"Twenty," I said.

"He's not eligible then."

My cousins jumped up and down. "We did it! We did it! Mystery solved."

Bill stared at them. "Enrique's eighteen. I sent in his package. His birth certificate says eighteen."

"It's fake," I said. "Tim and Robin faked it to make him eligible."

"You don't understand," said Robin between her sobs.

"Oh, I understand. You saw the dollar signs."

"No. It wasn't for us. It was for them."

"Them?" asked Dr. Watts.

"Enrique's brothers and sisters. We couldn't get them out. The government was pissed that we got Enrique. They didn't care that he would've died. They just cared that he left the country. Inez has craniofacial deformities. She needs surgery. Her brain isn't growing properly. The bribes we need to get Inez out are a lot more, and we don't have it. If Enrique gets a major league contract, he'll have the money and he can help her."

"There has to be another way," I said. "What about Doctors Without Borders or the World Health Organization?"

"Don't you think we tried? We tried everything!"

"Hey!" yelled Uncle Morty.

"What?" I said, tearing my eyes from the sobbing Robin.

"They did try. I got the trail. They're broke, living paycheck to paycheck. Enrique's their only chance to help that kid."

I glared at Robin. "She could sell her earrings."

"They're fake. I sold the real ones to pay for the camp," said Robin and Deanna gasped before throwing back the last of her wine.

"Yeah, well, something tells me that this lie isn't recent. They changed his birth certificate when they brought him to the States," I said. "Did you know about the prize back then?"

Leslie gave Robin his handkerchief and she lustily blew her nose. "We didn't know that Enrique had talent. He was half dead. How would we know? We only wanted to save him. Ask Tim."

We all looked around and Tim was the only one missing.

"Where is he?" asked Robin, shoving Bill off her. His cap went flying.

"I haven't seen him since the library," said Leslie.

"Anybody see him leave?" I asked.

The answer was no.

Robin paled and her eyes darted around, searching.

"Parker," I said, slapping my forehead. "Of course."

"What?" asked Tiny, coming out of the armory and wiping the sweat off his face.

"Taylor and most of the boys were drinking that night. Everyone except Parker. He was drinking with Lane."

"So?" asked Dr. Watts.

Cory smacked her leg. "It still hurts. Can I get some more of that?"

"Sure. It's saline." She stood up and dropped the hypo in her sharps container. "What's any of this got to do with Cherie's murder?"

"Because Cherie figured out Enrique's real age in January when she was in Ecuador," I said. "She told Lane the prize was in the bag and that's why."

Robin went still, very deer in the headlights.

"She threatened Tim that night, didn't she?" I asked.

"No. No. He didn't do anything." She pointed at Cory. "He did it. He confessed."

"I take it back!" yelled Cory.

Jilly popped him in the head just like my dad was known to do. "No backsies."

Cory tried to crawl away and Pick dashed over to bark in his face.

"Shouldn't someone cuff him?" asked Bridget.

"Pick's got it," I said as the poodle showed all his large white teeth and snarled in Cory's face.

As we watched Pick's prison guard act, Robin tried to slip away, but Tiny snagged her arm. "You didn't answer Mercy's question."

She sucked in her lips.

"She doesn't have to. I overheard the fight in the sweat lodge. That's when Cherie told Tim that he'd have to pull Enrique from the competition or she'd tell, right?"

Robin didn't answer. I didn't really expect her to.

"Tim told you and one of you told Parker," I said quietly.

"Parker?" asked Sorcha.

"Enrique's brother," said Oliver.

Leslie's jaw quivered. "His catcher."

"Yes," I said. "And catchers take care of their pitchers."

"They do. Where's Parker?" Leslie asked.

Robin began frantically texting and ran back down the hall toward the library.

"Where's she going?" asked Dr. Watts.

"She figured it out," I said, feeling a bit sick. "Motive and opportunity."

"What?"

I pointed at Gerry. "You get Robin. Contain her. Do not let her out of your sight."

"I'll do it," said Tiny, looking much stronger.

"I need you here. Gerry go."

Gerry nodded and dashed off without a question. He was the only one. Everyone from Tiny to Phelong pelted me with questions.

"Quiet!" I yelled at them. "Oliver, where are the boys?"

"Down at the fields. Why?" he asked.

"Are Enrique and Parker down there?"

A deluge of questions hit me from all sides.

I put a hand up and told them to be quiet. "Who's down there with them?" I asked Oliver.

"Josh and Martin," he said. "Do you want me to call them?"

Cory howled again and I yelled, "Yes," over the pathetic complaining. Cory probably thought he was tough. But shoot him in the rear and all toughness vanished.

Oliver put a hand over his ear and walked away, talking into his cellphone. Everyone else lobbed questions at me again, which I ignored, except Anthony, who stayed silent. He rubbed his knuckles, slightly reddened from punching Bill, who was eyeing him while keeping his distance and twisting his cap in his hands. Anthony couldn't have cared less about Bill. He watched me with quiet appraisal. A calmness had come over him. He wasn't frantic and shocked like everyone else. He paid no attention to Cory, howling like a moron on the floor. For Anthony, it was over.

Oliver walked back. "All the boys are there. What do you want me to do?"

"Have them get Parker and Enrique and bring them up to the castle. Don't let Tim near them."

Robin ran back, dragging Gerry with her. She grabbed my arm and sloshed my hot chocolate over my fingers. Aaron gasped and took the mug from me with a reproachful look at Robin. How dare she waste chocolate? I put my hand down and Pick cleaned my fingers. He was almost useful.

"What did you say?" she yelled. "You have no right."

"I have every right. Tim's going to grab Parker and run for it," I said.

Mouths dropped all around me.

"But Tim didn't do it. He has an alibi," said Sorcha. "It's on the map. He was with Robin."

"I know. John, lock all the gates."

John got on his phone and a minute later he showed his first real expression, a frown. "One of the gates just opened."

"Which one?" I asked.

"The gate to the Shut-ins."

Dr. Watts touched my shoulder. "But he doesn't have the boys."

"Tim wouldn't leave us," said Robin. "He didn't do anything. Parker didn't do anything."

"You know he did," I said. "Oliver, do they have the boys? Are you sure?"

He nodded. "They're walking back right now."

John's phone dinged. "My head of housekeeping saw Tim near the spa."

"The spa?" asked Robin. "He wouldn't go to the spa."

"Oh my god," I said. "Anthony, where's Lane?"

Anthony stiffened. "The spa." He turned and jetted down the hall. Gerry started to go after him, but I stopped him. "She's not at the spa. Tim's got her. I need a car. I need a car!"

"Go! Go! Go!" yelled Uncle Morty out of my phone. I stuffed it in my back pocket and spun in a circle, spotting Tiny's .22, still on the floor, and grabbing it.

"We don't have a car," said Jilly.

I grabbed Leslie. "Give me a car. I need a car."

"A car won't help. It'll take a half hour to get there by car," he said.

"A golf cart," suggested Dr. Watts.

"I can run faster than that," I said.

"Do something!" yelled Uncle Morty out of my pocket.

"You'll never catch him on foot," said John. "It's too far. I'm calling the park rangers." John walked away.

"What's happening?" yelled Robin.

"Tim's got Lane, idiot woman," said Dr. Watts. "He's going to kill her."

Robin shook me. "No. Tim said she's Parker's girlfriend. He wouldn't hurt her. She's a child."

"And she's Parker's alibi," said Sorcha. "She told us she was with him all night."

"She *was* his alibi," I said. "I think she was drinking and fell asleep when her mother was attacked in the rock garden. She couldn't believe that Parker would hurt her mother so she said he was with her. Lane isn't going to stick with that forever and Tim knows it. The Shut-ins are perfect for Lane to have an *accident*. If she dies, her statement stands. She's worth more dead."

"That's insane," said Robin. "My son wouldn't hurt anyone."

"He would if it helped his brother."

John walked back to us. "They're going to keep an eye out."

"That's it?" I asked.

"They're forest rangers. What do you want?"

"He's going to kill her!"

"I'm aware."

"Go! Now!" yelled Uncle Morty.

"What else have you got? Four wheelers? Motorcycles?" I slapped my forehead. "Horses. Duh. You have horses." I pointed at Leslie. "Call Jamie and have him bring out Sly Dog."

"He'll kill you. That horse is insane."

"He's a racer. He'll get me there," I said, thrusting Pick's leash at Tiny and running off toward a random door.

"Wrong way!" yelled everyone.

"Dammit!"

Leslie waved to me and I darted back to him. We took left turns and right turns and somehow magically came out of the castle close to the stables. Jamie came out leading Sly Dog, who was prancing in anticipation. I tucked the .22 in my waistband and did a quick prayer that it would stay there.

"Get me a horse!" yelled Leslie.

"No time." I grabbed the reins and flipped them over Sly Dog's head before leaping on.

"Mercy!" yelled Leslie.

"Call the real cops!"

I rammed my heels into Sly Dog's side. He leapt forward and went into a full out run down the trail to the fields, the place where Jamie said never to ride that horse.

Here goes everything.

CHAPTER TWENTY-TWO

Sly Dog stretched out to his full length and galloped toward the baseball fields. The boys and the remaining coaches stopped what they were doing to watch us. I had the reins in my hands, but I didn't need them. Sly knew where we were going. Joy radiated off of him. No more gentle rides for delicate tourists. He chose the more difficult path, jumping gullies and threading through a small stand of saplings just because he could.

The boys poured out of the dugouts and pointed at a spot beyond the ballfields. Sly Dog went in that direction without a nudge from me. At some point, it occurred to me that the gate might be closed and with Sly going full out, how would we stop? The fence was too high to jump and electrified. Cory knew my code, not me. Just when I was about to pull back, I saw the gate, buried in a blackberry bramble. The gate was open. Thank god. Sly slowed on his own, but we were there in a blink. He slipped through the gate. It was so narrow my legs brushed the sides. If Sly noticed, he showed no sign. He cantered down the slim trail past a sign.

Johnson's Shut-ins State Park

3/4 mile

Tim had a good head start, but he didn't have Sly chewing up the distance with every hoof beat. I hoped Lane hadn't gone with Tim willingly and that would slow him down considerably.

Up ahead I saw blue skies through the thick trees.

Uh-oh. Drop off.

I squeezed with my thighs and pulled back. Sly wasn't interested.

Oh shit!

That thoroughbred pain in the ass knew what was coming and I felt a thrill go through his withers when I screamed. He launched us through the air over a set of stairs. It had to be fifteen down at least. Sly's position was perfect. Mine was less so what with me screaming and grabbing his mane. If horses could laugh, I'm sure he would've.

Sly hit the trail and in two paces jumped a tree that had fallen across our path. I didn't scream that time. Sly could do anything. He continued to canter down the trail, dodging small boulders and the occasional stump. At the end of the trail was a split-rail fence and another sign announcing that we'd arrived. The parking lot and campground beyond was empty. I could hear the sound of rushing water in the distance. The water must be super high to make that much noise.

Sly's muscles bunched and he jumped the fence instead of going through the opening. Showoff. Then he galloped through the Shut-ins campground toward the camp store and ranger station. A ranger stood on the deck watching us. The access gate was closed with a sign across it saying "Extreme conditions." I pulled up and Sly surprised me by actually obeying. He danced in a circle as I yelled at the young ranger, "I'm from the castle. Have you seen a man and a sixteen-year-old girl? She may be unconscious or in distress."

He shook his head. "I got the call, but I haven't seen anyone today. My boss went down to the water to look."

I nodded and gave Sly a light kick. He didn't need another invitation. He took off for the closed gate and jumped it easily. In the air, my phone started vibrating. No time for that. It stopped as we cantered down the trail and then vibrated again.

"I'm busy!"

We passed the last outhouse and the trail narrowed. The roar of dozens of waterfalls intensified. My phone vibrated again and I stood in my stirrups to get a better view of the water through the trees to the left. It was super high, up the banks and rushing around the trees. I'd never seen it like that. When I'd been there before it was always low and fairly calm. That day it was anything but calm.

I didn't see Tim or Lane. I urged Sly to go faster and we nearly mowed down a grizzly old ranger when we raced around a turn.

"Whoa there, ma'am!" he yelled after he jumped out of the way. "This isn't an equestrian trail."

"Sorry. I'm from the castle. Have you seen my kidnapped vic?" I asked, breathless.

He retucked his shirt and straightened his name that said Silver on it. "No sign of anyone. You can't get any farther on that horse. The trail's too skinny."

Sly pointed his nose at the underbrush. No more low branches, thank you very much. I slid off his back and he snorted at me.

"If you see them, detain him," I told Silver.

"You really think he's trying to kill that girl."

"Definitely."

Should I yell for Lane or not? By alerting her, I'm alerting Tim. I don't know. I don't know.

"Well, they're not here," said Silver. "I would've seen them come in. Not much happening with the park closed."

I scanned the water and my phone sang out, "Oh I swear to you, I'll be there for you."

Silver looked around. "What was that?"

"Chuck," I whispered and my hand went to my pocket as a scream echoed through the trees.

"Oh shit!" said Silver.

"Which way? Which way?" I couldn't tell. Was it behind us or up ahead?

A flash of black zipped by us and darted into the brush.

"Was that a poodle?" Silver peered into the brush.

"Yes!" I dropped Sly's reins and dashed in behind Pick. Another scream ripped through the air. I chased Pick through the brush to the beginning of the large rocks. He disappeared between two boulders as another scream came from up ahead. I knew where they were. The pool below my favorite sunbathing spot. I went right and took another path, slipping and sliding on the gravel in the forest of stone.

"Lane!" I emerged beside the rock tower and saw a flash of white. "Lane!"

Pick barked as I jumped into the rushing water. It was up to my knees where it was usually dry. Pick ran past me, jumping from rock to rock. I yelled for him, but the rushing water was so loud I couldn't hear myself. I climbed up on a tiny point of a rock and saw them downstream. I pulled out the .22, but I was too slow. Tim and Lane were both in the river being carried away by the force of the water through sluices and down waterfalls. They tumbled into a roiling pool and Tim lunged for Lane, dragging her under. Pick launched himself off a rock to land in the pool with a huge splash and came up swimming and snapping.

I jumped from rock to rock and made it to the edge of the pool where I slipped and dropped the .22. I lunged for it on instinct and fell into a sluice. The water battered me against the rocks and wedged me between a small boulder and solid rock. Something gave way and a searing pain went through my ankle.

I popped out into the pool and was dragged under by the force of the current. I took a burning blow to my cheek that I thought was Tim, but when I came up, I saw him and Lane going over another waterfall. Pick's jaws were clamped on Tim's arm and he was swept away with them. The water rammed me against rocks beside the waterfall. My nails dug into the algae as I tried to hold on. I went under and was carried away, shooting out into the air through the mist and pounding water. I landed in a great pool. Tim and Lane were on the other side, washed up on the rocky beach. I started swimming. One leg wouldn't work. I was getting nowhere fast. My arms weren't strong enough. I went under again and again. When I came up the third time, I saw Pick still had a hold of Tim's arm, but in his free arm he had a jagged rock. Lane was lying face down in the water. Pick pulled back and Tim smashed him in the head. The poodle yelped and let go. Tim raised the rock above Lane's head, Pick lunged, and two shots rang out. Tim's back arched and then he pitched forward to land on Lane's back, driving her face deep into the water. Pick jumped over Tim and clamped his jaws on Lane's arm, trying to pull the limp girl away.

I kept swimming and a wave of water pushed me forward. I dragged myself up next to Tim and pushed him off Lane into the pool. Between Pick and I, we managed to drag Lane onto the beach. I rolled her over and cleared her airway. Her mouth was full of water so I rolled her on her side. A good amount flowed out and I began CPR. After a few reps, Lane convulsed and a huge spew of water flowed out of her mouth and nose. She hacked and coughed. Pick gave her a couple of encouraging slurps on the face and then shook, spraying me with an amazing amount of river water. I collapsed beside Lane and heard yelling behind me. I rolled over and saw Silver swimming through the pool. Blood streamed out of his nose, but otherwise he was doing better than me.

I sat up and he crawled up on the beach beside me. "You rock," I said.

"Sorry. I couldn't be more help," he said, gasping.

"Are you kidding? You were great."

We watched as Tim's limp body was carried away downstream. It rolled over, revealing the ragged exit wounds in his throat. I kinda thought I should snag him, but my ankle said no way. Silver crawled to the other side of Lane and patted her shoulder as she coughed and wheezed. "You're okay. She saved you. Dr. Watts will be here soon."

Lane nodded and began a fresh fit of coughing.

I felt my ankle. It was already swelling and there was a large impact bruise on the side. Broken. Fantastic.

"I didn't save her. I tried, but that was you," I said.

"Me?" he asked.

"You shot him. Nice one by the way."

"I didn't shoot him. I thought you did."

Oh crap.

My eyes traced the path of the bullet and there they were. Leslie and John stood on the bluff overlooking the pool. Leslie waved and John stared down at me. Of course. I should've known.

Pick shook again and licked me on the chin.

"You were almost shot twice in one day," I said. "What would Chuck say?"

Chuck!

I yanked out my phone and my waterproof, shockproof case wasn't so much. My phone had died a watery, cracked death. All evidence of Chuck's call was gone, if it had happened at all. I lay down next to Lane and pressed my phone to my chest. The ranger stood over us, trying without success to get his walkie to work and then yelled up to John and Leslie about emergency airlift.

"We don't need that," I said. "John will find a way."

"That ankle's broken bad and you two are shaking to beat the band. We got to airlift you out. This is what we call an emergency." Silver yelled up to Leslie and John about calling for help.

I looked at my dead phone again and then tossed it away on the rocks. Lane coughed hard and brought up some water. Her brown eyes were trained on me and her lips formed the words, "He told me Parker needed me. I shouldn't have gone with him. I knew I shouldn't. Sorry."

I rolled over and pushed her wet hair out of her eyes. "No worries."

"I knew what my mom was doing."

"You mean the blackmailing? She told you?"

"No. I kinda figured it out. I didn't know what to do. Parker's family was cheating and Taylor deserved the prize, but Enrique's sister...they needed him to win for her. I let it all happen. I pretended it would be okay."

"Parker left you that night in the barn, didn't he?"

Lane coughed and nodded. "I woke up and he was gone. I didn't think...it wasn't very long."

"Parker did hurt your mom, but he didn't kill her. That was one of the Viper parents. It was about something that happened when she was in high school. It's nothing to do with you. It's not your fault, Lane."

Her battered face screwed up and she began to cry between coughs. I pulled her cold, shaking body to mine and cried, too.

"Ah, hell," said Silver. "The ladies are crying. Somebody get me a copter!"

We kept crying. Through it I could feel Tim's body, all bodies, being washed farther and farther downriver.

CHAPTER TWENTY-THREE

No copter came. We didn't need it. Leslie carried Lane out over the rocks and John carried me. Sly Dog had worn himself out galloping up and down the trail while we were being bashed against rocks and was calm enough to carry us back to the castle. He got the good oats. Dr. Watts checked us out. Lane had a minor concussion and a multitude of cuts and bruises, but nothing too serious. My ankle was broken and hurt like hell. The only x-ray in town was in the basement of Flincher Funerals. Dr. Watts got it through a grant from a women's health organization. I was surprised she didn't have an MRI, but that grant was still under review. I guess being a retired Vietnam vet doing everything from stitches to autopsies in a rural Missouri town for free was pretty damn persuasive.

Dr. Watts herself was a force not to be denied. She told me to hush up and quit my moaning, gave me some hydrocodone, a temporary cast, and put me in Elizabeth I's bed in the Tudor Tower with orders to go to sleep instantly. I obeyed. I was scared not to.

Three hours later, I woke up with a headache and an audience.

"Miss Watts," said Silver, dried out but very rumpled with a dab of blood on his nose, "I thought you'd never wake up."

"Has it been that long?"

"Long enough. Springfield will be here any moment and we have to get our story straight."

I yawned and rubbed my eyes. "What story?"

When I looked at him again, I got it. Behind Silver stood John and Leslie, showered and in fresh suits. My grandmother would say that butter wouldn't melt in their mouths.

"Oh. You mean the story where I shot Cory in the butt and Tim in the neck," I said.

Silver blew out a breath. "Good. That's all settled. You dropped the gun in the river by the way."

"Not in the right place. I dropped it when I slipped up in the rocks." I went up on my elbows. "They'll find it if they look."

Leslie nodded. "It's in the right place now."

"They have to be the same caliber. Did John use a .22 on Tim?"

"Of course."

"And let me guess. You already told Springfield that I shot Cory and Tim."

"It was necessary," said John.

"For you, not me," I said.

Silver came to my bedside and stuck out his hand, "You're a good man, taking one for the team."

How do I get off this team?

I shook his hand and he left. John and Leslie stayed at the foot of my bed, still as stone.

"So we're a team now?" I asked.

"You'll be the face of this," said Leslie.

"I never said I'd do it. You're taking it for granted."

"Naturally," said John. "You owe us."

"Not that much," I said.

They stared at me.

I crossed my arms. "Are you saying I have no choice?"

"None whatsoever," said John and he turned to go. "Your father would agree."

"Wait, wait, wait," I said. "How come you didn't end up in the water with me? Were you just standing on the bluff watching it all happen?"

Leslie smiled. "No. We came in at the end. You were too fast for us."

"That doesn't happen often," said John. I couldn't tell if he approved of my speed during the chase or not.

I laid back on my fluffy pillows. "I'm guessing you were made for stealth, not speed."

"Innkeepers are multi-taskers," said John.

"I'm a good accountant and a master distiller, for instance," said Leslie.

I threw my hands up. "Oh for crying out loud. You're spooks, retired spooks."

They didn't blink.

"You've been watching too much TV," said John.

"Yeah, right. Morty can't break through your firewall and the castle has better security than international airports."

"That's not saying much," said Leslie.

"Fine. How about your backgrounds? They're perfect, complete with speeding tickets and inaccurate medical histories."

"Inaccurate?" asked John, showing a spark of interest.

"Your nose has never been broken, but you have had plastic surgery. That's not in your history. And Leslie's appendectomy didn't happen in 1980."

"Now how would you know that?"

"I glimpsed his abdomen and he didn't have a significant scar. If he actually had an appendectomy, it was a laparoscopic procedure. Those weren't used in '80, so it was much later."

They didn't confirm or deny. So frustrating.

"Leslie already told me that he's Shaun so obviously he didn't play quarterback in high school in Pennsylvania to get a torn meniscus."

He shrugged.

"You may as well tell me. You're counting on me to tell the cops I shot two people for you," I said. "You're spooks. The truth will set you free."

"The truth never set anyone free. Evidence maybe. The truth, never," said John. "And no one uses the term spook. That's a journalist's invention."

"What do you call yourselves then?" I raised an eyebrow at him.

Leslie smiled. "Innkeepers."

"Oh my god!"

"Nothing," said John.

"Nothing?" I asked.

"Nothing."

"You have no name, no title?"

"No."

"That's disturbing," I said, and it was. Presumably they worked for our country. They must be something.

"Names aren't important," said Leslie. "Only results. You should understand that."

"I can't separate myself from my name, but I agree on the results thing. So what did you two do to get stuck out here?"

"We survived," said John.

I glanced around my sumptuous room. "And surviving comes with rewards."

"And penalties."

"Was it worth it? You can't even use your skills anymore."

Leslie gave me his most charming smile. "You mean like accounting."

"Yeah like accounting," I rolled my eyes, "and shooting—"

My door flew open and Uncle Morty stomped in with Pick. The poodle whined when he saw John and Leslie and then jumped on my bed, still damp and stinky. Uncle Morty tugged on his brand-new sweats blazoned with the Cairngorms Castle logo. "I mighta known I'd find you two in here like a couple of spiders with my girl in your web." He dropped a plastic bag on my bed and paced. "You don't have to do a damn thing that they say."

"I know," I said.

"Do you?"

"I'm not an idiot."

"That remains to be seen. You didn't shoot either of those guys." Uncle Morty glared at the spooks or innkeepers or whatever they were. "Beat it, *John* and *Leslie*. Those names suck by the freaking way."

"What would you have called us, Dekth and Arubus?" asked Leslie.

Uncle Morty's hand went to his heart. "You read my work."

"Don't get excited. Book three sucked. You shouldn't have killed off Mirba. You screwed up your whole arc, and what is with the Merenda? Were you just horny when you wrote that?"

Uncle Morty went purple with rage and charged them. He might've caught them if he hadn't been limping. "I will kick your asses!"

John and Leslie hurried out the door. John left without a backward glance, but Leslie gave me a couple of looks before he exited. First was a smirk. He really enjoyed poking Uncle Morty. Second, he asked me to keep his secret with a glance and it was a package deal. If I denied their assertions to the police, I'd open up what my dad would call a shit storm. They already said I'd shot Cory and Tim. I didn't deny it after John said it in front of my cousins and the other guests. If I denied it now, there would be an investigation and the same thing would happen with the Tim situation. I wasn't fool enough to think it would be easy or comfortable. The cops would need an answer. Who did shoot Cory and Tim? Why didn't I deny it before? Was I lying? Did I lie in New Orleans? Did I lie in my depositions about The Bled Collection? My family, the Bleds, Leslie, John, Lane, nobody needed the attention and I didn't want anyone cross-examining me about New Orleans again.

"I shot them," I said.

"Oh yeah?" The purple faded from Uncle Morty's face and he leaned on my four-poster bed.

"Yeah. What's going to happen?"

"Not a damn thing. You shot two dirtbags. Cory confessed to strangling a brain-injured woman in front of multiple witnesses. Lane's lucky to be alive. The ranger will back up everything you say and he's a great liar. They'll probably give you a medal."

"Pass on the medal. I just want to go home."

"Not gonna happen. They haven't nailed the Costillas yet."

"Great. What's in the bag?" I asked, hoping for chocolates.

He tossed the bag onto my lap. It was light, not at all like chocolate. "I got the stuff."

Please don't be what I think. Please don't be what I think.

"What stuff?"

"Watts brought the dressings. For my butt."

"Are you kidding me?" I asked.

Uncle Morty yanked down his sweatpants. "Look here. I got ooze."

"Oh my god. I've got a broken ankle."

"Your hands ain't broken."

"They will be after I punch you. Get out," I said, crossing my arms.

"Tommy wants you to do it," said Uncle Morty.

I snorted. "You told Dad that you have bedsores?"

"Fix my butt!"

"That's what I thought."

His lower lip poked out. "It hurts."

"I don't doubt it. Give me that bag."

Dr. Watts had given me everything I needed. I took out a stack of moist gauze packets and a piece of folded paper slipped out. My name was written in copperplate script. Uncle Morty didn't have that handwriting. Nobody I knew did.

"What's wrong?" he asked.

"Nothing. There's probably a trash bin in the bathroom. Can you get it for me?"

Uncle Morty went to get the bin and I opened the note.

I have the answer you seek.

F

"F?" I waved the paper and a slight odor came off of it. Abacus Flincher.

"What was that?" asked Uncle Morty coming out of the bathroom.

"Nothing." I stuffed the note under my covers. "Come here. Let's get this over with."

"Some nurse you are."

"Beggars can't be choosers."

"I ain't beggin'."

"I have a different point of view. Pull down your pants," I said.

I can't believe I just said that.

"So is Flincher still here in the castle?"

Uncle Morty dropped his drawers and he did, in fact, have some ooze I'm sorry to say. "Yeah, that guy's been lurking around your room since you came back."

"Really?" I snapped on a pair of gloves and peeled off the old dressing.

"What's he want with you anyway?" he asked.

"Nothing good, I suspect." I did some minor cleaning. I should've done a better job, but my ankle started seriously aching when I rolled over onto my hip.

"Stay away from that guy."

Nope.

"No problem," I said.

My door flew open and banged against the wall. "What on God's good earth are you doing?" yelled Dr. Watts. "I told you to leave her alone. I'll take care of your issue."

Uncle Morty growled. "I don't want you to do it. It's Mercy's job."

Dr. Watts marched in and whacked him with an ancient golf umbrella. "Get away."

"She's not done!"

"Oh, she's done alright. Get outta here."

"I'm not leaving."

She brandished the umbrella. It had a wicked brass tip. "I will poke you right in your pus."

"What kinda medical professional, are you?" he yelled.

"The kind that works on dead people. Get out!"

I waved a wad of stained gauze. "He has to have a new dressing."

Dr. Watts whacked Uncle Morty one more time for good measure. "I'll do it then, you lethargic lump."

"I am not lethargic. No wonder Ace divorced you. You are a huge pain in the—"

"Ass? I'm about to be. Get over here. Stop trying to hide."

Dr. Watts and Uncle Morty did a strange dance around my bed. She with her dressing packets and he with his rear hanging out.

"No!" he yelled.

"Yes!" she yelled back.

Just then the real cops showed up. Two detectives that probably had forty years of police work between them, but they'd never seen anything like that. They stared without blinking. How often do you see an old doctor trying to chase down an obese man with bedsores? I'm going with never.

Silver came back into the room, wearing a fresh uniform and a bandage on his nose. He took one look and laughed. "Holy cow! This is the cherry on the cake of my day." He wiped his eyes and pointed to the bathroom. "Take it in there. We've got business to attend to."

Uncle Morty was purple again, but marched into the bathroom with something like dignity, as much dignity as a man can have with his rear hanging out.

Dr. Watts hung back and eyed him through the door. "Say please."

"Woman, get in here or I will bludgeon you to death with a toilet seat."

"Close enough." She went in and closed the door.

The cops stared at me and I waved. "Hi. Welcome to my world."

"I don't know what to say about that," said the one on the right. He was mildly handsome, bald, and wearing a suit that had seen better days.

I smiled and summoned up the Watts get-out-of-trouble charm. It worked for Dad. Why not me? "I'd be surprised if you did."

They recovered quickly and introduced themselves as White and Logsdon, up from Springfield and none too happy about it. They went on about procedure for a good ten minutes until I interrupted, "Can I get something to eat?"

"No, you can't. This is an official interview," said Logsdon, loosening his tie.

Dr. Watts hustled out of the bathroom. "You're hungry? Since when?"

"Now, I guess," I said.

She beamed. "Excellent. I'll order you a burger and fries. Aaron knows what you like, correct?"

Before I could answer, White elbowed Dr. Watts away from my bed. "No food until I get some answers."

Dr. Watts glared at him and pulled out her phone. White and

Logsdon proceeded to interrogate me about every moment since I got to the castle and my answers weren't what they were looking for. It was a bloody weekend and I'd stolen the win from them. Pissed didn't cover it.

Uncle Morty came out of the bathroom. His pants were up, thankfully, and he watched me getting bashed with an increasingly dark expression.

"I don't know what you want me to say," I said with my hands folded over my stomach.

"How about the truth?" White was as purple as Uncle Morty had been. It was weird with his dark skin and grey hair.

"I told you the truth."

"According to the innkeepers, you shot two men today?"

"Don't answer that," said Uncle Morty.

Silver stepped up. "I'll answer it. She shot that guy in the river. I told you what happened. She saved that girl."

"We haven't found the body yet," said White.

"You think he's alive?" asked Uncle Morty.

Logsdon colored. "No, but we need to confirm her story with forensics."

"Like what?" asked Silver. "The bullets from the river? Good luck with finding that."

White flushed and turned to the door. "Get in here, Emmett."

Emmett was a crime scene tech and he skulked into the room like he'd committed a crime himself. "Yes, sir."

"I want her tested for gunshot residue."

Emmett brought in his case and set it on the bed next to my ankle. He apologized when I winced.

"Don't worry about it," I said with a winning smile and he looked grateful.

"Don't apologize to her. She's a suspect," said Logsdon.

Dr. Watts sat on my bed between me and the cops. "A suspect in what crime? Did she strangle that woman? Did she try to murder that girl? I don't think so."

"She claims to have shot two men today, one of which she killed. Test her, Emmett."

Emmett got out his kit.

"Go ahead," said Dr. Watts. "But she's been in the river, and those gloves are filled with talc."

"Shit!" exclaimed White.

"What are you complaining about?" asked Dr. Watts. "She handed you motive, means, opportunity, and three perpetrators tied up with ribbon. You have two confessions."

"Two?" I asked.

Dr. Watts picked up my wrist and took my pulse. "Parker admitted to hearing Cherie calling for Lane that night. Lane was asleep. I gather some alcohol was involved. Parker went out to talk to Cherie. He pushed her after she refused to back off on Enrique. He claims it was an accident and he didn't know she hit her head."

"She was unconscious."

"It was dark. He panicked and ran." Dr. Watts shot a smug look at the Springfield cops. "Wrapped up, nice and neat."

"You should've called us!" yelled Logsdon.

"We obviously didn't need you!" she shouted back. "We handled it just fine without you big city boys sticking your noses in."

"You're not supposed to handle it. You're retired and she's a—"

"Watch it, detective," bellowed Uncle Morty.

"Who the hell are you?"

"Morton Van Der Hoof. I work for Tommy Watts. Remember him?"

"Watts doesn't count for shit down here. He's just a glory hound."

Uncle Morty walked over, pointed at Emmett's kit and said, "Swab her and get the fuck out."

"We're running this interview," said White.

"This interview is over."

"We're not done."

"Are you going to arrest her?"

"We haven't decided yet."

"Decide now. And remember she just saved a sixteen-year-old girl's life. She broke her ankle in the process and she's got claw marks on her face."

"I do?" I asked, touching a bandage on my cheek.

Dr. Watts shushed me.

"Mercy is stunningly beautiful. She photographs like a freaking dream and she gives good interview."

No, I don't. No interviews.

"We'll interview, too," said White, but he sounded less sure by the second.

"I'm not talking about local. You want to explain to Nancy Grace, FOX, and whoever else why you arrested Mercy? You who bungled the takedown at that meth lab last year. What's that toddler got? Burns over sixty percent of her body. I'm sure Nancy'll be interested in that."

White swallowed hard. "Are you threatening us?"

"I'm giving you the facts. If you question them, go talk to Anthony Marin and the rest of the guests. Go talk to Lane. Mercy did good. Ain't nobody gonna think otherwise. Least of all the media."

They left. They didn't say another word. I told Emmett to test my hands. He peeled off my gloves and swabbed me, saying it was pointless. At least he did it. That was the point. He asked for my autograph and I signed his glove. I hoped the detectives didn't see it. They'd make his life hell.

Silver shook my hand again. "Proud to know you. Don't you worry. I got it all covered." He nodded to Dr. Watts. "Dinner tomorrow?"

"Are you cooking?" she asked.

"You think I'm eating your cooking again?"

She made her sneezing noise. "I make good tacos."

"That's all you make." Silver gave Dr. Watts a kiss on the cheek and left, muttering about women that couldn't cook.

"Alright now. You go back to sleep," said Uncle Morty. "I need a beer."

"Actually," I said. "I think I'd like that x-ray now."

"Why?" asked Dr. Watts. "What about your burger?"

"Eating can wait. You need the x-ray to cast the ankle."

"Yes, but you'd have to go to Flinchers. When you're ready we'll drive over to Avery, they've got a decent clinic."

"After today, Flincher doesn't worry me." I swung my legs over the side of the bed and winced when my temp cast touched the floor. No matter. Time to see what answer Flincher had to give me.

CHAPTER TWENTY-FOUR

Dr. Watts pulled up in front of the castle behind Flincher's hearse in her Morris Minor. "Your chariot awaits, my girl."

I hopped over and peered into the backseat. It was minuscule and I had to lie down back there.

"What about Phelong and Gerry's car?"

"You don't like my Morris?" She glowered at me.

"No, no. I love it. I'm just not sure I'll fit."

She snorted and got out. "You're fine." She opened the passenger door and flipped up the seat. It was a good thing I lost all that weight or I would never have gotten in. As it was, my spine will never be the same.

"See," said Dr. Watts. "You fit just fine."

"Do you have any Oxy on you?" I asked.

"How much pain are you in?"

A lot more now.

"I put too much weight on the foot."

She got a pill out of her purse and gave it to me with a bottle of water. I didn't ask what it was and I didn't care. She covered me with a wool army blanket that smelled like feet and was about to slam the door when a picnic basket got in the way.

Aaron leaned in. "You hungry?"

"Oh my god, yes."

He put the basket on the floor and served up an herb-roasted turkey sandwich on parmesan focaccia, little bread ball things that had caponata inside, balsamic-roasted carrots, and a sippy cup of Chianti.

Aaron put the straw to my lips. "Good for what ails you."

"I just took a painkiller."

Dr. Watts got in the Morris and made her sneezing noise. "Please. Wine's good for you."

"You're not supposed to mix painkillers with alcohol."

"I'm a doctor. Are you questioning my know-how?"

"Er..."

"Drink it and eat that sandwich before I do. It smells better than sex feels."

Ew.

I decided to drink the wine because she was a doctor and I wanted to. Aaron got in the front seat, gave Dr. Watts a vanilla latte, and filled the Morris with the smell of hot dogs.

"Wait," I said. "What about Tiny? I hope you didn't make him get in with Flincher."

"I wouldn't do that," said Dr. Watts. "Tiny's staying here."

"Why?"

She didn't look at me. "He doesn't fit in this car."

I protested, but she put the Morris in gear with a bit of grinding that masked my voice. So I settled back and ate on the way to the funeral home, which isn't something people normally do. I didn't care that I was going to one of the creepiest places on Earth. I ate. Food. I'd forgotten about food in the last two months, the way it feels to eat something exceptional, to smell it, and not to feel a bit guilty in the process.

"So you're eating again," said Dr. Watts, pulling into Flincher's garage after what felt like thirty seconds.

Can't talk. Eating.

"Uh-huh."

"So it's over. Your mother will be pleased, not to mention all visually-oriented males."

"Huh?" I swallowed the last caponata ball. So good. "What's over?"

"The punishing."

"I don't know what you're talking about."

Dr. Watts turned in her seat to look at me. "You were punishing yourself for New Orleans and now it's over."

"I had to eat lettuce." I said.

"And now you don't."

She and Aaron got me out. It wasn't easy. Between the Chianti, the pills, and the calories, I was feeling no pain. I leaned on Aaron. "I don't remember why I thought I needed so much lettuce."

"It doesn't matter," said Dr. Watts. "You balanced the scales on the Black river. You did it in the worst way possible, but you did it. That's the important thing."

Flincher pulled up beside us in the hearse. He got out and I felt instantly sober. It was a good thing, too. I doubted Flincher did anything for free and his information would cost me.

"Ladies," said Flincher. "Shall we?"

"*We* aren't doing anything," said Dr. Watts and she got out her key. "You're going to keep your distance."

"Am I?" He steepled his fingers and leveled his gaze at me. The whites of his eyes were yellow and he looked jaundiced in general.

"You should see a doctor," I said.

"I see her all the time."

Dr. Watts gave me a cane and turned me to the stairs. "Ignore him."

I hopped up the steps and we went a different way than the way Flincher had taken me the last time. There was an elevator, a small one just big enough for a gurney and one person. We rode down to Dr. Watts' area. Cherie wasn't on the slab anymore. I breathed in the clean air after the stench of Flincher's possum and whatever else.

Dr. Watts led me to a small radiology suite that included digital mammography and ultrasound. "Why do you need all this?" I asked.

"I do all the mammography around these parts," she said, helping me up on the table.

"Women come to the funeral home where you do autopsies to get their mammograms? Are you serious?"

"It's better than driving hours to do it."

I glanced back at the autopsy suite. "If you say so."

"I do. Lie down. This will only take a second."

Dr. Watts removed my temp cast and did my x-rays, maneuvering my ankle around in painful ways, but the break was clean and she had me hop out to the lab section and sit in her office chair.

"Is there anything you don't do?" I asked.

"Colonoscopy. That's where I draw the line." She got out her supplies. "What color do you want?"

"You have colors? How many of these do you do a year?" I asked.

"Five or six. What'll it be? Pink, purple, green, neon green, or black? I had orange, but the Jasper twins used it all up."

"Purple."

"Good choice." She casted my ankle with expert hands and put on the outer layer of bright purple before saying, "An hour before putting weight on it."

"I know," I said, glancing at Aaron who was examining her bandage scissors. "What are you doing?"

"These would be good for cutting bacon."

"No, they're not. I tried it," said Dr. Watts. "Do you want some tea, Mercy?"

I shifted in my chair and tried to look like I wasn't up to something. "I'd love some, but do you have a kitchen?"

"Down the street at Mrs. Mahoney's house. I can't keep anything in here, except bottled water. It's a pain but there's Flincher to consider," she said.

Perfect.

"It's a long way. Do you mind?" I asked.

She shrugged. "Not at all. Alicia has MS and I like to check on her a couple of times a day anyway."

I smiled. "Do you have peppermint?"

"Is your stomach upset?"

"A little," I said. "I'm not used to so much food anymore."

"Alicia has peppermint and every other flavor that exists." She got up, ordered Aaron to watch me, and left by the elevator.

"You're not sick," said Aaron, not bothering to look at me.

"How do you know?"

"My food makes you better."

Dammit.

I pretended to burp. "You know what. I think you're right. Can you tell her that I'd like Sleepytime instead? If I have to be here for an hour, I'd like to snooze through it."

Aaron didn't move and I had to get rid of him quickly or Dr. Watts would come back before I could talk to Flincher.

"What are you waiting for?" I asked.

"You sure?"

"Of course. Go on. Sleepytime, if she has it, or chamomile."

Aaron gave me my cane, a bone saw, and the bandage scissors. "Five minutes. Don't eat anything."

Oh crap. He knows. How does he always know?

"I'll be fine." I waved the cane.

Aaron went out the door to the elevator and a scant ten seconds later Abacus Flincher, town ghoul, came in carrying an ancient blue tackle box. "I thought they'd never leave."

My stomach went into a complicated sailor knot. Being alone with Flincher was worse than I expected. His smell was unspeakable in the enclosed area and the harsh lighting made him look like he was on death's doorstep, knocking.

I sat up straight and raised an eyebrow. "Exactly what answer do you have for me?"

"The only one you can't get for yourself."

"And that is?"

"The identity of a certain individual who may or may not be fertilizing Mrs. Mahoney's begonias."

I shuddered. Not my finest moment, but I couldn't help it. I knew he'd done away with the body from the woods. Hearing him say it made it real, too real.

"Ah, and what will it cost me? I might as well tell you that I'm not eating or drinking anything."

He rubbed his hands together and I heard the knuckles crack. They sounded like cellophane. "I only require samples."

"Of what?" I narrowed my eyes at him.

"Of you, naturally. You are a lovely specimen."

Specimen? Yuck.

"What kind of sample? Better hurry. If Dr. Watts catches you in here, she won't be happy."

He smiled, showing his ragged gums. There was blood in his teeth, they were so wrecked. "She won't catch me."

I swallowed hard. "What do you want Flincher?"

"Blood, skin cells, a cheek swab, hair with root, and a fingernail clipping." He coughed and some sputum landed on the floor with a splat. "Nothing you can't spare."

"I'll be the judge of that. Why do you want it?"

"Just a little hobby of mine." He shook his tackle box. "I'm ready."

"I'm not. Why do you want it?" I asked.

"Does it really matter? I have what you want."

"It matters. Tell me or get out."

He pulled up a chair and a tray table, sitting with his bony knees jutting out. He laid out his collection swabs and a phlebotomy kit with several vials. They were all new and clean, but there was no way he was touching me with anything he brought in. Then he pulled out a sheath of papers covered in graphs and complicated chemical analysis. "I thought you might require more than my other subjects."

"I'm not one of your subjects. What is that?" I asked.

He sat up straighter than I would've thought possible with his hump. "My work."

"That doesn't strike me as mortician stuff."

"Because it's not. Funerals are a means to an end." He laid the papers in my lap and tapped them with a long bony finger. "This is the end."

Flincher's papers looked sort of like a drug study, but I didn't recognize the chemical compounds or the methodology. "Are you studying something?"

"Death," he said, leaning over and spewing fumes in my face.

"Whose?"

"Everyone's. I'm going to cure death." He clasped his hands together and beamed at me.

Oh dear lord. Where's that tea? Aaron! Dr. Watts!

Flincher pointed to a chemical compound on the first page of his papers. "There it is. It's taken me forty years, but I've finally got it."

"Um...great," I said. "What is it?"

"I can't tell you that. It's proprietary."

"Of course. And what do you need my samples for?"

"Testing. I'm always testing. A scientist must always be striving for the next discovery."

"As long as you're not using live subjects," I said gently.

Flincher blinked. "Oh, I am. I must."

Oh my god!

I gripped the cane hard. "Do they know you're using them to test your...discovery?"

"No. Of course not. They'd never agree. But science can't wait for fools to acquiesce. We'd never advance."

"It must be difficult to operate under those conditions."

He glanced around. "Yes, it is. No one will accept my little treats anymore."

I'm shocked.

"So how are you continuing your work?" I asked.

"I use the ultimate subject," said Flincher, sticking out his bony chest.

Please don't say the neighbors' pets.

"Myself."

Thank god.

"Um...how's that working out for you?" I asked, glancing at the door.

Flincher gestured to his ravaged body. "As you see, but once I perfect my serum all will be well. I project that I will return to my seventeen-year-old self immediately."

Great. The year you killed your parents.

"Sounds...good. Seventeen is good."

"So you agree?" he asked, his eyes going all watery.

"What evidence do I get regarding the body?" I asked.

"Photographs, blood, and fingerprints. I was thorough. I knew you'd want it."

"All right then. Let's do it."

Flincher picked up the needle.

"Nope. Back off. I'll be using Dr. Watts' stuff," I said.

"If you must."

"I must."

I hopped out to the autopsy suite and, without turning my back on Flincher, I collected everything I needed. He was impressed with my ability to draw my own blood, a skill I never thought would come in handy. I learned it in nursing school when my blood drawing partner kept passing out. I'd swabbed my cheek before Dr. Watts banged on the door to the elevator. "Mercy! Mercy!"

"I'm fine!"

"Is Flincher in there?" she yelled.

I looked at him and he at me.

"I don't know! Where's Aaron?" I asked.

"Looking for you. I'll come around to the other door."

"Okay!"

I collected Flincher's other samples, he gingerly put them in his tackle box, and stood up with every joint creaking. "Thank you, Miss Watts. You've been a great help to science."

"And my evidence?"

He handed me a small packet. I stuffed it under my hoodie and he left through the door to the elevator seconds before Dr. Watts came storming in.

"Are you alright?" she asked.

"Perfectly fine."

"And Flincher didn't come down here?"

"Haven't seen him."

"Thank god. I thought he'd make a play for you."

I shrugged. "He wasn't here. Where's the tea?"

She slapped her forehead. "I forgot it at Mrs. Mahoney's place. I had the most terrible feeling about you and ran back. But you're fine."

"I am."

"My intuition must be out of whack."

Aaron walked in with a thermos of tea and I gave him a wink behind Dr. Watts' back. We drank it while my cast dried and I tried not to think about Flincher injecting himself with toxic substances.

What was I going to do about him? I had no clue, but I couldn't leave it alone. Someone that crazy was capable of anything.

I didn't open Flincher's packet until I was in bed with my cast propped up on five pillows. It throbbed and ached, but it wasn't time for another painkiller. Aaron prescribed chocolate and ran off. Pick woke up, licked my toes, and went back to snoring. Dr. Watts fussed around, straightening my covers and muttering about Pick smelling like river.

"You're welcome to wash him if you want," I said.

"That's not much of a thank you. He did risk life and limb today."

"He's a water dog. Why do you think he leapt right in?"

"To save Lane. I think he would've jumped into fire for her."

We looked at the poodle, who promptly gassed and rolled over with all four legs in the air.

"Looks like a hero to me," I said.

Dr. Watts picked a moldy leaf and a stick out of his fuzzy tail. "He looks like a goof, the very best kind of hero, but the smell has to go."

"Pick," I said. "Bath."

The poodle flipped over, jumped off the bed, and scratched on the door frantically.

"I thought you said he's a water dog."

"He likes baths. He just forgets until he actually gets in the bath."

She ran her hands through her spiky hair. "How do I get him in there? He's too big to drag."

"Go in the bathroom and say sausage."

"That's a mean trick."

I rolled my eyes. "You can give it to him after he's clean."

"He gets at least five then."

"Fantastic. More gas."

Dr. Watts cackled, went in the bathroom, and said, "Sausage."

Pick stopped and darted in after her and she closed the door.

"What a sucker," I said, pulling the packet out of my hoodie. Inside were a set of five pictures of a middle-aged Hispanic man. In the first two pictures, he was dressed in black Under Armour athletic wear and

Reeboks. I couldn't see any blood and his face was intact. In the last three pictures, he was completely nude. No tattoos. No identifying marks. I winced. This guy had been murdered and then he ended up in Flincher's hands. I couldn't imagine anything less respectful. The victim had two gunshot wounds to the center of his chest. No stippling so the shots came from a distance, but I already knew that from the marks on the fence. The worst part was what had been done to him after he died. Flincher had taken samples. From what I could tell, he took pieces of skin, liver, kidney, one eye, and the brain.

I swallowed the bile that rose in my throat and turned the pics face down on the bed. No more of that. Thank you very much. I dumped out the rest. Flincher had been thorough and generous if I could reconcile that word with the ghoul. I got several evidence collection tubes with blood, a cheek swab, and a tooth. The last thing was a fingerprint card with all ten digits on it. Everything I needed to find out the victim's identity, but suddenly I didn't want to. He probably had a family. I didn't want to know their names or his story.

Toenails hit the tile in the bathroom and Dr. Watts exclaimed. I stuffed everything back in the packet and under the blankets. She opened the door and glared at me, drenched. Pick ran in, yipping and shaking.

"That is why I'm never getting a dog." She squeezed out her scrub top.

Pick scratched at the door.

"What now?" she asked.

"He wants to go out."

"And I'm supposed to take him."

"Would you?" I asked.

Dr. Watts grumbled and let Pick out, crossing paths with Aaron, who came in with a large mug of hot chocolate with a swirl of whipped cream on top. He gave it to me and bounced up and down on the balls of his feet, watching me while rubbing his hands together. I'd missed that. I really had. I took a sip and closed my eyes. French. Whole milk, bittersweet chocolate, and a dab of vanilla, probably cognac. "Delicious."

"You still hungry?" he asked, bouncing like crazy.

"I could eat."

He ran for the door and I yelled out after him, "Wait. Can I borrow your phone?"

He tossed the phone on the bed without a word and closed the door. First, I texted Chuck, telling him why I didn't answer his call. Chasing a would-be murderer seemed like a good excuse, but who knew what Chuck thought because he didn't answer. I didn't call my parents though I should've. I called Spidermonkey. It was late so he should be out searching for clues about The Klinefeld Group, but he didn't answer. I left a message, telling him my phone was dead and I needed his help immediately.

Spidermonkey called back a minute later and I told him what happened. I took pictures of Flincher's pictures and asked him to see if there were any missing person reports matching the description. I didn't have much hope considering the number of missing people in the U.S., but Spidermonkey said he had a couple of guys that were good in such cases and he'd have them give it a shot.

"Are you in much pain?" he asked.

"It's not too bad and, before you ask, I'm eating."

"Really?"

"Yep. Did you get anywhere with the first Jens Waldemar Hoff?" I asked.

"I did, not as much as I would've liked, but the picture is somewhat clearer."

Spidermonkey told me what he found out and I forgot about my ankle, Chuck, Tiny, and everything else for a bit. Through some business contacts, he'd gotten access to the Berlin records. Most were a dead end, except for the coroner's report. Hoff had no arrests, tickets, or trouble with anyone before he turned up dead in his office in October 1963. The death certificate said death by misadventure, but the coroner, Dr. Johan Traub, took notes and filed them. Spidermonkey had to sift through hundreds of Traub's reports in the moldy basement of a neglected office building that was near the former Berlin Wall.

Hoff's so-called misadventure was actually autoerotic asphyxiation. He was found hanging, nude, in his office surrounded by sex toys and magazines, but the doctor had his doubts. Hoff died at approximately ten o'clock the night before he was discovered. Dr. Traub noted that the drapes weren't drawn and the windows were open, leaving the body in full view of the neighboring office, which was how the body was discovered first thing the next morning. The doctor made a comment that this was odd. The behavior that Hoff was supposed to have engaged in was normally hidden, not put on exhibition. Also, the lights were on and anyone could've seen him at night. It was amazing that no one did. Plus, the toys and magazines were completely clean with no fingerprints or body fluids. Hoff had cuts, scrapes, and bruises on his upper torso and arms that couldn't be explained by the hanging.

Traub's notes were factual, but, reading between the lines, it was easy to see that he doubted that Hoff did this to himself. There was an interoffice memo tucked in the file informing Dr. Traub that no more inquiries from him would be tolerated. He was ordered to finish the paperwork and move on. Dr. Traub named the cause of death on the same date as the memo and made no more notes. Message received.

"So he was murdered," I said.

"Traub thought so."

"Did you get into the police files?"

"I did, but Hoff's file is missing," said Spidermonkey.

"Fantastic. A big fat dead end."

"Not exactly." Spidermonkey was lucky. His wife, Loretta, was very tired after so many museums and her naps were long so he was able to dig into the cops. Traub named Frederik Meyer and Werner Richter as the lead investigators. Both were dead and childless. Werner Richter was killed by a hit and run driver in1965. No one was ever prosecuted. Meyer quit his job three days after the funeral and became an alpine goat herder, only to die six years later of throat cancer. Spidermonkey had a feeling that something was off about Werner Richter's death, but he couldn't find anything to connect the accident to the Hoff suicide. Richter's twin brother, Paul, had inherited his worldly goods, including what was called work files in his will. Paul was alive and living in Paris.

"Are you going to Paris?" I asked.

"Not on this trip. I'll leave that to you."

Paris. I could be talked into that.

I looked at my cast. "I don't know when I can get over there."

"There's no hurry. Paul Richter may have trashed his brother's files or they may have nothing in them."

"But you think there's something there."

"I think the police knew Hoff was murdered and they knew who did it."

I put another pillow under my foot and slid down six inches, trying to get comfortable. "If they didn't, there was no point in covering it up. What does your Israeli contact say?" I asked.

"He wasn't active at that time and he's never heard of Hoff, but he has found out that there was an operation in Berlin in 1963."

"Nothing more specific?"

"Not yet."

"If Hoff was a Nazi and the Mossad killed him, why would the German police cover it up?"

"I'm not the detective. You'll be the one to discover the motivations. I deal in facts."

"You do much more than that."

"Mercy, you flatter me. Are you ready for the rest?" he asked.

"There's more?"

"Always." Spidermonkey decided to look into Hoff's wife when his trail petered out. Her name was Claudine Schmidt Hoff. She fell off the map shortly after her husband died. Their apartment was abandoned and their landlord filed paperwork to take possession of their goods after months of missing rental payments. On a hunch, Spidermonkey decided to check flight manifests and he found Claudine or a least a woman with her exact birth date and birthplace flying to Argentina one week after Hoff died.

I smiled. "The Nazis liked Argentina."

"Yes, they did."

"Am I supposed to go to Argentina?" I wasn't sure if I wanted the answer to be yes or no. I'd never been to Argentina. It could be interesting.

"At this point, no. Claudine Hoff aka Geraldine Homburg committed suicide in 1967."

"Autoerotic asphyxiation?" I asked.

"She jumped out a window. Nothing suspicious about it."

"This makes my head hurt."

Spidermonkey laughed. "Mine, too, but we are getting somewhere."

Are we? I can't tell.

"If you say so," I said.

Spidermonkey did say so, but I wasn't persuaded, especially after he told me what he found out about the break-in at the Bled Mansion. Some computer nerd along the lines of Spidermonkey and Uncle Morty breached the security company from a cybercafé in Bangalore, India.

Please don't make me go to Bangalore. It takes forever to get there and diarrhea is mandatory.

"So who is it?" I asked.

"We're not going to find out and it's pointless to try. I doubt he knows who hired him or why. He just opened a door in St. Louis. That's it."

"It could be a girl, you know," I said.

"Absolutely, but this particular subject searched for 'hot girls' while he was routing his commands through multiple IP addresses. He likes you by the way."

"Ew. What about the guys who went in the mansion?" I asked.

"No luck there either. One of the neighbors saw the car and got the plate number. The men rented the car under a fake name at the airport and somebody has a sense of humor. The name was Mr. Nichts Hier."

"Wait," I said. "Not here. The name was Mr. Not Here?"

"Or Nothing Here. Very funny."

"Hilarious," I said. "What about descriptions? The renter must've been seen."

Another dead end. The clerk didn't remember the man that called himself Mr. Nichts Hier, according to the police report. The car was dropped at the airport forty-five minutes after the break-in at the Bled's and the men in suits vanished. The general consensus was that they got on a plane, using different identification, but no one knew for sure. The case was at a standstill and, barring new evidence, it would stay that way.

"Do you know how Lester's doing?" asked Spidermonkey.

"Not well. I doubt he'll survive. They murdered him to get the inventory. It seems so pointless. Lester would've slept through the whole thing. They didn't have to kill him." My eyes filled and got hot.

"I didn't see anything in the police report about it but have the families been warned?" asked Spidermonkey.

"Families?"

"Some of the objects Stella smuggled out were returned to their owners, right?"

"Yes."

"How many?"

"Oh my god." I hadn't thought about that. Very few people survived the Nazis, but the Bleds had returned objects to those that did or to their relatives.

"Was that information on the inventory?" asked Spidermonkey.

I shook my head. "No, it's not. I used a copy to check the house. I never thought about those other pieces. What they're looking for could've been returned to one of the families. I'll tell Dad."

"Do that. Then we'll have to wait and see what they do next."

"Unless we can figure out what they're after. What are you going to do?"

Spidermonkey sighed. "I'm going to Salzburg."

"Are you looking into my dad and Josiah while you're there?"

"Yes." He sounded glum.

I looked at the clock. Almost time for a painkiller. Hooray. "You don't think you'll find anything?"

"I might, but I have to pay a significant price for this side trip. Loretta wants to do *The Sound of Music* tour. I'd rather get a root canal."

I laughed and felt like I could hold off on the painkiller a while longer. I told Spidermonkey that the tour was fun in a way, but he wasn't any more convinced about the tour than I was about The Klinefeld situation.

I hung up as just as Tiny knocked and came in. "How're you doing?" he asked, a little shame-faced.

"Fine. What's up with you?" I asked.

"Sorry about earlier."

"Er...what happened earlier?"

He stared at his belly. "You don't remember?"

And that's when my ankle started really hurting again. "You're going to have to give me a hint and a glass of water."

Tiny got me water and I took my pills. "So?"

He held up his phone. "You gotta call your dad." Tiny's screen showed about sixteen million missed calls and texts from Tommy Watts. Great.

"What'd you tell him?" I asked.

"Nothing," said Tiny, still not meeting my eyes. "I told him to ask you about that whole river thing. He didn't like that."

"No kidding." I bit the bullet and called Dad, ready for some serious yelling, but I didn't get it.

"So," said Dad. "Up to your old tricks, I hear."

"I don't know what you're talking about," I said using my innocent-as-the-driven-snow voice.

Dad snorted. "Haven't I taught you anything?"

Nothing I wanted to learn.

"Mercy, why do you insist on doing this for free?"

This?

"We own a small family business."

I don't own anything. What's this we?

"Do you hear me?" he asked.

I grimaced at Tiny and he shrugged. "Sort of. What did I do wrong?"

"You didn't charge. Small family business. Think, Mercy," said Dad.

"First of all, your business isn't small and, second, charge for what?"

"Detectives don't come cheap. You caught three, count 'em, three criminals. Do you know what we could've charged for that?"

"Dad, there's nobody to charge. Cherie's family's broke and I'm not a detective. I don't work for you."

Dad ignored the facts he didn't like as usual. "How about John and Leslie?"

"You want me to charge them? I thought they're your friends. I never noticed you charging friends for your services before."

"We have a particular kind of friendship. Never mind. It's all settled. They're comping the weekend for you all."

"Why are we even talking about this then?" I asked, praying that the pills would kick in and make talking to my father less excruciating.

"Because you can come home. I'm sending Terrance out tomorrow morning to pick you all up," Dad said.

I wanted to be happy, but Dad's tone made that impossible. "What's the hurry?"

Dad's tone didn't change and there wasn't a hurry. The news was good though. The Costilla brothers had been picked up in New York and their organization was in turmoil. They dropped the price on my head.

"When did this happen?" I asked.

"Homeland Security picked them up on the first day you were gone."

"You lied to me."

"Absolutely. They increased the bounty on your head after they were picked up and wouldn't deal. You were completely off the table for them."

"What changed?"

"Benny Costilla got shanked in the shower room and one of their lieutenants decided it was a good time to take over the operation. He's making serious headway with no one there to get in the way."

"What about the other lieutenants?"

"There's one other one, but the Feds think he fled to Mexico when the brothers were picked up."

The pill kicked in and I yawned. "Did Costilla die?"

"No. It was a precision shanking. Maximum pain, non-lethal," said Dad, not as triumphant as I would've expected.

"So why are we coming home early. Bridget won't be happy."

Dad paused and I listened to his breathing. It wasn't like him to hesitate. Then there was a scuffle and Mom said, "Mercy, it's Mom."

This is not an improvement.

"Are you going to tell me what's going on?" I asked.

"Your father doesn't like delivering bad news."

"Since when?"

Dad yelled in the background about how he'd deliver anything about anything. Mom groaned. "See what you did? Your father's upset."

What is happening?

"So why am I coming back early and angering the Troublesome Trio?"

"The Girls want you back." Then more softly, "And we want you back. Lester's not improving and the doctors don't believe he will."

"Are they going to take him off life support?"

"The family's considering it. I think they'll wait a few more days."

I told Mom I'd be ready to go bright and early and tried to hang up, but Mom stopped me. "Talk to Tiny. He wants to quit."

I said I would and Mom said she loved me, a rare occurrence. Lester's situation must be even worse than she was saying.

Tiny stood next to my bed, looking at his phone but not doing anything with it. His hands had a slight shake.

"We're going home tomorrow." Then I told him about the Costillas and Lester.

"I'm not going to St. Louis with you," he said.

"No?"

"I'm going back to New Orleans."

I sat up and tugged my foot off the pillows with a wince. "Why? We did good. Everything's fine."

He shook his head and began to wring his hands. His breathing went rapid and he flushed. "Naw. When you needed me, I freaked."

"When?"

Tiny told me that he wasn't good with blood. Cherie's body was difficult, but since she was strangled, he was able to stay mostly calm. Cory's rear shot was barely bloody and he hyperventilated over that. When Lane and I came back with blood all over us from various cuts, he lost it. I gathered that he broke down, crying and having flashbacks. Dr. Watts ended up sedating Tiny, which was why he didn't go to Flincher's. I didn't remember any of that, only the pain from the ride on Sly Dog and Lane convulsing with sobs.

"I'm no good to you or anybody," said Tiny.

"Not true. You're of great use to me. I hear you can kill people with your thumbs. That could come in handy." I grinned at him. "As long as they don't bleed."

It worked and I was rewarded for my impudence with a wry smile. "You can't count on me."

"It'll get better. Your meds aren't right. We should think outside the box. There's a doctor getting ready to do a marijuana study on PTSD. Maybe we can get you in."

"I don't want to get high." His voice went down. "I'm already drinking too damn much."

"You're drinking? When?"

"To sleep. I got to have something...a lot of something. Here I been using vodka so you wouldn't notice. It makes me snore more though."

"Well, I noticed that. Tiny, we'll figure it out," I said. "It'll get better and we'll have you on background work until it does."

"This shit ain't gonna get better. I can't get in that study. My next appointment at the VA isn't for three months and those docs just put me on more drugs or different drugs. I get fatter. I don't sleep."

Three months? That's crazy.

I texted Mom and asked her about our insurance. Tiny wasn't on it because he said he wanted to stay with the VA. I suspected that he thought Dad would find out about his PTSD if he went on the company insurance. That was moot now. Mom said she'd handle the insurance and told me I'd better get Tiny back to St. Louis or else. Like I could wrestle the giant into the limo or something.

"Okay," I said. "You're going on the company insurance. It won't take three months to get you in, more like three days."

"I don't know any docs in St. Louis," said Tiny, his hands shaking violently.

"You've met my mother?"

"Yeah."

I slipped out of bed and hugged him. "Then you know how determined she can be and she's well versed in PTSD specialists. She found me a guy and he had credentials out the yin-yang."

"It didn't help. You were starving yourself," said Tiny, barely controlling his hands. He was going to cry and I wished he would go ahead and do it. So much pain begged to be released.

"I didn't go," I said.

"Huh?"

"I didn't go to the therapist. I told Mom I did, but I didn't. She found out and has been pissed at me ever since."

"Why'd you lie?"

"I thought I could handle it. I thought I would stop seeing his face."

"You see his face?"

"I do. Not eating helped so I stopped eating. It was a simple solution," I said.

Tiny pushed me back from him. "It was crazy ass stupid."

"You sound like my mother."

He raised an eyebrow, but I didn't take it back.

"If you go, I'll go," I said. "Deal?"

He hugged me like I've never been hugged before which is to say I was nearly smothered and my vertebrae got realigned. Aaron came in with a double cheeseburger and more hot chocolate and we talked while I ate. That is, Tiny and I talked. Aaron sat there and looked confused. I don't know when I fell asleep with half a burger on my chest, but it was without scream-worthy dreams. A nice change of pace.

CHAPTER TWENTY-FIVE

It's hard to pack with a cast on one leg and even harder to shower. Dr. Watts helped me with both, taking our sweet time because the Springfield cops were back and waiting to talk to me. I wasn't interested. If I could've thought of a way to get off the property without talking to them, I would've done that. I hadn't actually admitted to killing Tim or shooting Cory. It was time to decide and I wasn't into it.

Aaron helped with the delaying by feeding me until I almost couldn't breathe. Nobody should eat that much food. Nobody. But Aaron was watching and I couldn't disappoint the little weirdo. He'd gone all out. Cheese soufflé, corned beef hash, eggs benedict. It was ridiculous, but oh so good.

I finished the last bite of hash and he held out his phone. "You got a message."

It was from Spidermonkey saying, "Is this the guy?" with a mugshot attached.

"Oh shit!"

"What?" asked Dr. Watts, hustling over.

I pulled Flincher's packet from under the covers and dumped it out. She pointed at the nude pictures. "Who is that?"

"Our mysterious dead guy from the woods," I said, comparing the mug shot to the pictures.

"And just how did you get those?"

"Er...well..."

She scowled. "Flincher."

I decided to tell her what happened, the blood for information deal, and she wasn't happy. She really wasn't happy when I told her Flincher thought he was going to cure death.

"What am I supposed to do with that?" she asked.

"Like I know." I held up the phone and a picture. "These are the same guy, right?"

"Definitely. Who is he?"

I texted Spidermonkey that he had the right man and he texted back, "Brace yourself."

"Tell me," I sent back.

"Alphonso Nunez. Lieutenant in the Costilla organization."

"Oh my god. John killed my assassin." I texted a thank you to Spidermonkey and pushed the remainder of my breakfast away before tucking the fat packet under the covers again.

"Are you sure John did it?" asked Dr. Watts.

"Yes. He practically told me." I looked at her hard. "You know who they are, don't you?"

She shrugged. "I may have been enlisted to help with, shall we say, community acceptance."

"And Flincher knows."

"He has little interest in people other than their pieces parts, but he might," she said. "What are you going to do?"

There was a pounding on the door. "Miss Watts, enough is enough." The door rattled. "We'll arrest you for obstruction if we have to."

Yeah, right.

"Unlock the door," I said and Aaron did, practically being bowled over by Logsdon and White.

Logsdon glanced around. "What are you doing?"

"Going home," I said calmly.

"That's not authorized."

"I don't need permission. I'm not under arrest. Where are Cory and Parker?"

White paced around the room. "Awaiting arraignment. The kid's seventeen and he says it was an accident. He's going to family court. Cory's denying the confession and he'll get a high bail."

"Is everyone else gone?" I asked.

Logsdon pulled up a chair and decided to be all friendly like I wasn't the daughter of a cop and used to interrogations that started out friendly. "The Marin family has decided to stay for the time being. I get the feeling they don't know what to do without the mother so the innkeepers offered to let them stay while they sort out the funeral arrangements in St. Seb. You're concerned about them?"

"Of course. The kids' have lost their last remaining parent and Anthony's no spring chicken, but I'm sure Leslie and John will look after them," I said.

"Taylor has been awarded the prize."

"Good."

The cops watched. I had no idea what they were looking for. I really just wanted a nap.

"Are you prepared to tell us the truth now?" asked White, acting all bad cop. I was so not impressed. Dr. Watts was tougher than him by a long shot.

"I haven't told you anything," I said.

That stopped them and they reconsidered. "Tell us what happened yesterday."

Before I could reply, John and Leslie came in.

"Dr. Watts, is your phone off?" asked Leslie.

She checked it and it was. "What happened?"

"The Jasper twins rigged a zip line in their backyard and the cable snapped."

"For crying out loud. Those boys are a menace to themselves." Dr. Watts came over and planted an unexpected kiss on my forehead. "You are my favorite ex-granddaughter. Call me when you get home."

I said I would and she left after telling the cops to behave themselves. The minute she was gone, they hustled Tiny and Aaron out of the room and glared at me. They tried to get John and Leslie to leave, but they didn't know who they were dealing with. Neither innkeeper could be moved, citing their loyalty to my father.

"Well, Miss Watts," said White, "tell us what you did or didn't do."

I glanced at John and Leslie's placid faces. I owed them. There had been an assassin at the fence with my name in his brain and they took care of it.

"I shot them both," I said.

White and Logsdon didn't believe me, not for a minute, but they had no choice. Everyone, including people who didn't actually see Cory get shot, said I did it. They even claimed that he was coming at me, yelling threats and whatnot. As for Tim's death, they thought the ranger shot him. Silver was a competition skeet shooter and he'd roughed up a few campers in the past and threatened a poacher with a .22. They couldn't believe little old me could've shot Tim in the back of the neck so perfectly. I pointed out with umbrage that I had recently shot a gang member in the face, but they were undeterred. They'd decided what happened and didn't want to be confused with facts. I *had* killed someone and there was no reason to believe I couldn't do it again. It was a fact they weren't interested in.

I didn't waver from my story and, of course, Lane and Silver backed me up. I doubted Lane knew what happened since she was about to be murdered at the time, but it was nice to have her vote.

"So are you going to arrest me or what?" I asked.

White gritted his teeth so hard I could hear it. That guy was going to need some dental work in the near future.

"You can go," said Logsdon. "But you have to be available for further questioning."

I shrugged. "I'll be in St. Louis if you need me."

"Gentleman," said Leslie, indicating the door.

White and Logsdon left and Leslie closed the door behind them. "So what tipped the balance in our favor?"

"John killed Alphonso Nunez to protect me. I never would've thought he'd be so sentimental," I said with a raised eyebrow at John.

"He attempted to breach our property," he said.

"To kill me."

"I assume."

"How did you know he wasn't here for one of you?" I asked. ,

Leslie picked up my breakfast tray. "Tommy gave us a dossier of known associates of the Costillas."

"And Flincher just agreed to incinerate him. No questions asked."

"He was well paid," said John, pointing at the lump under my covers. "I'll have the evidence now."

"Did you erase that video of me drunk?" I asked.

"Yes."

I sneered at him. "Why do I doubt that?"

John gave nothing away. "I couldn't say. The evidence, Miss Watts."

Here's hoping that video never surfaces.

"I'll have to trust you." I handed over Flincher's packet and grabbed John's wrist, "Thank you."

He stopped and looked down at me, the tiniest expression flickered in his eyes, making him almost human. "Anytime."

John left and Leslie stood there with my tray for a moment. "Thank you, Miss Watts. It was illuminating."

"I thought it was messy. Where do you get illuminating?" I asked.

He smiled, charming as always. "Let's just say things are clearer now."

"Fine with me. Bye, Shaun. I'll miss you."

"I will definitely miss you, Miss Watts." Leslie turned to leave, but I said, "Hey, what about my money?"

He laughed and adjusted his vest. "I thought you'd forgotten our little bet."

"Hand it over, bub."

Leslie peeled four fifties off a large wad of bills and gave them to me. "Good luck, Miss Watts."

"With what?" I asked, tucking the bills in my pocket.

"Nothing in particular. You just need luck in general." Leslie winked at me and left, leaving the smell of his cologne lingering in the air along with the stink of White and Logsdon's nervous perspiration. I finished packing and was about to call Tiny for help getting out to the limo when my door flung open without a knock.

The Troublesome Trio marched in with full makeup and four-inch heels.

"You," said Bridget.

"Can I help you?" I asked, backing up.

"You could've, but you didn't." Jilly admired yet another fresh manicure on her long fingers.

I backed up further. "Help you with what?"

"The truth," spat Sorcha. "You lied to me."

"What? When?"

Pick, who'd been sleeping on my bed, rolled over and gave out a half-hearted bark.

"Quiet, you," said Bridget, glaring at the poodle who in a fit of extreme bravery buried his nose under his paws. "This weekend was so perfect. Everything I could've asked for."

Jilly waved her hand at me. "And it ended up like this."

I looked down at my cast. They were mad that I broke my ankle? What the hell? It's my ankle.

"Look I'm sorry we have to leave early, but Les—"

Sorcha put her hand in my face. "You said it was a mystery for us to solve. Together."

"Er..."

They crowded in around me, a triumvirate of angry redheads. Jilly poked me with her sharp nails. "It wasn't a game."

"I never said it was."

"You said it was a murder mystery," said Sorcha. "I was there."

"I told you Cherie got strangled in the love garden." *You freaking nut.*

"You didn't say it was for real," yelled Bridget.

I backed up and bumped into the wall, rattling the artwork. "I thought it was implied."

"You let us think that it was one of those murder mystery theatre things," said Sorcha. "And you sent us out to interview murderers. We could've been killed and chopped up into little tiny pieces."

"You actually thought that everyone at the castle was putting on a show for you?" I asked.

"We didn't think there was a real murder," said Jilly.

"I told you there was. Weren't you paying attention? Everyone was freaked out." I said.

"We thought the crying was part of it," said Jilly.

Bridget rolled her eyes. "And here I was saying you did such a good job making this elaborate game for us to play together like real cousins."

I crossed my arms. "We are real cousins."

"Oliver thinks I'm an idiot," said Sorcha, bursting into tears.

Well, if the shoe fits.

"You lied to get us to do your dirty work," said Sorcha.

"You wanted to help."

"Because we thought it wasn't real. Because you lied."

That's when they pounced. I didn't have a chance to scream. I never do.

At least they used pretty duct tape. The green and blue went really well with my purple cast. I was trussed up good with alternating stripes before my cousins tossed me in the closet.

Jilly took her hand off my mouth and I said, "You can't leave me here."

"We can and we will," said Sorcha. "You need time to think about what you've done. Two hours should do it."

I struggled with my bonds. They'd gotten very good. My hands were duct taped together and then to my waist. "Two hours. What happens in two hours?"

"The maids will come to clean your room and let you out. By that time you should be very sorry."

"I'm very sorry right now," I yelled. "I'm sorry you're..."

Don't say it.

"Idiots that think that I would fake a murder for fun. This wasn't fun. I have a broken ankle and claw marks on my face."

"That's all you. Going around involving yourself in things that aren't your business," said Jilly, holding up a hand. "Oh, I chipped a nail."

I took a deep breath. "I'm sorry I involved you in Cherie's murder. It wasn't intentional."

That sounded pretty sincere.

"You're not sorry," said Bridget.

I guess not.

"You'd do it again if it helped solve the crime. You're just like Uncle Tommy."

"That's a low blow. Dad goes looking for crime. Crime comes to me," I said.

My cousins looked at each other.

"She needs some serious self-reflection," said Jilly. "We could tell the maids not to come until noon."

"No, no. I'm self-reflecting like crazy. I am like my father and I'm going to work on that. Please let me out," I begged.

"No," said Sorcha, bursting into tears and buckets of snot. "You've ruined my chance with Oliver and you must pay."

"He'll get over it. I'll take the blame. I'll tell him that it's all my fault."

"And you'll do it after the maids come."

"No! This is not happening. You think Uncle Morty isn't going to notice that I don't get in the limo."

Bridget smiled wickedly down at me. "He's staying to finish his book."

"Okay. What about Tiny and Aaron?"

"Aaron is staying to teach Leslie how to make that gross andouillette stuff."

Jilly looked at her phone. "Terrance is here. Time to go."

"What about Tiny and Terrance?"

Sorcha blew her nose, using about twenty tissues, then she reached down and patted my shoulder. "We'll lie. We can be very convincing. It runs in the family."

"We'll say you don't feel well. That you want to stay until you're better and you're sending us on ahead," said Bridget.

"They won't believe you," I said.

"Yes, they will," said Jilly. "We look honest."

Dammed if they didn't. Nobody looked more innocent than my cousins.

"Okay. Fine. What about Lester? He's going to die. The Girls and my parents want me home. They're going to notice when I don't show up."

The Troublesome Trio shrugged.

"You'll only be a few hours behind us," said Jilly.

"They can't really blame us," said Bridget.

"Yes, they can. I do." I tried to wiggle out of the closet, fell over, and bonked my head on the hardwood.

Bridget propped me up against the back of the closet. "Once you're done regretting your actions this weekend, you should have plenty of time to plan my bachelorette party. Here's a hint. We can have strippers, but they have to be classy like in *Magic Mike*."

"I think we should go to Vegas," said Jilly.

I kicked the wall and pain rocketed up my leg. "I'm not planning your party after this! Not in a million years would I do that!"

Bridget gazed down at me calmly. "You have to. You're my maid of honor."

With that, she slammed the door.

CHAPTER TWENTY-SIX

So here's the thing. The maids did not come after two hours. They did not come at noon either. I screamed until I was hoarse for all the good it did me. The Troublesome Trio left Pick in the room and I tried to get him to howl, alerting the staff that something was amiss. Instead, that worthless poodle sniffed at the door and then lay down in front of it blocking all of my light.

Screaming really wears a person out and, at some point, I went to sleep. I woke up when Pick moved and let light flood under the door. He yipped and then I heard something. Maybe a door opening. Then a zing of fear went through me. What if it was Flincher? Or another assassin. Dad could be wrong. He screwed up the security at the Bled Mansion.

The closet doorknob creaked and I bit my lip. The door opened and I was blinded by light. I blinked like crazy up at a tall form leaning over me.

"I should've known," said a warm, familiar voice. It couldn't be. Not possible.

I kept blinking and my eyes adjusted slowly.

"Have you got anything to say for yourself?"

"I..." I whispered. My voice was shot.

"You can't talk," he said. "This is working out for me just fine."

I blinked furiously and Chuck, my Chuck, came into focus. He wore a shiny track suit and a heavy gold chain around his neck. His hair had grown out and looked like it'd been slicked back with Brylcreem. In short, he looked terrible, weird and terrible. I was so happy to see him, I blubbered and then burst into the ugly cry, sounding just like Sorcha at her worst.

"Where...have...the...maids..."

"Oh, the maids were supposed to let you out." Chuck hauled me out of the closet and laid me on the bed. "I heard they're working on your last bedroom. Something about feathers."

Dammit, Pick!

As if he could sense my thoughts, the poodle jumped on the bed and licked me on the lips. Yuck. Chuck leaned on the bedpost and grinned at me. "So it wasn't just a ploy to get me to come back. There really was a murder in a gothic castle in the middle of the night."

"Uh-huh," I squeaked out. "Can you?" I wiggled my wrists.

"No, I don't think I will," he said running his fingers through his greasy hair. "You and I have to have a talk."

I tried to sit up and failed. "About what?"

"Us."

"Hmm...there's an us?" I asked, batting my eyelashes.

Chuck's blue eyes darkened. "There better be or I'm throwing you back in that closet. It's you and me together or I'm done."

"You already said you were done." I don't know why I said that. I did not want him to remember that.

"That was before you begged me to come back," he said.

I glared at him. "I didn't beg you to do anything."

"Now we both know that's not true." He bent over, taking me by the shoulders. "How much did you miss me?"

I looked away. "I might've missed you. A bit. Let's not go overboard."

"I got all your texts. All 232 of them."

"I was keeping you up-to-date."

"About you. Because you missed me so bad you couldn't stand it."

"Perhaps."

His lips brushed mine and I blushed.

"What about Pete?" asked Chuck. "Is that over?"

I nodded like a bobblehead. "Very."

"Do you want me to kiss you?"

"I wouldn't say n—" And he kissed me. Nothing mattered. Not that I was covered in duct tape or that a poodle with hideous breath was licking my hair. Nothing. Kissing was the only thing I wanted and then it was over.

"Don't stop," I whispered.

Chuck tapped the duct tape covering my wrists. "It's going to be hard to take off your top if you're taped."

"You're going to take off my top?"

"Do you want me to?"

"Okay."

Chuck had to borrow a pair of scissors from the maids that finally showed up and, even with their help, it took a half hour to get me untaped. The maids took the huge tape ball with them and were persuaded by Chuck's charm to take Pick out for a walk. He closed the door and I said, "You and me."

"Together? None of this cousins and we're gross stuff."

"We're not really cousins." I barely got it out. I sounded like Kathleen Turner with vocal cord damage.

"I like the sexy voice."

"I hate that track suit. Can we burn it?" I asked.

"Then I'd be naked." Chuck grinned at me.

I mirrored his grin with my own. "Works for me."

Three hours and a shower later, Pick was back on our bed, snoring with his paws in the air. Chuck traced my ribs with his finger. "Didn't use to be this way."

"Puhlease. He always snored. The vet says he has a septum issue," I said.

"I mean this." He flicked me in the rib.

"Ouch. What was that for?"

"Lettuce." He flicked me again.

"Stop it, you freak."

Another flick. "And carrots."

I smacked his hand.

"Green smoothies that taste like crap." Flick. Flick.

"I will beat you to death." I flipped over and sat on his chest.

"Oh you will, will you?" he asked.

I put my nose in the air. "I'm tough. I chase homicidal maniacs through dangerous rapids and save teenaged girls."

Chuck snorted. "He was trying to kill a sixteen-year-old girl and failed at that. He was a wussy."

"You weasel!" I pummeled him with an embroidered pillow until he gave up.

"Alright. Alright. This Tim guy was one tough bastard and you brought him down with one hand tied behind your back."

I whacked him one more time for good measure. "That's right." Then I collapsed next to him and closed my eyes. "I wish we could stay."

"I think we should," Chuck said.

"What about work?"

"I'm off for the next week. I'm supposed to see a therapist to make sure I'm adjusting after the assignment, but that's it."

"Will you go?" I asked.

He cupped my cheek. "Of course. Are you going to eat?"

"I already am."

"Good."

I reluctantly sat up. "But we can't stay. There's too much going on. I'm expected by The Girls." I looked at Chuck's lean body. "Besides there's a mortician around here that would love to get a hold of you."

"What do you mean by that?"

"It's a long story."

He coiled an arm around my waist and kissed my ear. "One more day. The parents won't mind. Now that you're in the clear and the Troublesome Trio are gone you can enjoy the castle."

I got up and slipped a sundress over my head. "Maybe. I'll call Mom for an update. Are you hungry? I'm starving. Let's see what Aaron's cooking. I hope it's something with butter."

Chuck laughed. "It's always something with butter."

I went in the bathroom and combed the snarls out of my hair. I had curls in all the wrong places. Headband. Definitely. Some music sounded in the bedroom, "Danger Zone" from *Top Gun*.

Please don't be work. No work. No work.

"Who's that?" I asked.

Chuck didn't answer and my stomach tightened. I stepped out and found him standing in the middle of the room wearing his favorite jeans and holding his phone like he'd never seen it before.

"Chuck?"

He looked up. "It's your dad."

"'Danger Zone'? That's funny."

"Hm...I don't know how to tell you this."

The smile fell off my face. "What?"

"Lester died." He walked across the room and pulled me to his chest.

Died. He's not supposed to die. Not yet.

"I didn't even know he was sick," said Chuck.

"He wasn't," I whispered.

"He was incredibly old."

I nodded, unable to speak.

"We'll leave right now. Okay?"

I nodded.

He sat me on the bed and packed up the rest of my stuff. "How well did you know him? I know he's worked for The Girls forever, but my mom has a gardener and I don't know him at all."

"He went with us on some of our trips," I managed to get out.

"Really? I didn't know that."

I smiled wanly. "The Girls would sometimes go out to restaurants that I couldn't go to and Lester would stay with me. We'd play checkers. He really loved checkers."

Chuck gathered all my stuff and put the luggage outside the door. "You did not pack all this stuff. Let me guess. Your mom did it."

I nodded.

"I'll call your crew. They'll want to come."

Uncle Morty marched in with his laptop bag, smelling like a cross between a men's locker room and antiseptic wipes. Dr. Watts had been working on him. "Hell yeah, we're coming. What's taking so long? Let's move."

"We're ready," I said.

He looked between me and Chuck. "So it's finally happened. About time. Does he know?"

"Know what?" asked Chuck.

"That Lester was murdered," I said.

Chuck didn't pause to take it in. No hesitation whatsoever. He called the front desk, ordered his car to be brought around, and asked about Aaron and Tiny. Aaron was coming up from the kitchens and Tiny was getting dressed after a massage. Chuck picked me up off the bed and carried me through the castle with Pick following close behind.

We went out the front door and I saw his car, a brand new Mustang in ice blue. "When did you get that?" I asked.

"Yesterday. Like it?" Chuck asked.

"Gorgeous, but the guys aren't fitting in there."

He looked at his car with adoration. "John, you got a car Morty can borrow?"

John stepped out of the shadows and Pick hid behind us, whining. I hadn't seen John there, but nothing got by Chuck. "Will a Mercedes coupe do?"

Morty walked up beside us. "What color is it?"

"Does that really matter?" I asked.

"Aesthetics matter."

I rolled my eyes. "Says the guy who wore the same smelly sweats for days."

"I suffer for my art. What color?" asked Uncle Morty.

"Black," said John like there was no other color possible.

"That'll work. See you at home, Mercy." He stomped back inside.

My eyes met John's and I said, "Thanks for everything."

"My pleasure."

I got the feeling he meant that and, considering that I was

thanking him for killing someone, it was fairly disturbing. Chuck looked back and forth between us. A shadow came into his eyes as he put Pick in the back of the car and me in the passenger seat. He got in and squeezed my thigh, his long fingers wrapping around the muscle. It felt so good, so safe. "Now you're going to tell me everything I missed."

I buckled up and thought about it. So much to say and how little I wanted to say it. Two months was a long time and it felt even longer.

"Is it The Klinefeld Group?" asked Chuck.

Among other things.

"Yes."

He peeled out, speeding down the long drive. I glanced back and saw someone on the parapet, but then they were gone. Lane, Taylor, and Anthony came out of the big black walnut doors with Leslie and watched us drive away. I didn't say goodbye. Another regret to think about another time.

CHAPTER TWENTY-SEVEN

The funeral was two days later. I wore my Valentino suit and a '40s style hat with a big ostrich feather. Lester loved women in hats. He said they classed us up.

He was laid to rest at Jefferson Barracks since he was a Korean War vet, and the wake was at the Bled mansion against everyone's advice. Lester's widow, Mary, wanted it there and The Girls insisted. The security was a nightmare for Dad. The wake was invitation only and streets were blocked off to keep the press and the general public at bay. The mansion was rarely open to that many guests and Dad was afraid The Klinefeld Group would make another move. Mourners had to present their invitations and go through a metal detector to even get on Hawthorne Avenue. It was crazy, but, I suppose, necessary.

Chuck and I threaded through mourners gawking at the art in the foyer and found Mary in the receiving room with a bowl of untouched boeuf bourguignon on her lap and an empty whiskey sour glass in her hand. Her red-rimmed eyes didn't seem to recognize me at first, but then she thanked me for coming in her gentle South Carolina accent. I almost lost it right there. Mary's nickname was Fireball. Lester always said she had a temper hotter than the fourth of July. She was known to throw plates and occasionally dumped all his clothes on the front lawn.

She and Lester were in love, a fiery kind of love. They were rarely apart, only when he traveled with The Girls. It hurt to see her there, alone and diminished somehow.

My shoulders quaked and Chuck led me away through the throng. "How many people are invited?" he asked.

"Around three hundred I think," I said before cheek kissing Lester's daughter, Sunny, and expressing my sympathies.

"That many?"

"Lester was well loved."

"No kidding." He ducked as a server came through with more bowls of bourguignon followed by another with a tray of tacos. "Who planned the menu?"

"We're serving Lester's favorites." I patted the back of one of the maids, Holly. She was practically howling and was quickly led away by my Aunt Tenne, who rolled her eyes at me. Her job was to keep people calm and it wasn't an easy one. The news that Lester was murdered had broken a couple of days ago and it was all people could talk about. A Bled employee being murdered was big news and the fact that nothing of value was taken fanned the flames. That the inventory was missing hadn't been reported and wouldn't be. Everyone who had pieces from the collection, the Bleds and the Holocaust victims' families, had been informed of the danger, but nothing had happened. No more break-ins or visits from The Klinefeld Group. It made me uneasy. But it probably made them more so. News commentators all over the world were questioning The Klinefeld Group's lawsuit and whether they were behind Lester's death. They were a shadowy group and now the spotlight was on them.

Chuck steered me into the formal dining room. "So it's tacos and bourguignon."

"And fried chicken and quiche."

"He was a renaissance man."

I took a deep breath. "He was. Look at that." I nodded at the buffet at the end of the dining room where the servers were loading their trays. People weren't expected to serve themselves, but Uncle Morty was there with a plate, trying to get at the tacos. My mother stood between him and paradise.

"You heard what Mercy said. If you're going to eat this stuff you have to move. No more sitting."

"Get out of the way, woman," growled Uncle Morty, trying to dodge her and failing.

"You have a condition," Mom said.

"Yeah, hunger." He juked to the right and she blocked him.

Mom saw me and we exchanged nods. "Morty, so help me god. Let me see your pedometer. Are you walking enough?"

"Leave me alone," he bellowed.

Chuck put his arm around my waist and squeezed. "I think your mom should've had more kids."

Mrs. Haas from next door called out to Mom and distracted her for a second. Uncle Morty dashed over, stole an entire taco tray, and made a break for it toward the hall.

I laughed. "I'd say she has plenty of kids."

Mom focused back on the dining room and then glared, her eyes searching for Morty. Chuck pointed at Morty's retreating back just as he went through the hall door.

I elbowed him. "You big snitch."

"It's for his own good," said Chuck, grinning at me. "Besides, I don't want you working on his sores every day."

"I am a nurse. It's what I do."

He waggled his eyebrows at me. "I've got better things for you to do."

I elbowed him. "Quiet. This is a funeral or have you forgotten?"

"Lester would approve. He once told me that before he married Mary, he dated four or five girls at the same time."

"Don't get any ideas," I said with a glare.

"You're all I can handle." He squeezed my rear.

I smacked his hand. "Stop it. People will see." I scanned the crowd, looking for disapproving frowns, probably my mother's, but instead found only one person looking at us and his expression was amused. Oz Urbani smiled slyly at me over a trio of old ladies wearing enormous going-to-church hats. I sucked in a sharp breath and Oz turned quickly before Chuck followed my gaze.

"What?" he asked.

"Nothing. You're just bothering me senseless," I sighed. "I need a drink. Can you get me a...strawberry margarita?"

Chuck kissed my forehead and patted my rear. "Be right back."

With any luck, he wouldn't be right back. Rodney, Aaron's partner at Kronos, was making drinks to order in the morning room and he liked to talk. I hobbled toward the hall with my cane and hoped Oz would follow. He caught up to me in the left conservatory. There weren't many people lingering in among the banana trees and palms. The temperature stayed at a humid 85 for all The Girls' tropical plants and the sun streamed in through the three-story glass held up by the Egyptian hieroglyphic ironwork, making it even steamier. I ducked behind a huge pot of ferns and Oz followed. He managed to look cool in his pin-striped suit while sweat beaded on my upper lip.

"What are you doing here?" I asked. "You definitely weren't invited."

"I wanted to talk to you," he said, gazing up at the wavy glass. "This is impressive."

"Whatever. How'd you get in?"

Oz smiled, his white teeth gleamed in comparison to his permanently tanned skin. "You never fail to surprise me. As resourceful as you are, you still have to ask me that?"

"Well, how?" I asked, feeling as dumb as dirt because I had nothing.

"I had 500 dollars in my pocket, no weapons, or a camera. That's the concern around here."

"You bribed the security guys?"

"One guy. The other went to pee. You have to pick your moment," he said.

I slapped my forehead. "Nobody can see you here. Dad and Chuck'll know it's because of me knowing your sister. I don't want them to think I'm involved with the Fibonaccis. The very thought freaks them out."

"I'm afraid you are involved."

"No, no. I saved your sister and your aunt helped The Girls with Brooks' lawsuit. We're even." My heart was beating faster by the second.

"You were even. Now you're not."

I peeked around the plants to make sure nobody had come in. "Why? What did I do?"

"You didn't do anything. Aunt Calpurnia decided to help you with the Costillas."

My heart skipped about six beats. "Oh my god. What did she do?"

"She had a friend of the family send a message to Benny Costilla," said Oz. "It wasn't my idea."

"The shanking in the shower? That was Calpurnia?"

"For all intents and purposes. She made it clear that you are a friend of hers and weren't to be touched."

"And they just agreed? What about their brother?" I asked.

"The boy is dead and business is business. He shouldn't have come after you, given your connections, and the Costillas recognize that. Besides, she helped him out with a certain lieutenant who'd gotten above himself. She would've helped him with the other one, but no one can find him."

And nobody ever will.

"So I owe your aunt big." I got a little light-headed and Oz pulled over a chaise lounge for me. "What happens now?"

"Nothing," he said. "If she needs something, she'll let you know."

"Will you be the one to tell me?" I asked.

He shrugged. "I'm not really a part of the family that way. This all happened without my knowledge. She told me this morning to tell you in person so I'm here."

Oz gave me a soft linen handkerchief and I patted my lip and forehead with it. "Well, the price is off my head. I guess I can't complain too much."

"You can't complain at all. It's done. This is how Aunt Calpurnia works. We don't have to like it. If it makes you feel better, your father couldn't have gotten the Costillas off you. He doesn't have the type of power it took."

I nodded, at a loss for words. What was I going to do? This was not supposed to happen.

"Are you going to tell your father and your new boyfriend?" asked Oz with a twinkle in his eye at the mention of Chuck.

"That'd be a no. They would freak and, as you say, there's nothing anyone can do," I said.

"Wise decision," he said. "I better go. I have a feeling that Detective Watts will be keeping a sharp eye on you from now on."

"You're probably right. Why didn't you just call me? This is risky."

He smiled a lazy smile at me. "But fun and it's not like I'll ever be invited in to see The Bled Collection."

My phone rang. It was Spidermonkey. I waved Oz off and he went around the foliage the other way just as Chuck called out my name. I hoisted myself out of the lounge and waved around the ferns.

He marched over, his eyes darting around suspiciously. "What are you doing in here?"

I pointed to the phone. "Shush. Spidermonkey."

"Oh," said Chuck and he gave me my margarita.

I sat back down on the lounge and said, "So you were saying."

"Using me as a cover?" asked Spidermonkey.

"Maybe. It's Lester's wake."

"Oh, right. I'm sorry to bother you, but I have news I thought you'd want immediately."

"What is it?" I sipped the margarita, icy and calorie laden. I loved it.

"The Klinefeld Group filed papers to drop the lawsuit."

I looked up at Chuck's face and he mouthed, "What?"

"Did they state why?" I asked.

"Change of heart or so they say. Out of sympathy for Lester's death."

"That they caused," I spat out.

"I believe so, but we'll never prove it." He sighed and said hesitantly, "Do you want me to stop the research, Mercy. I know it's been a financial burden and now there's no point."

Chuck sat down next to me and put his arm around my shoulders.

"There's still a point. They killed Lester and we don't know why," I said.

"Do we need to know?" asked Spidermonkey.

"I do."

He laughed heartily and with considerable relief. "I was hoping you'd say that. Because I can't stop until I figure this out. I can't live with the mystery."

"Me, either."

I hung up and told Chuck. He put his elbows on his knees and steepled his fingers. "You know what this means, right?"

I gulped half my margarita and felt the icy lump go down into my chest. "Either they found what they were looking for or they know we don't have it."

"Exactly." He took my glass and finished the margarita.

I leaned on him and was careful not to meet his eyes, afraid of what I might see. "You once said you were right behind me."

"It's my favorite view."

We laughed and I knocked into him, nearly dislodging him from the lounge. "But seriously."

"I did say that and I meant it."

"I don't know where this is going to take me," I said.

He cupped my cheek and raised my lips to his. I kissed him softly, tasting the sweetness of the margarita and the salty sweat from his upper lip. He pulled back. "I don't care where you go as long as you let me follow."

"I love you," I said.

"Tell me something I don't know."

I wrinkled my nose. "You are one smug bastard."

"But I'm your smug bastard."

For better or worse.

The End

The Wife of Riley (Mercy Watts Book Six)

I stared at the wide double doors along with everyone else in the clinic. Unlike everyone else, I didn't know what I was waiting for. From the expression on the practice receptionist's face, we were waiting for doom.

The Columbia Clinic was usually a friendly place but not that afternoon. I was seven weeks into an eight-week temp job as a nurse for the clinic's nurse practitioner, Shawna Davis, a tireless woman with four kids and a husband with so much energy she had to walk him every night or he'd take apart the microwave. Even Shawna's shoulders sagged when she saw the schedule. I'd taken a look but could garner no clues about what was coming. One of the other nurses suddenly discovered that her toddler had a fever and left after she saw the schedule. Nobody would tell me anything and I'm usually good at getting information out of people.

The Columbia Clinic was a normal general practice in a small picturesque town just over the Illinois border and I was lucky to get the gig. I needed a steady paycheck after having to take a couple weeks off for a broken ankle and the clinic was a prime place to work by everyone's account. I was filling in for the regular nurse, Kellie Greenwald, who was out on maternity leave. Kelly's newborn had a raging case of colic, but I'd heard several people say they wished they were her for the day.

That wasn't a good sign. Colic could drive parents to the brink of insanity—just ask my mother. It also wasn't a good sign when the entire place flinched whenever the doors rattled. Neither was the huge sigh of relief when a harried mother managed to open the doors with a double baby stroller while holding a screaming four-year-old on her hip.

Karen, one of the other nurses, ran over, calling out, "I've got her." Karen helped Mrs. Bellringer with a big smile on her face as the twins in the stroller started screeching and tugging at their ears. I went to help and Karen panicked, holding up her palm. "No, no. I've got it. You stay right there."

"Why do I feel like I'm being set up?" I asked Steve, the receptionist.

He gave me a blank look. "I don't know what you mean."

"Yeah, right."

"Don't let this affect your decision."

"It won't. Believe me," I said.

The whole office had been trying to talk me into going back to school to get my masters and become a nurse practitioner. The main argument was that I could give up dangerous detective work and not have things happen like broken ankles and the occasional murder attempt. They made it sound like I had a choice. I did not. I was Tommy Watts' daughter, and there weren't a lot of choices left up to me. He was a famous retired police detective who had opened his own shop, and I, as his only child, was expected to support the family business for free. The office thought I was making money chasing down lunatics, but it was costing me in more ways than one. Crimes showed up unannounced and demanding attention whether I wanted to give it or not.

"Mercy," said Steve. "You really should consider it. You'd be great. The patients love you."

"Let's just see how this goes."

More patients showed up, eliciting the same flinch and sighs of relief, until there was only one left. Stanley Cadell. Stanley was the one, but I had no idea why. He was a sixty-seven-year-old diabetes patient in a wheelchair, but the man could clear a room. There was a thump on the doors, and all the sudden, I was alone behind the desk with Steve, who immediately picked up the phone, saying, "He's here." There was a pause. "Mercy." Another pause. "Right away."

Steve looked up at me. "Can you get the door?"

"Sure," I said, not moving.

"What are you waiting for?"

"For you to read me the warning label."

"It's better if you don't know."

"Nothing good comes after that sentence."

Steve shook his head. "I know."

I got the door and found a thin man with the pallor of the recently deceased waiting outside. His comb-over had flipped up and was waving at me in the breeze.

"Mr. Cadell?" I asked.

He brightened up and ran his eyes up and down my scrubs a couple of times, not in a creepy way more like he was sizing up the competition. "So...you're the one they've been talking about."

"Are you Mr. Cadell?"

"I don't want one of those others," he said, shifting in his seat to peer through the open door behind me.

"Others?" I asked.

"I want the girl, the pretty one with the big eyes."

"Shawna?"

"That's the one. I don't want one of those useless doctors, and I'm not going over to Dr. Sidaway. You can't make me. She has a mole. A big one with hairs."

Definitely the dreaded Stanley Cadell.

"Okay. I don't think that'll be a problem, Mr. Cadell. You have an appointment here. Let me help you in," I said.

"I'm not a cripple. I get around fine on my own."

I glanced out into the mostly empty patient parking lot. There was no one waiting and no car with a handicap tag. "How did you get here?"

"Taxicab. Uber won't take me anymore, the commie bastards," said Mr. Cadell, laying the stink eye on me like I too might be a commie bastard.

"Alright then." I opened the door wider for him to wheel through. "Come on in."

"Aren't you going to help me? I'm missing a foot here or didn't your fancy medical training teach you to detect that?"

"I thought...oh, never mind." I wheeled Mr. Cadell in and Steve braced himself on the desk and plastered a patently false smile on his face.

"Good afternoon, Mr. Cadell," said Steve.

Mr. Cadell grumbled as I wheeled him past the desk and muttered something about faggots under his breath. Steve gave me his chart and whispered, "Check the chair."

I nodded, but I had no clue what he was talking about. The chair seemed fine to me. It rolled well and had serviceable brakes. I took him into Room Three and took his vitals. They weren't great, matching how he looked and probably felt. Mr. Cadell had one of his feet amputated since it started to rot as a complication of his diabetes and he was released from rehab the day before. I thought they'd jumped the gun on that. He had pretty much every complication you could get, from diabetes from coronary artery disease to impaired kidney function. The man was a mess and he knew it. He glared at me, questioning my technique for taking his blood pressure and lecturing me on why the new-fangled thermometers weren't accurate. I never wanted to escape a patient so much and that's saying something, considering I have a tendency to get vomited on.

"Can you dance?" he asked when I'd finished.

I jerked upright from looking at his stump. "What?"

"You look like Marilyn Monroe. I guess you got the surgery. Did you take the dance lessons?"

"I didn't get surgery, Mr. Cadell. This is what I look like."

"You look like a slut. What did your mother say about this?"

I swallowed and took a breath. It seemed pointless to say that my mother and I both were spitting images of Marilyn Monroe through no fault of our own. Mr. Cadell wasn't interested. "She didn't say anything. I'll see what's keeping Shawna." I had a pretty good idea what was keeping our big-eyed nurse practitioner—a sense of self-preservation.

"Well, can you dance?" he insisted.

"I never thought of Marilyn as a dancer," I said, heading for the door.

"Can you sing?"

"Not if I can help it." I left the room and found Shawna standing in the hall, twisting her white coat in her hands.

"Is he ready for me?"

"It's more a question of are you ready for him," I said.

She sighed. "Let's do it. Come on, Mercy."

"What? He's all yours. I'm done, unless you have a procedure."

Please don't have a procedure. Please don't have a procedure.

"I need a witness and it's your turn," said Shawna.

"A witness?"

"In case things go bad."

"How bad can they go? He's a 130-pound amputee in a wheelchair."

"He bites. There's pending litigation."

"With us?"

"Not so far. He likes me."

"God help you."

"He hasn't so far. Mr. Cadell is still my patient."

Shawna went in and I reluctantly followed. The checkup went pretty well until Shawna got to Mr. Cadell's stump. It wasn't healing as it should. Shawna had me clean and bandage the wound as she started talking about sending him to a dietitian. I got the feeling this wasn't the first time they'd had this talk.

"I don't need some woman telling me how to eat," said Mr. Cadell.

"What have you been eating?" asked Shawna.

"Food."

"Be more specific. Did you bring your food diary?"

Mr. Cadell started plucking at his American flag lap blanket. "I don't need to do that. I know what I eat."

"Fantastic," she said. "What did you eat for breakfast?"

"Oatmeal," he said with a triumphant look.

"What was in the oatmeal?"

My alarm bells went off. This was when things were going to go wrong. I finished the bandaging and backed away slowly.

"A little sugar. You have to have sugar in oatmeal," said Mr. Cadell.

"Did you test your blood before you ate?"

"I forgot."

Shawna rubbed her forehead. "Mr. Cadell, diet is a major factor in your disease progression."

"I'm not fat," he said with a certain amount of pride. In my opinion, he could've used some fat.

"We've discussed this," said Shawna. "In your case, weight isn't a factor. Diet is."

Mr. Cadell rummaged around under his blanket and I was afraid he'd come out with something I very much didn't want to see. In a weird way, he did. Mr. Cadell pulled out a Twinkie.

"Mr. Cadell!" exclaimed Shawna.

He ripped open the Twinkie and stuffed half of it in his mouth. Shawna smacked the rest out of his hand. "You can't eat that."

"I can eat what I want!" he yelled, pulling out another Twinkie.

I should've checked the wheelchair.

Shawna lunged for the Twinkie and I lunged for Shawna. I managed to hold her back from throttling the old loon.

"Do you want to lose another foot?" she yelled.

"It's your job to make sure I don't!" he yelled before ripping open another Twinkie.

"You make my job impossible! You must control your diet!"

"I am controlling it!"

She snatched the Twinkie away. "This is the opposite of control!"

"I want some Xanax!"

"Not unless you get therapy," said Shawna, panting with my arms around her middle.

"I'm depressed!"

"Then get some therapy!"

"No!"

That's when it broke loose. Twinkies were everywhere. Dingdongs and HoHos, too. Mr. Cadell had a whole Quick Mart under his blanket. It was a real sugar storm.

Read the rest in
The Wife of Riley (Mercy Watts Mysteries Book Six)

USA Today bestselling author A.W. Hartoin grew up in rural Missouri, but her grandmother lived in the Central West End area of St. Louis. The CWE fascinated her with its enormous houses, every one unique. She was sure there was a story behind each ornate door. Going to Grandma's house was a treat and an adventure. As the only grandchild around for many years, A.W. spent her visits exploring the many rooms with their many secrets. That's how Mercy Watts and the fairies of Whipplethorn came to be.

As an adult, A.W. Hartoin decided she needed a whole lot more life experience if she was going to write good characters so she joined the Air Force. It was the best education she could've hoped for. She met her husband and traveled the world, living in Alaska, Italy, and Germany before settling in Colorado for nearly eleven years. Now A.W. has returned to Germany and lives in picturesque Waldenbuch with her family and two spoiled cats, who absolutely believe they should be allowed to escape and roam the village freely.